THE
PERFECT
SON

THE PERFECT SON

BARBARA CLAYPOLE WHITE

LAKE UNION
PUBLISHING

Text copyright © 2015 Barbara Claypole White

Published by Lake Union Publishing, Seattle

www.apub.com

Amazon, the Amazon logo, and Lake Union Publishing are trademarks of Amazon.com, Inc., or its affiliates.

ISBN-13: 9781477830048
ISBN-10: 1477830049

Cover design by Shasti O'Leary-Soudant / SOS Creative LLC

Library of Congress Control Number: 2014921694

Printed in the United States of America

For my agent, Nalini Akolekar,
because thank-you notes are never enough

No one is perfect . . . that's why pencils have erasers.

—*author unknown*

What was silent in the father speaks in the son, and often I found in the son the unveiled secret of the father.

—*Friedrich Nietzsche*

ONE

Passengers in the row behind muttered the Lord's Prayer. Ella, however, had no plans to make her final peace with God or die in the clouds. She had a battle to conduct on the ground, after she'd cleared baggage claim at the Raleigh-Durham International Airport.

The plane lurched and a baby screamed. Eyes closed, Ella inhaled through the heartburn that had stalked her since Felix's text had dinged over the flight attendant's directive to power off electronic devices. Delivered with perfect timing—no possibility of retaliation—her husband's message had been a declaration of war. Signed without a kiss.

The young man next to her grabbed the armrest. "Rough flight," he said. "Think we can blame the polar vortex?"

The fuselage rattled as if about to rip into a billion fragments.

"Flying, still the—" Words clumped in her windpipe like a drain clog; statistics memorized to soften her son's fear fogged up her brain. She forced out a breath. "It's still the safest way to travel."

"No offense," the guy said, "but you don't look too convinced about safety records."

A stereo of heartbeats thumped in her throat. Boom, boom; boom, boom; boom, boom.

"Heartburn. Killer attack." Ella tried to smile, but her stomach began to bubble worse than a cauldron of boiling acid.

"I don't mean to be rude"—he glanced up at the call button and back at Ella—"but you've gone a strange color. You sure you're feeling okay?"

"Bit churned up with all the—" Ella made exaggerated roller-coaster movements with her arm, then paused to breathe. "Don't worry, I'm not going to start projectile vomiting."

"Good to know, because I might."

"A guy unafraid to discuss puking." She pressed her palm against her chest. "Admirable."

"Could you explain that to my wife? She thinks I'm a total wuss."

Ella gave a sympathetic huh that seemed to say, *Spouses, eh?* Felix had always believed she was strong enough for both of them, and he'd been wrong. After seventeen years of marriage, she was so tired of being the family fulcrum.

The stranger stared at her from behind thick, black-framed glasses—very Elvis Costello, very late-seventies London pub scene. Very Felix. She turned to the window, faking interest in cloud formations. The memory flashed anyway: a muggy Saturday on the London Tube; a wave of light-headedness followed by the certainty that she was going to faint; a different stranger with thick, black-framed glasses. A beautiful young Englishman with floppy hair and a hesitant smile: Felix Fitzwilliam. Who could resist that name weighted with authority, with nobility, with ancestors—she would learn later—who had signed the Magna Carta? Who could resist the laserlike intensity of concern channeled through those huge blue eyes? He'd caught her; he'd stopped her from falling in more ways than one. But that was the past, and nostalgia had no place in the present. Not after Felix had texted:

    Talked with the president of Harvard
    about Harry's admission.

Ella coughed back nausea. For sixteen years, seventeen next week, she alone had been responsible for the decision making that affected Harry's life. She had been his advocate and mental health coach, his full body armor. The parent who'd educated teachers and set up code words that enabled Harry to leave the classroom when he had excess energy to burn; the parent who had battled the family's health insurance provider over services, drugs, and appointments; the parent who had monitored Harry's sleep, nutrition, stress, and meds. She alone had given their son enough praise for two parents. Felix had been the breadwinning workaholic. That's what he did: he worked, while she parented to the point of collapse. And then Harry achieved perfect SAT scores, and Felix, no longer content to ride in the family backseat, snatched the parental car keys and reset the GPS for Harvard. Harvard, when she'd been pushing for the University of North Carolina so Harry could stay close to everything that mattered to him, everything that kept him safe. And now Felix had begun to confuse Harry with comments about how only losers stayed in state and attended public universities.

I'm an Oxford man, Harry. That means something.

Yes, if you allowed it to mean something.

The discomfort in her throat and chest eased, but the anger had returned. *Good.* She would nurse it, stay strong despite the exhaustion that crept into her thoughts, her bones, and her muscles. Had she ever been this weary?

Maybe she should flag down the flight attendant and order a Bloody Mary. A double.

What-ifs multiplied like a combat-ready squad of *Star Trek* Tribbles: cute, furry, and armed with bazookas. What if, when Harry went to college, she took Katherine's advice and moved out? Every time Ella and her best friend opened a bottle of cabernet, Katherine accused Felix of being a control freak, which he was. But could Ella Fitzwilliam do that—break apart her family after she'd fought so hard to keep it balanced on the imaginary high wire of raising an exceptional child? If not, could she at least rip up every one of Felix's to-do lists, those neat, color-coded notes of perfection that ruled their lives?

Her stomach flipped and flopped as the plane took another plunge, this one dislodging her Holly Aiken tote from under the seat in front. She nudged the bag back into place with her foot. Felix had taken six months to notice the bag, and once he'd discovered that Holly Aiken was a Raleigh designer and the bag was not a T. J. Maxx special, he'd launched into a diatribe on financial irresponsibility and the state of the college fund. She had explained, calmly, that the bag was a gift from her dad. Felix had never apologized.

"I'm going to hug my little girl so tight when I get home," the stranger said. A dad who offered hugs and probably declared every piece of finger painting to be a van Gogh—as did most fathers. Not Felix, though. He had never found anything worthy of praise in Harry's early artwork. One blemish, one flaw, and the whole was ruined.

Ella shook her head. A bit too hard, given the aura of dancing lights. She turned back to face her neighbor, and the world took a few seconds to catch up. "How old is she, your daughter?"

"Three."

"A fabulous age." Three-year-old Harry had been all boy, all energy, all the time. Admittedly he'd been more energetic than anybody else's kid, and there hadn't been many repeat playdates. And yes, the president of the preschool PTA had publicly denounced Ella's parenting skills after Harry had charged into the table at the annual ice-cream social and destroyed all the ice cream. But at three, Harry hadn't been branded or bullied; he hadn't become the Tourette's Kid, also known as "Jerky" to less sympathetic classmates.

"My son's a junior in high school," she said. Although if six-foot Harry were with them, he would be squirming worse than a kindergartner trapped inside on a rainy day. Plastic seats triggered his sensory issues. The ones on short-haul flights such as these were the worst.

And then—because how could she not share?—she leaned toward her seatmate.

"He just scored two eight hundreds on the SATs. Perfect scores in critical reading and writing."

"Impressive."

Doubly impressive given the neurological disorder that doesn't play nice with stress and the ADHD thrown in for shits and giggles. Plus the quirks that come from a patchwork of other diagnoses.

The guy fiddled with his wedding ring. "I'm dreading the teenage years."

"Don't. They're loads of fun. I have the best conversations with Harry—that's my son—but he still has a little kid's sense of wonder. I can't wait to see him at the airport."

She and Harry? Their lives had been soldered together by the rainbow of special needs. Five whole days they'd been apart! They'd never been separated that long before.

"He sounds like a very special guy."

"He is." The two years of rage attacks that had destroyed furniture and left holes in drywall didn't count. The à la carte menu of Tourette syndrome could offer up anything except choice.

The plane held a steady path, and people fidgeted in collective relief. Her neighbor, the good father, retrieved a Tom Clancy novel from the seat pocket and began to read. Soon they would start their descent into Raleigh-Durham, and when they landed, Harry would rush toward her with arms akimbo and deliver a Harry hug. He was the best hugger.

Ella sank back into her seat. Maybe she just needed a break from family stress. The last week had brought such guilt—juggling her dad's need for a postsurgical dose of daughter love with abandoning Harry to Felix. Although technically Felix had been the parent in charge for less than twenty-four hours, since Harry had been staying with his friend Max while Felix bashed out the prospectus for some bond issue.

According to Felix's business partner, Felix was "a friggin' rock star at bringing together a syndicate of underwriters." *A syndicate.* Amazing how the world of corporate finance co-opted the language of organized crime.

The muscles in her chest clenched as if squeezing through a contraction; she gasped.

"Heartburn getting worse?" her neighbor said.

Pain shot between her shoulder blades, scorching a path along her bra line. "Uh-huh."

She was sweating now. Not heartburn, then. Did she have a fever? She felt her forehead. Clammy. Had she picked up the flu?

She never got sick. Not since she'd quit smoking and started exercising daily. She watched her salt intake, kept an eye on her blood pressure . . . and she'd had her cholesterol checked only last month. Given her family history, she had no choice but to be vigilant. Maybe it was just menopausal crap. The last few days in Fort Lauderdale, she'd been sweating enough for a whole mob of middle-aged women.

I am not sick, I am not sick, I am not sick.

She couldn't get sick. Not right before Harry's birthday and the weekend college trip she'd planned to Asheville. And what if she'd passed on germs to her dad's caregiver? Or to her dad? He was still going to physical therapy to build up his muscles, to break through the scar tissue, to get the new knee working. He couldn't get sick. *She* couldn't get sick.

Felix would freak out if she got sick. He couldn't cope with anything that wobbled the building blocks of family life. Crap, what if he had to take Harry to the UNC Asheville open house? No way was she letting *that* happen.

She shifted, pushing down on her seat. The plastic had become hot and sticky; she peeled her palms free. Even though it was January, surely this dilapidated plane had air conditioning. And the oxygen, was it thinning? Ella sat still as everything around her slipped into slow motion. The hum of engines faded. The flight attendant, who had remained seated through the turbulence, glided backward down the aisle, holding up a white trash bag, claiming refuse. Her bangles jingled, chiming a death knell.

Judgment Day.

Sounds receded as Ella slipped into a dream, holding the armrests with weak arms, heavy arms that refused to move. A body no longer controlled. Pressure built between her breasts, an imaginary parasite swelling as it drained her oxygen, as it crushed down, as it suffocated her.

A fire-burst of pain shot through her jaw. Her eyes popped open; her breath came in short, sharp jabs. Her chest was being squeezed in a vise. Tight, tight, tighter.

Her heart began pumping adrenaline, pumping pain, pumping death.

"No," she whispered. *No.*

A deep voice, a stranger's voice from another time. *Felix?* "What's wrong?"

She had to stand, had to get air, had to get out. Couldn't free herself. Why was she wearing a seat belt? Why was she burning up? Who was the man clutching her arm too tightly?

Dying, she was dying. Was it too late to join the other passengers in the Lord's Prayer? *No, no.* History was not repeating itself. "You're so like your mom," her dad had said that morning. No, she had tried so hard to not be like her mom. Her heart was not meant to fail after forty-seven years. She was not her mom; she would not die and leave her child. She couldn't. No one loved Harry the way she did; no one knew how. Who would keep Harry safe, protect him from people who were stupid or cruel or both? Who would protect him from his own father?

"Can't . . . breathe."

A guy, fuzzy at the edges, faded in and out. He yanked her up; they were in the aisle, moving forward into first class. Felix would never make such a bold move . . .

"Miss!" the man shouted. "We need help!"

Someone reached for her. Women's voices—two of them. *Good, that's good. Women will understand: we aren't our mothers. History doesn't have to repeat itself. Mothers and daughters can share shoes. They don't have to share defective genes; they don't have to both die of heart attacks before their fiftieth birthdays.*

A narrow, metal space—everything stored away, everything secured. Except for her. Was she floating? No, someone was holding her by the waist, keeping her upright.

"Ma'am? Are you okay? Can you tell me what's happening?"

Burned coffee, she could smell burned coffee. Tried to cover her mouth; tried not to gag. The baby cried again. Harry; was Harry okay?

"Dizzy. Very dizzy. Short"—she sucked in air—"of breath. Pressure in chest. Pain in jaw."

"I don't think she's been feeling well since we took off," the good father said. Now she remembered him.

"How long have you had these symptoms, ma'am?"

"An hour? Maybe longer. Suddenly got worse."

"Do you have any current medical conditions? Are you on any medications?"

"No." Ella's legs buckled.

"Let's get her out of the galley—move her to the door where there's more room. Are you traveling alone?"

"Yes," the good father answered. "I think her son's meeting her at the airport."

Arms eased her to the floor.

Someone called for a doctor over the intercom. Three times.

"Ma'am? Can you hear me? Have you consumed any alcohol?"

Her head lolled to the side. "No."

"Get the oxygen and the AED. Call the cockpit, tell them we have a medical emergency." The voice softened, became angel-like. "Ma'am, I'm going to put an oxygen mask on you."

A plastic mask covered her face. It smelled funny.

"No one answered the PA," a woman said. She sounded worried. *Why?* "We can't use the enhanced medical kit."

"Call for a first responder. A fireman would do."

"I used to be a lifeguard." The good father again. He took her hand.

"Let's get the defibrillator on," the angel said.

Couldn't die on dirty, fake carpet, staring at a splat of gum. Couldn't die looking at anonymous feet. Wanted, needed . . . to touch Harry's face.

Harry. I won't leave you, Harry.

A ray of sunlight, and her mother's voice, singing a lullaby.

Please, Mom. Help me get home to Harry.

Hands ripped her shirt open; cold fingers stuck cold patches on her skin.

Then the world went black, silent but for an electronic echo: "Stand back. Monitoring heartbeat. Shock advised."

TWO

"You do realize, Harry"—Felix kicked his son's Union Jack Dr. Martens boot into the shoe cabinet, even though he'd been aiming for a nudge—"that this delightful piece of Scandinavian ergodynamic design has one job and one job only. To keep the hall clear of shoes. Hall, empty. Shoes, in here. It's a simple rule."

Harry, who was sprawled on the wood floor, puckered his nose and blinked repeatedly. "Don't you mean"—he stuttered through a series of short, shallow breaths—"ergonomic?"

"No. I don't. Ergonomic plus aerodynamic equals ergodynamic." Felix swallowed the *okay?* tickling the back of his throat. Harry never challenged him, but still, his son had a touch of smart aleck that could scratch the most even-tempered person raw.

Hair flopping forward, Harry fumbled with the laces of his Converse. Sixteen, with an above-perfect GPA, and still Harry struggled to tie his shoes. To stop himself from lunging across the hall and saying, "Oh for goodness' sake, let me," Felix shoved his hands into the pockets of his old donkey jacket—a classic bought on London's Carnaby Street in 1984.

Every day for the last sixteen years—Felix frowned; nearly seventeen—he'd prayed fatherhood would get easier. It hadn't. When he looked at this person who'd stolen his heart with the first gummy smile, Felix saw nothing that made sense. Harry's mind could leap from one subject to the next at chaotic speed while his body sparked through a rapid succession of spasms. He was a vortex of energy, the disruptive force of the kindergarten class, the only kid in first grade without the rosette that proved he had mastered the art of shoe tying. The boy who never blended in.

Before hopes and expectations had vanished, before the endless reports of inappropriate behavior had come home from school daily, Felix had imagined a future of parental bragging filled with father-son bonding. Of standing on the edge of a chilly soccer field saying, "That's my son who scored the winning goal." Of an annual father-son critique of the cricket at Lord's. But Harry hated soccer and denounced cricket as boring. Of course, he had no attention span for sports unless the Tar Heels were on the basketball court. Felix didn't understand basketball, nor did he want to. What he did understand was parental disappointment.

Had the SAT scores, combined with his connection to the president of Harvard, another Oxford man, brought a second chance for fatherly pride? Felix had always deferred to Ella on matters of Harry, and she'd been adamant that Harry couldn't cope with the pressure of an Ivy League school. And yet . . . and yet there was that grain of hope for redemption: *Oh yes, my son's at Harvard.*

He and Harry were night and day, yin and yang. No shared interests, no connection beyond name, and a bond neither of them seemed able to comprehend. Because if Harry understood one thing about his father, he would know to put his Dr. Martens where they belonged. It was an inarguable fact: the sky is blue; shoes go in the shoe cabinet.

Felix counted backward from ten, a calming technique he used at work when nothing was going in the right direction, and focused on his fiftieth birthday present. Stylish and functional, the cabinet had proved an adequate solution to the hazardous clutter of shoes in the hall, but as a gift it had been overly extravagant. When he'd pointed this out to Ella, she had pursed her lips, then walked away. That reminded him, he needed to ask her about the fifty-dollar charge on her last credit card statement from somewhere called hankypanky.com.

And still she hadn't replied to his text, even though his phone had marked the message as read. Ella knew he liked messages acknowledged immediately, but these days everything he did seemed to provoke her disapproval. Was it because of Harvard, or was a darker force at work, one that undoubtedly involved Katherine, the wine-drinking, marijuana-smoking, divorced she-devil?

"Harry, could you please hurry up?" Felix pulled his hands from his pockets and tapped his palm.

Harry glanced through the screen of blond hair that was reminiscent of Ella's hair twenty-three years ago. Or rather, it was until Harry had returned from Mad Max's with a purple streak and matching sparkly nail polish. Was his son trying to make a statement about sexuality, or was this merely the behavior of the socially challenged? With Mad Max involved, anything was possible. Supposedly a math genius, Harry's BFF dressed like a yobbo, stenciled on his arms with Sharpies, and burped far too loudly. Where *was* Max on the autism spectrum?

Felix pulled out his to-do list and checked. Yes, he had written *buy nail polish remover* at the bottom. He could have asked Harry to take care of this, but what was the point? Harry would forget and end up going to school tomorrow looking like a performer in the Ringling Bros. Circus. Given Harry's taste in clothes, that was entirely possible even without the nail polish.

"Harry, have you brushed your hair today?"

"Nope."

"Don't you have any self-respect?"

"Tons, Dad." Harry blew sideways out of his mouth, and what had once passed for a neat fringe ruffled. "Just none related to my hair."

A blast of ugly, harsh music blared from Harry's phone. "Hey, dude," he said in the singsong voice he used with his friends, but not his father.

"Harry!" Felix didn't mean to yell. Hustling Harry never ended happily, but late wasn't an option.

Harry swiveled round to face the wall, his upper body convulsing through a bout of tics that contained the power to strain muscles and joints. A complex tic was never a good sign. What would Ella do? She would give Felix the look—eyebrows raised, corner of her mouth dimpled—that either meant *I've got this covered* or *Really? You think you can help?* Then she would turn her back on Felix and exile him with an elegant wave. It was impossible not to feel irrelevant around those two, but he and Ella had made an agreement when Harry was first diagnosed: Ella, as the full-time parent, would take sole responsibility for Harry's therapy and treatment; Felix would follow her lead and never countermand that agreement. When he felt the urge to interfere, Felix would force himself to retreat into the havoc-free den he had designed and built at the far end of their 1950s bungalow. Ella and young Harry had a separate den, where there was always at least one toy in the middle of the sofa. Felix had rarely ventured inside.

If only Ella were here right now, taking care of this—of them. Yes, she babied Harry and pushed him to consider colleges that were an insult to his academic abilities, but Felix had missed her. Really missed her. Ella was always here, in their home, making sure their lives ran smoothly. Without her or Harry, the house had been cold and quiet, an abandoned shell. Loneliness, a forgotten emotion, had been Felix's only companion.

"Harry. We have to park, go inside the terminal, and get to baggage claim. If we don't leave right this minute, we will have failed to pick up your mother on time and she will be stranded like Orphan Annie."

"Gotta go, dude." Harry giggled. "Yeah. Dad's waiting."

Something about the way he said *Dad's waiting* niggled. At least Harry had a father who wanted the best for him. What was Harry thinking, agreeing to look at UNC Asheville? What was Ella thinking, suggesting it?

Harry pocketed his phone and headed for the front door. "You're wrong"—he paused with his hand on the doorknob—"Mom's hardly Orphan Annie. Annie Oakley, maybe."

Struggling to pay attention to anything after the word *wrong*, Felix followed Harry outside, slammed the front door, and snapped the key round in the lock.

Let it go, Felix. Let it go.

He pulled a small bottle of Pepto-Bismol caplets from his pocket, dumped two pink pills into his palm, and swallowed them dry. When had his stomach *not* been a dicky mess? Did he have an ulcer?

Walking down the steps of their freshly painted porch, Felix frowned at the combination of hot-tin-roof red against Westchester gray. All those hours spent agonizing over paint chips and still he'd chosen the wrong colors. However, the brushed-steel pots Ella had found at a going-out-of-business sale were close to perfect. She had stuffed them with ornamental cabbages and budded red pansies, as he had requested. Thankfully, his wife understood the importance of detail and never questioned his decisions regarding the house, which he had been rebuilding cabinet by cabinet, window by window, door by door since the day they'd moved in.

A pair of tiny, black-capped birds rose from the empty metal feeder, also painted in hot-tin-roof red. Ella would, no doubt, tut and ask why he hadn't filled it. But why would he? He had his domestic jobs; Ella had hers. He pictured her raised on tiptoe, pouring sunflower seeds into the feeder, her huge hoop earrings dancing at her neck. When they met, he used to say no one designed earrings like Ella. Now he said no one wore earrings like Ella. *Ella Bella.*

A herd of white-tailed deer sauntered in and out of his sight line. The wildlife of Durham, dubbed the "flower of the Carolinas" by English explorer John Lawson, still amazed and thrilled the city boy in him.

With a backward glance, Felix headed for the street. As always, part of him yearned to stay in their shady house, his very own castle hidden on the edge of Duke Forest and connected to the city cul-de-sac by a narrow wooden bridge. Such memories he had of kite flying on Hampstead Heath with his big brother, Tom; but tame London parks could never compare to the primal wonder of Duke Forest. During their first year in the house, back when Harry had been a giggling baby and Ella a picture of motherhood, Felix had longed for the world beyond their half acre to disappear. He'd wished they could cross the bridge, close their front door, and never leave.

A hawk gave a single, haunting cry; its mate answered. Passing through shadows cast by towering, ivy-wrapped pines, Felix stepped onto the bridge. The water in the creek beneath was still and clear, but reflected nothing. He wobbled the railing that needed replacing. Maybe this spring, after the toads and the bullfrogs returned, and the dogwoods and redbuds brought color back to the forest, maybe then he would take the time to rebuild this bridge.

Felix aimed the key fob at his cream and black Mini Cooper, which bleeped to unlock. After yesterday's washing, waxing, and interior cleaning, it sparkled. A four-hour job well done.

Harry bounced up and down with one hand on the passenger door, a human pogo stick set to hyperdrive. Plaid shirttails flapped from under his black leather biker jacket. How hard was it to tuck your shirt inside your jeans?

Felix stared at a discarded Christmas tree on the curb, with a solitary strand of tinsel bobbing like a snared snake. No, he would not comment.

"I've decided we're both . . . incorrect about your mother." *See, Ella? I'm trying.* "She's more like Annie Lennox."

Harry cracked his knuckles. Twice. Felix sucked on his bottom lip. Of his son's many irritating behaviors, this, surely, was the worst. And one, surely, that he could control.

"Harry. Please stop doing that."

"Doing what?" Harry jiggled worse than a squirrel planning an attack on the bird feeder. "And Annie Lennox? No idea who that is, Dad." Harry's face twitched, again and again.

How many tics in five seconds? The first trip back to England after Harry had been diagnosed—after they'd lost a year to misdiagnoses—Felix counted and charted the tics every day, seeking nonexistent triggers that could solve the mystery of where the Tourette's came from. He stopped when Ella pointed out that his hovering made the tics worse. The holiday had been ruined then, lost to the knowledge that he'd inflicted pain on his child.

In the power lines above, a murder of crows cackled.

Felix cleared his throat. "Annie Lennox is an English rock star. Cropped peroxide hair like your mother's. Drop-dead gorgeous."

"Gross," Harry said. "Next you'll be telling me Mom's sexy. Don't you think I spend enough of my life in therapy?"

An image formed of Ella wearing nothing but lacy red knickers. Felix eased his jeans away from his groin, but the sensation coiling in his gut was not desire.

How long since they'd had sex? She was in bed by ten thirty, and he never finished work before midnight. Her alarm went off at six so she could go on a power walk with some retired neighbor; his alarm went off at eight, when she was weaving through Durham's historic tobacco district, driving Harry to school. Could he blame conflicting circadian rhythms for their dwindling passion, or had something fundamental shifted in recent months? And if so, why was his gut hinting that the failure was his, that he was the one at fault?

The Coheed and Cambria song from Harry's iPod continued playing through the car stereo as Felix slowed down for the exit ramp off I-40. Music had always been problematic—so many wrong notes and bad lyrics. He'd faked an interest in punk and new wave as a teenager because doing so seemed appropriate, but until New Order's "Blue Monday" hit the charts in the early eighties—with its orderly, repetitive pulse—no song had resonated. Music, however, was a sedative for Harry. Although that screamo stuff Harry and Mad Max blared through the house could hardly be classified as music.

In the passenger seat, Harry was folded in half. What a gift to sleep that way, as if his constantly flailing body were finally unplugged. Once he'd become mobile, young Harry had stopped napping, and the broken nights had lasted through most of middle school. This new ability to conk out anywhere seemed to have coincided with Harry's starting high school. On random nights, however, he still shuffled into their bedroom, whimpering, "Mom, I had a nightmare. I need a hug."

Felix's own mother had stopped hugging him when he'd turned five. *Mother.* She had never been the easiest of people. Since turning eighty, she had become downright unpleasant. Harry had nicknamed her Moaning Myrtle, which was kinder than her cleaning lady's mumbled *miserable old trout.*

As Felix turned right onto Airport Boulevard, sirens advanced toward him like an approaching thunderstorm. He pulled over and stopped, and a bright-orange ambulance shot past, heading back toward the highway, lights flashing, siren howling.

Some poor bloke was probably strapped to the gurney inside. A wiped-out businessman who'd stayed over the Saturday night to save his firm money—an honorable thing to do—then risen early, showered and shaved, unaware that this flight would not be the carbon copy of every other trip home. Hopefully, the poor bastard would survive. Rotten luck to be taken ill at an airport.

Looking over his shoulder, Felix inched back onto the road and continued two miles an hour below the speed limit. He began spotting signs for Terminal 2 hourly parking. It was easy to get distracted by the traffic flow and end up in the wrong lane heading for the wrong car park. And when that happened? You had no choice but to exit the airport, circle back to the beginning, and start over. Another ten minutes would be wasted.

Five minutes later he found the ideal parking space adjacent to the pedestrian walkway and lined up the car perfectly between the parallel white lines. *Brilliant.* The car juddered into silence, and Harry slept on. Ella always woke him gently, easing him through the transition. Even so, Harry often woke up with fists clenched as if ready to box his way through another day.

Felix took a deep breath and squeezed Harry's knee. "Time to wake up."

Harry shot awake. "Mom?"

"It's Dad. You need to wake up now so we can—"

"Where's Mom?" Harry's head jerked from side to side. "She was calling my name. Something's wrong, very wrong—"

"Just a bad dream. You've been asleep since we left Durham. Come on." Felix unbuckled Harry's seat belt, but his son cowered.

"Harry. Shake off the dream. We need to find your mother."

Eyes glassed over with fear, Harry stared at Felix as if he were a stranger. Had Ella ever talked to the psychologist about these nightmares? Felix glanced at his watch. Ella's plane had landed ten minutes ago. The luggage would already be spewing down onto the carousel.

"Hazza—time to go."

Harry blinked, the spell broken. "You haven't called me Hazza in years."

"Because you're a little old for nicknames."

"You really believe that?" Harry cleared his throat. Part of his original tic repertoire, this vocal tic had been the one constant in the ever-changing world of Tourette syndrome.

"Harry, you're—"

"Nearly seventeen, I know." Harry opened the car door. "Old enough to start mapping out the rest of my life. So you keep reminding me."

What? Felix got out of the car. What had he said? Now he was the bad guy for trying to prepare his son for the future? Fatherhood was an active minefield.

A plane roared overhead, zooming up into the heavy blanket of gray clouds. Felix shivered and snuggled into the cashmere scarf knotted around his neck. For a nanosecond he was back in London, trapped in one of those gloomy January days when summer was an unattainable dream and you believed sunlight would never again warm your skin.

Heads ducked against the glacial wind, they crossed the road and entered Terminal 2. Felix patted Harry's arm to signal a change of direction, and they headed for the down escalator. People buzzed around them while an announcement drummed from invisible overhead speakers. Harry winced, then stopped to listen.

"Dad?" He grabbed Felix's arm, nails digging in as his elbow started to flap.

No. Not now. Not in public. Could Harry not hold in the tic for two more minutes so Ella could deal with it?

"Dad, why are they talking about Mom? Something's wrong, I told you. I told you. Something's wrong!"

"Harry. Stop this nonsense right now and—"

"Would the family of Ella Fitzwilliam please go to the Air Florida desk? Would the family of Ella Fitzwilliam please go to the Air Florida desk?"

Felix stood still and tried not to let his mind tumble through a series of worst-case scenarios as Harry's always did, but the thought trickled out like slow-working poison: *Who was in the ambulance?*

THREE

Mom was in trouble. Even without the nightmare, Harry knew, he knew. This wasn't the wacky part of his brain flashing through catastrophe. No, this was tangible fear; this was certainty. Mom was big on constant contact: *Text me when you and Max get there so I know you're safe; text me as you're leaving; just text me, okay?* Truthfully, it could get a bit annoying, but that was her way: to worry about him. All the time. And now he was worrying about her. She hadn't texted him when her plane landed. She wasn't safe.

A herd of travelers split around them and scattered. Everyone was going someplace except him and Dad. Why was Dad standing there not moving? What was he waiting for?

"Would the family of Ella Fitzwilliam please go to the Air Florida desk? Would the family of Ella Fitzwilliam please—"

"D-dad!" The stammer vibrated through his chest, through his arms, through his fingers. Pressure built in his throat: an unstoppable urge, an itch that had to be scratched. *No.* Now was not the time for a new tic. Dad couldn't deal with, with—

"G-go!" Harry tried to say more, but the words stuck in his throat.

Dad's chest rose and fell like he was panting. Beads of sweat escaped from his hairline like he was melting. He leaned up close, so in-your-face close that Harry almost gagged on the aftershave. Shouldn't a father know that his son was practically allergic to perfume?

"Harry, please, don't do this to me. I can't cope if you start ticcing."

Seriously? Mom needed help and this shit was still pushing Dad's buttons? Did he ever consider anyone but himself?

I have Tourette's, get over it already.

Harry tried to push against the mudslide of demeaning sound, tried to focus on those years of habit reversal therapy with Mom when she'd refused to quit, refused to let him quit no matter how hard they'd both been crying.

And where were you, Dad? Always wherever I wasn't.

Harry's head jolted sideways and his jaw made a cracking sound, like a bone breaking. *Ow.* Then he clucked. Twice. Always in pairs, had to be pairs. Relief—warm, comforting relief. He grabbed his jaw. Yup, still in one piece.

"I've got this," Harry said. "Go, help Mom."

The pressure regrouped, turned around for a second swing. But it was okay, okay because Dad was heading for the Air Florida desk. Finally, he was going to help Mom.

Harry's jaw popped in and out, popped in and out with sharp, jarring movements. Shockwaves of pain raced up through his face. *A clusterfuck of motor tics, a regular clusterfuck.*

He shoved his fist in his mouth and bit down. Blinding pain—Harry rocked back and forth—he would focus on the blinding pain. A woman grabbed her little boy's hand and yanked him away. The kid continued to watch over his shoulder, mesmerized. Two girls in skinny jeans giggled. Did they think he cared? He had no inhibitions—how could he? But they were cute girls, popular girls. And their stares hurt worse than the tics.

If Max were here, he would walk toward them, jab his finger, and say in the loudest voice possible, "*Eeew.* What's wrong with you, you fucking weirdos?" Then he would look around to make sure he'd drawn the fire from Harry.

Without Mom or Max as buffers, Harry was trapped in his own worst nightmare: just him and Dad against the world. He concentrated on walking, not hopping, twirling, or kicking. Most of the time, he didn't know when he was ticcing. But the complex tics that manifested as demonic possession? Those built up inside like tremors warning of a volcanic explosion.

Good, that's good, Harry. Focus on science. Focus on anything other than Mom.

Dad had reached the desk. He was talking to some airline lady with carrot-colored lipstick. Now they would get answers. Women responded to Dad—to that arrogance everyone mistook for aristocratic Brit, to those razor-blue eyes that could gut you.

Lipstick Woman watched Harry walk toward them, her eyes huge and white.

"Sclera!" Harry shouted. "Sclera!" Sclera—the white of the eye. A word he'd learned in biology; a word he'd never used until now. His jaw popped again. Pain ricocheted up into his eyeballs. He clamped both hands over his mouth and tried to hold his jaw still.

Her jaw, Lipstick Woman's jaw, kept moving as if she were some actress in a silent movie. *For real?* Lipstick that color and she thought *he* was the freak show?

Tell us about Mom.

Dad balled up his fists but didn't turn round.

"I'm sorry to have to tell you this, sir—" Lipstick Woman leaned over her desk, eyes flicking toward Harry. Her right hand hovered as if waiting to pound on some imaginary panic button. "But your wife collapsed on the flight from Fort Lauderdale." The woman lowered her voice. "I've been told she's on her way to Raleigh Regional."

Collapsed? Raleigh Regional? The pressure built again—hot, bubbling lava.

"Can you be more specific?" Dad used his monotone voice, the one that gave nothing away.

"The crew thinks"—more eye flicking in Harry's direction. *What is her problem?*—"it may have been a heart attack, sir. Obviously we don't know for sure."

Heart attack? How was that possible? But his grandmother had died of a heart attack at forty-seven. Mom had just turned forty-seven. But Mom couldn't have a heart attack. Mom couldn't die.

The volcano erupted and Harry started spinning.

"Sir, I realize this is a difficult time for you, but I need you to control your son."

"Control my son?" Dad's voice was jagged ice. "And how do you propose I *control* a young man with Tourette's after you just informed him that his mother may have had a heart attack?"

Did Dad have to repeat the words *heart attack?*

"There's no need to take that tone." The woman picked at her tightly fastened top button. "You need to calm down. Sir."

"I'm perfectly calm. *Ma'am.*"

Spinning around and around. Spinning, clucking. Repeat, repeat.

"If you can't control your son, I'll have to call my supervisor."

Shit, no. Dad would go ballistic and make the situation a thousand times worse. Could it—Harry strummed his fingers, pranced on his toes—get any worse?

The tics ended like a twister hauling ass back into the sky. Exhaustion replaced chaos.

"Harry." Dad stalked past him without making eye contact. "Ignore this woman. We're leaving."

Poker players had tells; so did Dad. No other way to read him. Dad did quiet anger, suppressed anger, with his fingernails digging into his palm. Until he blew. What to say that wouldn't set Dad off? Not the truth. Not, *Are you as scared as I am?* Because this was Dad, not Mom. Dad didn't believe in trading emotions.

"Dad?"

"Mom's tougher than a marauding Celt in a kilt. She'll be fine."

"You really believe that?"

Dad slowed to a normal pace, but he didn't answer, not even as they walked back out into the gray Carolina afternoon. Drizzle fell from the sky; pinheads of rain marked the lenses of Dad's glasses. Dad, who wiped his glasses so frequently that Harry often wondered if it was a compulsion, seemed not to notice.

The cop on traffic duty blew his whistle, and Harry imitated the sound. Sometimes it was easier to give in and release the tic before it transformed into a full-blown hurricane. The tic lasted only a few seconds; the stare from the cop, longer.

"I have to go to the hospital." Dad stepped into the crosswalk without looking. "Can you handle this, or do we need Max to pick you up?"

Mom had taught him to ignore critics, but how did that line of thinking work when your toughest critic was your own dad?

"You remember about me and hospitals?"

Dad sighed. "I'm your father. I know that you're phobic about hospitals, being behind the wheel of a car, spiders, and flying."

Right, like Dad knew much about that last one.

"But you never sit with us on a plane. How do you know?"

"I don't sit with you because Mom—" Dad swallowed a sob.

Can't fool me. I've been disguising vocal sounds for years.

"I don't sit with you because your mother insists I don't. She can focus better on you that way. She knows I don't like to fly, either."

"But you fly all the time for work."

"It's part of my job, Harry. Failure isn't an option."

For a moment, Harry had almost believed they were having a father-son confidence. But Dad was wrong. Failure was always an option, because the knowledge that you couldn't win every time gave you the courage to try. Effort should always be enough to earn gold stars. Ask anyone with a shitload of defective brain wiring.

Dad fumbled in his pocket, took out his car keys, dropped them, picked them up. His hand shook. "Can you do this, Hazza—come to the hospital?"

There it was again, *Hazza*. A name once spoken with affection.

"Yes," Harry said, leading the way to the car.

He would force himself to go to the hospital for Mom—the ultimate exposure to his phobia; she would be so proud. But he would also do this with the hope—a hope he'd never been able to ditch—that one day Dad would be proud of him, too. For something other than fucking SAT scores.

FOUR

Felix pulled onto the freeway off-ramp and headed into Raleigh. Navigating narrow London streets might be a nail-biting exercise, but these grid-planned divided highways with rows of town houses and interchangeable strip malls were so contrived. So falsely happy. He and Harry could have been skirting the center of any city in America— trapped in a suburban prison with Ella beyond the razor wire.

He needed to meet with the cardiologist, investigate the man's credentials, start the process of transferring Ella to Duke. Or Memorial in Chapel Hill. Or he could look into taking her back to England, to Papworth Hospital in Cambridge. Wasn't that the best of the best? And phone calls—there were phone calls to be made: to Mother; Ella's father; Katherine, who always looked at him sideways as if to say, *I know more about your marriage than you do.* And Robert; he should call his partner and say, what—I need a day off? He never took a day off. And what about Harry's school?

"Could you slow down, Dad? I'm feeling carsick."

"I thought you outgrew that when you hit double digits."

"So did I," Harry said.

Felix eased his foot off the accelerator, and the needle dipped from sixty miles per hour to forty-five. The last thing he needed was vomit inside his clean car. Or a speeding ticket. His right leg began to shake, making it almost impossible to keep pressure on the pedal. Should he be driving? Probably not. He glanced around. Where in God's name were they? Had he taken the wrong exit? He knew how to get to Raleigh Regional. How could he be so incompetent? How could he fail his wife so abominably?

"You do know where we're going, right?" Harry said.

Be quiet, Harry. I need to think.

"Want me to figure it out?"

"No." How had he managed to screw this up and get them lost?

Harry was messing with his phone. "I see what you did." He bounced in his seat—kinetic energy barely contained by a seat belt. "Easy to fix. Turn right here. Here, Dad. Here!"

"I'm turning round, Harry."

"No, you don't have to. We're so close. Look!"

Harry waved his phone in front of Felix.

"Harry, I'm driving."

"But we're super close and we can be there in like two minutes. It's a shortcut!"

"I don't want to take a shortcut, Harry. I want to turn round and put us back on the road we're meant to be on."

Harry jolted forward, nose almost touching the windshield. "Hospital Drive! Turn right—the next right. Please?" He cleared his throat multiple times. "For once, Dad, can you just trust me?"

But Harry didn't understand. This wasn't about trust; this was about making the best decision. Decisions flew out of Harry's mouth the second they entered his brain. He didn't agonize, didn't edit, didn't weigh pros and cons to reach a responsible, informed course of action. He did whatever his mother suggested he do, which was the real reason Felix had to take control of the college applications.

If he could just read the damn street signs . . . Traffic shot past, cars driven by people who knew where they were going. Felix slowed to thirty miles per hour, and the person behind blared a horn. They should be on their way to Raleigh Regional, and instead they were stuck on some never-ending dual carriageway. Felix glanced in the rear-view mirror. The huge pickup truck behind moved up almost to the Mini's bumper, flashed its lights, and tore past.

Felix felt nothing, not even a flicker of his usual road rage.

"There's nowhere for a U-turn." Felix dug around in his pocket and located the Pepto-Bismol. Wait. He'd already taken two, hadn't he? Focus, he must focus. His stomach gurgled.

"We don't need to retrace our steps, Dad." Harry's voice was quiet and flat. "Take the next right. I can get us there."

What the hell? It wasn't as if they had many options right now. Besides, there was a BP gas station up ahead. He could turn around in there. BP, British Petroleum. If he believed in omens, which he most definitely did not, that would mean something.

Felix flicked on the indicator and maneuvered.

"There it is, Dad. On the left—Raleigh Regional!"

Dammit, Harry'd been right.

"Should I spot signs for the ER? Is that where we go? You think Mom's in the ER?"

"I don't know, Harry. I swear, I don't know."

"I think we need the ER, Dad."

This time, Felix listened to his son.

A gust of January wind roared in their faces as they trekked across the hospital car park.

"I'm calling Max," Harry said.

Felix nodded. The rain had turned into hard nuggets of frozen precipitation that battered the tips of his ears. Should he call someone? If Tom were still alive, he would have called Tom. Even when they were children, his brother knew what to say, knew how to comfort.

He could call Saint John, his friend from Eton days. *God, I hate having to explain his name is pronounced Sinjun. Will I ever stop feeling like an alien in this country?* Should he call Saint John? No, no, it was nine English time. Far too late to disturb on a Sunday evening. There was no one else.

"'S me." Harry sniffed into his phone. Felix glanced round to see if anyone was listening. "Mom's in the hospital. She got sick on the plane." Harry paused to tic. "They think it's her heart. Yeah, I'm really scared. Shitting myself. Doesn't sound good." Another sniff, this one louder. "Would you? Okay. I'll call when I know what's going on. Love you, man."

Harry pocketed his phone. "Max is coming over when we get home." He continued snuffling as they walked toward the brightly lit "EMERGENCY" sign.

"Would you like a tissue, Harry?"

Harry shook his head, then wiped his nose on the back of his hand. He stopped as the door whooshed open. "I-I don't know if I can do this."

I don't know if I can, either. Felix hadn't been inside a hospital since Tom's last months.

Felix was six; he was standing in Pater's study with his legs crossed. (He really, really needed the loo.) Pater was grilling him on capital cities, making sure Felix was ready for his school interview, ready to follow in the footsteps of four generations of Fitzwilliam men: Shrewsbury House until he was old enough for Eton. Mother had already bought the tuck box and the

trunk with his initials on the top. Failure was not a possibility. He had to succeed—had to—because if he didn't, he couldn't be with Tom for his final year before Eton. If only Tom were here now. Tom had magical powers. He always knew when Felix was alone in Pater's study. Always knew when to burst in. Pater couldn't get mad at Tom because Tom was Mother's favorite. And strong. He had big muscles from those weights he lifted.

Who cared that Tom was Mother's favorite? Not Felix. He was Tom's favorite, and that was all that mattered. When he was grown up at twelve—double digits!—he was going to be just like Tom. Tom was always laughing about being in detention. Nothing scared Tom. Nothing! Not even Pater. If Tom were here, Felix could be as brave as a World War I soldier in the Battle of the Somme.

He really needed the loo.

The curtains were drawn; it was dim and stuffy. Pater's green leather chair looked black. Everything looked black. How could Pater work in here with so little light and the gas fire turned up high? The room stank of stale cigars; the overhead light flickered. Felix shivered. The boys in his class were always making up scary stories about hell, but Felix didn't have to use his imagination. He knew what hell looked like.

He stared at Pater's blotter, covered in splodges of black ink like dried bloodstains, and backed up into the bookcase. He didn't want to think about the last time he'd been in here alone.

Pater raised his voice; Felix's tummy felt all growly. His fingers were slippery, too. He tapped his palm, which he always did when he was anxious. Pater called it his annoying habit, but it always made Felix feel better and reminded him to not suck his thumb, which no one but Tom knew he still did. Sometimes he dug his fingernails into his palm hard. Hurt loads, but it stopped him from raising his thumb to his mouth.

The capital of Finland? Pater slammed his hand down on the blotter.

Felix knew this! Too hard, though, to remember everything: the sequence of his annoying habit, the capital of Finland . . . Too late. Thumb at his mouth. Quick! Think, Felix. Chew nail! Yes, chew nail. See. I'm not a baby!

I've told you a thousand times, Felix. Keep those bloody hands still. You're not some nervous little girl. Or are you? Are you another fairy, like your brother?

What did Pater mean? Tom was a boy, not a fairy.

Take that thumb out of your mouth! Pater's face was red.

Felix screwed his eyes shut. Capital of Finland, capital of Finland.

Helsinki! he called out, but it was too late. He was always too late. Pater was going into the locked drawer at the bottom of his desk.

No. Daddy, no.

Bend over.

Helsinki, Daddy, Helsinki!

You know the routine.

He was crying and tapping his palm and all he wanted was to suck his thumb. He couldn't run away. He was jammed up against the bookcase. Trapped.

Pater moved out from behind the desk. He tightened his grip on the riding crop.

Please. I'll work hard. I'll get rid of my annoying habit. I will. I don't mean to be "the big disappointment."

Take your trousers down, and your underwear. Bend over. Pater's voice was cold and hard.

No.

Pater stopped and panted as if he were a bull about to charge. And Felix couldn't help it, he wet himself.

Everything happened fast. He was on the floor, facedown on the stinky old Oriental rug. He screamed, but the house was empty. No one would hear him; no one would rescue him. Mother was away for the weekend; Tom was off with friends.

Pater tugged at Felix's trousers. The whip cracked.

Pain sliced him in two.

Another crack, another. Would Pater kill him this time?

The door crashed open.

Get off my brother. Get off! You ever touch him again, and I'll call the police. Right after I tell Mother and Grandmother.

Scuffling and chaos followed, but Felix kept his eyes shut tight. He couldn't move, couldn't do anything but cry. His legs were cold and wet; his bottom was on fire.

Tom was lifting him up. His hero, his savior.

He would never love anyone the way he loved Tom.

Felix gasped for air.

"You okay, Dad?"

"Yes." Felix stabbed his left palm with his fingernails. Again and again, until his hand was pockmarked with pain. "I have to go inside. You can come with me, or you can wait in the car."

"For real, Dad?"

"I can't baby you through this, Harry. I'm not your mother, I—"

"Why d'you think I called Max?" Harry said, and strode past him through the open door. Then he stopped in the foyer, his body writhing, jerking, contorting, dancing to the weird tempo Harry alone understood.

"I need help," a woman inside shouted. "Why aren't you helping me?" She collapsed into the arms of a security guard and screamed in Spanish.

The security guard wore a holstered gun on his hip. Instinctively, Felix moved between him and Harry. He could live in America for another seventeen years and never adapt to the sight of an armed cop. He looked up at a sign banning concealed weapons. This was not a world he could comprehend; this was not England. He didn't want Ella in a place with armed guards.

Harry stared at the woman and began to shake.

"Go through the metal detector," Felix said, "and sit in the far corner of the waiting room. Watch the game." Felix pointed at a huge flat screen TV, which was showing players running around in powder-blue and white basketball uniforms. "The Tar Heels are playing."

"Now you want me to watch television?"

"I'm doing my best, Harry."

Behind him, the woman grew hysterical. Voices muttered and she was gone.

"I know, Dad. I'm sorry. I didn't mean to be . . . I'm freaking out. Really freaking out."

"I'll see if I can get us somewhere private to wait."

Harry's head bobbed with short, jerky nods.

Felix turned to the receptionist, a bank teller look-alike behind bulletproof glass. "My wife was brought in earlier from RDU. Suspected heart attack."

The woman scanned a clipboard. Good God, was she incompetent? How many women could have been brought in from an airplane?

"Name?"

"Felix Fitzwilliam."

"No, sir," she said gently. "Your wife's name."

"Ella." *Ella Bella, Ella Bella.*

"Ella Fitzwilliam?"

"Yes. Is she—?"

"I believe they took her to the cath lab. Let me get some information for you." She picked up the phone.

"And my son." Felix swallowed. "My son has Tourette's and a hospital phobia. He's quite . . ." Sharing personal information with strangers was not within Felix's definition of normal social interaction. "My son is quite distressed. Could we wait somewhere private?"

Somewhere with a door. A door meant Felix could contain Harry the way Ella used to during the rage attacks that, on some level, Felix had understood. After all, if you were going to lose yourself in one emotion, anger was the least complicated.

"I'll go ask," the woman said. She finished her call and moved away from the glass.

In a private room, they could disappear. "Disappear," Tom always told him. "Out of sight, out of Mother's mind. Don't bother her unless it's to say good night." Mother had no interest in the emotional life of her family, only in maintaining appearances. Her life was perfect; her children were perfect. Her husband was not an abusive bully. Her elder son did not appear to be a homosexual. God, he missed Tom—every single day. He couldn't miss Ella, too.

The future flashed before him. A kaleidoscope of unlived memories without Ella. A future in which he had sole responsibility for Harry. A future in which he had to prove that, unlike the two role models he'd grown up with, he could be a decent parent.

Felix glanced over his shoulder. Harry was rocking back and forth, one hand digging into his hair, the other clutching his iPod. Of course—music.

"Harry," Felix said loudly. "Plug in."

When Harry stared, uncomprehending, Felix mimed putting in earbuds.

He turned back. A second woman had appeared behind the glass, and she was watching Harry as if he were a curiosity in a zoo.

Felix had to be clear; he had to take charge. "My son has several neurological disorders and a phobia about hospitals. I need to get him somewhere secluded right now. If I don't, he'll create a distressing scene, and you will wish you had listened to me." Too much information?

The woman continued to stare at him. Did she need sign language?

"It will create a huge disruption in your waiting room," Felix said slowly.

The woman nodded. "I'll see what I can do."

"Thank you."

She smiled. A smile laced with pity, a smile he'd seen when Tom was in hospital.

Felix signaled Harry over. He shot out of his chair, grimaced and blinked, grimaced and blinked, and hurtled toward Felix like a heat-seeking missile. Harry grabbed the edge of Felix's jacket and tugged. Felix tried to wrap an arm around Harry's shoulder, but Harry was taller than he was, and Felix couldn't reach. He had missed the hug-gable years. He settled for Harry's waist, and they both went rigid. A pair of robots with shared DNA.

The two receptionists slid back into their stations, and a nurse appeared through a door. "Fitzwilliam family?" Her voice boomed, a surprisingly powerful voice for a petite woman with a bouncy ponytail and a bright smile. "We're preparing a room in the CCU for your wife. It's not quite ready, but I can take you up there."

"Thank you," Felix said.

They followed her through endless corridors rank with the stench of disinfectant, and up three floors in an elevator. How would they ever find their way out?

Finally, they stood in a vast, macabre version of an anonymous hotel room. One wall had a built-in media center with cabinets, shelves, and a large television. The recliner in the corner was covered in Tar Heels–blue vinyl. Harry glanced at it and moved to the opposite side of the room. The nurse fiddled with the venetian blinds. Not yet four o'clock and the day was fading.

"When can I see my wife?"

"It's going to be a while," the nurse said. "But once she's done in the cath lab, they'll bring her up here."

"What in God's name is a cath lab?"

"It's where they take pictures of a patient's coronary arteries and open up any blockages they find. It's not nearly as scary as it sounds." The nurse smiled at Harry. "And by the time patients arrive here, in the CCU, they're pretty stable."

"What's her prognosis?"

"You'll have to ask the cardiologist, sir. But I can tell you that people who get to the cath lab quickly enough often have nearly full recovery of their heart function."

Often, nearly. Those were empty words. "When can I meet with the cardiologist?"

"He'll be by after the procedure."

"What procedure?"

"Angioplasty. That's how they open up the blockage. I'll find you a pamphlet that explains everything."

No, he didn't want a pamphlet, and he didn't want reassurance from Florence Nightingale. Felix needed information and statistics; he needed facts and figures; he needed a plan of action. Maybe he should start making a list while they were waiting: questions to ask the doctor, people to call, things to be arranged. First and foremost: see the doctor.

"I really need to see the doctor."

"The cardiologist is still with your wife, sir."

"Will you at least tell me if she's . . ." He lowered his voice. "Conscious."

"Oh, yes, she is."

Harry paced around the room like a caged gerbil without a running wheel. "Is my mom going to die?"

"Good heavens, no," the nurse said. "She's very lucky, you know—to end up here. Raleigh Regional has the best heart center in the state. We see more heart patients than any other hospital in North Carolina."

Really. Well, this sure as hell wasn't Duke.

"When you see her, your mom will be groggy from the sedative and antianxiety meds." The nurse kept smiling at Harry. "'Quietly happy' is the phrase we use. Can I get either of you anything while you wait?"

Harry shook his head. "No, thanks."

"No, thank you," Felix said. What he meant was "Yes, I want my wife." *I want her to walk through that door, smile, and say, "Let's go home."*

*

An hour passed. Harry listened to music and played *Angry Birds*. There had been several phone conversations with Mad Max, which was hardly surprising. The boys seemed incapable of navigating a day without multiple phone conversations. Some of their daily chats shared asinine observations—"Dude, the camping episode of *SpongeBob* is on!" Others led to laughter and clipped sentences in Harry-Max language. This afternoon, Harry had told his best friend over and over, "Still no news." Felix was prepared to smash the phone if he heard that phrase one more time.

When squeaking wheels in the corridor moved closer and closer, Felix leaped to attention. Harry glanced at him and bounced up to stand by his side, rolling on the balls of his feet. Two orderlies pushed in a gurney; a nurse followed alongside. No one spoke.

Felix retreated into a corner, and Harry followed his lead.

The white mannequin lying rigid on the gurney with a tube taped to her wrist, a plastic cone hooked over her finger, a tube jabbed into the pale skin under her neck, pads taped to her chest, and what appeared to be a sandbag on her groin, was his wife. And her mouth was covered with an oxygen mask.

A memory flickered: Ella in Jackie O sunglasses, laughing at a shared, private joke. Felix stared at the oxygen tank and tasted bile.

Ella raised a palm and waved her fingertips. Harry jumped forward, but Felix put out an arm to restrain him. "Let the nurses get Mom settled," he said.

Harry grimaced and blinked, grimaced and blinked.

People swarmed as orderlies grabbed the gurney's sheet and, in one swift tug, slid Ella onto the bed along with a startling amount of paraphernalia. Felix recognized most of it from Tom's last weeks: the monitor, IV fluid bag, catheter bag, and blood pressure cuff. The orderlies disappeared with the gurney; the nurse transferred Ella's oxygen tank and began messing with leads, hooking up everything to the large monitor on the wall. Felix stared up at the words until he'd memorized them: heart rhythm, MAP, and O_2 saturation.

"Are you having any chest pain, dear?" the nurse asked Ella.

Ella shook her head so slowly it barely moved. The nurse took Ella's vital signs, listened to her lungs, and then checked the sandbag on the groin.

"What's she doing?" Harry whispered.

"This is the arterial insertion site," the nurse said. "It's where they inserted the catheter that went into your mother's heart. We keep the sandbag in place for a few hours to apply pressure and prevent a hematoma from forming. You must be Harry." She turned with a smile. "Your mother told us all about you."

Harry glanced at Felix, his lips almost as pale as his cheeks.

"Are you comfortable, dear?" The nurse turned back to Ella.

Ella nodded, grabbed at her oxygen mask, and missed.

"You can talk to your family for a minute." The nurse slid the mask off. "Then we need to put this back on."

"Hey, baby." Ella smiled a lazy smile and reached for Harry. He shot toward her, rubbing his left eye with the heel of his hand. "Don't be scared. Everything's fine. I'll be home soon. So proud of you for coming to the hospital."

They threaded their fingers together, and Felix stood frozen in place. An outsider watching through an invisible window.

Finally, her eyes settled on Felix; she squinted as if staring directly into the sun. "Take Harry home. Doesn't need to see this."

"I had to come." Harry tugged on his shirt—hard enough to rip it. "I had to. What did they say? Are you going to be okay? Are you, Mom?"

Harry's breath sped up; he pounded his chest. Any minute now he could explode into a tornado of tics. Ella gave another punch-drunk smile. How much sedative had they given her? Was she too looped to calm Harry?

"*Shhh.* I'm fine. No pain." She gave an odd laugh. "Treat this as an excuse to skip school. Stay home tomorrow, play video games."

"No." Harry clucked. Again and again. "I have a calculus test. And I don't want to stay home." Harry glanced at Felix. His look clearly said, *With you.*

Felix fixed his attention on the top line of the monitor, the heart rhythm line. "Why don't all the heartbeats look the same?" he asked the nurse. "Is that something bad?"

Harry started twitching. His left elbow flapped in several short, sharp bursts.

"Certainly not, sir," the nurse said as she slid the oxygen mask back into place. "You're seeing skipped beats, or what we call premature ventricular contractions. They look a bit different than normal beats, but I can assure you they're very common in this setting. Nothing to worry about." She fussed with Ella's sheets.

"What does MAP mean?" Felix said, still staring at the monitor.

"Mean arterial pressure." The nurse puffed up a pillow. "And the bottom one is oxygen saturation."

"Yes. I figured that out." Felix paused. "What do you know about the cardiologist, Ella? Do we need to get a second opinion?"

Ella closed her eyes briefly. She loosened the oxygen mask. "Take Harry home. I'm fine."

No. For once, could she need him as much as he needed her?

"Not until I've talked with the doctor." Felix turned to the nurse. "Why isn't he here? Where is he? Is he the best? What are his credentials?"

The nurse's head jerked back, creating a stack of double chins. "You need to be patient." She spoke as if addressing a non-English speaker. "He'll be in shortly."

Felix clenched his fist. Shortly was not good enough; shortly was not a call to action. "I'll phone your father while we're waiting for the cardiologist."

Ella shook her head.

"No? But what should I do if he calls the house and asks how your flight was?"

More violent head shaking, and then Ella pushed up the mask.

"I'll call Dad tomorrow. Phone Katherine," Ella said. "Tell her to come here. You guys leave. Katherine will . . ."

"Mom?" Harry became a spinning top wound too tight.

Felix ignored him. "I'm not leaving until I've talked with the doctor." He walked to the bed and rested his hand on Ella's leg. "Nurse, why did the oxygen saturation just drop from ninety-eight to ninety-six percent? What does that mean?"

"Nothing, sir."

"It means something, otherwise—"

Harry grabbed his neck as if trying to strangle himself. His head did the weird sideways tic he'd released at the airport. A new tic.

"Our son has Tourette's," Felix said to the nurse.

"Shhh." Ella reached for Harry, but her hand swam through air. "Felix, please. Harry needs to leave. Call Katherine. She'll stay with me."

"I'm not leaving. Not until someone tells me what's going on. I will not trust your life to people I don't know. Suppose they've been sued for malpractice."

"Thanks for the vote of confidence," the nurse muttered.

"Felix, I'm in good hands. One of Harry's teachers"—Ella closed her eyes—"had heart surgery here. I know you're trying to protect me, Felix. But I'm fine. Everything is fine."

Could she please stop staying that? Every corner of his being told him things were not fine. They were far from fine.

"Call Katherine. Go home. She'll tell you everything. Later." Ella's chest rose and fell. Her mother had died of a heart attack at forty-seven; Ella was forty-seven. Had nature's bullet hit the genetic bull's-eye painted on her chest? He tapped his palm with ferocious speed.

"I need to talk with the doctor." His voice split. "I need to . . ."

"I know you do," she said quietly. "I understand."

Ella always understood—just as Tom had.

"But we have to . . . think about Harry. Take him . . . home . . . before this becomes . . . too much."

Too late.

Harry's elbow flapped, then his right arm shot out, nearly catching on one of Ella's tubes. Felix and the nurse rushed forward. Harry's arm flung out a second time, and Felix jumped back before he got walloped.

"Maybe you should listen to your wife, sir," the nurse said.

"Maybe you should get the cardiologist so I can find out whether my wife is going to die."

"Felix!" Ella tried to sit up, suddenly massively alert for someone shot with what had to be horse tranquilizers. He couldn't imagine anything else keeping her down when Harry was in this level of distress.

The nurse eased her back. "Ella, you need to lie flat. You"—she glared at Felix—"are upsetting your wife, and I cannot allow that."

Harry, huddling against the wall now, continued to tic. "Mom, I'm sorry. I—"

"*Shhh*, baby," Ella said. "I love you, my amazing son. Everything's fine. But you guys shouldn't be here. It's going to upset . . . both of you . . . for no reason." Ella wheezed and closed her eyes again. "Felix, please."

Chaos, he was surrounded by chaos, and no one was doing what he needed them to do.

Felix looked down at his hands, clawed and ready to inflict pain if he didn't get what he wanted. On his pinkie was the family signet ring that had belonged to Pater and Grandfather. And Tom. Every day it connected him to Tom. He raised his fist to his mouth and caught the family crest in his teeth. He would not be a monster; he would not be his father's son.

He moved up the bed, blocking out Harry and the nurse with his back, trying to collapse the world to him and Ella. Despite the sedative, her eyes widened with the truth. *I'm afraid,* her expression said. The false bravery had been for Harry's benefit.

"I love you so much, Ella Bella," he whispered into her ear. *Don't leave me.*

She grabbed his hand and squeezed.

I love you too, she mouthed.

He pulled back. "Say good-bye to your mother, Harry. We're leaving." Felix placed Ella's hand on the bed and walked to the door.

Behind him, Harry's voice, small and childlike: "I love you, Mom."

Felix kept walking. How many times had he told Ella he loved her? Not enough. He'd never expected a woman to love him back; he'd certainly never expected the woman of his dreams to vow to love him for all eternity. After they met and she left London to be near her father, he had never dared to hope for a different outcome. When she left the second time, after returning five years later, it was as if a part of him had died. And he knew, without doubt, that if she left him for a third time, he would not recover. Without Ella, he could not exist.

FIVE

Mad Max was waiting for them on the doorstep. "Dude—" He rushed forward to give Harry a hug that was all arms, boy odor, and limp, unbrushed hair.

This bizarre relationship seemed to operate beyond the boundaries of normal guy friends. Heterosexual or homosexual, Felix didn't care, but he couldn't imagine having a friend he wanted to hug. Nor could he imagine ending a phone call, as Harry had earlier, with *love you, man*. It was hard enough to say *I love you* to Ella.

Felix unlocked the door, and the boys bolted inside before he'd canceled the alarm. Harry's bedroom door shut with a slam that said *Do not enter, don't even think about entering unless you know the secret handshake.*

The only secrets Felix knew were his own.

He slid the pizza box onto the hand-poured concrete island in the kitchen. Picking up a large pepperoni pizza on the way home had made perfect sense. Although he wasn't remotely hungry and neither, apparently, was Harry. Maybe the boys would scavenge later.

Time to start on those lists. An organized mind was the key to survival. Lists comforted; lists screamed *I am in control*. First up, though, call Katherine. Her phone went to voice mail; he didn't leave a message. He started dialing Robert, who was likely in the office, then changed his mind and sent a text.

> Ella had a heart attack. She's in
> the CCU at Raleigh Regional. I won't
> be in tomorrow.

An immediate reply:

> What room? We'll send flowers. Keep
> me posted.

He was about to type *thank you* when his phone rang.

"Hey, Felix," Katherine said. "I gather you caused quite a scene at the hospital. Has the nursing staff blacklisted you?"

Felix flicked up the entire row of kitchen light switches. A horrible waste of power, but he had a sudden need to flood the house with artificial light. "It's been a long, hard day, Katherine."

"Longer and harder for your wife, I can assure you."

Cradling the phone between his neck and shoulder, Felix tapped his palm. "What did the cardiologist say?"

"He reiterated what happened and said she did great in the cath lab. They put in a stent, which I gather is how they unblock the artery."

"I know all this. I want—"

"The location of the blockage means she has something called a widow-maker lesion. Basically, she's pretty damn lucky to be alive."

Felix's left hand began to convulse; his wedding ring became a blur of gold.

"Bottom line—big heart attack, and she's critical but stable," Katherine said. "They'll likely keep her in the CCU for the next twenty-four hours, and then move her onto the cardiac floor with something called telemetry monitoring."

"What's her prognosis? How long will they keep her?"

"I couldn't weasel much out of the doc on either front. He was annoyingly vague, despite my best romance novelist charm."

Felix nearly said, *I thought you wrote porn for a living.*

"She could be here for up to five days—it all depends. As for big-picture thinking, if she learns to manage her risk factors and does well in cardiac rehab, she'll likely be fine, yada, yada, yada. I get the impression these heart docs don't like to commit. But the point is that she's a survivor. That's what's important. Oh, and the cardiologist assigned to her will be here at nine thirty in the morning," Katherine continued. "You might want to arrive in time for that. Without Harry. Ella is adamant that he's not to return to the hospital."

"Harry's going to school tomorrow. His choice," Felix said.

"How's he doing?"

"Max is sleeping over. They're currently barricaded in the Bat Cave."

Katherine gave a hollow laugh. "How are you doing?"

"Not well. You?"

"Total shit. I'm on deadline but I can't write. My thoughts aren't lining up. Know what I mean?"

Actually, he did.

Music—loud and raw—came from Harry's bedroom. Ambient noise from the CCU drifted down the phone line. Outside, a neighbor's dog barked.

"And Ella?" Speaking her name, feeling the vibration of *Ella* on his lips . . . He crumpled onto a barstool and tried to support the weight of his head in his hand. But his elbow slid along the top of the island, threatening to knock the pizza to the floor. "Is she in any pain?"

"She's asleep again. They gave her a ton of happy pills."

"She doesn't like taking pills."

"Oh, she's enjoying these."

No matter what he said, Katherine had to contradict. "Would you do me a favor?"

"What?" She sounded wary.

"Stay with her until I get there tomorrow. I don't want her waking up alone."

"Do you have to ask?"

"Katherine, can we call a truce?"

She gave another laugh, this one even less sincere. "Sure. But if you upset her again, I'll beat the shit out of you. And you know I'll win. Good night, Felix." And she hung up.

Katherine had a point. Now that she'd taken up boxing, she could pulverize him, but who—male or female—would seek pleasure with a pair of boxing gloves?

Pushing himself away from the smell of pizza, he stared into the living room. Seventeen years of creating this perfect, open-plan cocoon for his family, of grappling with 1950s electrics, of tearing out to rebuild, and suddenly it all seemed pointless. Above the empty fireplace hung the portrait of Ella painted by one of her arty college friends. Felix had never liked oil paintings—real life embellished with heavy brush strokes and globs of paint. This one was particularly grotesque: Ella distorted into *The Scream*.

Felix walked across the living room and faced the night on the other side of the sliding patio doors. Beyond the glass lay an impenetrable screen of mature trees and undergrowth—the black wall of Duke Forest. Since he was a boy, he'd been drawn to small, dark places. A true Brit, he loved to sit in the sun, but he needed shade to feel safe. Ella had wanted a modern colonial with a wraparound porch, a lawn, and a cheerful sun garden—preferably in rural Orange County, outside Chapel Hill. Not Felix. The moment he'd discovered the tree-lined roads of flickering shade that surrounded the Duke campus, it was as if some missing piece of his life—that he hadn't even known was missing—fell into place.

She had conceded, but not happily. Did she regret her decision? If she had the choice, would they move? He looked down. A foot up from ground level, a raccoon had smeared paw prints on the glass. At least, he assumed it was a raccoon, or some other woodland critter living on the outside, looking in as he had done in the hospital with Ella and Harry.

A small, dark shape with red-glowing eyes lumbered between the trees. A creature existing on nothing but instinct. The security light came on and illuminated an opossum snuffling around. Was it searching for food? Was there a nest of opossum babies to feed? Was the mother guarding the nest? Even in the wild, male and female creatures had their roles. The male was the provider, the mother the nurturer. He had always provided—school fees, a good standard of living with annual trips to England, money for stuffed Christmas stockings. And now?

Felix glanced back at the unopened pizza box. If the top of tomorrow's to-do list was *send Harry to school on a nutritious breakfast*, the entire day would be ruined before 8:00 a.m.

Felix dragged himself out of bed at six, as Ella always did. Not that he'd slept. He unwrapped himself from the duvet, slipped his feet into the sheepskin slippers Ella had given him for Christmas, and padded down the hall to turn up the thermostat. The compressor rattled to life; heat whooshed up through a floor vent; the humidifier hummed. Moisture levels in the house were down to thirty-three percent. He would fill both water tanks before leaving for the hospital.

He peered through the thin strip of glass that ran the length of the front door. The hand of frost had painted the ground white. Mother would call it a hoarfrost. Harry would need layers for school—something more substantial than the beaten-up leather jacket he treated as a second skin. And a woolly hat. And gloves. And a scarf. Did Harry own winter clothes? They rarely needed them in North Carolina, but this winter was closing in with arctic cold and too many memories of a childhood spent desperate for warmth.

Shivering, Felix wandered into the kitchen and flicked on the recessed lights and the electric kettle. Tea was the way to start the day. And tea wasn't tea unless it was served in an English bone china mug. He reached up into the cabinet and found his favorite: a Susan Rose Merton College Mug Full of History. Felix brewed his tea and, raising his mug, read the hand-painted words about the city of Oxford. Words that took him back to another place, another time, another life.

He headed into the master bath, the room he had gutted and rebuilt so Ella could have a state-of-the-art shower with multiple jets. It had been her fortieth birthday and tenth wedding anniversary present. He reached inside the shower and turned the dial as far round as it would go. Then he put the mug down on the vanity, slipped his T-shirt over his head, and stepped out of his pajama pants. Catching sight of his flat stomach in the mirror, he sucked it in until his ribs showed. He would never develop a paunch like Pater.

His plan was to shower and shave as he did every morning. Keep moving forward. Wake up the boys, he supposed. Offer them breakfast and push them out of the door. What time did Harry normally leave for school? Should he allow longer if Max was driving? Were student drivers meant to get there early? He didn't know the routine; he didn't know the rules.

The day loomed ahead as an unmoored horror. Investment banking, putting together deals, issuing bonds . . . those were in his marrow. Without the structure of work, without the bond market, he wasn't Felix Fitzwilliam. Today he was someone he'd never been before.

Felix stepped into a cloud of steam. Water vapor misted up his shaving mirror and turned the glass shower doors opaque. He braced his arms against the tiled wall and let needles of scalding water pummel his body. But still he couldn't erase Katherine's words from the night before: "Harder for your wife."

Returning home after a girls' night out the other week, Ella had said, "Why do you make everything so hard, Felix?" Had he made her life too hard—driven her heart to fail? Decisions were hard, relationships were hard, life was hard, and according to Ella, he made it harder.

For seventeen years, he'd been waiting for his wife to wake up and say, "You know what? I deserve better than you." And he would have agreed. That's the thing—he would have agreed. He wished she had left him, because then she might be healthy: Ella Bella without the stress of being Mrs. Fitzwilliam.

Rocking back, he slammed the flats of his hands on either side of his head. All the thoughts, he needed them gone.

Everyone would expect him to weep and wail, but he hadn't cried since he was six years old and Tom saved his life. He knew, with certainty, that Pater, who'd never lashed him more than once before, would have killed him that day. Felix was twenty and up at Oxford when his father died. He'd felt nothing. Even when Tom was diagnosed with AIDS, Felix hadn't cried. He'd become the master of concealed emotions.

Felix slid to his knees. On the floor of his shower, with his skin beginning to burn, he prayed to be numb.

Harry was dreaming about Sammie, the hot new girl in tenth grade. It was summer and they were at Kerr Lake, and she was wearing a red bikini. But Dad was rising out of the lake like Godzilla, cawing at him, "Get up, Harry! Get up!"

Harry shot up, heart pounding on jackhammer overdrive. No hot tenth grader, no summer weather, and Mom was in the hospital. And Dad . . . Dad was standing in the bedroom doorway, weaving around looking totally batshit. His hair was wet and sticking up like he'd been zapped with a high-voltage cable. Eyes bloodshot; skin beet red. Had he tried to boil himself like a lobster?

The numbers flashed 7:30 a.m. on his digital alarm clock. For real?

Harry sprang out of bed. "Why didn't you wake us, Dad?"

"I just did."

"Wake up, Maxi-Pad!" Harry grabbed and jostled his psychedelic beanbag. Max was buried in a nest on top of it with the duvet from the guest bedroom. "Dad let us oversleep."

Dad glanced down at the pile of clothes on the floor, then glanced back up with lips curled back in disgust. Didn't even bother to fake it. Mind you, Dad often gave him that I-can't-believe-we-share-the-same-gene-pool scowl. "You've got plenty of time to get to school, if you can extricate yourself from this pigsty."

"But we normally leave at seven forty-five."

"Why?"

"Traffic." A white lie, but Dad would never know differently.

Harry pulled his jeans off the back of his desk chair. "Dude." He nudged Max with his foot. "Wake the fuck up."

"Harry! Language!"

"Sorry, sorry. Did you talk to Mom last night? Is she okay? How's she feeling? Did you learn anything else from Katherine? I texted Mom before we went to bed, you know, to say good night, but she didn't answer."

"Apparently, your mother has done little but sleep since we saw her."

"Is that bad?"

"Harry, she's been heavily sedated."

"And Mom always says sleep is nature's cure. So I guess that's good. Right?"

Dad didn't answer. "I'm driving straight to the hospital after you boys leave. Do you want me to call the school if there's any news?"

"Really? You'd do that?"

"Of course I would."

"You'll tell me the real truth, the whole truth, and nothing but the truth?" Harry paused. "Even if it's humongously bad?"

"If that's what you want. Is it?"

Wow. Mom never gave him the option. She saw herself as his personal film editor, passing on truth with bits edited out. "Yeah." He looked Dad in the eye. "That's what I want."

"Fine." Dad turned to leave. Harry tugged off his pj pants and pulled on his boxers. He hopped into his jeans and followed down the hall. "Uh, Dad, do I get lunch today?"

Dad looked at him like he was an orc. "How the hell should I know?"

"Mom marks it on a calendar in the kitchen. Every other Monday, I get lunch through school. Mexican."

"Did you have it last Monday?"

Harry shrugged. "Can't remember."

"For God's sake, Harry." Dad began rifling through the kitchen drawer, the one where Mom kept the really important shit. "The calendar, the calendar," he was muttering, "where the hell is the calendar? I can't find it, Harry. Harry, I can't—"

"Here." Harry reached past him. "No, I don't get lunch."

"Meaning?"

"Can you make me lunch?"

"Lunch, as in—"

"A sandwich?"

"How about a bagel with cream cheese?"

"O—*kay*. Can you fix one for Max, too? And Dad? Maybe you should call school and tell them Max and I will be late. Maybe if you explain about Mom they won't mark us tardy."

Dad scowled. *Uh-oh. Oversharing.*

"Do you get marked tardy often?"

If he expected Dad to be honest with him, he had to return the favor, even though he was betraying Mom and breaking the let's-not-tell-Dad code. Mom had been adamant when he'd brought home the warning. It was a total brain blitz, juggling all the things Mom told him to pretend hadn't happened. *You can tell your dad X, Y, and Z, but not A, B, and C.* Mom had always encouraged him to be himself around everyone except his own father. On what planet did that make sense?

Harry gave a big sigh, nodded. "Don't be mad at Mom. It's my fault. That's why she started waking me up at seven fifteen. I have a hard time getting organized in the mornings. But we'll get it right tomorrow, Dad. We will." Mom would be super proud of his positive attitude. She loved the whole glass-half-full thing. And really, finding a positive thought was way easier than the yoga shit she'd tried to force him to master. Who had time to slow down for meditation in a crane pose? Life was way more fun at warp speed.

"Is there anything else you would care to share with me?" Dad reached for the phone.

"I need a permission slip signed for a field trip to Barnes & Noble for AP Lit. And breakfast would be good." Harry pasted on a smile. "Mom keeps chocolate croissants in the freezer."

For one whole moment, Harry truly believed Dad's nostrils flared. "You know what, how about I take care of breakfast?"

"Yes, how about you do just that."

SIX

Voices hovered beyond her eyelids. A nurse muttered about preventing bedsores and then stuck her with a syringe; Katherine whispered into a cell phone.

Sleep reached out, wrapping her close.

Sit up, Ella. Sit up.

An invisible force—a formless being—pinned her to the hospital bed. Sound shimmered into waves of light; lips moved through soundless words; a ghostly mirage leaned over to kiss her with icy breath.

"Mom?"

"Honey, you okay?" Katherine; it was Katherine's voice.

"I think I'm hallucinating."

"Seeing the dead mother again?"

Ella nodded slowly. The only part of her that didn't ache was her head. She planned to keep it that way.

"Damn, you need to share those drugs," Katherine said. "How do you feel? Like a gang of Hell's Angels partied all night in your chest?"

"Pretty much." Ella stared at the breakfast tray. *When did that arrive?* "Water?"

"On it." Cradling Ella's neck, Katherine raised her head and held a plastic cup to her lips.

Ella sipped through the straw, then eased her head back onto the pillow. "Throat like sandpaper. On the positive side, I didn't croak. If my breath would hold out, we could sing Gloria Gaynor's 'I Will Survive.'"

"That's my girl." Katherine packed away her laptop and started winding up the cord.

"Your deadline. God, I'm sorry, Kath."

"You're kidding, right? I've been on my very own writer's retreat for the last twelve hours. I should be thanking you." Katherine smiled. "Felix will be here by nine thirty. Are you still sure you want to meet with the cardiologist alone?"

"Positive. Thanks for covering for me."

"Hey, what are best friends for, if not to lie to husbands?"

"I owe you."

"Honey, I owe you a thousand times more." Katherine picked up her writer's bag and headed toward the door. "I'm going home to shower and then I'll be back."

"Wait. How did Felix sound—when you talked to him last night?"

"Concerned about you, which won't do him any harm. And Harry's fine, so no worrying about him. Velcro Max is refusing to leave his side."

The ringing in Ella's ears became a thunderous waterfall. She was tumbling into nothingness, falling into rapids. She grabbed the bed rail.

"Should I call the nurse?"

"No." Ella closed her eyes and visualized the horizon. Nothing was moving; she was not moving.

"I should text Harry. Say good morning." Ella grappled for her cell phone, and it clattered to the floor.

Katherine dove down to retrieve it. She placed the phone out of reach on the chair. "Harry's fine. He's in school with Velcro Max, and you, missy, need to rest and get your strength back. Your mission, should you wish to accept it, and you will, or else"—Katherine raised her eyebrows—"is to focus on no one but yourself. Got it?"

"Yes, ma'am." Ella adjusted the bed so she was sitting up.

"Want me to help you freshen up? I hear the cardiologist is a hottie. Dr. Beau Carlton Beaubridge, what a heroic name."

"You spent last night eavesdropping by the nurses' station, didn't you?"

"I couldn't help myself. The CCU is fodder for character research. I may have to give my next heroine a heart attack. Okay, I'm outta here. Love ya." Katherine paused in the doorway to greet the doctor. Not exactly a hottie, but he was good-looking in a bland, predictable way.

"Good morning. May I come in? I'm Dr. Beaubridge, your cardiologist." He closed the door and moved to her bedside with a confidence that stated, *I own this place.* A young nurse followed in his wake.

"How are you feeling?" He whipped the stethoscope off from around his neck and warmed it on his hand.

"Like I was run over by a freight train," Ella said. "Possibly a whole battalion of them."

"Yes, it was a substantial heart attack."

Dr. Beaubridge began to examine her in efficient silence. When he pulled up her gown to inspect the site of the catheter insertion, she looked toward the nurse.

"Nice work," he muttered. "Dr. Wilson did this?"

The nurse nodded.

Dr. Beaubridge sat next to the bed and read Ella's file. Her mind wandered to Harry in his dress-up scrubs, the ones he'd worn to kindergarten every day for a week—until a brute of a five-year-old had ripped them in a playground incident. Calhoun Junior, Cal for short. She'd memorized the names of all of Harry's bullies.

She would listen and obey; she would do whatever Dr. Beaubridge told her to do so she could get home to Harry. But first, she had to ask the question.

"I have a disjointed memory from the plane. At least, I think it's a memory, not a nightmare." Ella stared up at the ceiling tiles, found a focal point, and kept staring, despite the prickling dryness of the air. "My heart stopped and I was shocked back to life. Is that true?"

"Yes." Dr. Beaubridge rustled papers. "It happened again in the ambulance."

"My husband won't be able to handle this. He mustn't know. Please don't refer to it if he turns up before you leave." Dr. Beaubridge had been late; Felix would be early. The chances were high that they would meet.

"There's no reason why he should know unless you choose to tell him. You're of sound mind and able to make your own medical decisions. What your husband does or doesn't know is between the two of you."

"I need to understand something." She glanced at the door. Felix could walk in at any time. "Was this incident"—she couldn't say the words heart attack; they belonged to her mother—"life-threatening?"

"Yes, you dodged a bullet, Ella. The STEMI—or ST segment elevation myocardial infarction—had a proximal location such that the area of the heart muscle provided for by this artery was quite large. Maybe greater than fifty percent of the heart muscle of the left ventricle, which, as you probably know, is the pumping chamber of the heart."

Ella nodded.

"When the blockage is very proximal—which means before any branches come off that artery—it's sometimes called a widow-maker lesion. For good reason. A blockage at that site can be high risk."

Widow-maker, widower-maker.

"But you were also extremely lucky. The plane was close to landing, and you were brought to one of the best heart centers in the country. I'm not sure if anyone has explained this to you, but not every hospital has a cath lab." He paused. "Now we focus on healing."

"And I can assure you that I'll do whatever it takes." She stopped to catch her breath. "But I also have a high-maintenance family, which means I always need a plan B."

Her monitor bleeped with a slow, steady rhythm.

"Am I at risk for another one, Doctor?"

"There's always a possibility, yes, but we'll teach you how to aggressively manage your risk factors to lower the chance of a recurrence." He glanced down at the file. "Losing weight isn't an issue for you. Do you exercise?"

"Every day."

"Smoke?"

"I quit five years ago."

"And your cholesterol is fine," he said with a frown. "I see your mother died of a heart attack at the same age."

The young nurse coughed.

"Meaning I'm screwed?" Ella said.

"Meaning we can likely blame a genetic condition."

∗

Ella's door was the only closed door in the section. Once he opened it, Felix would be a step closer to the truth about her prognosis, to confirming or denying the terrifying statistics he'd gleaned from the Web. He tucked the yellow legal pad under his arm. From now on, he was compiling a written history. He didn't trust this hospital—inner-city incompetence waiting to happen—and he didn't trust his own memory to get the details right. Plus he was towing a U-Haul of questions. The cardiologist better be packing answers, because if he didn't come with a wall of shiny plaques that bragged of his expertise, this man was not going to treat Ella.

Braced for impact with Katherine, Felix opened the door and discovered his wife sitting up in bed. The oxygen mask was gone, replaced by a tube under her nostrils, and she was chatting to a blond, blue-eyed, all-American male doctor. A young nurse stood behind him.

"Felix—" Ella blushed as if he'd caught her red-handed. "This is my cardiologist."

"Beau Carlton Beaubridge." The doctor rose, shook his hand, sat back down.

Felix flicked the "Mute" button on his phone. "I'm sorry if I'm late, but I was under the impression that you were due at nine thirty."

Dr. Beaubridge frowned. "I was explaining to your wife that it was a substantial infarct."

"A fart?" Felix said. Clearly, this man was not qualified to treat his wife.

"A myocardial infarction, or MI. A heart attack to Joe Blow."

Did he, an Oxford man, look like a Joe Blow? Felix flexed his fingers.

"I was also explaining that the angioplasty was successful." Dr. Beaubridge checked his pager. Really, the man could have been discussing a picnic in the Hundred Acre Wood.

"Can she be transferred to Duke or Memorial?" Felix asked. *Can I confiscate your pager?*

"Felix, I'm not changing hospitals."

"Ella, please. Let me handle this. You need the best care available."

A muscle twitched in the doctor's neck. "If Ella wants to move, that's her prerogative, but if you're concerned about the level of care, I can assure you that Raleigh Regional has the leading heart center in the state. I myself transferred here from Duke. Your wife is in excellent hands, Mr.—"

"Felix," Ella said.

"Fitzwilliam," Felix added. "Her prognosis?"

"Your wife is relatively stable at this point, Mr. Fitzwilliam, but she's still in critical condition. A normally functioning heart ejects about sixty percent of the blood in the pumping chamber with each contraction. Ella's heart is operating at thirty percent. You see—" Dr. Beaubridge swung his chair round and pulled a small pad and a pen from his pocket. "The heart muscle provided for by the blocked artery lost its blood supply for a period of time." He began drawing a diagram. Really? Did Felix look like someone who needed visual aids?

"By the time the blockage was opened up with the stent, the damage had already been done. That heart muscle may recover in time; it may not. Obviously, we hope for the former."

"Yes, I did my Internet research last night." Felix scowled. "Did your staff not get her to the cath lab quickly enough? Was the door-to-balloon time not up to par?"

Dr. Beaubridge exchanged a glance with the nurse. "We don't advise Internet research. In our experience, it generates misinformation and unnecessary distress. Door-to-balloon time, for example, is no longer relevant. These days we work directly with the EMS. They faxed us your wife's EKG from the ambulance, and it revealed ST elevation. Since timing was an issue, we couldn't treat her with thrombolytics—superstrong blood thinners—so my colleague arranged for her to go straight to the cath lab."

Dr. Beaubridge resumed his kindergarten sketch, this time angled toward Ella. "Your artery here got blocked, so we unblocked it with a stent, a small tube placed across the blockage. That opened up everything so blood could flow to the heart muscle again." He drew something that looked like a bridge, then pulled back to admire his artwork. "Dr. Wilson, who treated you yesterday, managed to get a good look at the rest of the coronary arteries, and you do have severe blockages elsewhere. We'll deal with those later, after the heart has healed some—"

"Why didn't he deal with the other blockages yesterday?" Felix said.

"We need to do things step by step in an acute setting." Dr. Beaubridge paused. "Outcomes are worse if we try to fix all the blockages at the time of the initial heart attack."

"No open-heart surgery?"

"Not at the moment, no. The muscle is too compromised."

"Compromised?"

"Mushy."

More Joe Blow definitions?

"But it is likely that Ella could return after a recovery period of one to four weeks for a subsequent cardiac catheterization. Our goal right now is to stabilize Ella's condition, and start her on medication that will take the load off her heart and enable her to breathe more easily."

Something attached to Ella bleeped.

The doctor slapped his knees and stood. "We'll educate you about managing your risk factors, Ella, and when we're convinced you can handle basic self-care, you can recuperate at home. We'll treat you with a statin to lower cholesterol—"

"My wife has high cholesterol?"

"No, but we need levels below normal. Less than seventy. And you'll need a beta blocker, Ella, and Plavix to prevent clots from forming at the site of the stent. Plus aspirin. And we'll refer you to a cardiac rehab program several weeks after discharge. No driving for a while." Dr. Beaubridge checked his pager again. "You'll probably be back to work in three to six weeks. Resume sexual relations in about four."

"It could be six weeks before she can return to work?" Felix said.

"Is that a problem?"

"Yes," Ella said quietly.

"What is it that you do?"

"I'm a stay-at-home mom."

"Well, I'm sure friends and family can help out."

I'm sure they can't.

Ella gazed up at the ceiling. She didn't move; she didn't make a sound. And Felix knew what she was thinking, because he was thinking it, too. *Life will never be the same again.*

"Ella needs to focus on building up her strength, recuperating, and, as I've said, learning to manage her stressors," Dr. Beaubridge said.

Manage her stressors. Was that a cardiologist's get-out-of-jail-free card, the one that allowed him to blame everything on a patient's failure to rein in her risk factors?

"I'll see you at the same time tomorrow, Ella."

"Thank you, Dr. Beaubridge," she said.

"Wait! You're leaving her with a bunch of nurses?" Felix stood tall and put a hand on his hip.

"Extremely well-qualified nurses, Mr. Fitzwilliam."

"You're not coming back later today?"

"I do my rounds in the morning, before patient office hours. Do you have any questions, Ella?"

Felix moved to barricade the door. This guy was not leaving. They had barely scratched the surface of Ella's diagnosis. "Are there any problems we should be aware of—with stents?"

"Dissection, sometimes. It's very rare."

"But it can happen."

"In less than one percent. And a small tear can heal itself." Dr. America checked his pager again, and Felix imagined pulverizing it under the heel of his boot. "Mr. Fitzwilliam, I understand how frightening this situation is for you and your family, but I don't think this conversation is helpful."

"When can she come home?"

"That all depends on her condition and her recovery, but I'd say in a few days."

"So she can't come home tomorrow?"

"Definitely not, Mr. Fitzwilliam."

"The next day?"

"Unlikely."

"The day after?"

"Let's wait and see, shall we?"

But Felix needed answers, he needed solutions, he needed absolutes. He needed someone to say, "Yes, she'll be home in four days, and her chances of making a full recovery are ninety-five percent." This man was not telling him what he needed to know.

"Your wife is in excellent hands here at the Raleigh Regional CCU, Mr. Fitzwilliam."

Brilliant, so now Dr. Beau Carlton Beaubridge sounded like a cheap car salesman. Felix scribbled on his pad: *check doc's credentials.*

Dr. Beaubridge shook Felix's hand. "I suggest running a Google search. That's the easiest way to check my credentials. I think you'll be impressed." And he left. The nurse, eyes lowered, shuffled out behind him.

Felix turned and stared at the blank television screen and the vase of flowers next to it. Unlike him, Katherine had thought to bring flowers. They were ridiculously gaudy and horribly inappropriate for January. Also far too sweet. He would bring ones that didn't nauseate; ones Tom would have approved of. Was it too early for *jonquilla*?

"How's Harry?" Ella said.

As Felix moved to her bedside, a memory ambushed him: holding Ella's hand during labor. Drug-free labor at Ella's insistence, although Felix, who'd believed he would die from the horror of watching her suffer, would gladly have taken any drug offered.

"Harry's in school. Max drove him." He reached out and twisted her wedding ring round and round. It was warm and smooth. "Did you know that after two teenage boys share a bedroom, the stench is worse than when Saint John's gun dog rolls in manure?"

"Welcome to my life." She gave a laugh that disintegrated into a cough. Felix poured water into the plastic cup and held the straw to her lips.

She lay back on her pillow. "Is Max doing school pickup?"

"No, I am."

"Good. Keep Harry on his normal routine as much as possible. He needs routine." Ella looked up at him with huge brown eyes, eyes that normally reflected passion, humor, anger. This morning, they were dull and lifeless.

Her mobile dinged with a text; she ignored it. "Felix, I need you to look after Harry."

"Harry doesn't need looking after. He's practically a man."

"He's a sweet, all-over-the-place kid who needs help structuring his life and a lot of parenting." Ella smoothed out the edge of her sheet. "Tag, you're it."

Felix dug his fingers into his hair and was shocked to discover its softness. He must have forgotten to use gel. He never forgot the gel. "Our son is a brilliant teenager who needs to learn independence. You baby—"

"He's a remarkable person who should be full of insecurity but isn't—partly because I work hard to bolster him, to praise him, to show him what an incredible person he is, to reinforce that his challenges give him strength, not weakness. I never stop, Felix."

"I know. You're a remarkable parent."

"I need you to be one, too."

Her mobile dinged again. Felix waited two seconds. "Ella, your phone—"

She dismissed him with a limp wave, but how could he ignore a message? *Look at me, look at me,* it seemed to scream, until he reached over and grabbed the phone.

Harry. How did he get access to his mobile during school hours? "Harry's sending you a virtual hug."

"Send him back the heart sign."

Felix stared at the keyboard. "There's no heart sign."

"Type the less-than sign followed by the number three."

Felix typed and squinted. "That doesn't look like a heart sign."

"I can assure you it does to Harry's generation."

He hit "Send"; Harry replied immediately with the same sign. Overhead, helicopter blades thumped through the air; voices moved down the corridor.

"Do you know how messed up most teenagers are," Ella said, "even without a slew of diagnoses?"

"Harry isn't messed up."

"Exactly. But take away his anchor, and it could undo everything. All the years of therapy, of learning coping skills, of—" She hesitated and her monitor continued to bleep. "I'm his go-to person twenty-four seven, and I can't be that person right now. I can't even pee by myself." She stopped to breathe. "He's blessed to have devoted friends, and thank God for Max, but Harry's going to need you like he's never needed you before. You have to take over, Felix—provide the infrastructure that lets Harry be Harry." She closed her eyes briefly. "You have to promise to apply all that focus you direct toward fixing up the house to becoming Harry's emotional rock." She sucked in a breath. "When I'm on my deathbed, I want my final thought to be 'Harry will be okay.'"

"But you're not on your deathbed."

"I didn't say I was."

"Did Dr. America tell you something he didn't tell me? I don't trust that man. I need to get you moved to Duke or Memorial. We can get you the best, we can—"

"Felix, I'm not moving. The end. I won't consider anything that slows down my recovery time and delays my return home. I just need you to promise me—"

"You're asking me to attempt something doomed to fail."

"You don't know that."

"Yes, I do."

"Look, can we just be practical for a minute? What about the fact that I live in my car, transporting our nondriving teen to school, music lessons, parties, the child psychologist, the psychiatrist, the neurologist . . ." She shook her head. "It could be weeks before I can drive."

"How can I become you, Ella?"

"You don't have to become me. You just have to try and . . ." Her eyelids fluttered. "I'm tired, Felix. Exhausted."

"Sleep." He took her hand. "I'll sit with you."

"Tell me a story. Talk to me about how we met, about how you saved me."

"I didn't save you, Ella."

"Yes," she said. "You did. I was so lost after Mom died. And then all I wanted was a family of my own . . ."

Ella drifted back to sleep, and Felix held her hand. What else could he do?

Felix sat in the hospital car park, shaking an empty Pepto-Bismol bottle. Ella had slept, woken up, and slept some more. Katherine had arrived a little after eleven, and Ella suggested he leave—try to work until school pickup. But he could hardly go to the office in jeans. Besides, Nora Mae, the office administrator, would mace him with concern. He could, however, call his assistant.

He briefed Curt on the upcoming meeting for Life Plan, the hundred-million-dollar deal that would allow their client to buy a Research Triangle Park company on the cutting edge of medical device invention: 3-D organ printing. Would computers one day be able to create digital hearts? Curt's final comment, "I've got your back, Felix," was not reassuring. When he'd hired Curt, he'd been attracted to the young man's ability to schmooze. Felix hated that word and everything it implied, but Curt's social charm kept people calm during deals. It had worked well for both of them: Felix handled the numbers; Curt handled the people. But an industry filled with money and greed generated its own healthy supply of sniveling weasels, and Felix didn't trust anyone—including Curt.

Should he go into work and keep an eye on his overly ambitious assistant? Should he go home and fold laundry? Do a food shop? How did one fill a Monday stripped of routine? He had been yanked out of his world and dumped into one with alien vocabulary: MIs, stents, fatherhood.

He pulled onto the road and headed toward the interstate, his mind circling two questions: What was Ella hiding? And why had Dr. Beaubridge been in her room half an hour ahead of schedule?

A signpost sped past and Felix cursed himself out loud. What a twit—he was on I-40 going east, not west. Above, clouds drifted like icebergs floating away from the shore. *He* was floating away from the shore, without a lifeboat. Without his wife, he couldn't even find his way home.

Of course. Felix thumped the steering wheel. He would do what he and Tom always did when they needed to escape: drive until the land ran out. Brighton Beach was a straight shot from London; Wrightsville Beach was at the end of I-40 east. No more than two hours away. If he found the ocean, maybe he would find Tom's wisdom.

"Come on, baby brother," Tom used to say. "We're going to drive until we hit the sea. Then it'll all make sense."

Life had been so easy for Tom—until the end.

As he drove southeast, Felix left behind the urban sprawl, and the speed limit switched to seventy. Forest stretched out on either side of the empty, straight highway. Tom would have loved this road. He would have played their escape song, "Rebel Rebel" by David Bowie.

Tom had songs for everything—a soundtrack for life. Felix lived without melody.

The Mini zoomed past a dead hawk on the verge. One wing was raised, and its tawny feathers ruffled in his backdraft. Briefly, Felix imagined the bird taking flight like a phoenix.

For the next hour, his speed didn't vary while his mind tumbled through disjointed thoughts. Did Ella want to be cremated or buried near her mother? Someone should rewrite the marriage service, elaborate on *till death do us part*, because a husband should know his wife's thoughts about death and the hereafter. He should have asked Ella to explain her final wishes years ago. Why hadn't he? Was this another failure as a husband? And why was he thinking about death? His wife wasn't dying. But what she was asking of him was a serious threat to his life. She might as well have said, "Stand still while I practice being a knife thrower."

The sun cast jagged peaks of shade across the empty lanes. No one was heading to the beach on a blustery January day. Turkey vultures circled random splatters of road kill—unidentifiable chunks of raw meat. And still Felix drove.

When Harry was finally diagnosed, Ella had handed out a pass from fatherhood, and Felix had snatched it up. He had chosen to walk. After all, if you had no hope of doing something well, of being the best, why would you even enter the race? And who could argue with his reasoning? Harry was an expensive child; Felix needed to be an above-average breadwinner. Caught in a web of thoughts, Felix tried to imagine the smell of salt air, tried to rewind his memories to find Tom.

One night, as they had sprawled on the pebbly beach at Brighton, watching stars, Tom handed him a small green bottle of Gordon's gin. Felix got drunk for the first time—hammered at fifteen. Tom, however, stayed vigilant and sober. Whatever their parents thought, Tom had always been the responsible sort. He'd just hidden it really well.

How different would this current situation with Ella be if Tom had survived? Tom would have jumped on a plane, would have taken charge, would have made Harry laugh. Tom would have been a natural father.

The interstate petered out into a road that bumped over a metal drawbridge and crossed the Intracoastal Waterway. Clouds consumed the Carolina-blue sky, and the world turned gray. He had reached the end.

Felix parked in an empty lot and, tugging up the collar of his donkey jacket, headed toward the roar of the Atlantic Ocean. If Tom were alive, he would applaud.

The beach and pier were deserted but for a handful of spindly-legged birds skittering in and out of the ocean. His Dr. Martens sank into waterlogged sand, and he became a blip—a tiny, colorless ant in a world without horizons. Monstrous gray waves reared up, crashed apart, and re-formed to barrel forward with the force of a marauding army. The sun appeared for a moment and cast his shadow across the sand, creating a distorted Felix with grotesquely long legs. Next to his left foot, the water had regurgitated the rotting carcass of a pelican.

Wind rustled the sea oats with a tinkling like chimes, but the moment he turned and walked away from the pier, it battered his eardrums and stole his breath. His eyes stung as if pelted by Lilliputian spears. Felix trudged across sand the color of wet concrete. With each step, he could have been dragging chains.

He zigzagged onto a thick layer of shells that crunched and splintered under his boots. Walking became easier, and he marched across the flat grayness as if he were the last soldier on a battlefield.

Mad dogs and Englishmen.

Except not even a stray dog was crazy enough to walk on the beach in this weather. There was no one around, just the mad Englishman. He laughed, actually laughed. But there was nothing funny about the sound. His hands tingled with cold, and he shoved them deep into his pockets. Maybe he should walk into the ocean and disappear. Would that be so hard? If he removed himself from the picture, maybe Ella would come back to her senses and be the Ella who would never do something as desperate as hand over care of Harry to him.

That was the truth she was hiding, and the reason she had met with Dr. Beaubridge alone. Rightly or wrongly, she believed her life was in danger. Which left Felix facing the real ghoul under the bed—his true self. If he did what Ella was asking of him, would he discover the cause of the anger that bubbled constantly under his skin? Would he discover he was indeed his father's son?

Colors leaped up from the compacted sand. Warm colors of amber and mauve, tan and russet. Felix stopped, bent down, and reached for a shell streaked with tones of caramel, vanilla gelato, and iced coffee with whipped cream—colors from another season. Brushing off the sand revealed not a whole shell but a fragment. The elements had turned the edges smooth like a river stone or a piece of sea glass. When he closed his fingers over it, the shell that wasn't a shell fit snugly into his palm.

More colors called to him from the sand. Soon his palm was filled with four, five, six shell pieces—each different in size, shape, and pattern. They chinked together like loose change in a trouser pocket, and he started walking again. These broken remnants made no sense. They weren't perfect, they weren't symmetrical, and yet, as he rubbed them, they became as warm and as comforting as his wife's wedding ring.

Ella might never heal, but maybe time would smooth out her broken edges, make her even more beautiful. Because the heart attack could never alter the truth: she was Ella Bella. Mrs. Felix Fitzwilliam. The only woman he had ever loved.

Eyes watering heavily, Felix planted his feet wide apart and turned to confront the Atlantic Ocean. The crash of waves obliterated the thunder of the wind. Of the two titans, the sea was stronger, an unharnessed force of nature that could rise up and annihilate him on a whim. And yet. Even the strongest wave was powerless to do anything but sigh and retreat when it reached the shore. He could do that; he could roar and retreat. Wasn't that what Pater always did? But he wasn't Pater.

His wife was critically ill; his son would never be classified as normal. But this damaged family was his family. *Mine.* He shuffled the smooth shell pieces until he had three in each palm. Coins from the ocean. Currency to buy back a life.

"Mine."

The wind took his word and carried it into the ocean, maybe all the way back to England. Back to Pater's grave, to his bones.

I will never be you. I will do better.

He pulled out his phone. It was one thirty already. He should get some lunch before driving back to Durham. He turned, and with the wind at his back other sounds broke through the din of the waves: a seagull crying, a distant car horn. Even the waves were less ferocious. He had two phone calls to make: the first one to the school secretary, to explain that Harry would need to stay for after-school care; the second to Robert. To tell him that he was taking the rest of the week off and would not be joining him for the client meetings in Charlotte on Friday night and all day Saturday. Curt would have to take over the Life Plan meeting, too, but Felix could finish hashing out the details from home. Curt would merely have to present his boss's work with confidence. Confidence was never a problem for Curt. But first, he stopped and typed with one finger:

```
I promise to make my life all about
Harry.
```

Then he hit "Send." He'd done it. There was no going back. His word, once given, was a titanium seal. Ella replied immediately with the symbol Felix now recognized as a heart. A shape that had new meaning.

Felix slipped his mobile into his back pocket. If he was going to do this, if he was going to prove to Ella that he could raise their child single-handedly, he needed to reassess his role in the family, step out from behind the desk job, and sign up for the frontlines of active father duty. If he was going to master the nitty-gritty of being an at-home parent, he needed a battle plan. A bloody good one.

Starting tomorrow? There would be no more after-school.

SEVEN

Harry was freeing his calculus textbook from the disaster that was his locker when the spitball thwacked him upside the head. He hadn't been targeted since second grade, but it was a feeling he'd never forgotten. Little kids could be unconscionably cruel. But there were no little kids around. Hardly any kids, period. Just after-schoolers, and none of them were meant to be up here except to get stuff from their lockers. One of those rules that made no sense, considering the upstairs hall was a huge room crammed with everything that didn't fit in the rest of the school. Kids and teachers were in and out constantly.

He bobbed his locker disco ball with his index finger, twice, and turned to corner his attacker with well-armed Tourette's facts. But there, on the other side of the big table that doubled as the art room, was Sammie. Wearing those skinny jeans that were tight enough to make him want to roll out his tongue and pant. She was also grinning at him like he was special. And not special in a challenged way. Which she might think if he did pant. With good reason.

Harry, you dork. Just say hello.

Harry grinned back, and for one whole glorious moment, his body did exactly what he wanted it to do. Nothing.

Then she gave a shy wave and skipped off toward one of the classrooms.

Shit, she was even hotter than she'd been in his dream. If that was possible. Why hadn't he said hello? That wasn't so hard. One word: *H, E, double L, O.* Guys had been saying it to girls for generations. No big deal.

His head jerked in the crazy-ass sideways nod, the new tic from the airport, and his neck cracked. *Vagina, vagina.* The word threatened to spew out like a hazmat spill. *Vagina, vagina.* He cleared his throat, made some weird gagging noise, swallowed the word.

The door crashed open, bringing a wave of cold from the stairwell. "Hey, man. What's up?"

Harry shrugged at Max. "Not much. Getting my stuff."

Max adjusted the messenger bag slung low across his torso, then plopped down in one of the wheelie chairs lined up around the table and slid back and forth, like he was about to start a bobsled race. And Dad thought *he* never sat still. Harry dumped himself into another chair.

"Any more news from your dad?"

"Just that he drove to the beach to clear his head, which is why I have to go to after-school."

"Your dad's a weirdo. You know this, right?"

Harry nearly replied with "Your dad is creepily normal." Which was bizarre. Never wandered into a pissing match over dads before. Max's parents were joined at the hip—always touching each other, which was gross. And Max's dad, Pete, was everything Dad wasn't: spontaneous, fun-loving, wanted to be friends in a slightly annoying, hey-I'm-the-cool-dad, have-a-beer kind of way. A parent should be a parent, not a friend.

"You're ticcing worse than a howler monkey on meth," Max said. "What's going on? I mean, other than your mom being in the hospital and your dad being MIA at the beach."

74

"Dad says she's going to need a long recovery time even after she gets home. What if Dad loses his job because he has to look after Mom, and I have to go back to public school? I can't go back to public school. I mean, this shit-hole is falling down around us, but it's home, you know? Like being part of the von Trapp family."

One hundred kids, kindergarten through twelfth grade, in a haunted, historic house in downtown Durham. Needed a complete renovation job, but what was not to love about their school? Best of all, the teachers totally got how Mom could fuss. After the parent-teacher conference when Mom had insisted on giving everyone the full update on how spectacularly he had flunked drivers ed, Ms. Lillian had taken him aside and said, "She just wants to keep us all in the loop, so we can be part of team Harry." But hadn't he outgrown team Harry?

"C'mon, dude," Max said. "Your dad probably has a whole to-do list of backup plans. Besides, hasn't he already paid next year's school fees to get that price break? I remember my dad bitching about it, and then being all excited because it meant they were down to one set of school fees. If my parents have done it, your dad has."

"I guess." Harry cracked his knuckles. "I miss talking with Mom, too. Trying to talk with Dad's worse than falling into a copperhead's nest. You know me, I like to talk things out. But Dad starts tapping his hand and says—" Harry cleared his throat for his upper-class Brit voice. "You have already told me that *twice*."

Max cracked up. "I know, dude. But you can always talk to me. Want me to drive you home so you can become a latchkey kid like the rest of us?"

"Nah. I'm good. Why are you still here?"

"George asked me to help out this fifth grader. Poor kid is practically math dyslexic." Max elbowed him. "Oh wait, I get it. You *want* to go to after-school. Doesn't Sammie Owen go to after-school?"

"Does she?" Harry looked at his groin.

"When're you gonna actually talk to her, man? Say, 'I think you're super hot. Want to hook up?'"

"Max!" Harry glanced around. "Walls have ears."

"Dude, it's not complicated. You like her, I'm pretty sure she likes you. One plus one equals earth-shattering grope session. If you don't make a move, I will."

Harry scowled. "What the—"

"On your behalf, dude." Max punched the air. "Ha! I knew you had the hots for her. Well played, Max. Well played."

Harry blushed. He and Max talked about everything. Mom always said they were two halves of a whole; the teachers joked they were Siamese twins separated at birth. They didn't keep secrets from each other, but this was different. The way he felt about Sammie was different. Fragile and private. Not for sharing. But Max had figured it out anyway. That's what best friends did, figured out life when you couldn't.

"I really like her," Harry mouthed.

"Well, duh. Tell me something I don't know. By the way"—Max leaned closer—"she thinks you're pretty chill."

"How do you know?" Harry whispered.

"Can we stop whispering like little girls?" Max pushed back his chair and put his feet up on the table.

"She's super hot, isn't she?"

Max shrugged. "I guess. Not dark and twisted enough for me. I bet she's a virgin."

"Come on, so are you."

"Yeah, but let's be real. We're the only two people in the eleventh grade who haven't done the deed. And I, my friend, plan to fix that next weekend."

"No! She said yes?" With the Mom Situation, he'd forgotten about Max's date.

"Oh, it gets better, dude." Max winked. "Her parents are out of town."

The door banged open a second time, and Mr. George, the math teacher, barged into their tête-a-tête. "What are you boys doing up here? And Max—feet off the table."

"Harry needed some quiet time, Mr. G." Max sat up as if he had all the time in the world. "We're talking about his mom."

"Of course." Mr. George held up his hands in surrender and backed out of the door.

Harry tried to hold in the giggle, but it escaped through his nose.

"As I was saying before we were interrupted"—Max frowned at the door—"unlike you, I actually talk to Sammie."

Max had better luck with girls than Harry, which didn't mean a whole lot. But Max could catch their interest because he was funny and smart and an awesome lead guitarist in a punk band called The Freaks. Teenage girls, however, seemed to care more about the packaging than the contents. And Max's features looked, well, to quote Max, "splattered together on a supersized pumpkin."

But now that he'd dyed his hair black, grown it over his sticky-out ears, and started creating full-sleeve tattoos up his arms with Sharpies to tick off his dad, Maxi-Pad was looking pretty rad. He would definitely get serious girl action soon. Enough to blast his giant-sized math brain into orbit.

"Tell her about your mom," Max said. "Play the sympathy card. Chicks love that shit."

Harry squeezed his eyes together in a series of deliberate, exaggerated blinks. An aftershock of pain from his neck snap migrated up into his temple. He imagined a dwarf on a stepladder pounding a mallet into the side of his head. Could he bash out the recurring images of Mom in a hospital bed, too?

"Sorry, dude. That was way off base."

"Don't worry about it."

"She's going to be fine, your mom. She doesn't take shit from anyone."

"But this is different. This she can't control." Harry rested his face on the table. "I'm scared, and I know Dad is, too, but he won't talk about it . . ."

Max patted his back and then leaned over him. "Man hug."

"Guys? Am I interrupting?" Sammie entered the room.

Harry shot to his feet, rubbing his eyes. Suddenly, he just wanted to be alone.

"His mom's in the hospital. He needs a little TLC, you know?"

"Omigod." Sammie put her head to one side.

"Yup. Heart attack," Max said in a slow, exaggerated way.

Harry turned in circles. Needed out. Couldn't breathe. "She—she's going to be fine."

"She sure is, buddy," Max said. "You should meet Harry's mom. She's great. You know, for a mom. She likes me way better than my own mom." Max stood, straightened his messenger bag, picked at his nail polish. "Well, kids, gotta run. You look after him for me, Sammie."

The fucker! Was Max smirking? He *was*. He was smirking.

And then they were alone. Him on track to graduate as the most fucked-up kid, and Sammie Owen, hands down the most beautiful girl in the school. In the town of Durham. In the state of North Carolina. On the planet.

Sammie stood in front of him and placed one hand on his shoulder, and then pulled it back. He wanted to grasp her wrist, shove her palm into his face, inhale the essence of Sammie Owen.

"How can I help?" she said.

A simple question that told him she was the one. The one and only. His first true love. Random acts of kindness—his favorite thing in the world.

"I-I don't know."

"Maybe we can be there for each other." She paused. "My dad has lung cancer. Stage four. Incurable."

Harry stood still. "I didn't know."

"No one does. I wanted it that way, so I could have a normal life."

"Why tell me?"

"Because I knew you'd understand. Even without—"

"Yeah," Harry said, and his head did the sideways tic again. Her gaze didn't falter.

"We moved down here so he could go to Duke hospital. They don't know how long he has. He responded pretty well to the chemo and radiation. They think he could have as long as three years. Or he could be gone before spring break. But I don't want to think about that. I want to be a normal teenager, you know, thinking about this beautiful junior"—she paused and her cheeks glowed—"called Harry." She twisted her feet. "Can we sit together at lunch tomorrow?"

He was a lot to handle. More energy than a whole power plant when the meds ran out. That was a turnoff for most girls, at least the ones who'd been classmates since third grade. No one had asked him for a lunch date before. (It was a date, right?) No one had ever called him beautiful, either. Except for Mom. She always said, "You're going to grow up to be such a heartbreaker, Harry." But moms had to say that crap, didn't they? And his wasn't exactly impartial, since she overcompensated for the fact that he was, well, Harry. She never judged him, never criticized. But then again, Dad did enough of that for both of them. Why was he thinking about his parents? He didn't want to think about anything except Sammie Owen. He moved toward her slowly, focusing on her lips. Shutting out the world.

"Stop right there!"

They jumped apart and Mr. George waved a heavy-duty stapler at them. "No PDA. Time to come downstairs. Both of you. Now." And then he held the door open and shepherded them through, still waving the stapler.

Sammie looked at Harry and they both giggled. And in that shared moment, nothing mattered beyond the school rule about personal displays of affection. And his *almost* first kiss.

When could he try again?

EIGHT

At 5:30 a.m., Felix studied the daily and weekly to-do lists Ella had dictated over the phone the night before. Armed with color-coded guidelines, he felt marginally less like he was starting life over as an amputee.

Robert had not taken the news well. There had been much huffing and puffing on the other end of the phone line and a muttered comment about why Felix couldn't be a normal dad and give his son a house key, a car, and a credit card, and "let him get on with it" while they went to Charlotte for the weekend. Felix tried to imagine what Harry getting on with it would mean.

He hadn't expected sympathy from his partner, but tolerance would have been an acceptable response, as would a little faith that someone with such a highly developed work ethic as Felix could still deliver. Felix snapped the elastic band he'd slipped on his wrist the night before. Katherine had suggested it as a stress reliever. Bizarre as it sounded, she'd been right.

And he had to-do lists. To-do lists were good; Ella knew this. It was one of the many reasons that he had never doubted their marriage would work: she was a list maker, too.

He walked to the fridge and took out the required sandwich-making supplies.

Thank God she'd packed away the Christmas ornaments before flying to Florida. He knew only two things about Christmas decorations: they had to be hung by Christmas Eve and taken down by Twelfth Night. Mother had always insisted. Over the years, he had fallen into a habit of moving ornaments around while Harry, their tree decorator, slept. Neither Harry nor Ella had ever commented, but several times Felix had caught Ella staring at the tree with raised eyebrows.

Felix laced his hands together, twisted his palms heavenward, and stretched. Let day one of full-time fatherhood begin. First task: pack Harry's lunch.

Harry had said he wanted a turkey sandwich, which, according to Ella, involved a smidgeon of mayonnaise spread on one side of the bread (white from that funny little bakery in Chapel Hill), turkey sliced so thin it was almost shaved (Whole Foods in-house roasted turkey), one crunchy—not limp—piece of iceberg lettuce, superthin Swiss cheese, and two rashers of bacon.

He and Harry had done a small shop at Whole Foods on the way home from school. Ridiculously overpriced, but Ella was big on organic fruits and vegetables. They all were, but really, could Harry's brain chemistry detect the difference between a Pink Lady apple from Whole Foods and one from Harris Teeter? Still, they had picked up supper—barbecue ribs that had been quite tasty. Although a tad too salty.

Felix laid out everything on the counter.

The first sandwich didn't look right, so he made a second. Then they both went in the bin, after he'd extracted the lettuce for the composter and the turkey for his own lunch. He moved on to sandwich number three.

Handling bread was rather disconcerting—Felix had given up carbs for his fiftieth birthday. He didn't miss bread, but he did miss potatoes, especially Ella's potatoes au gratin. He eyeballed the generic fat-free yogurt on the counter. His breakfast. Next to it, the horrifically expensive chocolate croissant for Harry. Surely Harris Teeter pastries were a perfectly acceptable substitute—and cheaper?

The third sandwich was satisfactory. Not overstuffed. Nice layers that worked. Paying attention to the position of the knife, Felix cut the sandwich down the middle, then sliced off one crust, turned it round, and sliced off the other. Repeated. After spearing both halves with toothpicks, he wrapped the sandwich in heavy-duty aluminum foil. Twice—to make sure it was properly secured and therefore able to withstand the abuse Harry heaped on his lunch box. After pausing to double-check Ella's list, Felix added the organic apple, a bottle of water, a small Tupperware of baby carrots, and an individual bag of salt and vinegar chips that stimulated saliva and nostalgia for pub lunches.

Felix glanced at the clock. In two minutes, he would wake Harry. Perfect. He flicked on the kettle. This stay-at-home parent thing was much easier than he'd suspected.

Ten minutes later, he was standing in Harry's bedroom, yelling, "Get out of bed! Now!" Harry, the little rotter, had gone back to sleep. Why had Ella not included that—*Make sure he gets up*—on the list?

"Five more minutes, Dad."

"No." Felix yanked back the duvet and slipped an ice cube down Harry's T-shirt.

"What the fuck!" Harry shot out of bed.

"Your language is appalling."

Harry grabbed at his back as if he were on fire. Then he stopped and threw the ice cube onto the carpet. "But you were torturing me."

Felix's head jerked up; he took a breath. Had he—had he tortured his son?

"It was just an ice cube, Hazza." Was his voice shaking? Did Harry remember? Did Harry hate him? On the day Harry was born, Felix had sworn he'd never raise a finger against his son. But he had crossed that threshold once, just once. He must never do so again.

Harry scratched through his hair and yawned. He didn't look traumatized, but then, as Felix knew only too well, it was hard to tell. Felix's heartbeat returned to normal—for now.

"We're leaving in twenty minutes. If you're not dressed, I'll take you in your pajamas. Do you have the folder for your voice lesson?"

"Yes, Dad."

"And your bag is packed?"

"Yes, Dad."

"And you printed out your English essay?"

"Yes, Dad."

"Breakfast in five. And please pick up that ice cube before it melts all over the carpet."

"Yes, Dad."

Harry said only two more words before they left: "Thank you." And the moment they got in the car, he folded himself in half and went back to sleep.

Once they arrived at school, Felix had the pleasure of waking Harry in front of an audience of other parents. Competent parents who slid through the carpool lane like pros and deposited vanloads of little people plus backpacks, lunch boxes, and musical instrument cases in thirty seconds, tops. Parents who didn't have to abandon their cars to leg it up the school steps after discovering their child's lunch box sitting on the back seat. Tomorrow he'd forgo humiliation and the carpool lane, and park in one of the designated parking spots.

Felix was about to pull out of the parking lot when his mobile rang.

"Hey, it's me," Katherine said.

They were now well enough acquainted to identify themselves as *me*?

"What time are you going to the hospital today? I thought we could coordinate so we don't overlap. Nothing personal, but with this killer deadline, I want to visit, chat with Ella, and get out."

Interesting. He would never have pegged Katherine for someone with a professional work ethic. After all, she wrote bodice rippers. How much self-discipline could that involve? Felix tried not to imagine Katherine typing sex scenes. Did she plot them out or just let them happen? Maybe she got high first. Maybe that was why she smoked pot with Ella. Once, he'd caught them smoking inside the house. He'd never trusted Katherine after that.

"I thought I'd visit Ella now," Felix said. "Then run errands before school pickup."

"Excellent. I'll work till four and go over there before dinner. So, Felix . . ."

Felix ground his teeth.

"You do know Ella's friends are calling me incessantly, asking how they can help? Have you listened to any of the messages on your landline?"

"No and no." Really, how did she expect him to know what Ella's friends were up to? Ella was always reminding him of their names and how their lives intersected, but he'd never been interested.

"We need to come up with a system so people can help out."

Yes—systems are good. No—people helping out is bad.

"I don't need help, Katherine. I've got this covered."

"You know that Ella is supermom on steroids, right?"

"Yes, I do know this about my wife."

"And you know her life is all about Harry, twenty-four seven?"

"Yes, I am fully aware that my wife is a miracle worker. However, I have taken a leave of absence from the office and am confident that I'm more than capable of handling her job." He glanced in his rearview mirror. "Katherine, I really need to hang up and drive."

She gave a smoky laugh. Coming from anyone else, it would have been sexy. "How are your cooking skills?"

With a sigh, Felix turned left, drove back into the school parking lot, and parked.

"A bit rusty, but I was a bachelor for over a decade. I can cook." Scrambled eggs on toast and English trifle counted, right? Tom had taught him the latter one Christmas as they drank an entire bottle of sherry, minus the healthy serving added to the trifle. And he'd just mastered crustless turkey sandwiches. "I'm sure cooking is like riding a bike." Although he'd never learned how to do that, even at Oxford. Another secret no one knew.

"Then I'm going to organize a list of people to drop off meals every night this week."

"Katherine, I don't want—"

"This will give you one less thing to deal with and stop everyone from calling me."

Ah, so it was really about Katherine. He might have guessed.

"I'll make sure they know to leave the food in a thermal bag on the doorstep by six and to not ring the bell or otherwise engage with you," she continued. "How about that? And I made a lasagna for you last night. I'll drop it off after my hospital run."

"I don't eat pasta anymore."

"Then pick out the pasta. Problem solved."

"Are you taking the piss?" *Wow.* Where did that come from? He was reverting to Britishisms he hadn't used in nearly two decades.

"Am I what?" Her voice hardened.

"English expression. To make fun of someone," Felix spoke slowly.

"No. I'm not making fun of you. I'm presenting a solution that might enable you to enjoy a home-cooked meal that *you* didn't have to prepare. And yes, I know Harry doesn't eat mushrooms, so it's fungus free. It's a gift, Felix. Take it."

Then she hung up before he could say, "What time shall we expect you?"

*

Crawling through traffic in the Brightleaf District, Felix stared at the giant Liggett & Myers Tobacco Company sign. The early lunch crowd, muffled up against the day's windchill factor, drifted in and out of historic tobacco warehouses now filled with trendy shops and restaurants. The century-old red brick buildings always pulled him back into the past, into life before Ella. Not unlike London's docklands, downtown Durham smelled of rejuvenation and reinvention. And survival.

Felix took a deep breath and turned right. When he'd left the hospital, he'd told himself he was going to run errands until school pickup, but that wasn't true. Neither was he avoiding an empty house that resonated with Ella's absence. Although that was partially true. No, he was navigating city streets that would lead him back to Harry. Even while listening to Dr. America explain that Ella was making slow, steady progress, Felix had been worrying about Harry. Quite simply, Felix could not move through his day, could not progress down his to-do list, until he'd reassured himself that he had not traumatized their son.

"You were torturing me."

Felix turned onto the tree-lined residential street behind Harry's school and formulated a plan. He would ring the doorbell, tell the school secretary he needed to give Harry an update on Ella, and take it from there.

He was pulling into the car park when sounds of recess assaulted him—the wild screams and explosive energy of children out of control. This changed everything. Suppose Harry was on the playground? Would he embarrass his son if he strolled across the gravel and said, "A word, Harry?" Felix reversed into a space under the spreading branches of a gnarled old oak, turned off the engine, and watched. It began spitting with rain. How very brutal to make children go outside when it was cold and drizzling. How very British.

Spotting Harry was easy. Other kids were in motion—chasing, jumping, shooting hoops—but there was something about Harry's bobbing head that singled him out, that screamed, *I am not normal.* Felix tapped his palm. Was there a new, more complex element to Harry's head tic that meant his son was indeed traumatized?

Wow. Felix's hand dropped to the steering wheel and he leaned forward for a better look. *Wait a minute.*

A blond girl sitting next to Harry at the wooden trestle table edged sideways to whisper into his ear. She was extremely pretty. In fact, she and Harry made a handsome couple. At least his son was good-looking. Think how hard life would be if you had a face like Max's. The girl touched Harry's shoulder, and he turned toward her with a love-sick puppy grin. Felix felt his mouth flop open as if his jaw had magically unhinged. Why hadn't Ella told him their son was besotted? What other secrets had she kept from him? Was Harry failing calculus, too?

Were Harry and this girl sexually active? Did he and Harry need a man-to-man talk about sexual responsibility? Felix tightened his grip on the steering wheel.

Harry dangled his arm behind his back and reached for the girl's hand. They linked fingers in a way that suggested they were attempting to avoid detection. Being the product of a single-sex boarding school education, Felix had no point of reference for dating behavior on school grounds, but he could only assume this sort of activity was banned. Which probably explained why Max sat on the wall behind them, watching.

Harry reached around with his other hand and touched the girl's shoulder. Another of Harry's embarrassing habits: if he touched a person's right side, he had to touch her left side and vice versa. Something to do with balance. The girl seemed not to notice or care.

A pair of crows cawed, and the drizzle now smothered his windscreen, impeding his view of the children. The scene on the playground took on an oddly dreamlike quality. His son, who had never—to his knowledge—expressed interest in girls, was in love. And those feelings were reciprocated. Truth be told, he had never expected teenage Harry to have a girlfriend. Did that make him, Felix, shallow and judgmental? Yes, it did. Because here was a beautiful teenage girl who could accept what Harry's own father could not.

Why had he promised Ella he'd make his life all about Harry? Clearly, he wasn't wired for parenthood. Maybe he should forget the tasks Ella had assigned him and go into the office to do what he was meant to do: put together deals.

Felix had been a working stiff his whole life and had never once used up his quota of paid holidays. He'd been earning a salary since he'd taken up carpentry at sixteen—Harry's age.

"Coming from money doesn't mean a bloody thing," Pater had always said. "I don't care if you want to follow in your grandfather's footsteps and be a banker. Haven't you studied the Great Depression in American history? You need manual skills so you can provide for your family whatever the situation. You don't want to be some slacker sponging off the welfare state."

Slacker was not a word associated with the Fitzwilliam name, even though Mother had happily lived off the family inheritance for decades. Felix had never been a slacker, nor was he about to become one.

He glanced at his watch. Three hours to school pickup. Should he head to the office? Eliminating travel time and the obligatory chat with Nora Mae, that would leave two hours at his desk. Less if he ended up in a confrontation with Robert. Hardly worth going into work, then.

What he did need to do, however, was exit the parking lot before Harry turned and spotted the Mini. After all, it was evident that he had not tortured his son.

His phone chimed with a text from Ella.

You need to collect your dry
cleaning. Forgot. Sorry to give
you one more thing to do. Feeling
pretty useless and exhausted. Dr.
Beaubridge was a ray of sunshine,
wasn't he?

Felix texted back:

He's an arrogant prick. Every time
you look at him, imagine a giant
penis.

Ha! That's a good one!

Had he made her laugh? When was the last time he'd made her
laugh?

Going back to sleep, Ella typed.

Good night, Sleeping Beauty.

He started the engine. Back to the errand-running plan, then. He
should begin with the dry cleaner's before he forgot to write it on his
to-do list. Wait. Where the hell was the dry cleaner's?

NINE

The nurses had dimmed the lights at her request, but Ella couldn't sleep. Light found its way into her room, seeping under the door and through the venetian blinds. After seventeen years of sharing a bedroom with Felix, she, too, could no longer sleep with the slimmest crack of light. He had trained her well. The nighttime sounds of Duke Forest—the occasional owl hooting, deer padding up to their bedroom doors to nibble her azaleas, raccoons nosing around—were replaced by traffic, sirens, and trolley wheels squeaking along the corridor. She missed her woodland garden; she missed her morning power walks with their elderly neighbor, Eudora. She even missed their house, which she'd condemned to Katherine as a twisted fairy-tale nightmare cottage after a record number of copperheads had slithered out of the forest and onto their patio one spring.

Ella had wanted to live in the country, in a modern colonial with a wraparound porch and enough land cleared for a sun garden, despite being vehemently opposed to clear-cutting. Felix had been the one who'd lusted after the 1950s fixer-upper bungalow trapped on the edge of civilization.

She had never liked that dark, hidden house, and now all she wanted was to hear the birdsong in the forest—the wood thrushes, the mockingbirds, the eastern whip-poor-wills, even the jeer of the blue jays. The shadows from the trees, the flickering sunlight that lay across her bed mid-morning, the Monet-inspired bridge that led over the creek to their front path—she missed them all. And soon her camellias and hellebores would be blooming.

There was so much to look forward to, if only she could get home.

Dr. Beaubridge had told her to be patient, but relearning basic self-care was slow and demoralizing. She wanted nothing more than to rise up like Lazarus and go pee unaided, but the effort tied her to the hospital bed with imaginary ropes. All day she'd felt suspended in a weird in-between state of existence. Her mind would tell her to wake up, shake off sleep, move, and yet her body refused to cooperate—except for her heart, which danced a never-ending rumba.

Ella closed her eyes and imagined the softness of her goose-feather duvet. They'd brought it back from London in the days when you could check two fifty-pound bags for free on a transatlantic flight. They used to return home with such precious loot: Dr. Martens, chocolate, candy, Wellington boots, English bone china . . . Would she ever have the strength to travel again?

She had done nothing for two days; nothing had become her new normal. If she had the energy to care, she would be crazier than a shithouse rat. Maybe she was already, since whenever she slept, in snatches, she heard, smelled, and touched her mother. Not a single haunting or symbolic dream in twenty-three years, and now her dead mother was flesh and blood living in Ella's subconscious.

Maybe she needed a brain stent.

How were the boys coping this evening? They were so different, her guys: Harry, tactile and demonstrative; Felix, someone who lived life with hands firmly in his pockets—unless he was reaching for her. Felix had always been a tender lover, a generous lover who took his time. When had they last hugged with passion, not obligation? And whose fault was that—who was the one who'd reset the ground rules in the bedroom? She might just as well have spray-painted *back off, buddy* on the bedroom walls.

Ella picked up her cell phone and hit "Favorites."

"Hello, darling," Felix said. After all these years, his smooth, quietly sardonic English accent still surprised her, still warmed her with desire. Even now, when she was confined to a sterile hospital room.

"I was missing you."

"Me too," he said.

"How's homework going?"

"I have a double single malt in my right hand. Does that answer your question?"

"You don't have to supervise. Just check his assignment notebook, write due dates and deadlines on the dry-erase board, and vaguely oversee."

"Vague isn't in my repertoire, Ella."

She smiled, imagining his lips on her breasts.

Ice chinked against his glass. "How can he accomplish anything when he won't sit still?"

Ella sighed as their shared moment slipped away. "It might look as if he's not working, but movement is part of Harry's thought process. He literally cannot think if he sits still."

Felix slugged his drink. "How the hell does he manage in school?"

"Legally, the teachers have to let him get up in the middle of class, so I established a code word to make it less distracting for other students. Then he goes outside and runs a few laps."

"Oh," Felix said. She could almost hear him frown. "I should have known that, shouldn't I?"

"No, Felix. We chose to be on different tracks because we did what works for our family. Life isn't perfect, but we've been managing, haven't we?"

Three days ago, she wouldn't have asked that question because she wouldn't have cared how he answered. But this evening, here in this ugly hospital room that wasn't dark enough for sleep, it mattered. She wanted it back—her life. All of it, the way it was.

Felix seemed to be walking around; a door closed. "Why did you never leave me, Ella?"

"Why would you ask that? I love you." How could he doubt her?

"Is marriage really that simple?"

"It has to be. How else would couples survive? Marriage never runs on an even keel. We love each other and we've created a life together. What else matters?"

"Do you ever wonder what might have happened if we hadn't both been on the Tube that day, in the same carriage, six feet apart?"

"Of course not. It was destiny and it led to Harry."

"Right." Felix drew out the word as if he were trying to make sense of it. "Do you want to speak with him, say good night?"

"Not just yet." Ella held the phone as close as she could. She had to compose her next sentence with care. Felix was overly sensitive about anything he classified as criticism.

"I'm pretty anxious—about everything. You worry," she said quietly. "A lot. How do you cope?"

"One has to face one's demons and keep going. Channel the British war mentality."

"I'm not British."

"Close enough." He hesitated. "We will get through this, darling. Despite your cardiologist and his God complex."

"You'd have one, too, if you held people's hearts in your hands."

The void slunk back into place and threatened to swallow her whole. "I'm pretty beat. I should talk to Harry. 'Night, Felix."

"'Night, Ella." Felix paused. "Harry! Come talk to your mother."

And Felix was gone. Ella rested the weight of the phone against her cheek and waited.

"Mom! How're you feeling? How's the food?"

"Crap and crap. How's school?"

"Awesome. Everyone's being fantastically nice. And I got one hundred five percent on that calculus test."

"One hundred five percent?"

"Bonus questions. Didn't you get my texts?"

"Sorry, baby. I must have been asleep." He'd sent so many, and she didn't have the energy . . .

"That's okay. I wondered why you didn't answer them, but Dad said they keep you busy in there. So. Whatcha doin'?"

"About to go back to sleep. I'm training for the world sleep record."

Harry giggled. "Mom . . ." She knew that tone. He had a secret. "Remember the new girl in tenth grade?"

"Sammie Owen?"

"Yeah. I think she likes me. You know, like *likes* me."

"I hope you've asked her to a movie or something."

"I'm thinking about it."

"Sweetheart—this is one of those cases when you should act first, think later. What if you hesitate and someone else asks her out? Do it. I dare you. No, I double dare you." Ella stopped to breathe. Such exhaustion. "How are you and Dad getting along?"

"He's a little scary as Mr. Mom. Cuts the crusts off my sandwiches."

"Ask him not to."

"But he's trying really, really hard, and I don't want to, you know, upset him." Harry gave a Harry sigh, which was more of a warp-speed snort. "When're you coming home?"

"We're shooting for Saturday. Have you talked with Dad about the sleepover?"

"No, I figured I'd cancel it."

Harry clicked his tongue, a tic she hadn't heard in a while. Was he regressing? Were Felix and Harry not trying hard enough to connect? Her heart picked up its pace, pounding as if through a megaphone.

"Ask Dad what he thinks. He might surprise you." Maybe she should interfere, issue them a hold-the-damn-sleepover directive.

"I dunno, Mom. Me and Dad? We're like that Simple Minds song you played for me the other week, 'When Two Worlds Collide.'"

She and Harry were always sharing music. Ella closed her eyes and listened to the dissonant bleep of her monitor. "You should play Dad some Simple Minds."

"Why?"

"Just something from way back when . . ." But she couldn't grasp the memory. Even thinking drained her energy. "Listen, baby, I'm fading. It's been another action-packed day for us cardiac patients. Finish up your homework and get to bed."

"'Kay. Love you."

"Love you too."

Ella lay back down, but within seconds her phone trilled with a text alert.

can you ask dad about the sleepover

No.

please ☺☺☺☺

Nice try. Answer still no. This week you and Dad have a special assignment: figure out how to deal with each other without me playing piggy in the middle.

She flopped back. Texting was exhausting.

suppose he yells at me

```
Dad doesn't bite, you goon! He's
just a little quirky.

i'm a lot quirkier

Yes and no. Dad needs a lot of
support right now. Be nice. HUGS.
xox
```

The pale gray bubble came up, the one that meant Harry was still typing. Ella groaned. She never said no to Harry, but she needed rest. And really, if Felix was willing to put his life on hold, Harry had to meet him halfway.

If she was ever going to get home, she had to start listening to her body; she had to start rethinking life as a woman with a heart condition. Katherine had nailed it when she'd told Ella to stop worrying about Harry and put herself first. She needed to unlearn her mothering instincts, become a bad mother. And she needed to believe in Felix, trust that he could be the father she'd always hoped he would be.

The gray bubble was still pulsing. Harry had more to say, and she was making the decision to ignore him. Midconversation, and she turned off her phone. The worst part? She had no guilt.

TEN

Harry gobbled a large smiley-face cookie—crumbs shooting everywhere—and stopped briefly to slurp hot chocolate. He swallowed with a gulp before hunching forward to resume his maniacal munching. Felix watched. Could his son not slow down to eat? In fact, could he not slow down for life?

The Mad Hatter had been Harry's choice, not his. Felix would have preferred a café with less buzz and fewer students, but at least they had a satisfactory view of Duke. Parts of the campus always reminded him of Oxford.

Felix crossed his legs and brushed a piece of lint from his thigh. Fifteen minutes until they had to leave for Harry's after-school voice lesson. Plenty of time to ask about the girl and throw in a quick tutorial on table manners. Should that preempt the condom conversation?

"Dad, I want to—"

"Harry, please. Not with your mouth full."

The waitress squeezed past to deliver a plate of scrambled eggs, home fries, and toast to the old geezer sitting next to them. Breakfast food at three thirty in the afternoon? How utterly absurd. Maybe it wasn't just his son who confounded him. Maybe it was people in general.

"How's your girlfriend?"

Harry's chin jutted up in a salvo of tics. "I-I d-don't have a girlfriend."

"Cute, blond, mismatched Converse. Five foot four, if I had to guess."

"She's not really . . ."

"You're not doing that casual hookup thing, are you? You do know that's how kids get STDs." *Or AIDS, like your uncle.*

"Dad. I'm not interested in flings."

"So how does she fit into your life?"

"You really want to know?" Harry blushed.

"No, Harry." Felix scratched at the label on his small bottle of Perrier. "That's why I asked."

"I think she's, like, amazing." Harry paused to clear his throat. Of all the tics, this one bothered Felix the least. It could easily pass for an allergy symptom. "But she has serious family stuff going on."

"Might I point out that so do you?"

"But what if that's all there is? What if it's just a connection of need?"

"Does it matter? Harry, your life will be filled with women. Don't overthink first love."

"Suppose it's not first love?"

"Suppose you take a risk and find out?" As he did when Ella got pregnant.

"Dad, what was it like when you met Mom, when you first saw her?"

Felix glanced up at the decorative red light fixture hanging above their table. "She was beautiful. It was passion at first sight." *And a whole lot of lust.*

"Not love?"

Someone behind them coughed. Felix frowned and leaned across the table.

"That took longer. Your mother also had 'serious family stuff going on' the first time we met. Your grandmother had just died, and Mom left London shortly afterward to go home and be near your grandfather. We didn't really get together until five years later, when she returned for her thirtieth birthday. It all happened quite quickly after that."

"Wow." Harry bobbed in his chair. "Mom never told me that bit."

"Which bit?"

"About you meeting and then being apart for five years."

"What exactly did she tell you?" *And which part did she leave out?*

"That she fainted on the Tube, and this handsome Englishman raced to her rescue. It sounded very romantic."

"Indeed. Although I'm not sure about the handsome part."

Ella, as pale and delicate as a fairy in an Arthur Rackham illustration. Ella, so vulnerable and needy. That moment she'd started to crumple, to sink without a sound, he'd barged through the rush-hour crowd so he could catch her before she hit the dirty floor of the carriage. Thought had drowned out all reason: "No, you can't die. I haven't met you yet." He'd wanted to keep her safe, protect her. Had he? Had he done any of those things?

"Did you have many girlfriends before Mom?"

"I thought we were talking about you."

"I'm curious, Dad. You and I never talk about this shit."

"Unlike you and your mother, I choose to not talk about my feelings, Harry." Felix's left foot tapped the floor. "To do so makes me intensely uncomfortable."

Felix pulled out his phone to check his messages before remembering he'd taken a leave of absence from work. Robert still copied him on everything, but Felix was forcing himself to not engage. Either you were in or out, working or not working. He had never felt so redundant.

"But did you date women? You know, before Mom."

"Of course I did. I was twenty-seven when we met."

"So?"

"So?"

"Other women?"

"Harry. I'm not good at relationships." Felix looked round to make sure no one was listening. The tables were far too close together. Anyone could be eavesdropping. Harry thumped his elbows on the table and leaned forward, eyes wide and eager. "Let's put it this way: yes, I dated a lot of women. Some beautiful, some smart. But I never understood them and they never understood me. I tried to do what a boyfriend was supposed to do. Compliment them, be chivalrous . . . But your mother was different. From the beginning."

"How so?"

"I don't know."

"Yes, you do." Harry grinned. "C'mon, Dad. Boy talk." He twitched through a grimace and blinked compulsively. "It's all a big mystery to me. Girls aren't exactly rushing to date the weird guy."

"You're not weird if you hide it."

"That's not going to work for me. I'm more of a what-you-see-is-what-you-get person."

Felix picked up his Perrier and finished it in three swallows. "Maybe you could try harder to disguise the tics."

Harry didn't answer. He merely knotted up his napkin.

This was why confidences were bad, very bad. It was too easy to say something that could be misconstrued.

"Your mother understood me." Felix sighed. "That was the difference."

Harry glanced up through his hair. "What you mean is that she accepted you the way you were. Warts and all."

"I suppose."

"So you didn't really hide anything from her. Did you?"

Had Harry just outmaneuvered him? "We should leave in ten minutes."

According to MapQuest, the singing teacher lived 3.4 miles from the Mad Hatter Café, and they needed a few extra minutes to park. How he'd been talked into voice lessons that cost fifty dollars a week was beyond comprehension. According to Ella, singing was another form of therapy, but surely they had spent enough over the years on the neurologist, the child psychologist, the psychiatrist, and the medications. For six months straight, when Harry had been taking a drug that didn't exist in generic form and had to be ordered from Canada, his prescriptions had cost more than the mortgage. Much of Harry's care had not been covered by health insurance. Certainly not the acupuncture and the biofeedback. Ella had become something of an expert in alternative medical treatments for Tourette's. None of them had worked.

Harry jiggled from side to side, then drained his hot chocolate, literally holding the mug upside down for the last drop. Felix drummed his fingers on the table. If only he had emails to answer.

"Dad, did I thank you for my sandwich today?"

"No."

"It was perfect. Thanks. But you don't have to cut the crusts off. Really."

"It wouldn't be perfect with crusts on."

"But I like crusts."

"Then it wasn't perfect, was it?"

Harry frowned. "Can we just leave this at 'Thank you, I really appreciate what you did for me today'?"

Felix tried, and failed, to process the idea that a sandwich with crusts left on could be perfect. Mother had always insisted on crustless cucumber sandwiches made with soggy white bread.

"I . . . I also wanted to tell you that I'm canceling my birthday sleepover," Harry said.

Felix sat up. What sleepover? Ella hadn't put *sleepover* on his to-do list, and there had been no talk of a sleepover before the heart attack. Of course, he wasn't even supposed to be in town this weekend. Had Ella and Harry planned something and not told him?

"It doesn't seem right with Mom in the hospital, and it doesn't seem fair to you."

"What day was this planned for?"

"Friday night."

Felix glanced at his watch. "How many boys are we talking?"

"Five. Plus me. And Ginny and Stella, who were going to be picked up by eleven. And I would've invited Sammie, but I guess it's irrelevant now."

Felix nodded and almost said, *Too bloody right.* Nine teenagers, and he couldn't cope with one. But what if he could pull this off? Might it tie everything up with a bow? Might Ella accept that he'd fulfilled his promise? And if that happened, might the incessant worry about failure be replaced with a mission-accomplished mindset?

"You should invite Sammie."

"What?"

"Harry, life has to go on. Mom would want you to do this. You're only going to turn seventeen once."

"Seriously?" Harry shot up; heads turned. Felix made the down-boy-down motion with his right hand.

"Okay! You're the best, Dad. The best!"

"Harry," Felix dropped his voice. "Please sit down." *People are staring.*

"You'll need to organize cake and pizza and lots and lots of soda!"

Felix regretted it instantly. "How much is lots?"

Sitting in the music teacher's front room on a ridiculously low, sagging sofa, Felix gave up trying to read the *New York Times*. He refolded it, tried again to cross his legs—which was impossible given that his bottom was inches from the ground—and listened. Harry didn't sing much when he was in the house, but Felix was painfully familiar with the warm-up exercises. Even in a classroom setting, they sounded like a cat being strangled.

Zak, the teacher, began strumming an acoustic guitar while Harry jabbered away about school. *And I'm paying for this?* A discussion followed on the importance of thinking ahead for the switch to modality three at the end of the third line in "Pony Street." Elvis Costello's "Pony Street"? Tom had been a big Elvis Costello fan. Once, he'd taken Felix to see Elvis perform at the Royal Albert Hall. Felix sat up.

Then Zak started playing real music, and the unfaltering voice that accompanied him was Harry's. From the front room, it was impossible to imagine that such a powerful voice—clear and rich—belonged to a teenager with vocal tics. Felix never indulged in what ifs—because really, what was the point?—but he couldn't stop the thirty-second fantasy: What if his son had never developed Tourette syndrome? How different would their lives, his marriage, have been?

Felix closed his eyes, and when he opened them again, the music had stopped. Harry emerged, head bobbing, and tripped over air. His voice folder and sheets of music drifted to the floor.

"Keep up the good work, Harry. Same time next week," Zak called out, as an attractive young woman with pigtails walked in carrying a guitar case.

"Hey, Harry," she said, grinning.

Harry, who had been down on all fours, shot up with his arms full of paper. "Hey, Rach."

"Harry," Felix said, "please take two seconds to put those back in your folder before you drop—"

Too late.

Rach giggled. "You klutz!"

"Tell me about it." Harry laughed.

"Here, let me help," she said.

"Nah. I got it. My dad can help. Go have your lesson. The clock's ticking."

"Nice to meet you, Harry's dad," Rach said, and disappeared into the music room.

Harry was back on the floor, trying to retrieve a piece of paper from under the upright piano, where there was dust and God only knew what else. In a house this dilapidated and rickety, mouse droppings and dead cockroaches were likely candidates.

"Aren't you going to ask what I think?" Felix said to Harry's backside.

"Sure, Dad. What did you think?"

"Not bad. Except for that note you missed at the end of the third verse. And there was a bit after the second verse when your voice wobbled."

Harry stood, laid out all his pages on the piano stool, and stuffed his folder in an annoyingly haphazard way. "That's why I didn't ask," he said quietly.

They drove home in silence, except for Harry's vocal tics.

ELEVEN

Felix stared at his Thursday to-do list until a low-grade headache set up shop in his temple and started telegraphing little messages of pain across his forehead. Tugging off his glasses, he squeezed the bridge of his nose.

Midnight, and he had two things left to accomplish before bed: hang the happy birthday banner and blow up balloons. Were fifty too many? Ella had told him not to bother with balloons, but if he was doing this, he was doing it right. Besides, a quick Google search would, no doubt, debunk the mystery of how to hang balloons.

Due to the astronomical expense of party supplies, Felix had taken full advantage of all the deals. Thanks to the discovery of BOGOF—buy one get one free—they had enough paper goods for Harry's eighteenth. In fact, they would never need to buy paper plates or napkins again, which was why he'd chosen a timeless color. Black.

He should probably create tomorrow's to-do list before the headache crippled him. Suppose you had to do this task multiple times a year because you had more than one child? Unimaginable.

He pulled out a blank index card and started writing. Had Harry told everyone to bring sleeping bags and pillows? Could sixteen-year-old boys be relied upon to remember pillows? What if they forgot to bring bedding? He ripped up the list and started over.

Remind Harry:
1) All boys sleep in his room. (No louts sleeping on the sofa.)
2) Midnight curfew on noise.
3) Guests must be gone by noon on Saturday. No exceptions.

Felix glanced over at the three boxes of pancake mix sitting in the middle of the kitchen island. Could he pull off pancakes and bacon for six when he'd never cooked them for one? The mix came in a box labeled "just add water!" How hard could it be? He pulled out another index card, Saturday's to-do list, and wrote: *make test batch of pancakes while boys sleep.*

Back to tomorrow's list:

Get up at 5:30
Shower
Make Harry's breakfast
Pack Harry's lunch
Although really, Harry should be able to do those last two himself.
Drive Harry to school
Come home
Do a load of laundry
Go to Harris Teeter and pick up birthday cake
Clean the powder room
Hoover
Tidy up

Should he have hired Merry Maids? Ella had told him to not clean beforehand but merely "clear the decks." Which made him intensely nervous that (a) people would be coming into an unclean house and

(b) that he somehow needed to protect his possessions. Would they break furniture? Not use coasters? Sneak illegal substances into his house as easily as Katherine had?

He should probably stop by Pizza-To-Go on the way back from Harris Teeter. Meet with the manager and confirm that yes, they could indeed deliver four large pizzas at 7:30 p.m. (Should he have taken care of this yesterday?) Felix kept writing:

Stop at Pizza-To-Go
Put soda in fridge
Put candy in bowls

Had he bought enough soda? Should he have provided more choices for the kids? And when Harry said put out a few bowls of candy, how many did he mean? This was so unlike work, real work. This was the great unknown of vagueness, and it came without explicit instructions.

Felix got up, freed the stopper of his cut-glass decanter, and poured a healthy shot of Macallan. He went back to the sofa and added *hide the alcohol* to his list.

So many possibilities for disaster. And suppose Harry didn't have a good time? Suppose his guests didn't have a good time? Shouldn't there be more organized activities? Suppose the loo got clogged from overuse and he had to call Dickie the plumber on a Friday night? Suppose the kids stole the Mini for a joyride around the neighborhood? Did teens en masse devolve into mob mentality?

This whole event was ludicrously unstructured. The only definite was pizza at seven thirty: two cheese, one pepperoni, one Hawaiian. Although why anyone with half a brain, even a teenager, would choose to eat anything as disgusting as Hawaiian pizza was incomprehensible.

Felix pulled out the Pepto-Bismol bottle, unscrewed the top, and swallowed two pills with a chaser of single malt. A hive of stinging bees had surely taken up residence in his stomach. If only it could be this time tomorrow. No, not tomorrow, since there would be six large, smelly teenage boys camped out in the bedroom down the hall. This time on Sunday, then, with the house quiet and Harry asleep. When Harry was awake, the house was littered with the perennially half-finished: a glass of orange juice left on the island for two hours; soda cans moved to the sink but not rinsed out and dumped in the recycling; dirty crockery left on the counter and not scraped, rinsed, washed, and slotted in the dish rack to dry. (Felix refused to use the dishwasher. If he had his way, they wouldn't have one.)

The ghost of birthdays past hovered—the good old days when Ella organized extravaganzas for twenty children at a local museum and never once lost her cool.

Two more days until Ella came home and life could revert to the way it was supposed to be. The way it had always been. Well, not quite. He would still have to chauffeur Harry around and drive Ella to medical checkups and then rehab. Do the supermarket run and be the errand boy. So not exactly the same as before. In fact, nothing like before.

Harry nearly melted when Sammie rubbed her thumb along his palm. Holding her hand was the softest, warmest, safest, sexiest feeling ever. He would never tire of it. Seemed the Beatles actually got something right. Who knew?

Hand in hand, they walked across the school parking lot.

"Oh, your dad has a Mini. How cute," Sammie said.

Dad and cute? Really?

One good thing about Dad doing pickup—unlike Mom, he never got out of the car. Mom was always the only parent on the porch at pickup, and the only parent who drove for every field trip, and the only parent who volunteered for every school event. At the science fair, one of the little kids had actually mistaken her for staff. When she was back in charge of, well, everything, maybe he should grow a pair and finally set some boundaries. Ask her to wait in the car at pickup, like Dad.

Dad appeared to be asleep. Not surprising, given how hard he'd worked on the party. At this point, Harry just wanted it to be whatever Dad wanted it to be. Maybe they should have canceled. He and Sammie could have gone to the movies instead and held hands in the back row.

Harry knocked on the window. Dad shot up like Max had when Mr. George caught him napping in calculus earlier that day. "Are we boring you?" Mr. George had asked, and Harry had willed Max not to say yes. Thankfully, the psychic vibes must have worked, because Max had apologized. Seriously un-Max-like behavior.

"Dad, Dad." Harry knocked again, louder.

Dad opened the driver's side door. "Once would have been enough, Harry. I have a headache. No need to rap as though attempting to wake the dead."

Dad's eyes bored into Sammie. "The car is unlocked, you know. And since I'm not officially a chauffeur, I don't need to open the door for you."

Sammie squeezed his hand tight.

Be nice, Dad. Please, be nice.

"Sammie can't get a ride this evening *sooo* can she come home with us?" Harry knew he was talking fast, but Dad had to say yes, and he had to like Sammie. That last bit was super important. Dad didn't like surprises, and this was so totally off script, but he *had* to like Sammie.

"Nice to meet you, Mr. Fitzwilliam," Sammie said. So sweetly.

That had to thaw even Dad's heart. *Don't screw this up for me, Dad. Please.*

"I can help set up," Sammie said.

"I've done everything." Couldn't Dad fake it, just for once pretend to be the laid-back, "whatever, dude" parent?

"Oh." Sammie blushed.

"I'm assuming that's a yes?" Harry said with a mega dose of bravado.

"Do I have a choice?"

Harry sighed. "I need you to do this. For me."

Dad sighed, too. Two sighing guys in the school parking lot while the most beautiful girl in the world watched.

"Fine, yes." Dad turned on the engine. "Nice to meet you, too, Sammie."

"You'll get used to my dad. He can be blunt."

"You don't have to talk about me as if I'm not here, Harry." Dad gave him that look, the one that made Harry feel as if he were the size of a flea and even further down the list of life-forms. "What time did you say people were coming?"

They'd had this conversation. Several times. Why was Dad checking?

Harry opened the rear passenger door and let Sammie scramble inside, then joined her. No way was he sitting in the front while she was stuck in the back with Dad glaring at her in the rearview mirror.

"Six. Six sharp." Harry smiled. At least, he tried. Best get all the news out at once and be done with it. "And Josh's dad has a problem picking him up tomorrow. He asked if we could give him a lift home."

Dad angled his head and turned away. "No."

"Dad—"

"I said no, Harry."

"Not even if you dropped him off on the way to the hospital?"

"Are you arguing with me?"

Really? *Really!* Dad had to pull this shit in front of Sammie?

"No. It's fine. I'll tell him to ask one of the other guys." Harry looked at his lap. And Sammie reached over and wove her fingers through his. He knew Dad was watching. He knew, but he didn't care.

Sammie Owen, the most beautiful girl in the school, was holding his hand.

*

The kids turned toward Harry's bedroom the second Felix unlocked the front door and canceled the burglar alarm.

"Harry, wait. A word, please."

Harry looked over his shoulder. "Yeah?"

"Your door stays open."

"Excuse me?"

"A new house rule when you have a girl over."

"Great," Harry mumbled as he slumped off. "Another house rule."

"I heard that," Felix called after him. Would it be inappropriate to have a whisky before the kids turned up? Highly inappropriate. Suppose another parent came to the house because it was polite to say hello to the parent in charge, and that person smelled alcohol on his breath and assumed Harry's dad was an alkie . . .

No. No alcohol.

Felix focused on working down his to-do list. Everything was checked off by 5:45 p.m., and then he paced.

Guests arrived in dribs and drabs—the two girls came together—and Felix ordered the pizza. The kids had taken off their shoes in the hall, as Felix had requested, but they'd left them scattered. When the pizza delivery guy rang the doorbell, ten minutes behind schedule, Felix tripped over a particularly large white sneaker. The quintessential American sneaker, the ugliest shoe in the world, and it was defiling his hall.

He nearly yelled at the kids right then to leave. It took all his powers of concentration to swallow his irritation so that he could serve supper. An Oxford education reduced to slicing pizza.

The kids descended on the pizza like starving street urchins from *Oliver!* Trying to get them to line up led to failure, but he did force them to wait as he cut the pizza and handed it out one piece at a time, on double paper plates. Then they homed in on the dining room table, squishing into the six chairs. Two of the boys stood to eat. Why hadn't he covered the floor with drop cloths?

When Max helped himself to a piece of Hawaiian pizza directly from the box, and a small chunk of pineapple fell to the wood floor, Felix rushed at him with a paper plate. And two napkins.

"Uh, thanks, Mr. FW," Max said.

Felix couldn't take his eyes off the kids for a second, especially not Max, who was barely house-trained. There was even a can of Coke sitting in the middle of the coffee table without a coaster underneath. Felix rectified the situation and wiped down the entire table with a wad of paper towels.

Then he retreated to stand behind the kitchen island, where he waited with the pizza cutter for the next half hour—to make sure nobody pulled a Max. Occasionally, he snuck glances at Harry and Sammie snuggled together on the same chair. In part he did this for Ella, who loved Harry's birthday parties and would expect a detailed report. But he was also curious to see how Harry handled himself with a girl. At one point their foreheads touched, and Harry sat perfectly still—until he giggled at something Max said. Strange that Harry still had his little-boy giggle.

When the kids abandoned the dining room table to sprawl on the sofa, the floor, and the fireplace hearth, Felix started the cleanup with a black bin liner. Harry fired several blinking glances at him as he dumped all the paper plates and half-munched slices of pizza. Did this generation not finish anything?

Under the table, there was a snowdrift of candy wrappers. Why had he thought the bumper packs of individually wrapped candies were a good idea? He picked up one, two, three cans of soda, but they were all half- drunk. How could he rinse them out and recycle them when he didn't know whether or not the kids were finished? What a waste if they were; what a waste if they weren't. He dumped the cans anyway.

Someone cranked up the stereo, and Felix took out the trash. The hired help; he'd become the hired help. Even from outside, the house pulsed with teenage anarchy. And was *every* light on in the entire house? Did youngsters have any idea of the cost of electricity? He went back inside and barricaded himself in his bedroom.

The lunatics had taken over the asylum, and it was only 8:00 p.m. Two hours until he served the cake; three hours until the girls left; four hours until the implementation of the noise curfew. And then he would be alone with six boys. Would he sleep? Would they? Suppose they wandered off somewhere in the middle of the night, decided to go walkabout through Duke Forest at 2:00 a.m.? The evening stretched to infinity. He was not going to make it to noon the next day; he absolutely could not do this.

He called Ella's mobile, but she didn't pick up and the phone went to voice mail. Unsure what to say—other than *help*—he hung up. He could watch a movie, but suppose he got distracted and forgot to check on the kids? As the parent in charge of nine teenagers—*nine*—he had huge responsibilities. There would be no shirking of duty. He set the timer on his phone for thirty minutes. He would do a walk-through every half hour until the three girls left. Make sure there was no sex, no drinking, no smoking. Nothing that could be classified as monkey business.

By 9:00 p.m., Felix was contemplating breathing into a brown paper bag. His heart raced in one direction and his mind in another, galloping through a reel of nightmares that looped from one imagined catastrophe to the next: an uncoordinated teen tripping over his own feet and breaking a piece of furniture; a fight erupting, which seemed highly plausible given the boy-girl ratio; one of the kids—Max, no doubt—needing to be rushed to the ER for a stomach pump.

Someone yelled hysterically; feet pounded past his door. Kids were running inside his house. And Harry's voice drowned out all the others. Why was his son not the quiet wallflower? Why couldn't Harry blend in and *disappear*? Why couldn't all the kids disappear?

Wait—earplugs! Ella often complained that he snored—he didn't—but she kept earplugs in her bedside table. Earplugs were the solution!

As Felix rummaged around in the drawer, his fingers landed on a small wooden box. Too small to be a jewelry box; too small to be functional. Curious, Felix opened it, and there lay a half-smoked joint and a lighter. So Katherine was still sneaking pot into his house.

Despite the large number of illicit cannabis plants grown in his old dorm room, Felix didn't know much about dope. But yes, he'd seen *The Big Lebowski*. He picked up the joint. Right now, his world was too bright, too clear, too damn loud; he just needed to soften the edges. Mute everything to a manageable level.

Sitting on the carpet with his back against the bed and his legs stretched out, Felix stared at the innocent-looking joint. A few puffs wouldn't be that illegal, and no one would know. He just needed help coming down from the ledge so he could function for another—Felix glanced at his watch—two and a half hours.

In the hall, Harry screamed. There was energy, there was high energy, and then there was Harry. A whole subcategory of energy.

Felix put the joint in his mouth, lit the end, and inhaled. And nearly coughed up a lung.

He repeated. Nearly coughed up the other lung. The third hit wasn't as bad. And the fourth was nice, quite nice.

Weird—he'd never noticed before how red the bedroom walls were. Of course he knew they were red—he'd painted them! But wow, the color really popped. He made the Winston Churchill V-for-victory sign with his fingers.

Scary teenagers! What scary teenagers?

Felix had dated a pothead briefly in college. The fact that she'd been a pothead was the reason the affair had been brief. Although it hadn't really been an affair. Just lots of mediocre sex. She'd told him marijuana could make you paranoid, but she must have been lying, because his worries went *pop!* He put the joint on the bedside table, lay down on the carpet, and spread out his arms. A snow angel! The kids' music wasn't too bad, either. Humming along, Felix closed his eyes and let it throb through his muscles. He could feel every beat, every note. The music was in his bloodstream, drifting around his body, filling him with endorphins. Was this that Marilyn Manson guy? Not bad for a baby-eating psychopath. Eating! Felix got up. He was starving! Definitely had the munchies. Pizza! He needed a slice of pizza right now. And the strangest thing—he didn't even care if it was Hawaiian.

He rocked himself up to his feet and paused. Stood absolutely still. *Shhh.*

A scrabbling noise came from the bathroom. What was that? More scrabbling. There was a creature in his bathroom! Felix grabbed the doorknob and slammed the door shut. Then he shot back into the corner of his bedroom. Panic zoomed out of nothingness. Down the hall, the kids laughed—at him? Had they discovered he was stoned and were making fun of him? Blood pumped in his brain, in his guts, in his throat. Heart palpitations—he had heart palpitations. His heart was about to burst. He was about to burst. Vomit, pass out, burn up. Die.

Breathe, he must breathe.

Somewhere a bell rang. The doorbell? Was one of the parents early? They hadn't had cake yet. No one could leave—they hadn't had cake!

Breathe, Felix, breathe.

His hair follicles prickled; flashing lights danced before his eyes. Oh God, this was not good, very not good.

Knocking on his door. *Please don't let it be a parent.*

"Dad? Katherine's here."

The she-devil.

Another knock. "Felix? Are you decent?"

"Yes," he said, because he couldn't think and breathe and talk at the same time.

"Good, because I'm coming in." Katherine opened the door, then her eyes grew wide and she stepped inside, slamming it behind her. "Felix! Are you stoned?"

"I feel a bit funny."

She snatched up the joint. "How many hits did you have?"

He cowered in the corner. "Four?"

"Four. This is strong shit, buddy." She shook her head.

"Please don't tell Ella."

"What were you thinking?"

"The party, I was anxious . . ."

"Felix, honey." Her voice softened. "You shouldn't smoke when you're wound up."

He was a failure, a huge failure. "Please"—he nodded at the joint—"take it away."

She put it back in the little wooden box he'd dropped on the bed. A familiar routine, no doubt.

"You don't want a hit?"

"No, Felix." She frowned. "I never smoke if I'm driving. I'm not as irresponsible as you think I am."

"But you and Ella, you're always drinking wine and—"

"I never have more than one glass. I don't drink and drive, either."

"Oh." He couldn't think of anything else to say.

More banging on the door. "Dad! Katherine! Can we do cake?"

Felix crossed his arms and started rubbing his shoulders. "I can't go out there. I can't."

"Okay. Here's what we're going to do."

Felix nodded again and again. *Yes, tell me what to do.*

"I'm going to deal with the cake. Is it in the fridge?"

More nodding. "There are paper plates and cocktail napkins and black plastic forks on the counter next to the kettle. And candles. And matches. And a cake slicer. And here." He shoved his mobile at her, then huddled back into the corner. "You need to take a picture of Harry blowing out his candles and text it to Ella. I promised."

"I can do all that, but you need to sit in the chair and focus on calming down. And I'm going to get you a glass of water."

"No! Don't go in the bathroom." He dropped his voice to a whisper. "There's a monster in there."

"No, there isn't." She went into the bathroom and turned on the tap.

"No monsters?" he called out.

"No monsters."

"Swear?"

Katherine handed him a red glass from the bathroom. It had taken him six months to find the perfect glasses, ones that matched the soap dish and the tissue holder.

"Pinkie swear," she said. "No monsters."

Smoking a joint before interacting with Katherine was definitely the way of the future. She wasn't half bad when he was stoned. In a the-world's-gone-pear-shaped way. Except that he never, ever planned to do this again.

Felix sank into the big club chair and tugged Ella's cashmere throw around his shoulders. *Hmm.* Lavender, the scent of Ella's clothes. Tomorrow he would buy all-new lavender sachets for her drawers.

"Are you going to tattle about this to Ella?" he said.

"Of course not. She has enough to worry about."

"Katherine?"

"Yes?"

"Why are you here?"

"Ella asked me to come."

Finally, something made sense. "She wants a full report on the party. I get it."

But Katherine didn't answer. "Drink the water. I'll deal with the cake, and we'll talk later."

"Wait! What are you going to tell Harry?"

"That you have a migraine."

"You'd lie for me?"

She folded her arms over her breasts. Nice breasts, actually. "Do you have a headache?"

"Bit of one, yes."

"Then we're not lying. Ella wants Harry to have good memories of tonight. It's up to us to make sure he does. Your headache has suddenly become quite debilitating. I predict you won't be able to poke your head out of the rabbit hole for at least two hours."

Felix held up his glass and stared through the red prism at the still water. He sloshed it around, trying to create a mini tsunami, but the water moved heavily like viscous blood.

Felix woke up in the chair, cuddling Ella's cashmere throw like a security blanket. Katherine was perched cross-legged on the end of his bed, watching a barely audible movie on the television. The cable box flashed 11:30 p.m.

"Feeling better?" she said without shifting her eyes from the screen.

"Hmm." He rubbed his chin. "Sorry. I didn't mean to fall asleep on you."

She shrugged. "You've been under extraordinary stress, Felix. I think your body is trying to tell you something, but next time you want to get stoned—call me first."

"There won't be a next time. The girls?"

"Gone. The boys have retreated into Harry's room for manly activities." She covered up a yawn with her hand, and his guilt returned. She had to be as exhausted as he was, but she was still in motion.

"Thank you. You should go home now, Katherine; get some sleep. Will I see you tomorrow, when I pick up Ella from the hospital?"

"No." Katherine held up the remote to click off the television. "Ella won't be home tomorrow. That's what I came to tell you."

"Why?" He jumped up. "What happened?"

"Blood clot in the stent." She stood too. "And her ejection fraction dropped."

Ejection fraction, the percentage of blood pumped out with each cycle of the heart . . . and Ella's figure was already less than half of a normal person's. "You mean lower that it was—lower than thirty percent?"

She nodded. "Fifteen."

"My wife's heart is now seriously compromised, and you waited to tell me? How long have you known? When did it happen?"

"This afternoon."

"Dear God. This could put her in class three heart failure. I've done my research. I know what it means to have another blockage at the same site. I know how high the mortality rates are. And you've been sitting on this information. You hate me that much?" He spun round, hands digging through his pockets. "Have you seen my car keys?"

"I don't hate you, Felix. Although I'll admit, I had miscast you as the archvillain when you're actually more of the antihero. That's a huge difference."

"Really? Nothing personal, but I've never trusted you. And after tonight, I certainly never will. Now where are my bloody car keys?"

"I'm sorry. Please, can we not do this?"

He glowered at her. "Have you seen my car keys?"

"You can't go, Felix. Ella insisted you stay here with Harry. She made me promise. Nothing can ruin his birthday party—she was adamant."

Felix collapsed back into the chair. "Ella's mother died on her birthday."

"Exactly. She's fine, Felix. I wouldn't have left otherwise. And the nurses have my cell number. You need to stay here and supervise the boys. You need to honor Ella's wishes and make sure Harry suspects nothing until after the sleepover. I promised, and I don't break my promises."

So they shared something after all.

"Listen," Katherine continued. "I'm going to forget this little spat. But for Ella's sake, you and I have to start trusting each other. Are you with me?"

It was Felix's turn to nod.

"I'm returning to the hospital. I'll call when I get there, even if there's nothing to report."

"Is she . . . in the CCU?"

"Yeah." Katherine pulled back her hair, twisted it into a ponytail, and let it bounce free. "I thought she was having another heart attack, and I could tell the staff was worried. I mean, that part of her heart's already taken a hit. But they sucked out the clot and put in a second stent, and they're adding another blood thinner. Dr. Beaubridge says she could be in for two more weeks while they get all the medications adjusted. Now they move to medical therapy and watching and waiting."

"Waiting for what?"

"I don't know." Katherine threw out a brief smile. "I got the impression he'll know more by Monday. He wants to meet with both of you then."

Were there two repelling magnets inside of him? How did a person split himself in half to be a supportive parent *and* a supportive spouse? He needed to be in the hospital with Ella, and he needed to be here with Harry. And in front of him, making it impossible to move forward, was the mammoth concrete wall labeled "The Truth." He couldn't do this alone, could he? He needed Katherine, a person he wanted to hate for taking his place by Ella's side.

"That ruddy cardiologist." Felix wrapped his arms over his head and began rocking back and forth. "I knew he was an incompetent imbecile. I knew he was too good-looking to be a serious doctor. First thing Monday, I'm getting him fired."

"For what? Being arrogant? I checked his credentials, and he's some sort of cardio superstar. Besides, he's not that good-looking."

"He is. He's bloody gorgeous."

"Seriously? Don't you ever notice women watch you walk into a room, Mr. Colin Firth clone? Does anyone ever accuse you of being too gorgeous to do your job?"

Felix wasn't sure what to say, but it appeared that Katherine had given him a compliment. The dope must still be in his system. "When you call from the hospital, please don't use the landline in case you wake up the boys."

Katherine raised her eyebrows. "You expect them to sleep?"

Felix glanced at the door. "They won't?"

"Didn't you ever have sleepovers?"

Felix shook his head. "I stayed with a friend during the summer holidays to avoid going home. It was a somewhat large house. He slept in one wing, I slept in another."

"A word of advice. If you have Benadryl or anything that might knock you out, take it. Sleepovers get noisy."

Felix gulped. Although noise levels hardly seemed important. He shook off the image of Ella alone in her hospital bed, reconnected to all those tubes. Would there be another sandbag on her groin?

Katherine stifled a yawn.

"Can I make you a thermos of coffee to go?"

She shook her head. "What time are the kids leaving tomorrow?"

"Noon. I have to feed them pancakes and bacon." Felix visualized the pancake mix on the counter. All three boxes. Waiting.

"Then I'll tell Ella you'll be over at one. How does that sound?" Katherine picked up her bag.

"Thank you."

"You still don't get it, do you?" She flicked back her hair, a gesture that yelled, *I am peeved.* Or maybe, *You are exasperating.* Either way, he'd screwed up again.

"Get what?"

"You don't have to keep thanking me. Ella's my friend. I'd take a bullet for her."

Felix looked at the carpet and glanced back up. "I don't have many friends."

"That's because all you do is work, same as me." She put her head to one side and scrutinized him. "Most of my friends are up in New York. I never really had time to make new ones down here. But thank God I went to book club that night and met your wife. I figure you and I both hit the jackpot with Ella."

"She's the only person who understands me. I don't know what I'd do if—"

Katherine held up her hand. "She's stable, and she has excellent care. I'll call in half an hour. And we're good—about tonight. No one else will know." Katherine walked to the door and stopped with her back to him. "Try and get some sleep."

She closed the door quietly, and Felix stared at his empty bed.

TWELVE

Harry tore out of a nightmare he couldn't quite remember and fell back on his bed, heart racing. Man—he scratched through his hair—he was starving. Must've been out cold for three hours.

Post-sleepover coma!

Dusk already. It would be dark soon. Dark like it could only get in the forest. He shivered and burrowed under the duvet. The house was silent. Silent as a cemetery, which meant Dad wasn't back. Harry curled into a tight ball. Being alone was the worst state of existence. Being home alone was creepy as shit. Mom never left him home alone at night. She knew he was terrified of the dark. 'Course, Max said anyone with half a brain should be.

Dad would call him a spineless wonder.

Yup, a wimp and proud of it!

Harry poked out his head. There was some weird scratching noise in the wall, as if something was trapped in there. Threatening to explode through the drywall in a bloody mess like the creature in *Alien*. Not that he'd actually seen that bit, since he'd been cowering behind his Darth Vader cushion. He'd meant to hide it before Sammie came over, but turned out she was a *Star Wars* fan. A hot girl who liked sci-fi. Was that not the best?

Dumb, dumb to let Max pick the first of last night's movies. *So dumb.* Max made horrible decisions for himself. Why on earth had Harry thought his decision for the group would be any better? None of them had really wanted to see *Alien*. None of them really liked guts and gore.

Spineless wonders of the world, unite!

Harry snatched his phone off the nightstand, pulled it under the duvet, texted Max:

```
DUDE! dad still not back house scary
as shit walls are alive!!!!!!!!!
```

Max didn't reply. He was probably asleep.

Okay, so staying under the duvet and reliving horror movies, when there was probably some perfectly rational explanation for the—*gulp!*—noises in the wall, was lame. Mice!

There you go, Harry. Rodents. Curse you all, rodents!

Hopefully, mice weren't nesting in the walls because he'd been sneaking cookies into his room in the middle of the night. But really, Mom's friends had brought by some bizarro meals on wheels. Crap—now he sounded as ungrateful as Dad, who'd thrown the last offering in the kitchen trash, muttering, "Why would an American willingly cook shepherd's pie for a Brit?"

Harry sat up, listened. Nothing.

Was that a note shoved under his door? Harry jumped out of bed and grabbed the index card. *Clean your room before I get home. Dad.* Dad never tacked on kisses. A kiss would've been nice, though. A bit of father-son camaraderie. What earned an *xox* from Dad? What made Dad happy—work, fixing up the house, anything that didn't involve Harry?

When would Mom be home? Not tomorrow, not for his actual birthday. Mom was devastated—so Dad said. Harry had texted her that it was fine, all fine. Tomorrow was just another day, and they'd have plenty more birthdays together! But truthfully? He wanted her home so bad it hurt worse than when he'd had his appendix out. The house had no soul without Mom; there was no laughter. Dad didn't find much in life that was funny. On Christmas Eve, when they'd watched *National Lampoon's Christmas Vacation*, he and Mom had cracked up while Dad had muttered the occasional "banal."

Harry glanced at the index card in his hand. Dad had offered to give him the lowdown on Mom this evening, so it wouldn't be wise to upset him. Whatever Dad wanted would be done. Clean room? On it!

"Make it so!" Harry said in his most theatrical voice.

Although he didn't give a flying fuck about the state of his room. After all—his space, his choice. Three cheers for the liberation of "My Way" (the Sid Vicious version). Mom had a nasty habit of sneaking into his room and tidying up when he was in school. Not that she snooped, but she was always moving his stuff around. Putting it where she thought it should go. Suppose the mess made sense to him? He would never go into his parents' bedroom and start meddling. And really, did it matter if he threw his dirty clothes on the floor? At some point, the piles always made it into the laundry hamper.

If only Sammie were here. Or Max. Or anyone. If only he wasn't alone.

He texted Dad: where are you?

Normally he would type *U* instead of *you*, but abbreviations annoyed Dad.

I'll be home in one hour. Mom sends
her love.

His head jerked with the new sideways tic, his fingers strummed, his left foot tapped. Then his body stilled. *Enjoy the calm while you can, Harry.* He picked up his phone again. No texts from Sammie? He'd thought, hoped . . . But she had a truckload of family shit to deal with. Worse than he did, since his mom wasn't terminal.

hey how's your saturday

Instant reply! Want to get together tomorrow?

hell yeah!!!!!!!

Call me later.

Unlike Dad, Sammie added kisses. A whole row of kisses.

They'd kissed last night when Dad was shut away with his migraine. And the best part—no tics! The moment he'd put his hand around her waist and pulled her close, everything had gone still. Except for the fireworks in his brain. He wanted to spend the rest of his life kissing Sammie. And maybe doing a few other things. But only if she wanted to. He wasn't going to be one of those creeps who wanted to get inside her panties. Besides, the idea of sex was as terrifying as monsters in the walls. Suppose he ticced through the whole thing?

Harry texted back four rows of kisses. And four hearts, because one wasn't enough. One of anything would never be enough for Sammie Owen.

Max would say, "For fuck's sake, dude, play hard to get." But why? If Sammie was going to love him back, she had to love him all the way. Love him for who he was. Hiding shit wasn't working out so well for Dad, who pushed everyone away rather than admit he needed help. Harry wasn't falling down that manhole.

He should check the living room and kitchen. Make sure everything was cleared up from the party, even though it'd all looked "fine and dandy, dandy and fine"—to quote the elf in *Santa Claus: The Movie*—when they'd eaten the rubbery pancakes. Harry had briefed the guys ahead of time: "Even if breakfast is disgusting, eat everything and tell Dad it's fantastic." Everyone had thanked Dad tons. Maybe too much, since he'd given Harry that skeptical look, like he'd known it wasn't spontaneous. Couldn't Dad just accept that someone was trying to do something nice for him? Mom was right; Dad made life way too hard. For himself and others.

Harry shuffled into the living room. Dad had vacuumed, cleaned off the coffee table, even puffed the sofa pillows. A most excellent sign. If Dad had been worried about Mom, he wouldn't have taken the time for a thorough cleaning job. Nor would he have cooked pancakes and bacon for six starving teens. Something poked out from under the sofa. Harry dropped to his knees. Max had a habit of squirreling away candy as if he were storing nuts for the winter. Yup. There was Max's Starburst stash.

His phone made the clown noise. Another text from Dad.

```
I'm going to stay with Mom a bit
longer. I'll pick up Mexican on the
way home.
```

Dad hated Mexican. Complained that it was too heavy, that it sat in his stomach like concrete and gave him heartburn. Harry patted his stomach. Was he getting fat? Hadn't told anyone he was worrying about getting fat. Mom would be upset if she thought he was fussing about how he looked. She was always telling him horror stories about her high school friend whose kid had body dysmorphic disorder. "See, Harry? There are worse things than Tourette syndrome and a little ADHD." Had a lot of new worries since Mom went into the hospital.

Seemed like his head was jangling with anxiety. Was he getting fat? A little voice told him he was.

Wait.

Anal-cleanup Dad had missed the Starburst wrappers, and now he was offering to pick up Mexican. Harry tore off a hangnail with his teeth. Had something bad happened, and Dad didn't want to tell him? What if it was just him and Dad all the time, and he had to deal with Dad all the time, and Dad had to deal with him all the time, and it was just two of them *all the time*, and . . .

mom, he texted. i'm super anxious

Dad here. Mom's indisposed. Deal
with it, Harry. We'll talk later.

Harry stared at the phone. *Deal with it?* Like, for real? He was alone! Who was going to help him deal with it when he was freaking out and alone? Should he send Max a Code SpongeBob text, which meant super urgent emergency, come over right now?

And Mom was *indisposed*. And Dad was running interference.

Maybe Mom was the one who couldn't deal. Deal with him. Before she went to Florida, she'd gotten frustrated with him—she never got angry, just quiet and tense and her voice dropped a notch—and said, "Harry, you've got to stop dumping on me and start dealing with these things by yourself. What are you going to do when you're at college?" He'd grinned and said, "Text you?" But she'd just given him a sad look.

Was it his fault that she was sick? Was he too needy? She made his life easy—maybe a bit too easy—but he let her. He never said, "Please stop acting like my maid and minder." Why had he never learned to deal with shit by himself?

Alrighty, then. Time to flip this whole thing around. Rise to the challenge and prove to his parents that he could take charge of his life. Harry strutted back to his room to start the big tidy up.

He plugged his iPod into the speaker dock to blast out My Chemical Romance. Why not? He was alone; he could blare his music. And tonight? They were going to have nachos and fajitas. *Yum.*

Harry started to spin, to dance, to sing, to "get up and go," as the lyrics said. Dad would come home expecting chaos, and Harry would bowl him over with order. And when Mom came out of the hospital, she would be impressed at how independent he'd become, how organized, how neat and tidy . . .

Yes, he was lord of his universe—a guy who could *deal with it* by himself!

THIRTEEN

Felix sat cross-legged on the bathroom floor with Ella's green T-shirt in his lap. Did it belong in the light or the dark pile? He held it to his face and inhaled her scent, then created a third pile of clothes he wouldn't wash—just in case. Eleven o'clock on a Saturday night, and he was sorting laundry, tackling a mindless task that made more sense than Ella handing over her phone chock-full of unanswered texts from Harry.

"Take it home with you," she'd said.

When he'd asked how Harry would text her, her answer had made less sense than the laundry instructions: "For once, Felix, can we do something my way?"

Then she'd extended the embargo on Harry's visits. "He's not to see me like this, Felix. Promise."

He was handing out a lot of promises these days.

Harry had accepted these developments with quiet stoicism. Felix had even broken his own house rule and allowed TV with dinner— some moronic cartoon called *Family Guy*. An IQ off the charts, and his son still watched rubbish.

"Dad?" Harry's voice, hesitant and childlike, came from the master bedroom.

"I'm in here. Sorting laundry." Felix got up and stretched. "Be out in a sec."

"Does Mom really not want to see me for the next two weeks?"

Felix walked into the bedroom and stared. Harry was wearing slouch pants and a ridiculously small T-shirt with some demonic-eyed little pony on the front. The T-shirt didn't look familiar, but had he shrunk it in the wash and not realized?

"And why won't she let me text her? It's like she's punishing me. I want to go see her, Dad."

"Come. Sit." Felix patted the bed.

Harry slumped down and heaved a sigh of dejection.

"I know it's hard, Harry, but you and I have to figure this out. Getting home to you is all that matters to Mom. But she's pretty sick, thanks to the blood clot, and we need her to concentrate on taking care of herself so she can come home in two weeks." Felix took a deep breath. Two weeks, two more weeks.

"You mean I'm high maintenance and I distract her?"

"I mean she loves you so much that worrying about you can side-track her. We need her focused."

"Was this your idea—to sever communications with me?"

"No." Felix frowned. Why was he always cast as the bad guy? "This affects me, too, Hazza. We can still call her room anytime, but I think she wants to make phone contact a little less convenient, to encourage us to go to each other, not her."

"So we can do this for real if she dies?" Harry sniffed.

"Your mother is not dying. This is merely a setback."

Harry leaped up and bounced on the balls of his feet like a ballerina. Could he not stop moving for two seconds? Even a dog knew when to sit and stay. And there, right there, was the thought that made Felix Fitzwilliam a monster.

"Are you scared?" Harry pirouetted through a tic.

Felix opened his mouth to reprimand Harry for not controlling his own body, but nothing slipped out. The tic didn't even bother him that much. What really bothered him at this precise moment was the truth. "Terrified. You?"

Harry threw himself back on Ella's side of the bed, facedown. Then he grabbed one of her pillows and bundled it under his head. "Dad, what did you want from life at my age?"

"To pass my A-levels with all As and sit Oxbridge—the exam that would get me into Oxford or Cambridge."

"No, I mean big picture."

"Be the best."

"That was it? No dreams?"

"I'm not much of a dreamer, Harry."

"But wasn't there one thing you wanted more than anything else?"

Escape from my parents. Felix picked up the silver hallmarked photo frame on his bedside table. Ella on their wedding day, wearing a beautifully understated dress and carrying a bouquet that Mother had criticized openly. No veil, a simple hairdo, and dramatic earrings only Ella could have designed. Even then, Ella knew her heart. She had always known her heart. That was one of the reasons he'd fallen in love with her—her certainty, her confidence. Enough confidence for two. "I wanted to fall in love with the perfect woman."

"And you did," Harry said.

Felix smiled. "I did."

"Sammie's being really nice to me." Harry tugged on the hem of his T-shirt. "She gave me this."

Now the little pony on the very small T-shirt made sense. What a relief. A moment ago, he'd feared his son was regressing.

"She's cute, your Sammie."

"Yeah, she is, isn't she?"

The heating kicked on and a rush of hot air filled the room.

"Are you two officially going out?"

"Doesn't really work like that these days." Harry gave a lopsided grin.

"You like her, though."

Harry messed with the pillow. "I think I'm in love with her." Then he flipped over and lay on his back. "And the timing sucks. I feel horribly guilty, like I should be worrying about Mom, not thinking about being in love."

"I'm sure your mother is thrilled. Falling in love for the first time is a rite of passage."

"Mom doesn't really know about Sammie. I mean, she knows I have a crush on her, but we haven't talked—I mean, *really talked*—recently."

Harry had told him something before telling Ella?

Harry's arm flopped over the edge of the bed and swung back and forth as if he were lying in a boat, trailing his arm through the water. When they went back to England this summer, he would take Ella and Harry to Oxford, and they would punt on the River Cherwell. Maybe they'd have a meal at the Cherwell Boathouse. Or they could pack a picnic of cucumber sandwiches and fresh strawberries with clotted cream and champagne. He might even let Harry have a half glass of Moët, since he would be close enough to the English drinking age of eighteen.

"I want to be with Sammie forever. She's perfect."

"That may change. First love is a fickle monster."

"Do you remember your first kiss?"

Did he ever. "Playground." Felix ran his hands over the stubble on his chin. He hadn't shaved since Friday morning. "She kicked me in the shin, and it bloody well hurt. Have you and your mother talked about . . ." His voice dried up. He'd learned the facts of life from Tom. He'd learned everything useful from Tom.

"Talked about what, Dad?"

"Sex, drugs, rock 'n' roll—condoms."

"Yeah. Mom told me everything when I was little. And then I told Max and he got into trouble, and Max's mom had words with Mom in the school parking lot."

"Really?" It was as if his family had lived a whole life he knew nothing about. Felix jiggled his wedding ring. Actually—they had.

Harry smiled. "Thanks, Dad."

"For what?"

"Being honest with me about Mom. About how sick she is. It's worse when people won't tell you the truth, because your mind fills in the gaps. And"—Harry wriggled to get under the duvet, then molded Ella's pillow round his head—"it's reassuring. To know you're scared, too."

"Solidarity in fear?" Was this the big, amorphous *it* of the father-son relationship? Being honest even if it stripped you bare?

"I guess. This pillow smells of Mom."

I know.

Harry nestled deeper. "Does Gramps know about Mom?"

"No. It's not a decision I agree with, but your mother's very protective of your grandfather. Again, she's doing what she feels is right. We have to respect that."

"Dad, why don't you ever talk about your father?"

"I prefer to forget him." *If only I could.*

"Why?"

"He's not worth remembering."

The room seemed to shrink. Felix wasn't sure he could breathe. Would Harry have the identical conversation with his own son one day? *My father's not worth remembering.*

"I need to tell you something." Felix sat on the foot of the bed, his back to Harry. "On the day you were born, I vowed I would never raise a hand against you. But when you were a toddler, I broke that vow. I smacked you across the back of the knees. It only happened once, but that's not an excuse. I've never forgiven myself."

"I probably deserved it," Harry said, the tone of his voice suggesting a smile. "I was a lot to deal with, even then."

"Never say that. No one deserves to be hit. It was wrong and I knew better. But sometimes anger is the only emotion I understand."

"I nearly hit Mom once." Harry crackled his knuckles, and Felix turned sharply. "I mean, I don't think she realized. It was during the rage attacks, and I had my softball bat in my hand. The rage was burning me up. And I-I nearly took a swing at her."

Felix put his hands on the bed for support; they sank into the duvet. "But you didn't."

"No, and the rage attacks stopped soon after. But the knowledge of what I might have done was terrifying. I was this close to complete loss of control." Harry sat up and pinched his thumb and index finger together.

"Those rage attacks," Felix said. "I always thought they came from me, from my DNA."

"A lot of Tourette's kids have them, Dad."

"Do you remember much from back then?"

Harry hugged his knees. "Bits. It was like a different me. I was angry all the time, and when I wasn't angry, I was a hot mess of guilt. I would hear Mom crying and think I was the worst kid. You never cried, though. That made me feel better."

"Seriously?"

"You didn't get sucked in. It's like you were this force of control. Everything I wasn't, but needed. Does that make sense?"

Felix didn't dare say anything, couldn't risk ruining the moment.

"I would come out of my room after I'd trashed it and be totally freaked out by what I'd done, but the rest of the house would be, you know, orderly and predictable. Everything as it should be."

"Part of me understood that rage, Harry. I have blind anger. So did your grandfather."

"Dad, did your father ever hit you?"

Felix turned away from Harry and faced his reflection in Ella's full-length mirror. His father's eyes stared back. Cold. Hateful.

He whipped me. Like a dog.

Once, Ella had asked about the scars hidden low beneath the waistband of his jeans. He couldn't remember what he'd told her. Certainly not the truth, too shameful to admit to the woman he loved. Only two people knew the real story, and they were both dead.

"I can't talk about it, Harry."

"That's okay. I understand. But if you wanted to, you know, I'd listen."

"Are you good at that—listening?"

"My friends think so. Besides, when your best friend's Max, you have to listen a lot. Tension at home and all that."

"I imagine it's not easy having an autistic younger brother." Maybe he'd been too hard on Max. After all, not every big brother could be Tom.

"Oh, no, he and Dylan are fine." Harry flopped back, pulling the duvet up to his chin. "It's with the parentals, as Max calls them."

"Really? His mother and father seem so normal."

"Exactly. And, like, Max lives in a parallel universe." Harry paused. "Dad—why didn't you and Mom have more kids?"

We didn't plan for any *kids.* "We never really discussed it. You came into our world as a fireball, and our family was forged in nuclear energy."

"Right. Who'd want two of me?"

Harry snuggled under the duvet, and Felix tried to think of a comment other than "Yes. One of you was more than enough." Instead, Felix walked around to Ella's side of the bed and tucked their son in.

"It's nearly your birthday."

"Yeah, how about that?" Harry gave a big yawn.

"Your mother, of course, bought and wrapped your presents months ago."

Harry smiled. "Dad, I'm pretty comfy. You mind if I stay here for a while?"

"No. Happy seventeenth birthday, Harry Felix Fitzwilliam. Sweet dreams of Sammie."

Harry closed his eyes. "Thanks."

Felix turned off the lights and went back into the bathroom to finish sorting the laundry. Even on a Saturday night, an incomplete task had to be finished.

When he reemerged, Harry was asleep. Felix sank into the big club chair, Ella's reading chair. Ella used to watch baby Harry sleep, but Felix had always been too scared, because if he'd started watching over their son, how would he ever have found the strength to stop?

The terror had been constant: terror of touching the baby, terror of doing something wrong. And then Harry grew into a walking, talking whirligig of impulsivity who toddled into Felix's den one day when Ella was out and dumped the contents of Felix's files across the carpet. Felix smacked him hard enough to leave a handprint on the back of Harry's legs. By the time Ella came home, Harry had been bribed with ice cream and an expensive trip to the toy shop on Ninth Street. The next day, he had begun the process of retreating from Harry's life, because after that, he no longer trusted himself to be alone with Harry.

Felix hadn't planned to tell Harry about smacking him, but Harry had handled the revelation well. And yet, it had been little more than a pinpoint in time for Harry. The moment had held meaning only for Felix.

Midnight, and he was sleep deprived, yet wide awake, which made about as much sense as the rest of his life. He went into the living room, turned on Ella's phone, and started moving everything from her calendar to his: birthdays, anniversaries, a dentist appointment for Harry, and an alert to turn the compost. (He made a note to research that on the Internet.)

At two o'clock, knackered almost to oblivion with a mind that continued to churn, he went into her messages and scrolled through the barrage of texts Harry had sent in the last week. No wonder Ella had relinquished her phone. Felix went farther and farther back, through their never-ending conversation, through the intimacy and understanding that he could never hope to achieve with his son. His name rarely appeared. It was as if he'd been a footnote in their lives.

FOURTEEN

"Dad, Dad. Wake up!"

Felix shot off the sofa and reached for his glasses. Why was it light outside, and why was Harry standing over him wrapped up in the white duvet, looking like the Michelin Man with a full head of hair?

"What are you doing out here?" Harry grimaced and blinked, grimaced and blinked.

Good question. Felix swept his tongue round his mouth, which was dry and fuzzy and had a sour taste. "I was sorting through your mother's calendar, and I must have conked out." He massaged the crick in his neck. "Happy birthday."

"Yeah, thanks. Listen—" Harry lowered his voice. "We have a problem. Mice. Or maybe rats. I don't know."

"What?"

"Shhh." Harry grabbed his hand. "Quick, come now before they stop. They're in the walls."

The doorbell rang.

"Oh, that's probably Eudora. I saw her in the garden with flower clippy thingies."

"Who the hell's Eudora?"

"Our neighbor."

"We have a neighbor called Eudora?"

"You know." Harry mimed out something that could have been interpreted as power walking. Or maybe he was constipated. "She walks with Mom?"

"I thought her name was Eleanor."

"Dad." Harry rolled his eyes and then skidded toward the door, the duvet—Felix's duvet—dragging behind him. Trailing on the floor. *Wash the sheets* was definitely going on today's to-do list.

Harry flung the front door open and pulled a little old lady inside. She was wearing a hat with earflaps, a huge puffy jacket, what appeared to be denim overalls (he would have called them dungarees two decades ago), and men's work boots. And she was carrying purple gardening gloves and a pair of secateurs.

"Hey, Eudora," Harry said in a stage whisper as he eased the front door closed. "We've got a rodent infestation. Wanna come hear?"

"Harry," Felix said through gritted teeth.

"Lovely to meet you. You must be Felix. Eudora Jenkens." She took a step toward him in her boots, her muddy boots. Her very muddy boots. On his pale oak hall floor. She held out her hand and Felix shook it. A leftie, and she didn't wear a wedding band. "I sure am sorry to hear about your charming wife. Another two weeks in the hospital? My, my." She shook her head.

How did this unknown person find out about Ella—the jungle telegraph?

"Now, I don't want y'all worrying about the garden"—Felix hadn't been—"I'll keep an eye on it. I was fixing to cut back your hellebores, but I see they're quite fine."

"My hellebores?" Felix said.

"How silly of me. You probably know them as Christmas roses. Should you need references, I'd be more than happy to provide them, although I am an ambassador for the Blomquist Garden at Duke

Gardens and a former president of the Chapel Hill gardening club." Her voice was slightly breathy and her *r*'s soft; her tone dripped with old-fashioned southern hospitality. She gave a slow, genteel smile that said, *I bite.*

"But Lord have mercy, did you mention rodents? It sounds as if you need my expertise in other areas." She took off her jacket—not her boots—and rolled up her shirtsleeves. "Now. How can I help?"

Brilliant. Not merely a nosey parker, but a nosey parker do-gooder. Felix ranked do-gooders at the same level as Jehovah's Witnesses. "Thank you, but we don't need any—"

"To hear them, we have to go into the bedroom." Harry looked from Felix to Eudora with a shaky smile. "You might want to take your boots off first."

"Of course, child." Then she put the secateurs on top of the shoe cabinet and sat on the floor like an agile twenty-year-old. Her socks were neon orange.

Harry, jiggling from foot to foot and still mummified in the duvet, turned his back to Eudora and gave Felix a wide-eyed look that made less sense than a semaphore. Felix couldn't think of a response. Quite simply, his life was no longer his own. There were rodents in his bedroom, a pair of rusty clippers on his ash shoe cabinet, and some mad old biddy with hideous socks sitting on his floor like a limber yoga master. He'd heard a news report once about frozen waste from a transatlantic jet hurtling down through the sky and crashing into someone's house. Had frozen shit fallen on him right at that moment, it wouldn't have surprised him. At all.

Harry waved for them both to follow. Wordlessly, they did.

As they filed into the bedroom—his bedroom—Felix remembered something from the night of Harry's birthday sleepover. *Scrabbling.* Scrabbling was coming from the linen closet in the master bathroom.

"What do you think it is?" Harry's voice squeaked with excitement.

"Since there are no holes in the walls of our house and we have bird-proof cages over the outside vents"—Felix paused to inhale—"I can only assume the creature or creatures responsible chewed through the cedar siding."

"Squirrels," Eudora said.

"In my linen closet?"

"Nesting, if I had to guess."

Squirrels making babies in his clean linen. And he needed to change the sheets. "I hate squirrels."

"He does," Harry said helpfully. "Loathes them. They ate the back of one of our outside chairs in the fall, and they dug the plants out of Mom's pots. Made a terrible mess on the porch. Dad's at war with them."

"Have you tried sprinkling chili powder in the pots?" Eudora said.

Felix stared at her. "You don't make authentic Brunswick stew, do you?"

Eudora gave a deep laugh that made him think of dark, paneled bars and, for some reason, flappers smoking cigars. "We're going to become good friends, Felix."

"Really."

"Dad! We're not killing anything and we're not cooking it, either. And we're not eating squirrel."

"Squirrel is delicious," Eudora said. "Tastes like rabbit."

"Yuck, that's gross," Harry said.

Eudora made a move toward the bathroom. "Would you like me to have a look? I had squirrels in the attic last year."

"No. I can't let you do that." Felix flinched. Every now and again, he heard the ghost of Pater's voice in his own. *I can't let you do that.* Pater dragged out *can't* with a long imaginary *r*. So British and always a precursor to something bad.

"I'm not a fan of chivalry," Eudora said, her voice sweet as strychnine.

"Neither am I. But no one's going in there except for me." He'd seen *National Lampoon's Christmas Vacation*. He was not having a squirrel tearing through his house on a rodent rampage. "You're both staying in the bedroom."

"Whatever you say, hon." Eudora put her arm around Harry. "Holler if you need us."

"Don't hurt them, Dad."

"I wasn't planning a squirrel carnage, Harry." What he was planning, he had no clue.

"Wait! I know. I know! Max's dad has a wet vac they used when the basement flooded. We can, like, suck them up in the wet vac and release them in the forest. What do you think, Eudora?"

"Well, child—"

Felix closed the bathroom door on the conversation, and the scrabbling got louder. Suppose Eudora was wrong, and it was a bat? Bats carried rabies. He really, really didn't want a rabies shot. He hated needles even more than he hated squirrels.

He rummaged under the sink for Ella's bathroom cleaning supplies. Rubber gloves seemed a good idea if you were going anywhere near squirrel afterbirth. He snapped on the purple gloves. A bit small, but they'd work. Were mother squirrels aggressive? He should grab a weapon, too, in case the situation called for self-defense. He picked up the loo brush, and the scrabbling stopped.

"Dad? Dad? What are you doing in there? Should we call in reinforcements? One-eight-hundred-come-get-my-squirrels?" Harry sounded as if he were choking on a giggle.

Felix pressed his ear against the closet door. All quiet on the Western Front. Time to channel Macbeth and be bloody, bold, and resolute. He eased open the door and immediately gagged on the stench of squalid zoo cage. After this, he was taking a long, hot shower in Harry's bathroom. He wasn't coming back in here until the entire place had been hosed down with industrial-strength antibacterial cleaner.

In the wall behind the third shelf, half-hidden by sheets, there appeared to be a serious hole with jagged, gnawed edges. The hole at the back of the top shelf was bigger—approximately eight inches wide with twigs jammed across the opening. Rising up on tiptoe, Felix tugged gently on the pile of thankfully older towels. They were shredded and bloodied, and in the middle was a potpourri of leaves and grasses, sticks and insulation, and two baby squirrels.

Squirrels had eaten through the siding, eaten through the drywall, and carried twigs and leaves inside his house. To go forth and multiply.

He looked heavenward. *Don't I have enough burdens? You had to send me squirrels?*

A flash of fur shot at him, screeching like a demented Squirrel Nutkin. Felix swatted with the loo brush, missed, and slammed the closet door shut.

"Dad? Dad? Are you okay in there?"

"Not now, Harry—" Where was that little bastard? It had to be in the bathroom. He'd heard it plop to the floor.

The door to the bedroom opened.

"Stop mucking about, Harry, and—"

Too late. The squirrel legged it into the bedroom and began tearing round in circles, squawking like a hellcat. Then it shot under the bed skirt.

Eudora had the sense to slam the bedroom door shut; Harry stood there gawping.

"We have to drive her back in here," Felix said. "I'm not having a rabid mother squirrel loose in my bedroom."

"Squirrels don't carry rabies, son," Eudora said with another smile.

"It was a figure of speech." She might be next for the loo brush. Swear to God.

"Let's chase it back in," Harry said. "I'll go get a broom!"

"No!" Felix and Eudora shouted.

"Child, that bedroom door needs to stay closed." Eudora sucked in her lips and gave Felix a nod.

"This is a great way to spend my birthday!" Harry said.

"Your birthday? My, my. Is anyone baking you a cake?" Eudora said.

"He's celebrated already with his friends," Felix said.

"Nonsense. I'll bake for you this afternoon. What's your favorite flavor?"

"Carrot cake. I love carrot cake." Harry grimaced and blinked, grimaced and blinked.

"How many candles?"

"Seventeen."

Felix held up his rubber-gloved hands. "The squirrel, chaps?"

"On it, Dad." Harry tossed the duvet onto the bed.

"Working on the assumption that this mother is determined to get back to her babies, here's what we're going to do—" Felix turned on all the lights in the bathroom and slowly opened the closet door. "Harry, shut off the lights in here. Eudora"—she shot him a look—"if you wouldn't mind closing the curtains so we can darken the room? Let's hope her instincts call her home." Felix chose not to think about irony.

Harry started giggling again. Felix stood behind the bathroom door and held a finger to his lips. "*Shhh.* We need to be quiet and still."

Eudora dropped to her knees and disappeared behind the bed. Was she deaf, senile, or unable to follow basic instructions?

A hand reached up and removed the red glass from his bedside table. A bump and a flurry of squawking came from under the bed, and the squirrel—which Felix noticed for the first time was covered in bald patches and seriously manky—shot from under the bed and tore into the bathroom. Felix slammed the door and dusted off his hands.

"My," Eudora said, "all that excitement has left me tuckered out. At the risk of ethnic profiling, I'm assuming you're a tea drinker, Felix? How about a cup of Earl Grey? With lots of sugar to calm the nerves."

"You're in luck, Eudora. That's Dad's favorite."

She smiled as if she'd known all along. Had she gained access to their house, snooped in their cabinets, examined the contents of the tea caddy? Felix dragged Ella's bedside table across the bathroom door.

"Dad, you do know squirrels can't open doors?"

"I'm not taking any chances. Did you see her bald patches? She's probably a mutant."

Harry cupped his hand over his mouth and started shaking.

"Now what's so funny?" Felix frowned.

"You're, you're"—Harry hiccuped with laugher—"still wearing rubber gloves."

"Would you like me to go fetch Daddy's hunting rifle, Felix?"

"You're offering to shoot my son?"

Harry collapsed on the bed, hysterical.

"In case the squirrel escapes again. Daddy used to take me to the range on Sundays. I can hit a squirrel at fifty yards."

Brilliant. They were living next door to a squirrel sniper.

FIFTEEN

Felix stood in the middle of the cul-de-sac, hand raised in a solitary wave as Critter Rescue drove off with the squirrels. A truck rumbled in the distance, and then silence settled. The air smelled faintly of skunk and warmth. Sixty-five degrees on a Sunday in January, and yet the neighborhood was as quiet as the morning-after set of a disaster movie. He could pretend he and Harry were the only people in this corner of the Bull City.

A rabbit hopped toward a neighbor's dormant vegetable garden, and Felix's stomach bubbled and churned. Clearly, he needed an upgrade to something stronger than Pepto-Bismol.

He folded his arms behind his neck and stared up into the cloudless expanse. A hawk drifted overhead, screeching, and a flock of pigeons rose from the power lines and scattered. He blinked against the intensity of blue sky marred only by the laceration of a single vapor trail.

One week earlier, he would have denounced sky gazing as unproductive and self-indulgent. But in the last thirty-six hours, he had become a dreamer, a man who wanted his critically ill wife to come home looking like the woman he'd been preparing to collect from the airport a week ago. In seven days, someone had moved the goalposts of his life; someone had stolen the certainty that his wife would even come home.

A double yellow line divided his marriage into before and after the heart attack. And this person who now lived in jeans and Dr. Martens, who had given up hair gel and aftershave, was not someone he recognized. And neither was the nervous, frail person he had visited in hospital yesterday.

Turning his back on the Carolina sun, Felix stepped onto the wooden bridge and entered cool shade. A solitary toad croaked and water trickled down the small waterfall he had created for Ella out of indigenous river stones.

He crossed the periwinkle that threatened year-round to swallow the stepping-stone path, and headed for the clearing around the house. Years ago, Ella had told him that periwinkle was the flower of death. When Felix had suggested ripping it up, Ella had reminded him that the garden was her territory, and periwinkle was the perfect low-maintenance ground cover for the patch of woodland by the creek. The periwinkle had stayed, jostling for superiority with the equally invasive ivy that grew up and around the tree trunks. Felix hoped the ivy would win the battle.

As the sun warmed the back of his neck once more, Felix walked around the side of the house to the small patio that faced untamed forest—a protective barrier that afforded year-round privacy and solitude.

It would have been easier and cheaper to let Eudora blast mama squirrel into pieces. A week ago, he would have done exactly that. After all, he routinely decapitated copperheads without a qualm. Now he was paying Sunday rates to relocate nature's original psychos. And yet the squirrel invasion had been a problem he could fix. Had it also become an excuse to avoid the hospital? Was there a small part of him that said *enough*? Katherine had been more than happy to take today's shift, but it should have been him. Ella was petrified about tomorrow's meeting with Dr. Beaubridge, convinced he was going to prescribe the knife. Felix was terrified he wasn't, because if open-heart surgery wasn't an option—then what?

Inspecting the gray mesh patio chairs, he chose one that had not been gnawed by squirrels, dragged it across the concrete, and sat. He pulled out his mobile, tapped on the phone app, and selected the third number down. As usual, Robert picked up on the first ring.

"Please tell me you're coming in tomorrow," he said.

"I'm afraid not. Ella's back in the CCU." Explanations seemed irrelevant. The upside of working with Robert was that he never expressed interest in anyone's personal life but his own. "She's going to be in hospital for at least another two weeks."

"Sorry to hear that."

"Which means that starting on Tuesday, I'll have to leave the office by two forty-five each day for school pickup."

"Jesus fucking Christ, Felix. Are you kidding me?"

A nice attitude from someone who was, no doubt, fresh home from taking his family to the weekly service at the First Methodist Church of Raleigh. Robert Sharpe was partial to anything that contained the word *first*.

"My wife is in acute heart failure. I'm not exactly in the mood to joke."

"Neither am I, Felix. Do you have any idea what's at stake here, what will happen if we lose the Life Plan deal? What it will mean for the company and for us personally? The loss of revenue? I'm working my balls off here to hold up my end of the deal, and I need you to take the lead on the bond issue."

"I'm doing that; I—"

"I need you in the office every second of every day. I need you on call seven days a week. I need you to be the hot shit specialist I once believed you to be."

"I can deliver." Felix clenched his jaw.

"And how exactly do you propose to do that if you're leaving the office every day for school pickup?" Robert made the words *school pickup* sound like something that should be buried in the middle of a compost heap.

"I'll work at home in the evenings. As many hours as it takes." *Thwack.* Felix snapped the elastic band he was still wearing on his wrist at Katherine's suggestion. The woman clearly understood a thing or two about stress. "But part of my day will now revolve around my son's schedule."

"Have you considered allowing your son to take the bus, Felix, like most sixteen-year-old boys?"

"He's seventeen, and there is no bus. He goes to a small private school. I thought you knew this."

"No offense, but I don't keep up with the personal lives of employees."

"I'm not an employee. I'm your partner."

"Then act like one, man! What the hell's happened to you? You used to be a friggin' rock star, and now you're talking about school pickup as if you were a whiny kindergarten parent. This is a crock of lazy, slack shit."

Lazy. Slack. Felix pinged the elastic band so hard it snapped in two. And stung like hell.

"Hire a taxi service to drive your son to school."

"He has after-school activities."

"Then hire a fleet of taxis. God knows you earn enough money."

"No one is driving my son except me."

"Man up, Felix. Your son is sixteen—"

"Seventeen."

"My eldest had his first DUI at that age. When family shit happens, people like us hire domestic help, caregivers, whatever the fuck you call them. I am not losing this deal, do you hear me?"

To think he'd lost his temper with Ella a few weeks ago after she'd called his partner a philandering scumbag. Robert Sharpe was a man who didn't see obstacles, who saw only the prize, who had moved his mistress to an apartment five miles from his wife and kids to cut down on commute time, never once questioning whether the women would cross paths.

"I am not handing over the care of my wife, my son, and my house to strangers."

"Your son, Felix, is sixteen—"

"Seventeen." Felix spat the word out. "My son is seventeen."

"And he doesn't drive."

"No. And nor does he drink. He's a straight-A student without a police record." *Unlike your delinquent.*

"When I took you on board, I made it clear that family came second. That's why our wives are full-time wives." Robert's southern drawl grated on Felix more than usual.

"My wife"—Felix bristled—"was a talented jewelry designer who made a choice to stay home with our son because of his needs. Now I am making the same choice. My son is not your average seventeen-year-old. He has issues."

"We all have issues. Hire a therapist."

"He has several."

"Good, then let them do their jobs."

In the forest, a dog howled—an eerie yip and a yowl. Or was it a coyote? According to the local news, coyote sightings in Durham were increasingly common. The creature howled again, but this time on the move. Felix stood.

"This conversation is pointless. Need I remind you that if we were a bigger company, I would be quoting the family and medical leave act and taking twelve weeks of unpaid leave?" He would be chewing through his own siding if he had to leave his job for twelve weeks.

Robert momentarily turned away from the phone to talk to someone. *How rude.*

"Am I interrupting you, Robert?"

"Curt's here. He has some concerns about the Life Plan deal."

"Concerns that are unqualified. I've got this." Felix dug his fingernails into his left palm. "I have to hang up now and go buy industrial-strength cleaning supplies."

Robert gave a snide laugh. "You're cleaning your own house, too?"

"Squirrels ate through my cedar siding. I have to de-squirrel the inside of the house and squirrel-proof the outside."

"For Chrissake, Felix—"

"I'll see you on Tuesday morning. Nine o'clock *sharp.*"

Robert, the tosser, hung up. What had happened to common courtesy? Did no one say please, thank you, and good-bye anymore?

A squirrel rushed out from the undergrowth, stopped with its front paw raised, and looked at the house.

"Piss off," Felix said. "Otherwise, my next call is to Eudora."

The squirrel waved its tail frantically and then shot back into the forest.

Could this whole mess get any worse? If he lost his job, they'd lose their health insurance. God only knew what their medical bills would amount to when all this was done. And if he quit the partnership, he'd have to start over. At fifty. And do what? Become a corporate financial consultant—if he could brush off the stigma of failure? He would have nothing left but his reputation, which Robert was more than capable of shredding out of spite. Felix sighed. Everything he'd worked for since coming to North Carolina could flush down the lavatory if he crossed Robert.

The glass doors slid open and Harry appeared, carrying Felix's Merton College mug. "Thought you might need a refill."

"Thank you."

"You okay, Dad?" Harry plopped down in a squirrel-deformed chair. He didn't even bother to check.

"It appears my partner has become, to use your Uncle Tom's favorite word, a tosspot." Felix cradled his mug. "Although that is privileged information not to be shared."

"No offense, Dad, but Robert's always been a jerk. I mean, c'mon, he called on Christmas Day."

"He did?"

"You don't remember Mom going nuts?"

Felix nodded slowly. Work had never come with barriers. It had always spilled over into all aspects of their lives.

Harry cracked his knuckles; Felix ignored it. He just didn't have the energy.

"You're not going to lose your job, are you?" Harry grimaced and blinked.

"Robert stole me from Morgan Stanley because I'm an expert in my field. He needs me." Not strictly an answer, but close enough.

"That's a relief. I've never really understood what you and Robert do, Dad."

"We're investment bankers. We help corporations get financing by issuing stocks and bonds and arranging loans. Robert specializes in stocks and loans; I handle the bonds. Up until now, it's been a match made in heaven." Felix paused. "If you're worrying about the college fund, you needn't. It's safe, and so are your school fees. In fact, your school fees are paid through the end of senior year."

Harry sat up, rigid, and began kicking the legs of the table. Again and again.

"Harry, please. Stop that." Felix scraped the small metal table along the concrete, out of Harry's reach.

"I don't care about the college fund, Dad."

"You should."

"I was thinking about Mom's health insurance."

"Harry, I'm not going to lose my job." He couldn't afford to—on any level. "I won't allow that to happen, do you understand?"

Harry nodded. "So why *did* you become a corporate banker?"

"My grandfather was one. I admired him, and I knew it would be a good career for a provider. It's certainly helped us cover your exorbitant medical expenses."

"That's not exactly my fault, Dad." Harry spoke quietly, but his deep scowl suggested he had a great deal more to say on the subject. His right leg jerked sideways.

"I'm not blaming you. I'm merely stating a fact. I enjoy my work, I'm good at it, and we've all benefited. I'm not highlighting a problem." *So please think before you say anything critical.*

A blue jay jeered in the forest, and Harry gave his throat-clearing tic.

"Do you think Mom ever regrets giving up work to be a full-time parent?"

"She does work. Bloody hard, as I've discovered this week."

"You know I didn't mean that."

"Then you should have been more specific." Felix sipped his tea. It was too weak, but Harry was trying. They were both trying, and the effort was exhausting. "Your mother made choices, as did I. She didn't ask me to move to the States before you were born. I didn't ask her to give up jewelry design."

"What do you mean about moving to the States?"

"Pretty obvious, I would have thought. You know your mother was pregnant when we got married."

"I thought I was planned."

"Have you ever talked about this with your mother?"

"Yes. But I'm not asking her right now—I'm asking you. Was I planned?" Harry stood and stared at Felix without blinking.

"No," Felix said. "You were an accident. I assumed you knew this."

"And you followed Mom to America and married her because it was the right thing to do." There was no question in Harry's voice. And still, he stared.

"Harry, I have to get to Home Depot so I can fix the hole in the house before the light goes. I don't see the relevance of this conversation. I married your mother because I wanted to, and I have no regrets. I'm quite sure she doesn't, either."

"But did you love her?"

"I was passionate about her. I was obsessed with her, and I made a choice. Turns out I made the right one. And through that choice, I discovered what it means to be in love. Do I love your mother? Yes. With all my heart."

Harry turned and slid open the glass door. "I just can't believe neither of you ever told me the truth," he said, and disappeared.

Felix looked up at his house, disfigured by the large piece of silver flashing he had attached temporarily to cover up the hole. An ugly metal Band-Aid. The men from Critter Rescue had struggled to accept that Felix preferred they not seal up the hole—"Really, Mr. Fitzwilliam, it's part of the service." Really, but no thanks. He was the only person who worked on this house. If necessary, he would rip out and rebuild the entire bathroom. His eyes moved across the siding to the glass doors. Harry was stomping back and forth in the living room, yelling the f-word and playing the part of the disaffected teen Felix had just informed Robert did not exist. Dealing with squirrels was definitely the easiest part of this brave new world.

SIXTEEN

Felix looked up from his lined legal pad. "I have questions."

Ella, sitting upright in her hospital bed, picked at the weave of her white cotton blanket while her monitor bleeped.

"Of course you do." The corners of Dr. Beau Carlton Beaubridge's all-American smile wavered. Unlike Felix, Dr. Beaubridge had applied hair gel. Just another day at the office with the critically ill, the dying, and those unfortunate enough to be his patients.

An image flashed in Felix's mind, a perverted image of him ripping out Ella's tubes and bashing the monitor with the fire extinguisher. Or was it Dr. Beau-Beau he wanted to bash?

"Let me get this right." Felix crossed his legs. "My wife's stent got clogged on your watch."

"Unfortunately, these things happen, Mr. Fitzwilliam."

"Incompetence, you mean?" According to his research, a clog was a rare occurrence with a drug-eluting stent and, when combined with a widow-maker lesion, extremely dangerous. Someone was to blame— someone was responsible—and Felix was staring at that someone.

"Stent thrombosis is uncommon, but it can occur subacutely in the first thirty days. As I have explained before, your wife has been incredibly unlucky. A seemingly healthy woman with a dormant genetic condition. And now this second setback." Dr. Beaubridge shook his head.

"I hope you're not implying that luck plays a part in her medical treatment." Felix tossed the pad aside. "So what next? We hold hands and pray, because prayer seems a better option than Raleigh Regional at this point."

"Felix, please." Ella's voice competed with the bleeping of that bloody monitor.

Felix began scratching, the anger a mass of chigger bites inside and out, searing through his gut, burning off his skin. It was lack of reason; it was insanity.

Ten, nine, eight . . . to hell with counting down from ten. Try one hundred.

Ella started coughing, and Felix stopped breathing.

Dr. Beaubridge whipped the stethoscope free from around his neck and listened to her heart. "Can you tell me how you're feeling, Ella?"

"A bit breathless. That's all." Ella rested her head against her pillow with a hesitant smile. Her skin was ghostly gray, and her voice was cracked like a worn-out record.

He wanted to go backward in time. He wanted before.

"Mr. Fitzwilliam, I understand your sense of frustration, but we need to keep your wife calm."

Felix continued to count silently.

"Having this artery become occluded twice within such a short period of time was far from ideal." Dr. Beaubridge tugged down the cuff of his white coat. "Ella's heart is severely damaged as a result."

Felix nodded, kept counting.

"However, she did well over the weekend. We're moving her back to the cardiac step-down unit this morning, and our focus now is on adjusting the medications to their optimal doses. But it could take two weeks."

"And during that time she will be here, in this hospital." Felix spoke slowly, calmly. It was no different than walking: left foot, right foot; one word, next word. "Then what happens?"

"We often see remarkable results with careful medical therapy, watching, and waiting."

"And the cases that don't fit the remarkable-results category?"

"The heart can also continue to get weaker."

"What are my options if that happens, Doctor?" Ella said.

"Possibly an implanted battery-powered device called a left ventricular assist device, or an LVAD for short. This would be a bridge to a transplant."

"Transplant?" Ella whispered.

"You would make an excellent candidate, Ella. You're young and healthy—"

"Why not bypass surgery?" Felix said.

Dr. Beaubridge laced his fingers together, palms down, and placed them on his thigh. "Unlikely in your wife's case. Her initial infarction was extensive, and muscle damaged to that degree will likely not recover. This recent incident extended the MI, and given the anatomy of your coronary arteries, Ella, I believe you would not benefit from a bypass operation. The arteries are diffused and narrowed, and there isn't enough normal heart muscle left to save. To be blunt"—he looked at Ella; she nodded—"we're talking inoperable heart disease, which is why a heart transplant might be the solution."

The door banged opened, and a cleaning lady began to wheel in a large trash can.

"Not now, please," Dr. Beaubridge snapped.

"Sorry, y'all," the woman said, and backed out of the room.

Did this cleaner have family, a husband? Did she understand what it meant to stare into the abyss of unimaginable loss? Were there other spouses in this building, maybe even in the room next door, in the same state of utter despair as Felix?

"Thank you, Dr. Beaubridge," Ella said.

The doctor walked toward the door. "I'll leave the two of you alone. Ella, I hope you'll consider going on the transplant list. I'll see you tomorrow on my rounds. Keep up the good work, and be assured that we will continue to treat you to the best of our abilities."

And he left.

What if Ella started crying? She hardly ever cried, and when she did, she took these huge, gulping breaths that jabbed his heart like red-hot pokers. Leaning over the bedrail, Felix took her hand and raised it to his lips. His mouth lingered on her wedding ring. "I love you, Ella Bella," he said. Why hadn't he told her that every day? People said *I love you* all the time. Look at the way Harry tossed it into the air like a badminton shuttlecock. *I love you, Mom! Love you, Maxi-Pad! I love Sammie.*

I love you: the three hardest words to say, unless you believed your wife was dying.

It was a death sentence with a timer. There were no guarantees that her heart would hold out until she could get a new one. She knew it; Felix knew it. Why else would he say *I love you*, words he rarely spoke?

Ella grabbed a tissue from the box by her bed and dabbed at her eyes.

"Don't cry, darling, please."

"I'm not. The air in here is too dry. Makes my eyes water."

Felix gave her one of his laser looks; he wasn't falling for it. But if she told him the truth, if she screamed, *What else do you expect me to do*, it would be harder for both of them. He would fall to pieces, and that wasn't an option. Finally, it was his turn to be strong enough for two. He had to be the strong parent, because otherwise, what would happen to Harry? And what would happen to Felix? Her thoughts circled like turkey vultures. Who should she worry about first?

"I think it's time to call Dad." Once she told her father, there would be no going back. She was stepping up to the plate, admitting she could die. Until the clogged stent, it hadn't felt real. This was as real as it got.

"Do you want me to take care of it? I could call him from home."

Ella shook her head. "If it comes from you, he'll worry more. He'll want to hear my voice, gauge how I'm coping. I have to be the one to tell him." After Felix left, she would sit with this, try her death sentence on for size, find words that wouldn't bring a rush of memories for her dad. Then she would pick up the pieces and discover her fighting spirit. Tell herself that she was a good candidate for a transplant. If she'd been lucky to survive on the plane, she was lucky still. Unlike Felix, she had no problem with luck.

"And what if you break down on the phone?" Felix said.

"I won't do that to him. I can fake it when I have to."

"That's not a reassuring thing for a husband to hear."

Ella stared at the tissue. "For the record, I've never faked anything with you."

Felix shot up and darted around the hospital room as if the walls and ceiling were closing in on them, shrinking. "Please consider transferring to a better hospital. If I pull every IOU, I can get you a bed at Memorial before the end of the day. I've played golf with the chief of cardiology. I'd prefer to get you moved to Duke, but—"

"No. We're done with that conversation, Felix." Ella closed her eyes. "I'm still competent to make my own medical decisions. I'm not starting over with a different team. I like the staff here, and I want to continue the conversation with Dr. Beaubridge about a heart transplant."

She reached for Felix, pulling him down until his head rested on her chest. She buried her face in his hair. "I like the nongel look." His hair, so soft, smelled of lavender. Had he been using her shampoo?

"Once I get home, things will seem brighter."

Felix straightened up, took off his glasses, and rubbed his eyes. "I think you're being overly optimistic."

"Please, Felix. I need you to support me in this. I'm not changing hospitals, and I don't want to argue."

"Because life's too short?"

"Quite frankly, yes. I could croak at any time."

"Ella, that's not remotely funny. Nor is it appropriate."

"Seems to me we can laugh or cry. Right now, I choose laughter. Is that so wrong? You can't control every situation, Felix."

"Neither can you."

"Touché."

"I can't lose you." His voice was so heavy that she nearly caved, nearly cried.

"Not ready to trade me in for a younger model with bigger boobs?"

"I've never wanted anyone but you, Ella Bella. There is no one else for me. I should have told you that a thousand times a day since we met." Felix mussed his hair. "Why didn't I?"

"Hey, I'm not planning on going anywhere. I'm young, I'm in good shape. You heard the doc—I'm healthy. Apart from the defective heart. Honestly, I believe that getting home will be the best medicine. How are you and Harry getting on?" She coughed to cover up the wheezing. Hard to breathe after all those words.

Felix squirmed.

"Want to tell me what happened?"

"You should have told me Harry thought your pregnancy was planned."

"Our pregnancy," she said softly, then listened as Felix explained.

"Let me talk to him," she said. "I'll call as soon as I get my new room assignment."

"No. This is my problem to sort out. I have to say, though, he out-maneuvered me like a pro."

"He's good at reading people. He always has been—ever since he was little. He probably picked up on some hesitancy."

"And went for the kill?"

"Followed his instincts. Harry's not shy about asking for what he wants or needs." She turned her head away from those icy-blue eyes, from the perfect bone structure that made her husband a classic male beauty, from the expression that was a mirror of their son's. Everyone said Harry resembled her, but that was because of the mop of dirty-blond hair. When you looked deeper, when you watched his mannerisms, he was all Felix. A child laughed outside her door, and she ached to hold her son.

Felix pulled a chair closer to the bed and sat. "You've lost a lot of weight."

"The food's crap." *I'm nauseated all the time, Felix. I can't eat.* "Tell me what Harry's doing today."

"I could go home and get him if you want me to, since there's no school."

"There isn't?"

"Martin Luther King Day."

She nodded. It was so easy to lose track of time in the twilight of hospital living. "No. Bad enough he's seen me in the hospital once. I don't want him stuck with images of me like this. Is he at home playing on the Xbox?"

"I believe Eudora's giving him a cooking lesson."

"Ah, so you've finally met our newest neighbor. Interesting, isn't she?"

"She turned up like Mary Poppins and refused to move on." Felix paused. "Harry seems to like her, though."

"He helps her from time to time with odd jobs, carrying in groceries, that sort of thing."

"He does?" Felix frowned.

"That's how we met. Harry saw her unloading groceries one day and rushed to her aid. All very sweet." Ella paused to catch her breath. "Of course, Eudora has a spine of steel and doesn't need help with anything. But I do think she's lonely."

"She has a gun."

"Most people in the South do, sweetheart."

"She's not some retired ax-murderer hiding out in a Durham neighborhood, is she?"

"Have you started watching *Criminal Minds* since I've been in here?"

"I don't know anything about her, Ella. And she's in our home, teaching our son to cook."

"She moved in last spring. Had a huge historic home in Chapel Hill, but decided to downsize for her seventy-fifth birthday. My guess is that she came from old money. She's a retired horticulturalist. Famous in her field. Single, and had a scandalous affair with a married Duke professor a few decades back."

Felix looked horrified.

"She's a good soul, and she's alone. Since we started walking together in the mornings, I've gotten to know her pretty well."

"Why did you never tell me about her?"

"When did I ever tell you anything about my day? I don't ask about your work; you don't ask about mine."

"We haven't done a good job of keeping up with each other's lives, have we?"

Ella shrugged. "We did what we had to do. Most families like ours end up in the divorce courts, but we didn't."

"Any regrets?" Felix said quietly.

Ella looked him in the eye. "Not one."

Felix seemed to think for a few minutes. "Do I need to put Eudora on my to-do list?"

An unexpected feeling grew in her throat like an iridescent bubble blown through a wand: laughter. "If anything, she'll put you on her list. You, Felix Fitzwilliam, may have met your match in Eudora Jenkens."

SEVENTEEN

Several hours later, Felix sat on the patio with Eudora Jenkens, retired horticulturalist of questionable morals. Spring had apparently arrived early in North Carolina. A chorus of spring peepers, jingling away like sleigh bells down in the creek, seemed to agree.

Eudora had welcomed him home with a glass of iced tea. In seventeen years of southern living, Felix had refused to drink iced tea as an abomination against the tea gods. And the stuff Eudora served him was sweetened. Felix never added sugar to anything. Except, of course, to English strawberries served with double cream. Real cream that was too thick to pour. Not the synthetic rubbish American supermarkets sold in spray cans.

Felix raised his glass, closed his eyes, and swallowed. If he could have pinched his nose without offending his elderly neighbor, he would have. And yet . . . this sweetened iced tea was surprisingly good. Quite pleasant, even refreshing. "I'm afraid I have rather a lot to take care of this afternoon."

"Of course you do," Eudora said. She turned her face to Duke Forest, where the sinking sun ignited the treetops with an orange glow. "And I haven't touched today's *New York Times*. Not always a pleasant experience, reading the newspaper, but I choose to not fret about things I can't control. Don't you agree? We can always find plenty to fret about."

His evening's to-do list was considerably longer than *read the paper*. Would he have to be blunt and ask her to leave?

"Such a delightful young man, your son."

"Thank you." Felix waited for the qualifiers: what the hell is wrong with him; does he ever sit still; why does he blink and grimace nonstop?

"And what a gift he has for dealing with the harsh realities of the world. I'm sure Tourette's has given him more than one disadvantage, but he sure doesn't act that way. I spent many years in mental wards, and—"

"My son is not mentally ill."

"I didn't say that he was. I believe Tourette's is classified as a neurological disorder, but I doubt that has always been the case. My twin sister was a paranoid schizophrenic. Well, we didn't know that for years. Sadly, neither she nor Mama handled the diagnosis with grace. She passed five years back. All in all, it was a blessing."

"How did your father handle it?" Felix had to ask.

"Daddy left to cohabit with the maid in quite the scandal. I don't think men of his generation knew how to handle women who were different, women who didn't conform. And when he discovered I was a lesbian—"

Felix choked on a mouthful of tea. Ella had omitted that part of the potted bio.

"Bless your heart, did I offend? I don't filter these days. Speaking one's mind is the sole advantage of age. Sad that we have to wait until our later years to figure that out."

"I was surprised, not offended." Felix slapped his chest. "My older brother was gay. He died."

Eudora eyeballed him. "I'm sorry for your loss."

"It's been twelve years."

"But time doesn't heal all wounds, does it?"

"No." Felix stared into his tea.

Furious rustling came from a drift of leaves on the forest floor.

"What a rumpus." Eudora sipped her tea. "This weather sure has every living creature fooling around."

Felix glanced at her sideways. Please God, she wasn't going anywhere creepy with this, was she?

"Harry and that young sweetheart of his make a fine couple."

On the other side of the sliding glass doors, Harry and Sammie lay entwined on the living room sofa, watching a movie. Harry was so still, he had to be asleep. Or maybe not, since he had just scratched his head. Intriguing. Maybe dopamine suppressed the tics; maybe love was a natural cure for Tourette's.

"I'm not sure they are a couple," Felix said. "Officially, that is." How could he explain something he didn't understand, and why would he even try?

"Youngsters have their own way of doing things. But those two are as much in love as I've ever seen. I bet you and Ella were one fine couple. Y'all still are. You so dark, Ella so fair. I didn't see a single picture of you in the house. Lots of photos of Harry—Harry as a baby; Harry sitting on a toy dump truck; Harry dressed for his first day of kindergarten, I assume, with a multicolored backpack and matching outfit."

Out of the corner of his eye, Felix noted Harry's red plaid shirt and clashing purple jeans. If Harry had a style, Felix couldn't identify it. "Hard to believe, but Harry used to like everything to match."

"Yes." Eudora trailed off. "So many pictures of Harry, but none of his handsome parents, and I had to wonder why."

"Were you snooping?"

"Wouldn't be much of a crazy neighbor if I didn't snoop, now, would I? Don't you have a good nose around when you're in a house for the first time—see what you can learn? See what's missing."

Was she finding fault? "I'm not one for photos. That's Ella's territory."

"And Harry can't take the occasional photo of his parents while y'all are on vacation?"

"We don't really have vacations." Holidays, spent in England, were classified as duty visits. When Harry was younger, they'd squeezed in the occasional sightseeing trip—to York, to Bath—but the last two visits had been devoted to overseeing Mother's affairs, and Harry and Ella had restricted their tourism to the Tower of London and the Imperial War Museum. And, from what he could remember, a number of rather expensive cream teas.

"Next time I come, I expect to see a picture of you and Ella on your wedding day."

"I'm not sure I know where the wedding photos are." The photo of his pregnant bride, the one he kept by his side of the bed so he could see it first thing every morning, was not for public viewing.

"Oh, I'm sure if you search you'll find something."

"I'm stretched a little thin, Eudora—"

"I bet she was beautiful. As a young woman."

"Yes," Felix said. "She was. Still is."

"Tell me how you met. In London, I believe?"

He gave her his hardest stare, but she merely raised her eyebrows. "How did you know?" he said.

"Ella told me once. I was telling her about meeting Dahlia. Love at first sight."

"And Dahlia was married?" *Two can play the Ella-told-me game.*

"Oh, yes. Happily married to her childhood sweetheart. But we met, and it was one of those life-changing events you can't ignore. Like a category five hurricane knocking on your front door. You can't really escape from that, even if you want to."

"Meeting Ella was life changing." The words slipped out unedited.

"I imagine it was." Eudora cocked her head to the side.

Felix smiled. He was back on the Tube, seeing Ella's face for the first time, knowing she held the power to break his heart and not caring. "We were on the London Underground, and the train was stuck in a tunnel during rush hour. Ella's claustrophobic, which of course I didn't know at the time, but I could tell she was anxious."

"How very astute of you."

"I'd been watching her; it was hard not to. She's never been a woman to blend in."

Eudora patted the back of his hand; Felix tried not to flinch.

"Her companion had his Walkman on and was singing along, oblivious. She was grabbing at the overhead strap and horribly pale. Once I realized she was about to faint, I made sure I was the first person she saw when she woke up. In fact, I caught her."

Eudora smiled her slow, easy smile. "And the man with the Walkman?"

"Her boss, a famous jewelry designer. They met in college, and when his career took off, he asked Ella to move to London to be his production manager. It was a step sideways for her, since Ella's dream was always to have a small jewelry shop of her own and do mainly custom work. It was the first time she walked away from her calling. The second time was for Harry."

"Were they romantically involved?"

"No, he's gay. He had a crush on my brother for a while." Felix's sigh lingered like acid reflux. "Everyone did—gay or straight."

A male cardinal dive-bombed the glass door and flapped against it frantically for several seconds before flying off. The bird had done the same thing several times this week. Either cardinals had no ability to learn from their mistakes, or this one had brain damage. Why keep doing the same thing, day after day, with no hope of a different outcome?

"Our timing was off when we met," Felix said. "Her mother had just died, and Ella's life was falling apart. She needed someone to tell her to move back home to be near her father."

"And you were that someone. How very honorable of you, son."

"Thank you. I can't say it was easy, but it was the right decision for her. Her boss was making it extremely difficult. Unpleasant, really. Threatening to blacklist her in the industry so she wouldn't find a job Stateside."

"And you encouraged her to see him for the asshole he was."

"More or less." Felix grinned. "We kept in touch over the next five years, dated other people, but never quite moved on. Her thirtieth birthday present to herself was to come back to London to see if I was the man who got away."

That encounter, almost as brief as their first, had been long enough only for Ella to conceive. Would Felix have moved halfway round the world for a woman he barely knew if not for the seed that would become Harry? Yes, he would. Huge decisions had always been danger zones, but not that one. Joining Ella after he learned of the pregnancy had been more than the right course of action. It had been the only course of action, because once he knew how they fit together, how they moved together, he couldn't imagine being with anyone else. If dopamine was the cure for Tourette's, sex with Ella had been the only drug to ever mute the endless static in his brain.

"How romantic." Eudora flattened her hand across her chest. "Now you *know* I won't let up until I see a picture of y'all as a young couple."

"I'll look tonight." Maybe Harry could help him, and then he could judge for himself that his parents' marriage had not been rooted in mere propriety.

Harry banged on the glass doors and mouthed something.

"Open the door, Harry."

Harry held up his hands.

Felix rolled his eyes. "Open. The. Door."

"Dad, Dad! The dryer just buzzed. Want us to fold the laundry?"

"N—"

"What a treasure you are, Harry," Eudora said.

Harry beamed.

"Okay. Yes, fine. Thank you." What was the harm? Harry needed to learn responsibility, and he could refold everything when Harry was in the shower.

Birds began chattering in Duke Forest, heralding the end of the day. "Time to start supper." Felix stood up.

"Oh, my stars, I nearly forgot! I left shrimp and grits in the fridge. You're not one of those picky eaters, are you?"

Mother had accused him repeatedly of being a picky eater. He wasn't. She was big on starch and stodge; he wanted quality and nutrition. Although he wasn't sure grits fell into any category that could be labeled nutritious.

"That's extremely kind, but you don't have to feed us."

"Yes, Harry told me you've been trying to deal with everything by yourself. Utter nonsense, of course."

Nonsense? Felix opened his mouth, but Eudora continued talking. "I'm a darn good cook, and I have no one to cook for since my Dahlia passed. If accepting the occasional meal puts you at a social disadvantage, you can lend me your son from time to time to help with projects around the house."

"That's extremely generous. Thank you." He glanced back through the sliding doors. Harry and Sammie had disappeared. Were they still folding laundry, or had they retreated into Harry's bedroom for who knew what? Like everything else in his life, the open-door policy had fallen apart. On the way back from Home Depot, he'd bought condoms and left them out on the counter in Harry's bathroom.

"You're welcome to join us for supper. Since you cooked, it seems only fair."

"Don't look so terrified, son. I don't bite." Her eyes twinkled. "Thank you kindly for the invitation, but I must decline. For now."

She expected to be invited again? This was why it was easier to refuse offers of help. *Just say no.*

The sliding door opened again, and Sammie appeared. "My mom's here to pick me up. Bye, Eudora, and thank you for having me, Mr. Fitzwilliam."

"You're welcome, although I think it's time you called me Felix."

Sammie grinned and ran off.

"Lovely girl," Eudora said. "Now, where were we? Oh, yes. Dinner. I sense you and Harry need some alone time. The poor child has so many worries about his mama, and bless him, he doesn't want to keep troubling you. But before I go, maybe a quick drink? You keep bourbon in that wooden liquor cabinet of yours?"

Felix glanced at his watch. Five o'clock. "It's a bit early for me."

"Son, you need to learn to be a good southerner. Slow things down a bit."

"At this point, Eudora, I'd settle for simply making it through this week." He picked at his fingernails.

"What's making you so nervous, son?"

He didn't have to answer. He had already shared too much; he really didn't need to make it worse, tell her the one thing he was scared to verbalize. A pair of cardinals flitted in and out of one of Ella's camellias and flew off together. Did cardinals mate for life like swans?

"What if she comes home as an invalid? What if she stays that way until the transplant? How on earth will I cope?"

"Honey, I think we both need that bourbon."

EIGHTEEN

"And that's everything the cardiologist told you?" Harry picked up his fork, then put it down for a second time.

They were sitting at the dining room table, two half-eaten plates of shrimp and grits between them. Shrimp and grits were a rare treat, but Felix had no appetite—even for illicit carbohydrates. He pushed his plate away; Harry mirrored him.

"You know everything I know. Your mother is in class three heart failure, and she's on the transplant list. Dr. Beaubridge is optimistic that medical therapy will allow her to come home in two weeks, but she's going to be weak." Felix patted his mouth with his napkin. "And probably in a wheelchair. Any physical activity will exhaust her."

"This changes everything, Dad. I have to see her."

"No, Harry. Your mother was adamant." Felix picked up their water glasses. "Please clear the table."

Harry stood and started jiggling. "Class three heart failure, when there are only four levels? How can that be good? Anything can happen. Anything. I have to see her. Please."

"Your mother made me promise, Harry."

"Then break your promise!" Harry's voice cracked, not with a vocal tic, not with anger, but with raw desperation.

Felix rose to his feet, too. He carefully pushed his chair back into place and kept his eyes lowered. If Harry started crying, he didn't want to be a witness. "I will not do that."

"What if some promises are meant to be broken? I know you're trying to protect Mom's wishes, but—no offense, Dad—this is bullshit, and you know it. She's got to stop trying to hold me and Gramps at arm's length. She's got to accept that we have a right to be concerned. And what if seeing me actually helps, reminds her of—of"—Harry's head started jerking as if he were flicking a switch on and off, on and off; Felix waited—"all she has to fight for? When Uncle Tom was dying, you flew out to California to be with him, right?"

"Keep Uncle Tom out of this." Felix hadn't meant to threaten, but he was not prepared to relive bad decisions made while Tom was in hospice. "Your mother isn't dying, Harry. She's on the transplant list."

"I need to go see her." Harry repeated the head jerk. This time, the tic was more violent. "Please, I need to see her."

Felix turned away, unable to shake the memory of Tom's voice: "I need you to come, Felix." But he'd waited, made excuses because he couldn't accept that Tom wasn't Tom—unchanged and unchangeable. Another deal was in the works, he couldn't leave Ella and Harry, and then it was too late. Tom was dead.

Harry followed him into the kitchen, but without the plates.

"Harry, I asked you to clear the table."

"I know, but just listen. Mom's always talking about instinct—about following your gut. What's your gut telling you about this? You must understand, Dad. What kind of a person would I be if I didn't want to go see her?"

I need you to come, Felix.

"I'll make you a deal." Harry's fingers starting flicking through the air as if manipulated by invisible puppet strings. "If you take me once, just once, I wouldn't ask to go again. Dad, I need to touch her, tell her I love her face to face. This is something I have to do." He pounded his heart. "Bottom line, I'm going, whatever you say. Max will take me."

When did Harry become so contrary? Was this a new behavioral problem, or was he finally growing up, learning to be assertive? "If your decision is made, then whatever I say is irrelevant."

"Pretty much, but I'd rather have your blessing." Harry cleared his throat. "And I think one of us should tell her ahead of time, so she doesn't get upset. Which can't be good for a bad heart, right?"

So Harry had thought this through.

"Look, just take me one day after school. It can be super quick."

"But I visit her every morning after school drop-off," Felix said. He turned on the tap and rinsed their glasses.

"Maybe you could break routine? Special circumstances and all that?"

"I can't take you after school pickup, Harry. I have to get home as quickly as possible to return to work. This Life Plan deal—"

"Five minutes. All I'm asking for is five minutes." Harry put his head to one side and beamed as if he were a child saying, *You're the best.* "I'll take full responsibility and ask Katherine to plead my case with Mom. You won't even be involved!"

Felix realized he was still washing the glasses. What a waste of water. He elbowed off the tap. "The drive from school and back will stretch that five minutes into one hour."

"If you dump me in before-school care and go straight into work, you can easily compensate for that lost hour."

"A valid point, but have you forgotten what happened last time you were in the hospital? It ended quite badly."

"I'll take a Klonopin before I go and practice yoga breathing in the car. Hell, I'll even meditate." Harry spread his arms wide. *"Ommm."*

"I thought you hated yoga."

"But that's the whole point, Dad. Things change. You do what you have to do. You don't have to be like the kamikaze male cardinal that keeps head-butting the deck doors. What *is* that bird's problem?"

"Your mother—your very sick mother—was adamant." Now Felix was repeating himself, but his brain was too exhausted for original thought.

"So am I. Which means you get to make a choice. If someone told *you* you couldn't visit Mom, would you listen?"

Felix put the glasses upside down on the draining board and turned to stare into the darkness on the other side of the sliding doors. Despite the predominance of pines at the edge of their property, Duke Forest was filled with hardwood trees, all of them naked at this time of year. In three months, when everything returned to life with the bright-green touches of spring, would Ella be healed? Would she have a new heart? Could anyone tell him that in three months, this nightmare would be over?

"No," Felix said. "I wouldn't."

NINETEEN

Holy shit, spring had sprung. Harry whirred around. The birds were singing their adorable little hearts out, and look! Was that a butterfly? No—Harry snatched up the scrap of colored paper dancing across the yard. Hopefully, Dad hadn't noticed; otherwise, he'd be in for another lecture on securing the recycling. As Saint John would say, a real bollocking! When Harry had lugged the recycling to the curb the other day, he'd forgotten to snap the bungee cord over the top of one of the bins, and paper had blown everywhere. *Oops.*

Couldn't they be done with the whole squirrel fortification? He and Dad were checking every piece of siding, every nook and cranny on the outside of the house, and it was *sooo* boring. He should go finish his AP Lit essay. Due Monday. But it was warm outside, and cool and dark inside. The house felt like a tomb. Except when Sammie was over. Mom could meet her next weekend!

Ha! A wild turkey strutted across the yard. Didn't see those too often. *Gobble, gobble!* Man, he was *sooo* bored. Watching ice melt would be more exciting than this.

One week and counting till Mom came home. Seeing Mom in the hospital had been gut-wrenchingly awful. He cried; she cried; even the nurse cried. But they kept it short, and he'd chosen an awesome bunch of balloons and flowers in the gift shop, with a stuffed bear that looked like it needed its own transplant. Dad had complained it was too expensive, but Harry had offered to pay half. Never expected Dad to hold him to it. And now his piggy bank was empty. How could he afford to take Sammie to the movies?

He'd seen Mom and felt strangely better. Like staring down the enemy, like saying, *I'm scared shitless that my mom is dying, but I will see her and hug her and make her smile.* And he had—he had made her smile! Mom had called him the Harry Tonic.

Calling her room every night wasn't the same as seeing her, especially since she didn't always pick up the hospital phone. A bazillion times during school, he'd think, "I need to tell Mom this." But then the end of the school day came, and it was just him and Dad. And by the time he talked to Mom, he'd forgotten half the school gossip. Mom used to love school gossip. Funny, she didn't seem that interested these days.

Harry reached down and grabbed the basketball from where he'd left it in the middle of a fern. He ran his right hand up the fronds. (Wasn't that what Mom called them?) Did the same with his left. Gave him that calm, just-right feeling. Like when he'd been in kindergarten and he had that poking tic. Had to poke things until they felt right. When it was other people—that was problematic. But Mom had gone into the class and explained it to the teacher and all the kids. Then she'd told him—in private—that poking people wasn't acceptable behavior, and they'd figured out a way to stop the tic. Funny thing, he couldn't remember their strategy; he just remembered it had worked.

He pounded the ball on the concrete. Bounce, bounce; bounce, bounce. *Rise up on your toes, take aim, shoot.* Swish. Perfect shot. *Hell, yeah!*

A dog barked in the street. He'd wanted a dog. Used to pester Mom about it. Answer was always the same: "Dad says no." Never a discussion.

Bounce, bounce; bounce, bounce. *Aim, shoot.* Swish.

Bounce, bounce; bounce, bounce. *Aim, shoot.* Swish.

Balance. Life was about balance. The family had balance, they lost it, but Mom would come home and they would find it again. Although in the last week, he and Dad had fallen into a groove. In a totally dysfunctional, two-guys-home-alone kinda way. Maybe he and Dad had found their own balance. It wasn't so bad—just the two of them. Dad didn't hover, and he'd abandoned the open-door policy with Sammie. (Did Mom know about the condoms?)

Most amazing discovery of all, last night—when he was fooling around with Sammie—he didn't tic. Maybe for their one-month anniversary, they could christen the condoms.

Dad let him help out more, too—with the laundry and shit, although he refolded everything. Harry could tell because the creases were all different. Tonight, they were going to watch a movie if Harry got his homework done. *Death at a Funeral.* The English original. Dad wasn't big on remakes. Had huge purple bruises under his eyes. Worked every night. Did he sleep at all? He was still working when Sammie's mom picked her up at midnight. On a Friday! Dad had lost weight. Maybe that would change now that meal deliveries were coming from Eudora. Fantastic fried chicken the other night! And she'd made hummingbird cake. *Delish!*

Would Eudora still bring them food when Mom came home? Would things really go back to the way they had been? Did he want them to? Harry dropped the ball, and it rolled off into the undergrowth.

Dad walked over with a hammer.

"Wanna shoot hoops?" Harry said.

"No. We have to finish this."

Harry rocked on his feet, itching to move. "I'm bored."

"That's because you have the attention span of a gnat."

"But this is super boring, Dad. Let's do something fun."

"I need to get this off my to-do list before your mother comes home. And could you please stop doing that?"

"Doing what?"

Dad put out a hand. "Cracking your knuckles. It's driving me bonkers."

"Driving! That's it. How about a driving lesson?"

"Seriously?" Dad fiddled with his glasses.

"Seriously! I've got to get back on the horse. I don't want to be one of those guys who lets fear rule. And my learner's permit expires in three months." Harry tried not to think about the humiliation of going through drivers ed twice. First and only time he'd ever failed a test. "I need to hit the open road. Practice!"

"Does this have something to do with Sammie?"

Yeah. "Maybe."

Dad grinned. He didn't smile that much, but when he did, it changed everything: his face, his mood. Hell, the mood of everyone in a ten-block radius.

"Has Sammie been giving you a hard time about not driving?"

The blush rose up Harry's neck. Threatened to swallow his head whole. "She doesn't give me a hard time about anything. But now we're—"

"Facebook status changed to 'in a relationship'?"

"Okay, yeah, we're a thing. Which means it would be nice to be more independent."

Dad's smile disappeared. Serious Dad was back. "Have you taken a Ritalin pill this afternoon?"

Harry paused a second too long.

"Do you have any appreciation of how lucky you are to be able to take Ritalin?"

"I know, I know. I hit the Tourette's jackpot because Ritalin doesn't stimulate my tics. Lucky me."

"Exactly. So why didn't you take it?"

"Life's more fun on the cutting edge." *True dat.*

"Then no. We're not going driving."

"Dad—"

"You can't drive wired, Harry. You need to be calm, focused, and in control."

"'Kay." Harry ran toward the house. "I'll take one."

✳

"You're not going to crash and kill both of us, are you?" Dad gripped the side of the car, and they hadn't even pulled away from the curb.

"Gee, Dad. Let me consider that one."

At least they were in Mom's Honda CR-V. Bigger, safer; besides, she wouldn't care about dings.

"If you kill me, I will come back like Marley's ghost and haunt you."

Harry sniggered. "You believe in ghosts?"

"No. I believe you're alive and then you're not. I will, however, not go gently into the good night if you kill me." Dad looked both ways up and down the street. "Do you believe in ghosts?"

"Hell, yeah." Harry made exaggerated movements as he adjusted his seat, messed with his rearview mirror, checked his wing mirrors, tugged on his seat belt. Okay, so that last bit was unnecessary, but really? Did Dad think he'd drive off without checking that the road was clear?

"What's your evidence?"

"Too much crap that can't be explained. Besides, I had that incident after Uncle Tom—" *Shit, shit, shit.*

Dad's arm shot across him like the safety bar on a fairground ride. "What did you just say?"

"Mom told me to never tell you."

Dad turned off the engine. "A bit late for that, wouldn't you say?"

The mail guy stopped in front of them. Pulled down their mailbox, shoved in the mail, slapped the box shut. Drove on to Eudora's house.

Harry opened his window, closed his window, opened it a crack. He clicked his teeth together in rhythms of four beats. Dad stared out of the windshield, waiting.

"The night Uncle Tom died," Harry said, "I had some weird dream. Only it felt real, as if Uncle Tom were sitting on my bed, talking to me."

"What did he say—in this dream?"

"'I love you, Munchkin.' Then he said . . ."

"Said what, Harry?"

"That life hadn't been easy for you, and we should look after each other. That was it. Then it was morning. Mom was cooking blueberry pancakes and you were gone. She told me Uncle Tom had died, and I said that was wrong because I'd talked with him, and she swore me to secrecy. Mom said it would make you too sad. I'm sorry, Dad."

Dad was right. He should try to focus more. Words spilled out without passing through his brain first. And now, because he'd screwed up and was worse than a slug, Dad looked ready to cry, right here in the car. And it was his fault. Like he'd stuck Dad with a blade. Mom always said, "Don't mention Uncle Tom in front of Dad. It's too painful for him." So he didn't. And now he had. Slug. Total slug. Or some other slimy life-form.

"Your mother was trying to protect me." Dad shook his head slowly. "That's what she does—she protects us—but sometimes I wish she wouldn't."

Yeah. Totally.

"That bit about life not being easy for you. He meant Grandfather, didn't he?"

"Your grandfather had no patience and a great deal of rage, and I had various habits he deemed annoying." Dad flicked at some invisible spot on his black jeans. "He attempted to discipline them out of me."

"You mean habits like when you tap your palm."

Dad snapped his head around and glared. "I used to make a little clearing noise with my throat, too."

"You mean"—Harry hesitated—"a tic?"

"No, Harry, not a tic. A nervous habit."

But how could Dad be sure? Hadn't they always wondered about the genetic component? Hadn't Mom and Dad said, in the early days, "But where did this come from?"

Dad scratched his hands through his hair like he was shaking out nits. Or demons. Then he reached over and turned the key. The engine juddered to life.

"You, however, will have to learn to control your tics while you're driving. You must have absolute focus and two hands on the wheel. Can you manage that?"

Harry cleared his throat, clicked his tongue again—a *nervous habit*—and nodded.

"We're going to do a loop around the neighborhood." Dad adjusted his glasses. He did that a lot. Maybe it was a tic. From now on, Harry would watch everything Dad did. Every little gesture.

"Not going on the highway?"

"No. We'll drive around the neighborhood until I'm confident you know what you're doing. If you don't scare me, next time we can go on University Road and do a circuit around campus. If I decide at any point that you need to stop and let me take over, you will. Agreed?"

"Sure. Can we have music?"

"No. No distractions. You need laser focus. Read the road, Harry. Be mindful of idiots who drive while texting or using their iPods. Once,

I saw someone driving and brushing his teeth. Watch everything and everyone around you. Anticipate hazards."

Anticipate hazards. Harry rubbed his nose. His insides were wibbly-wobbly, like a thousand fleas were jabbing him with teeny-tiny spears. Jab, jab; jab, jab. And a thought stuck on repeat: *You drive, you die; you drive, you die.* A thousand things could go wrong. Drivers ed the first time had taught him that—when he'd pulled onto the Durham Freeway and nearly hit a school bus. The instructor had sworn; the kids in the back had sniggered. One of them had whispered, "Retard." What if he ran over someone's dog? What if he totaled the car? What if he hurt Dad? Sammie wouldn't care if he didn't drive, if he never learned to drive. Sammie wouldn't care, but he would. He wiggled in his seat, imagined crushing those fleas one by one.

Laser focus, laser focus.

Harry glanced over his shoulder and pulled out onto the road. "Let's do this thing, Dad."

Harry parked. Perfectly. "Who da man!" He punched the air, and Dad exhaled loudly.

"That was good, Harry."

For real? Dad had used *good* and *Harry* in the same sentence without irony?

"You didn't tic at all while you were driving."

"Can we do this again tomorrow, Dad?"

"If you take your medication."

The pressure started building. A tic that wouldn't be contained. *No, not now. Let Dad say* good *and* Harry *one more time. Please.*

He should have known. Compress all that energy, pack it together as if it were a bound and tied Slinky, and sooner or later it would spring free. Tics 101. Harry started jiggling from side to side. His foot stomped on the brake, stomped on the brake. Repeated.

Dad opened the passenger door and let out a sigh. It was a small one, but it was a sigh. And that *wow!* moment vanished. Replaced by the feeling you got when you were in the back of a car and it hit a speed bump too fast, and your stomach went *bleh* and you prayed you didn't hurl. Worst feeling in the world, topped only by the realization that if he wanted to win Dad's approval, all he had to do was not tic—not release any *nervous habits*—for the rest of his life.

TWENTY

Nudging the door open with his foot, Felix stood on the threshold of Hades. The doorknob would, of course, be sticky. Stickiness oozed from his son's pores.

Piles of books or papers didn't bother him, but the mayhem of Harry's room had no rhythm. Even the posters weren't hung straight. Coheed and Cambria definitely tilted toward the left, and the Tar Heels basketball team was decidedly wonky. It was clutter run amok; it was bedlam. And it stank of unwashed socks and leftovers.

The trail of disaster snaked from the unmade bed to the desk to the floor. An open family-size bag of salt and vinegar chips gaped next to Harry's laptop, and not one but two plates of toast crumbs sat on the floor. A third plate was upside down, as if kicked over in a mad dash to exit the room. An action that made perfect sense to Felix.

His son was living in a hell of his own creation.

Reaching around the doorjamb, Felix grappled for the light switches. He had returned from the hospital to discover the house in darkness except for the light blazing under Harry's door. Which meant the lights had been on since the boys had left for their Sunday matinee.

Felix hesitated. Was the dump of unopened mail under Harry's desk composed of college mailings? Trying to ignore the sensation that he was speeding down a helter-skelter ride, Felix stepped into Harry's lair.

A color brochure from Princeton peeked up at him, and—Felix squinted—there was an envelope from Harvard. He stepped closer, picked it up, and flipped it over. An unopened envelope from Harvard admissions.

Now he understood the old adage about blood boiling, because really, cut him open and he would bleed bubbling lava. *Of all the irresponsible, immature . . .* Felix made a sweeping gesture with his hands. Brushed away the red-hot anger; slowed everything down. He would be calm; he would be rational. He would get this sorted.

Felix walked into the kitchen and grabbed a black bin liner. Then he returned to Harry's room, scooped up the sliding pile of college information, and dragged his haul into the living room. He moved the coffee table to one side, dumped the contents of the bag on the floor, and, sinking to his knees, began making sense of chaos.

Out on the street, car doors slammed and a cloud of chatter raced up the walkway. Max and Harry were home. Felix stayed on his knees and continued his work.

One brochure, one breath; one brochure, one breath.

"Festering turd!" Max laughed as the front door crashed open. Dark and cold spilled inside. The weather had turned again: winter was back.

"King of the festering turds!" Harry yelled, then guffawed.

That was it. Felix jumped up. "Boys!"

"Sorry," Max mouthed. He glanced at Harry. "I should go."

"'Kay, dude. Later."

Harry collapsed on the hall floor like a toy that had been unplugged. He tugged off one Converse without unlacing it.

"Movie was great." He jumped up. Pulled a fistful of change from his pocket, dumped it on the shoe cabinet, and then levered off his left shoe with his right foot. "Whatcha doing, Dad?"

Felix folded his arms. "Creating order out of your college mailings."

Harry glanced up, looking wary. "You took those from my room?"

"Harry, most of these are unopened."

"What were you doing in my room?"

"Turning off all the lights that you had left on again."

"'Kay. But please don't mess with my stuff." Harry went through his pockets and then slapped the wall. "Goddammit."

"Harry! Language! If your grandmother heard you—"

"Lost my phone." Harry grabbed the portable phone, dialed. "Maxi-Pad! You shouldn't be answering the phone while you're driving. Ha!" Harry snorted. "Let me know if you find my phone in your car. Yeah, lost it again. Imagine that." Another snort of laughter. "Later, faggot."

"Harry!"

"What?"

"Don't call your best friend a faggot."

"Why not? It was a joke."

"Suppose Eudora heard you. Imagine how she would feel."

"She'd laugh, Dad. She has a great sense of humor. Or haven't you noticed?"

Felix counted backward from ten. "Your uncle was gay. I find that word deeply offensive."

"Sorry, Dad." Harry blushed scarlet. "I'm not homophobic, you know that. It's just not a word that means much to my generation."

"Talk to some of your friends who've been bullied for their sexual orientation, and I can assure you it will."

Harry looked at the floor. "Sorry."

"Now that you're home, you can help me sort through these brochures. Do you have a college file?"

"Uh—nope?"

"Harry, this isn't a joke. This"—Felix drew his arm through the air—"is your future. Tossed into something that resembles a rubbish dump in a third-world country."

"I would have sorted them out eventually."

"Sit down on the sofa, and we'll go through them now. Together."

Harry bounced toward the living room, then changed direction. "Love to, Dad, but I've got to work on my calc."

"No, Harry."

"Homework takes precedence."

"College takes precedence."

Harry grimaced and blinked, grimaced and blinked. "Dad, I've got to do my calculus. It's due tomorrow. I don't have time for this right now."

"You had time to go to the movies with Max, ergo you have time to do this."

A car alarm went off in the street.

Harry gave an exaggerated sigh and collapsed onto the sofa. "Shoot," he said. His knee jiggled, and he cleared his throat with a series of little ahems that could—or could not—have been a new tic.

"Let's start at the beginning. What are your top ten choices for college?"

Harry shrugged, and Felix's phone rang—Robert. *Bugger it.* He and Robert had planned to talk an hour ago, but he'd fallen asleep by Ella's bedside and completely forgotten. Unbelievable—his brain had become a bottomless sieve.

"I thought you and your mother had narrowed this down to an A-list?" Felix put his phone on "Mute." Robert didn't believe in voice mail, which meant he would keep calling until he got an answer.

"Not really. Mom was hung up on the idea of smaller, in-state colleges, so she organized the Asheville trip. That was as far as we got."

From somewhere in the sofa, Harry's phone made a ridiculous noise, like a clown's horn. "Ha!" He started tugging off pillows and dumping them on the floor. Then he burrowed under the seat cushions. Felix clamped his teeth together.

"Found it!" Harry held up his phone as if he'd just been awarded a ribbon at the state fair.

Maybe Harry should consider chaining his possessions to his waist.

"Can you please put all those cushions back where they belong?"

"What? Yeah. Sure." Harry started scrolling through text messages.

"Harry!" Felix snapped. "Will you pay attention?"

"Please don't get angry. That's not an appropriate response for my ADHD."

"Maybe if you were better about managing your meds I wouldn't need to raise my voice." If Harry said, "Yeah, whatever," honest to God, Felix would no longer be of sound mind or action.

"Truth is, Dad—" Harry stood up. "I'm thinking about UNC Chapel Hill. Go Heels!"

"That's a ludicrous idea, Harry."

Harry blushed again. "Why? It's my life and my choice."

"And my money."

"Fine. I'll apply for a Morehead-Cain Scholarship." Harry started playing *Angry Birds* on his phone, then put it down. "What if Mom doesn't recover? What if she never gets better—even with the transplant? If that's the case, I want to stay close to home."

"You are not to talk about your mother that way. Do you hear me? She's going to recover; she's going to get better. These things just take time." Why was he yelling? Did he believe that if you said something loud enough, it had to be true?

TWENTY-ONE

Felix waited in the school carpool line, engine idling. He had a date with his son at a good neutral location: the Nasher Museum of Art on the Duke campus. Art always calmed Felix. Or rather, paintings with blocks of neat, contained color did. Random paint splashes left him utterly confused. Hopefully, the art would also calm Harry—so they could have a meaningful conversation about Harry's future.

The lead car in the queue pulled away, and Felix inched forward. A woman wearing more layers than an arctic explorer cut in front of the Mini and waved. She even mouthed, "Hi."

From polar vortex to spring to record lows in the space of a few weeks. It was as if they were trapped in that film *The Perfect Storm*, when the characters thought they'd escaped, only to discover they'd been sucked back into the storm of the century. And a rogue wave.

Felix nodded at the woman, and then ducked down to fiddle with the heating controls, a preemptive strike against conversation for the "Ella update" grapevine. Not that there was anything to update. They were stuck in a holding pattern, running on fumes and waiting for permission to land. That had to change. The key was forcing Harry to think about the next stage of his life. If Felix could jump-start the college conversation, then he could give Ella something to focus on other than her ejection fraction and how far she could shuffle unaided. The college decision was about to become the family lifeboat. (Hopefully with no rogue waves on the horizon.)

In the last two days, Felix had started making a new set of lists. Spring break was looming and he had a plan, although he had yet to initiate negotiations with Robert for more leave. In the meantime, there were flights, hotels, and rental cars to book; tours to sign up for; and arrangements to be made so that Harry could sit in on classes. It was a logistical nightmare, and one that was going to necessitate hiring in-home help for Ella, unless she had made a miraculous recovery at that point. But if they were extremely well organized, they could keep the trip short. First off, he needed Harry's full attention and minimal distractions.

Since Harry processed life better on a full stomach, they would start in the café. At pickup each day Harry was cranky, which, Felix had discovered, was caused by hunger blended with bottled-up stress. Years ago, Ella had said Harry would suppress his tics and rage until he got in the car, and then everything would explode in a cyclone. Finally, Felix understood what she meant.

He poked his head up and glanced around to make sure there were no other school mothers on the prowl. He spotted Harry chatting and laughing, his arm draped around Sammie's shoulder. Had he forgotten their date? Felix frowned. Harry had no sense of time, no sense of urgency, no sense of the fact that his father had cut out of work early, despite another barbed comment from Robert. If Harry bounced up to the car and asked him to drive Sammie home, nothing would contain his anger. And then he would be forever labeled the father who'd lost the plot in the school parking lot. Maybe he'd get some form of parental probation. Throughout school he'd never had detention, unlike Tom, who'd treated any notice of disciplinary action as a merit badge. How would it feel to be a rule breaker?

Harry's head bobbed, but it was too controlled for a tic. Well, well, Harry was checking to make sure none of the teachers were looking. Then he kissed Sammie on the lips. Tom would have approved.

Harry started bounding down the front steps, then turned and rushed back to retrieve the lunch box he'd dropped during his illicit kiss. Felix raised his eyes. Since the beginning of the month, two lunch boxes had gone missing in the bowels of the school. One had been located after a week, but Felix had dumped it as nonrecyclable hazardous waste.

The cars lined up behind the Mini now snaked out onto the road, which meant he had become *that* parent, the one responsible for holding up the carpool line. Throwing the passenger door open, he waved Harry in.

"Hey." Harry, breathless and flushed, grimaced and blinked, grimaced and blinked.

"You haven't forgotten our arrangement, have you?" Felix didn't mean to say arrangement. Too formal, too stiff. Too un-Harry-ish.

"'Course not." Harry's shoulder and head twitched. "We can eat first, right? Starving." He tugged out his phone, pulled it close, and grinned like the village idiot.

"Something funny?"

"Text from Sammie."

Felix reached into the back seat and grabbed the bag with the small bottle of water and the pill container. "Here. Take a Ritalin." Then he inched out of the parking lot, checking in all directions. The school parking lot was a quagmire of potential disaster: student drivers backing out too quickly, little kids running to cars without paying attention, mothers tearing in late. The stuff of nightmares.

"How was school?"

Harry gulped back a pill. "Good."

"How's the homework situation?"

"Good."

Which projects had been due this week? He'd started adding Harry's deadlines to his phone's calendar, but there were so many to keep track of. "How did you do on that philosophy essay?"

"Good." Harry was typing a text.

"Are you even listening to me?"

"Uh-huh."

"What did I just ask?"

Harry gave him the *duh, Dad* look. "How my day was."

Felix swallowed the sigh.

"This going to take long? This art museum thing?" Harry jiggled in his seat, cracked his knuckles, started to wind down the window, then changed his mind.

"I just need your undivided attention for half an hour."

Harry didn't answer; he was scrolling through his phone, already moving on to the next distraction. He watched television the same way—getting up in the middle to race around the house. Trying to sit through a movie with Harry made Felix want to gouge out his own eyes.

Thank God for Ritalin, because if there had been no hope of sharpening Harry's focus, Felix would have lost his mind.

Harry toyed with one of the many key chains on his backpack, and then raised his muddy Dr. Martens toward the dashboard.

"Don't even think about it," Felix said.

Harry went back to his phone and started playing *Angry Birds*. Felix tried not to watch out of the corner of his eye. Distractions were so inconsiderate to drivers. He cleared his throat and attempted to put his mind elsewhere.

"Are you mad at me?" Harry didn't look up.

"Why would you ask that?"

Harry scratched through his hair until he resembled an electrocuted hedgehog. Had his son started wearing hair gel? "Avoidance, Dad. That's good."

"No."

"No, what?"

"No, I'm not mad at you."

"'Kay." Harry paused. "Why are you brooding?"

"I'm not."

"'Kay." Harry sighed.

Felix flicked on the right-hand indicator and they crawled onto Duke Street. "Are *you* mad at me?"

"Nah."

"Avoidance?" Felix couldn't help it; he smiled.

"Maybe we should agree neither of us is mad." Harry buried his phone in his backpack. He sat back and crossed his arms. "Let's start over. Hi, Dad. How was your day?"

"Are we playing truth or dare?"

"Yup."

"Total shit."

Harry grinned.

"How was your day, Harry?"

"Total shit. Can you keep a secret?"

"From my extensive friendship network that includes Eudora?"

Harry sucked in his breath. "Max has a crush on this girl who's involved with a narcissistic jerk senior and she knows it—"

"Knows that her boyfriend's a jerk?"

"No, Dad." Harry slowed down. "That Max has a crush on her. And she's flirting with him. It's not going to end well. I keep telling Max to stay away from her, but she's really hot and—promise you won't tell anyone this?"

"Scout's honor."

"You were a Boy Scout?"

Felix changed lanes. "I was being facetious."

"Right. Anyway. Max thinks he's in love. Like, totally in love. Like, the real deal."

Felix braked as the car approached a red light. "How's your love life?"

Harry blushed violently. "Good. Yours?"

"Complicated." Felix glanced up in the rearview mirror. "Hazza, can I ask you something?"

"*Surrre.*" Harry chewed the corner of his lip.

"Do you think your mother's depressed?"

Harry didn't answer for a few seconds. "Maybe. When we talk it feels, you know, forced. Like she's trying too hard. One of my friends has it bad. Depression, I mean. Had a horrible time finding meds that helped."

"And he talks about it?" The light changed and they started moving forward.

"She. To her friends? Yup. Why wouldn't she?"

"In my world, one doesn't discuss mental health. One pretends life is lovely and suffers silently."

"It's hard, isn't it, Dad?"

Felix wasn't sure if Harry meant the way their lives had turned out, depression, or this thing called love, but he agreed on all counts.

A concrete walkway with evenly spaced steps and handrails led them up a gentle, wooded slope toward the museum. Under the trees to his left, American robins, larger than their English counterparts, hopped through the leaves. Fallen leaves usually set Felix's teeth on edge. At home, they mounded up in inappropriate places and mixed with rubbish blown in from the street. But the leaves here created a perfect carpet that ran up to the steps and stopped. Not a single stray leaf defiled their path. Everything on the Duke campus was close to perfection. It was a place that spoke of an established world order, of tradition, of old money. Of things being maintained the way they should be. Felix inhaled. Even the air smelled fresher at Duke.

Harry ran ahead, and Felix followed him through the museum door.

"Wait." Felix stopped by the semicircular check-in desk. "Would you like to see the exhibits while we're here?"

"Sure, Dad," Harry called over his shoulder. "But can we eat first?"

Without a backward glance, Harry shot across the vast, empty atrium toward the nook with the café. He looked so small, so insignificant, and some unfamiliar instinct made Felix want to run after him, saying, "Wait. Don't leave me behind." Instead, he paid for two five-dollar tickets. Harry, it seemed, was an adult at seventeen.

Sunlight filtered through the angular ceiling of glass and steel to create a crisscross pattern on the far wall—a trellis of light and shade. A strangely calming sight that might have quieted his thoughts, had a passing cloud not momentarily blocked the sun.

Felix strode toward the café. Plates and silverware clattered in the kitchen behind the counter, and Harry jiggled amidst a row of empty chrome tables. He had chosen a spot in a patch of sunlight. As hoped, the place was semideserted.

"I knew you'd want the sun," Harry said with a huge smile. Even his smile was larger than life. Harry did nothing quietly.

A muted hum of voices rose from the small group in the corner, but it was impossible to distinguish individual words. Good—the acoustics favored privacy. Felix pulled out a chair, gripped the cold metal arm, and sat.

A young waitress in black trousers and a black shirt came over and handed them menus. "You're just in time," she said. "We have a limited menu after four o'clock."

She reached over to grab the chain on the blind behind Harry.

"Can we leave that up?" Felix said.

"Sure." She glanced at Harry.

"My dad's a Londoner," Harry said. "Winter sun's a novelty for him."

Felix frowned at Harry. Now he was giving out personal information to a stranger? What next—a full family bio on Facebook?

Harry's face contorted into a grimace.

"You okay?" she said.

"Was I ticcing? Sorry, I have Tourette syndrome." Harry spoke as if they were still discussing the sun.

"Good for you. I'm bipolar." She glanced at Felix with a hesitant smile. "Wow. I don't normally blurt that one out."

"I guess it's easier to hide than ticcing." Harry grimaced and blinked, grimaced and blinked.

Felix slumped back in his chrome chair and watched, amazed. In the window behind Harry and the waitress, traffic crawled to a stop.

"Not necessarily. You don't want to be around me when I'm off my meds and manic." She twirled the pen through her fingers.

"I bet it feels good sometimes, the mania."

"Yeah, man. It does. Not for other people, though."

"Yeah." Harry nodded.

"Right." Her voice brightened. "You guys need a few minutes?"

"Nah." Harry grabbed the menu. "Italian cream soda, please. Vanilla. And . . . oh yeah. One of those." He pointed at the words *warmed chocolate chunk cookie*. "Thanks for bringing me here, Dad. This is fantastic!" He rocked back and forth in his chair.

Felix picked up the menu, studied it, and put it down. "Perrier. Thank you."

"Coming right up." The waitress smiled at Harry and then disappeared.

"Dad—" Harry looked down at the floor and looked back up with big puppy-dog eyes. He cracked his knuckles, and Felix winced. "I haven't had my allowance for the last two weeks."

"Why didn't you tell me?"

Harry shrugged. "You've been kinda busy. I figured you'd catch on at some point."

"But I didn't," Felix said slowly.

"No biggie. Can I order some songs on iTunes when we get home?"

Felix pulled out his wallet and pushed a twenty-dollar note across the table. "If you lose that, I'm not replacing it. And you can order up to five dollars' worth of songs on my credit card."

"Thanks, Dad!"

"We have to learn how to do this, how to trust each other."

"You mean we need to be a family without Mom as the maypole."

"You remember?"

"The village Morris dancers? Hell, yeah! And Saint John took us to that pub for a real ploughman's lunch afterward, and Mom got wasted."

"Tipsy."

"Nah, Dad. She threw up in a rosebush, remember?"

"She underestimated the power of Pimm's, despite my warnings." Felix smiled. At the time, he had been furious, but now, with the power of hindsight, he saw Harry and Saint John giggling. He saw a family being a family. Warts and all.

His smile slipped away. There were so few memories with giggles.

Harry fidgeted and kept glancing toward the kitchen, his focus already broken.

Felix smoothed out the flyers he'd picked up at the desk. "There's a sculpture made from what appears to be a crushed car in the lobby. That looks interesting."

"Not really into cars, Dad."

"Me neither." Felix caught himself about to crack his own knuckles and stopped. "There's a special exhibit on Archibald Motley. Jazz Age modernist. And there's another installation with—hmm—impressive, if you like modern art"—he didn't—"Andy Warhol and Roy Lichtenstein that might appeal to you."

"Ooookay," Harry said.

Was this a standoff, like a game of chicken?

"Be right back, Dad. Gotta find the restroom."

And Harry was gone.

Harry ate the way he tackled life—fast, messily, and with lots of head bobbing.

The waitress came back to check if everything was okay. Felix replied, "Yes, thank you," before Harry could speak with his mouth jammed full of food. Why had Ella not worked harder on his table manners?

"Something wrong, Dad?"

"Admiring the fact that you eat with such gusto," Felix said. "While your mouth is wide open."

Harry stopped midchew, then swallowed hard. "Starving."

"Evidently."

"Did you see the gift shop? They have jewelry. You should buy something for Mom, for Valentine's Day." Harry shoved more cookie into his mouth.

"We don't celebrate Valentine's Day, Harry."

"Maybe this is the year to start."

"Maybe it is. Do you have a present for Sammie?"

Harry shook his head several times. (He never did anything once.) "Would you help me choose something?"

"Of course. Would you help me choose something for Mom?"

Harry beamed. "Yup. My pleasure! So. Shoot. Why are we here? Is there something going on with Mom that I don't know about?"

"You know what I know, Harry, which isn't a great deal. We're watching and waiting."

"Yeah, like you and I do that so well." Harry pushed away his empty plate, sat back, thumped his feet on the floor, sat forward. "You'd expect more from medical science in the twenty-first century," he said.

"You would indeed."

"Could we take Mom to England?"

"I have a call in to Saint John. His brother is on staff at Papworth, the leading heart hospital in England." Felix sipped his Perrier. "But I think we have to accept that a transplant is in her future."

Harry traced circles through the crumbs of his giant cookie.

"In the meantime, we need to create a plan."

"For what?" Harry's voice turned cautious. His face distorted through a series of tics.

"Your future."

"Could you make that sound a little less scary?"

"College."

Harry jerked his chair closer to the table, then pushed it back. "Can we talk about this when we get home?"

"No, Harry. Spring break is less than six weeks away, and I need to make plane reservations. We're going to do a weeklong college tour in the Northeast."

"What does Mom say?"

Felix wrestled the edges of a headache.

"You haven't told her, have you?" Harry said.

"No. Harry, she's too brittle to get dragged in. You and I need to figure this out on our own. Then we can involve her, and it will give her something uplifting to think about."

"My leaving home is uplifting?"

"Yes. College is a marvelous time in your life. You'll be independent without the responsibility of being a wage earner." In a year and a half, Harry would leave home. That gave Felix a year and a half to prepare him. And a year and a half to prove—or fail to prove—that he could be a good father.

Harry scratched the side of his head, rose out of his chair, plonked back down. He picked up his white linen napkin, twisted it as if he were squeezing out a wet rag, and dumped it on the table. "Can we put this off till the summer, when we have a better sense of the whole transplant thing?"

"No. Whatever happens with Mom, you have important decisions to make that will shape your future. The path you take now will set you up for the rest of your life."

"But I feel like the world's upside down and there is no future."

"That's rubbish. The future—your future—is out there waiting. You need to start looking at colleges, and you need to start making decisions."

"There isn't room in my head for all this."

"Make room."

Harry stood up. Felix leaned forward and dropped his voice. "Sit. Down."

"I'd like to go look at the art now, Dad. I have a lot of homework."

How could a good parent argue that one in public? The guy on his laptop—was he listening? Was the group in the corner waiting to judge? *Will that man be a good father and let his son do his homework?* Jazz played softly in the background. Trumpets with mutes. He'd played the trumpet at Eton. And had failed to make first trumpet in the school band.

Felix signaled the waitress. "Check, please?"

Harry got up and left. Clearly, they weren't going to the gift shop to buy Valentine's Day gifts.

Harry stopped in the middle of the huge, empty atrium, huffing out his breath. Was Dad trying to go behind Mom's back? Because if so, there was only one place this was heading: Harvard. And if Dad knew anything about him, anything, he would know that Harry would be miserable in a pressure-cooker bastion of whatever-ish-ness.

His thoughts scrambled. He actually wanted to growl. *Grrr.*

Like Max—well, not as extreme as Max—Harry was going to live outside the lines with the weird kids. With the freaks and ghouls, as The Smashing Pumpkins would say. Or somewhere with a really good basketball team. They probably made you wear ties at Harvard.

He turned left. Jazz Age modernist? Nah. Andy Warhol and iconic soup cans sounded better. He turned right into the other exhibit. The security guard welcomed him with an odd sideways glance.

Harry stared back. *My tics offending you?*

The guard looked away.

Harry scratched his chin, then stuffed his hands into his jeans pockets. This was a great space. Nothing crammed in overloading his brain. Art galleries could make his thoughts spin.

Wow! Harry peered at the sign: "Lichtenstein *Water Lilies (Pink Flower).* Enamel on stainless steel with painted wood frame." Pop art with reflective bits, like a mirror. *Bizarro!*

And that? On the far wall, a painting of an African American dude against a gold background. He was dressed in a suit, sunglasses, and a Superman T-shirt, and the words "aint nuthin but a sandwich" were scrawled in all caps across the top. Harry took a picture on his phone, texted it to Max. Fahamu Pecou was the artist. Harry started reading the wall sign. Something about teenage drug addiction and . . . Now that was art! An Andy Warhol silkscreen of a Campbell's tomato soup can. *Awesome.* He took another picture for Max.

Which way, which way? Harry turned, went back to the Pecou, and followed the far wall of the gallery. The picture of a mother and a baby caught his eye, a lithograph called *Worker Woman with Sleeping Child, 1927.* The kid looked peaceful, and yet the mom was watchful. Anxious. Harry remembered that expression from playgrounds and public spaces. Mom always on high alert.

As he walked through the medieval and Renaissance art and into the antiquities area, memories played: Mom losing it in the supermarket because he'd wandered off after she'd instructed him to stand still and not move; Mom frantic when he went on a dragon-slaying adventure in the park; Mom pulling him away from some dude in Target who'd said he was one cute kid.

His whole life, Mom'd had his back. And now everything was changing, and Mom was the one who needed protecting—and Dad? Dad wanted to push him out into the world and wave farewell. Home, his comfort zone, was disappearing into a sinkhole. And the future loomed like the monstrous black sculpture directly ahead—a towering nonfigure dripping scraps of black fabric, black branches, black flowers. It seemed more shadow than solid, except for the pair of black taxidermied fighting birds rising out of the middle section. Harry moved closer, transfixed by decay—a regular Dudley Dursley sucked into the Dementor's Kiss. Dad talked about the future, but what if there was no future? What if there was nothing but fear and death?

Footsteps echoed on the wood floor behind him and disappeared around the corner. With a final glance at the sculpture and the weird shadows it cast on the wall, Harry followed Dad. But then he hung back by a still image of a boxing match. "Between Sugar Ray Robinson and Randy Turpin," the sign said. Off to his right, Dad appeared to be writing on a piece of card.

Harry waited a few minutes, pretending to study Sugar Ray. When Dad moved off, Harry followed and stopped in front of some interactive thing called "A man is . . ." Above a small writing shelf with pencils and index cards were the words "Share Your Thoughts." People had tacked handwritten cards to the wall. Spotting the perfect calligraphy Dad had learned with a real fountain pen was easy.

Dad had written one word. *Alone.*

TWENTY-TWO

In silence, they walked across the bridge and through the ivy-wrapped trees that lined their path home. Harry had pretended to sleep in the car. Felix knew it was an act—even when Harry was curled into a ball, there were telltale signs of ticcing. Felix unlocked the front door. As he turned off the alarm, Harry schlepped in and tossed down his backpack. It landed on top of the shoe cabinet.

Unwinding his cashmere scarf, Felix banished the image of all those damn key chains scratching the blemish-free ash lid. He would not comment; he simply would not.

"Dad, I'm sorry." Harry fell to the floor and levered off his Converse. "I know how hard you're trying to make everything work, and I don't mean to make it harder. It's just that I'm so overwhelmed."

"Welcome to my life."

"I was thinking. In the car. What if I took a gap year? I could—I don't know. Get an apartment with Max and—"

"And do what, Harry?" Felix's left eye twitched. Brilliant. Now he had a tic. "What will you do for money?"

"I'll get a job."

This was a prime example of Harry not thinking, of Harry making illogical, uninformed decisions. This was a knee-jerk plan aimed to appease, nothing more.

"A job," Felix said. He hung up his scarf and coat. "And what job are you qualified for?"

"Lots. I could sell video games at GameStop."

"You have no life skills, Harry. In this economy, if you don't have a college degree, you might as well hold up your hands in defeat and say, 'Fine, I'll live in a cardboard box.'"

"That's stu—"

"Stupid?" Felix tapped his palm. "Were you going to tell me I'm stupid?"

Harry cleared his throat multiple times. "Can Sammie come over?"

"No. You have homework. And after supper, we *are* going to look at college brochures, and that includes the one for Harvard."

"Even if I don't want to go down that route?"

"This is not an option, Harry. You are going to college. You are going to a good college."

"I'm not disagreeing." Harry's shoulder shot up and down as his head ticced sideways. Again and again. "But no one's asking what I want here. Not you, not Mom, not the school. It's all about perfect SAT scores or my imperfect brain. And I'm sick of it. I can't do this right now. Everyone has to back off. Stop pushing so hard." Harry's entire body seemed to judder with a scattershot of tics. "When I get overwhelmed, Mom encourages me to break things down and set small goals. You should try it sometime—thinking small. Aiming low. Way cheaper than therapy."

Felix dug his fingernails into his skin until pain numbed his hand. "Now you're telling me I need therapy?"

"That's not"—Harry started stuttering—"what I said."

"Correct me if I'm wrong, but a few hours ago, weren't we talking about trust?"

Harry pulled out a barstool and collapsed onto it. A heap of Harry. "You . . . don't think . . ." His words came out slowly, with long gaps between as the Tourette's took hold. "This thing . . . you have . . . for order . . . is a little odd?"

"I'm a Fitzwilliam. We're all a little odd." Felix straightened his spine; his hand had begun to sting. "Yes, I'm a perfectionist. That's why we have this great life, why I have a well-paid job, why you go to a private school, why your mother could stay home with you, why we have this house. There is nothing wrong with being a perfectionist."

"You set standards no one can live up to." Harry sounded tired—deflated and defeated. "Standards I can't live up to with a GPA off the charts and perfect SAT scores. What else do you want you from me, Dad? Because I don't get it."

"It's not that simple, Harry. Not everything can be judged by test scores."

"By what, then? What am I doing wrong?" Harry paused and cleared his throat repeatedly. Felix waited. "Do you have any idea what half of the kids in eleventh grade are doing? Sleeping around, drinking, taking drugs. The other day, a senior offered me a shitload of money for a handful of Klonopin."

"I hope you said no." Kids were dealing prescription meds? He would have to report this to the school director.

"Really? You think I would deal drugs? I'm not irresponsible, Dad." There was a hard edge to Harry's voice that Felix hadn't heard before.

"Maybe not, but you have no sense of order, and you're unnaturally messy. You have only to *walk* through the kitchen, and every cabinet knob is sticky. And your bedroom looks like the city dump."

"That's not fair. I cleaned it just last week. You could eat off the fucking carpet."

"Given the crumbs, I sometimes wonder if you do."

"Excuse me?"

"Disorder follows you."

"Disorder, huh?" Harry shot up and slammed the stool into the concrete island. If he broke that stool, swear to God he would pay for it. "Gee, thanks, Dad. And being a Nazi neat freak isn't weird at all."

"Don't use that word, *Nazi*. It's abhorrent to me."

"Don't use *disorder*. It's abhorrent to me. I'm not a freak show because I'm wired a little differently." Harry had never yelled at him before.

"That's it." Felix threw up his hands. "I don't understand you, Harry. I have tried, but as God is my witness, we have nothing in common."

"How hard have you tried?" Harry's head was bobbing constantly now—tics blending into each other.

"That's not fair. I've put my life on hold for you and your mother. I'm bending over backward to take care of you."

"I can take care of myself!"

"Really? You can't even find your shoes half the time."

"What's this unnatural obsession you have with putting away shoes?"

"Don't turn this around. This isn't about me. It's about you."

"Funny, I thought everything in this house was about *you*. By the way, you're wrong when you say we have nothing in common. We have everything in common." Harry's hands moved every which way in a blur. "We're both fucked up in the head."

"Are you quite done, young man?"

Harry grimaced and blinked, grimaced and blinked. "Google 'obsession with perfectionism,' Dad. See what nasties turn up."

"Go to your room," Felix said.

"Gladly." Harry grabbed his backpack, went to his room, and slammed the door.

Felix picked up a cut-glass water jug that had been a wedding present—*it's a jug, a jug, not a pitcher*—and slammed it onto the floor. It shattered, and so did he.

✳

Harry threw himself facedown on his bed. Then he kicked the pile of laundry to the floor. The clean laundry Dad had put in his room. Maybe he should set up a Dad-free zone with a sign that said "Keep Out." Suppose there *had* been a system for all those college mailings? Did Dad think of that for one minute? No. Dad thought only in black and white: there was a right way of doing things—his way—and a wrong way—Harry's way.

Dad was breaking stuff. That couldn't be good. But maybe now he'd understand how it felt to be criticized. Harry pounded the pillow. Without Mom, this house was toxic. Waves of anger and despair bounced off the walls. He needed out.

His room was pitch black, but he didn't care. He didn't care about anything right now except Sammie. He pulled his phone out of his back pocket and texted her. No answer. Was she doing her chem homework? She'd been worrying about it at recess. (Science wasn't her thing.) Harry hadn't been sure how to help, so he'd told her the answer. Who knew that would be a mistake? He'd had to work pretty hard to get her to forgive him.

Sitting up, Harry tugged out his laptop. He turned it on, logged on to his Facebook page, hit the message icon.

```
hey whatcha doing dad's being a dick
can I come live with you LOL
```

Silence. He drummed his fingers on the side of his laptop. She was online; she'd just commented on a post of Max's. He sent another message.

```
hello anybody out there really need
to talk dad's a dickhead
```

```
No, he isn't.

pretty sure he is can I come over

You mean can Mom and I come get you
because you're too scared to ask
your dad for a lift?

yup
```

He sent her a sticker of an animated smiley face. His favorite one. The one that bounced up and down and looked psychotic. Made him smile. Nothing else made him smile right now. Except for Sammie. And Max. Harry picked up his phone, sent Max a text.

```
hey maxi-pad dad hates me

Mom hates me. Parent swap?
```

Harry cracked up. Went back to his Facebook page.

```
please? He added a row of hearts. i can give you
the full update on life with attila the
dad & we can be homework buddies

Your dad isn't that bad, Harry. He's
just being a dad.

your dad isn't a jerk

My dad's terminally ill, Harry.
```

```
sorry that was thoughtless
```

He couldn't get anything right today.

```
Don't worry about it.
```

```
so can I come over
```

This time he picked the robot sticker with lots of hearts.

```
Let me ask Mom.
```

Harry flopped back onto his pillows. Never thought that simple phrase, that one short sentence, "Let me ask Mom," could be so loaded, so precious. He would give anything in the world to be able to ask his mom.

Felix splashed cold water onto his face, pulled back, and stared into the powder room mirror; Pater's face stared back. As he aged, he looked more and more like the monster from his own childhood. And now the transformation was complete. For a moment back there, he had seen nothing but anger—a hot, seething mass that could destroy anything in its path. Felix slugged his second glass of Macallan, then carefully placed the tumbler down next to the sink. He flipped over his right hand and examined his broken lifeline, which disappeared as it snaked around his wrist. Tom had always joked, "Either you'll end up living two lives, or you're going to develop a split personality and become a serial killer."

His whole arm began to shake. For a moment, he'd wanted to hurt Harry. God help him, he had wanted to hit his own son.

Genetics will out.

A tornado of noise whooshed down the hall and stopped outside the powder room door. Harry knocked quietly. A timid knock, a scared knock, one that said, *I don't want to wake the monster.*

"Dad? Dad, are you in there?"

"Yes."

"I'm going to do my homework at Sammie's." Harry paused and then words rushed out. "I need to calm down and regroup and might be better for both of us if I go out for a while."

Felix put his hand on the doorknob. As he turned it slowly, the doorbell chimed. "Wait. It's a weeknight. You are not going out on a weeknight."

Harry grabbed his backpack. "We study well together. She helps me focus. Sammie's mom is here. She wants to say hi."

Felix glanced back at the mirror. Did he have a choice? He swallowed hard and walked into the hall.

Sammie bounced through the door and threw her arms around Harry's neck. Her mother followed, and Felix blanked on her name. Something beginning with . . . ? Gray and lifeless with pouches of loose skin under her eyes, she looked almost as wasted as Ella.

"Hi, Harry," Sammie's mother said. "Do you mind if we stop and pick up a pizza on the way home?"

"That sounds great, Mrs. Owen. You'll be okay, Dad? For dinner?"

Felix nodded. He'd planned to cook for them tonight, make a cottage pie using the recipe Mother had dictated over the phone. Maybe he'd skip food and have a liquid dinner.

"Felix, good to see you again. How's Ella?"

"She's fine, thank you." Felix kneaded his shoulder. The muscles, tight with tension, crunched under his fingertips. "How's your husband?"

"He's doing well, thank you for asking. The tumors aren't getting any bigger. Always a good sign," she said. "Would you like Harry home by a certain time?"

Felix almost said, *Keep him.* "Since it's a school night, nine thirty. We have a ten o'clock curfew."

"We do?" Harry was gripping Sammie's right hand with both of his hands.

"We do," Felix said. There had to be consequences for calling your father a Nazi. "And if you break it, you're grounded for the rest of your life."

Harry blushed.

Felix turned to Sammie's mother. "Would you mind if I talk to Harry in private?"

Sammie glanced at Harry, her bottom lip caught in her teeth.

"Of course," Sammie's mother said. "We'll wait in the car."

They disappeared into the night, but not before a blast of frigid air entered the house.

"You didn't think I'd ground you?" Felix asked Harry. "I would like to remind you that you are still a child. For another year. And that I am the parent."

"Dad—when have I ever disobeyed you? I may have focus issues, I may be untidy, but I've always followed your rules. If you say home by nine thirty, I'll be home by nine thirty. You don't have to threaten me." Head down, Harry hoisted his bag over his shoulder. "Can I go now?"

"Yes."

Had Ella ever grounded Harry? In fact, had Ella ever so much as raised her voice at him? The front door closed quietly, and Felix glanced at the space where the jug had been, the one that he'd swept up and dumped in the kitchen bin.

An empty house breathed differently. It wasn't the silence; it was the nothingness. The heavy, painful solitude that hung in every corner.

In the black forest beyond the sliding doors, eyes popped through the trees. The nighttime creatures were out.

An owl hooted, speaking the language of darkness, of despair. Of loneliness.

When they were first married, Ella had planned to get a dog and walk it in Duke Forest every day. But once Harry was born and brought chaos into the house, Felix said no, and the subject had never come up again. Should they get a dog? Not a puppy, but maybe a rescue dog. No, that would come with unknown problems. A dog with a pedigree, then, with kennel-club papers. A perfectly behaved, perfectly trained, perfectly housebroken dog. Would that make Ella happy? Would it make Harry happy? Would a dog give Felix the one thing that continued to elude him: a real family life?

Down the hall, Harry's door was flung open. As always, the lights blazed. Once his son left home and had to pay his own electric bill, maybe he'd realize what it meant to be wasteful.

Felix stormed toward the teen cave. Harry's laptop was open, and the clean laundry Felix had folded that morning—he'd done a full load at 6:00 a.m.—lay scattered over the floor. Drawing a deep breath, Felix entered the room and forced himself to ignore the empty lemonade bottle, the crushed soda can, and the half-eaten bar of chocolate. He stepped over the debris of shoes.

"What's this unnatural obsession you have with putting away shoes?" Harry had said.

It's called order, Harry. You'll never understand.

He refolded the T-shirts, repiled them on the bed, and picked up the open laptop to shut it down. As he clicked on the track pad, the screen opened to Harry's Facebook page with a message to Sammie: see you in a few. Followed by a crazy number of kisses.

His son needed a lesson on restraint.

Restraint had never been an issue for teenage Felix. Girls put out for him all the time, but he could never take it to the next level. Sex was not the problem. Love, however, confounded him. He couldn't make girls happy; they couldn't make him happy. He tried to be a good boyfriend, but after a while he couldn't see past their flaws, and then his attention would turn to the next pretty girl. The theme continued into his twenties, but everything had changed the day Ella collapsed on the Tube.

Still holding the laptop, Felix sat down on the bed. Harry's skull and crossbones alarm clock ticked its ridiculously loud tick and Felix scrolled through the messages. He would never understand why he had decided to pry. Maybe there was no decision. Maybe all he wanted was to understand Harry better, but once he'd read the phrase *attila the dad*, there was no turning back. He had to read all of them. Every last message between Harry and Sammie, between Harry and Max, between Harry and Ella. (As if Harry and his mother needed yet another line of communication.) He read the messages that called him a control freak, that linked the words hate and Dad, and—the worst ones of all—the messages without smiley faces, the ones that shouted loud and clear, *My dad terrifies me.* It was official: he had failed to be more than someone who instilled fear.

The phone rang, but Felix didn't pick up. He didn't even move. Down the hall, Eudora's voice played to the empty living room.

"Felix, honey, I know you're home. I can see your lights on, and I heard Harry leave. Pick up the phone." A long pause. "Felix Fitzwilliam. You have two choices. You pick up the phone right now, or I'm coming over. And since I'm in my nightgown, I know you don't want that vision of wrinkled beauty on your doorstep." A longer pause. "Lord, son, are you going to make me count? One, two . . ."

Felix ran into his bedroom and snatched the phone off the cradle. "Harry hates me."

"Why, of course he does. He's a teenage boy, and you're his daddy."

"We had a fight, and he said—" What the hell was he doing sharing family secrets with a neighbor? "I'm not sure there's a way forward for the two of us."

"Now, that's not true, son. It might take a bit o' doing, is all." Eudora paused. "Noon tomorrow, meet me at Duke Gardens for some of that . . . what's it called? My mind just fizzled worse than a . . . Brainstorming! That's the word I was searching for. Brainstorming."

"Eudora, I'll be in the office until school pickup. We have a deadline on this hundred-million-dollar deal, and I need to work every second Harry's in school. I don't have time to wander around Duke Gardens."

"Have you ever visited?"

"No." Felix tried to edit exasperation from his voice.

"Well then, it's all settled."

"Excuse me?"

"You and I need to talk, and tomorrow's one of my volunteer mornings. Did I mention I'm an ambassador for the Blomquist Garden? Such a joy to work with native plants."

"Yes, I believe you have mentioned this several times, Eudora. Unfortunately, I don't—"

"Meet me under the pergola at noon."

Would he have to be rude to a pensioner? "I can't. I'm in danger of losing my job. The well-paid job that funds this family."

"Honey, that job sure is pointless if you lose your family anyway." She paused. "Bye-bye!"

TWENTY-THREE

Felix drove through the matching stone balustrades that marked the entrance to Duke Gardens and slammed on the brakes with no thought to other drivers. Straight ahead, beyond majestic evergreens and plants with elongated leaves related—surely—to palms, the gothic spire of Duke Chapel rose like a monument to his past, to the one place that had always represented home: Oxford. Many times he'd glimpsed Duke Chapel from the Durham Freeway, and yet he'd never seen it from this angle. What a glorious surprise.

Ducking down for a better view, Felix inched toward the car park. He was in the middle of Durham, North Carolina, but he could have been looking at Magdalen College.

Elation vanished the moment he stepped from the car and discovered the out-of-order notice taped over the parking meter. *Brilliant.* He had timed his arrival perfectly—*perfectly*. Now he would have to take a diversion inside the Doris Duke Center to purchase a parking receipt. He would not only be a hated father; he would be a late hated father.

Parking receipt purchased, despite the painful negotiation with an elderly volunteer who appeared incapable of understanding his English accent, Felix consulted his map and strode toward the Historic

Gardens. The path was covered in sand. Sand would stick to his shoes, track into his car, and necessitate another cleaning. He hated sand.

With a quiet harrumph, he tugged up the collar of his cashmere coat—now in its thirtieth year—and adjusted his scarf. If only he had his cashmere-lined leather gloves, too. There was a definite nip in the air, a bite of winter. Maybe even snow in those heavy clouds, which would mean school delays and closings. One snowflake, and the entire Triangle shut down. Really, it was preposterous.

Workers in beanies milled round, quietly purposeful; a young man drove past in a golf cart loaded with gardening implements and hoses; two young women silently shoveled compost out of the back of a small truck. Several dog walkers passed him and smiled. No one seemed in a hurry.

According to the map, he had entered the Mary Duke Biddle Rose Garden. If he wasn't pressed for time, he might pause to admire the calm order of the artfully placed decorative urns and the well-spaced, well-labeled plants. Felix inhaled deeply, and the irritation over the parking dissipated into the icy air. Plant labels, what a marvelous idea. He would ask Ella to start labeling their plants.

Felix turned left onto a straight path lined with flower borders and trees. Most of the plants were dormant, but some pushed up through the soil: spiky black grass no more than an inch high and a low-growing plant with vivid, scallop-edged leaves. How unexpected to find color on such a raw, sullen day. He peered down at the labels: "Black Mondo Grass" and "Heuchera."

He pulled out his phone and typed a note: Ask Ella about heucheras.

Through the trees to his left, an orange Bobcat whirred away as it dug up the ground, as it destroyed to rebuild. Intriguing that this garden, which had been established for decades, was still a work in progress.

Turning right, he spotted Eudora sitting on a metal bench under a huge pergola made of thin strips of iron and a gnarled old vine.

"My, my, don't you look dashing, all dolled up for the world of high finance." She pushed off from the bench seat, then wobbled and sank back down. Felix rushed to help.

"Are you unwell?" He had kept an older woman waiting in the cold. What inexcusable behavior.

Eudora waved him off. "At my age, things rust up if I've been on my rump for too long."

Felix hung back, fighting the urge to tuck his arm under hers and haul her to her feet. "Apologies for being tardy. The parking meters were out."

"*Pfff.* Late is a fact of life. I had hoped you were taking time to dawdle and enjoy this remarkable local treasure."

"That too," Felix said, surprised to admit to the dawdling. Dawdling didn't fit his worldview. Of course, he no longer had a worldview, at least not one he understood. His job was in jeopardy, his wife was critically ill, his son hated him, and he was meeting a seventy-five-year-old spinster for parenting lessons under a pergola.

"I hadn't appreciated before how much Duke Chapel looks like Maudlin College."

"I'm not familiar with that—Maudlin, you said?"

"Spelled *M-a-g-d-a-l-e-n.*"

"Ah, Magdalen College pronounced the Oxford way."

"Indeed." Felix tipped back his head to glance up at the gray sky through the giant metal web covered in a latticework of sticks. Frozen precipitation was definitely heading their way. Should he check the school website and see if they were announcing an early dismissal?

"Asian wisteria," Eudora said.

"I'm sorry?"

"You're looking at Asian wisteria. Not up to much in the winter, but wait until the wedding season." She gave a low whistle.

"They have weddings here?"

"Lord, yes."

In front of them, terraced gardens flowed down to a large pond. "Is that a heron?" he said.

"Blue heron. It comes to dine on the koi. Magnificent fish."

Felix nodded. He knew nothing about fish unless it was being served to him on a platter.

"The original garden was built in 1934 at the instigation of one Dr. Hanes, an iris buff. He persuaded Sarah P. Duke to invest in a garden, and they planted an array of iris bulbs. But the land was prone to flooding, and everything rotted. Sarah died, and he convinced her daughter, Mary Duke Biddle, to construct a new garden in honor of her mother, but on higher ground." Eudora flashed her eyes at him. "I admire that kind of persistence, when combined with an ability to learn from one's mistakes. Don't you?"

Felix nodded. Was there some didactic meaning buried in her docent spiel?

"Mary hired Ellen Biddle Shipman, a pioneer in American landscape design, to create the Terrace Gardens in the Italianate style. The garden you see today was built by women."

"Impressive," Felix said.

"And this"—Eudora swept her arm to the right—"represents the globe with its lines of longitude and latitude. Quite fascinating when you consider the dedication of the garden was in 1939."

"On the eve of World War Two," Felix said. "And this year marks its seventy-fifth anniversary."

"Precisely, hon. And the pergola is the original structure."

The structure above them had endured over seven decades and any number of weddings. He'd never thought about history in terms of gardens before, despite listening to busloads of National Trust retirees twitter over Saint John's garden, designed by the famous English landscape architect Capability Brown. Continuity, longevity, places that had established a timeline: these were important. Felix had little interest in the contemporary.

"But we're starting in the wrong place," Eudora said. "As everyone does. To experience the true joy of the Historic Gardens, we need to be on the other side of the pond, by the original entrance. Come."

Eudora started walking, and Felix followed.

"We're stepping on Tennessee stone, although"—she pointed to a low, circular wall surrounding a small pond and a statue of Cupid holding a large shell—"that's Duke stone. Bless my soul, would you look at that?" Her voice turned girlish. "The tulips are coming up. I *love* tulips."

"So did my brother, Tom."

"He was a gardener?"

"A landscape architect. Much sought after by the rich and famous." The pride in Tom's success never abated.

"You miss him, don't you?"

Felix stroked his designer cashmere scarf, his last present from Tom. Tom had been an extravagant gift giver. *I miss him every day, every week, every month, every year.* The void created by Tom's death was a rip through the universe, an open wound that would never heal. "He died of AIDS. Hard to forget such a slow, painful death."

"Ah," Eudora said. "But even under the shadow of death, one can celebrate life. Each day with a loved one is a blessing."

"I'm not sure that applies to AIDS."

"Dahlia had a drawn-out death. Cancer. But we took joy where we could, right up until the end."

They climbed the slope behind the pond, and Felix forgot to check his watch. Eudora paused by a cluster of ceramic pots in grays and browns that spewed over with plants in eclectic shades of green, gold, and bronze. He looked up—across the green water of the pond, streaked with orange fish, to the white steps and multihued walls, and, finally, to the pergola and the backdrop of forest. The gardens were surrounded by naked trees, and yet the plant beds were filled with layers of life.

"Splendid view, isn't it?" Eudora said. He turned to find her watching him. "Do you have a favorite plant?"

"Everything I know about plants comes from Tom, from his tales of plant folklore. Ivy always appealed. In Celtic tree astrology, ivy is a tree—the strongest of them all. At Tom's suggestion, Ella had ivy in her bridal bouquet to represent endurance and fidelity. Mother, who believes ivy belongs in churchyards, was quite horrified."

"I often wondered why you folks chose not to rip up the ivy on your property. To most people, ivy is little more than a parasite."

"Tom taught me that it symbolizes survival—the ability to overcome all odds."

Eudora nodded. "Seems I learned something from you today, son. But oh, would you look at that!" A young man dashed past, carrying a backpack and wearing outrageously high stilettoes. "Only a man would wear heels to a garden."

"It would seem so." Felix laughed—a stolen moment of pleasure. This was another reason he loved the heart of Durham: the downtown pulsed with creativity, especially in historic Black Wall Street, where he worked, with its art deco buildings, funky cafés, and nonsensical one-way system that could appeal only to a Londoner.

He stopped by a spreading magnolia, its twisted branches whispering, *Come climb me.* Tom would have loved it, would have created a whole world of make-believe in its boughs.

Eudora kept walking. "And now I'm taking you to the best part," she called over her shoulder. "The Blomquist Garden, started in 1968 by the first chair of the botany department at Duke."

With the cold stinging his cheeks, Felix jogged to catch up. For an older woman, she walked at a fair lick. "And what makes it special?"

"Nine hundred species of native plants. I have a feeling you're someone who will appreciate that we grow the real beauties here,"

Eudora said. "Not the gaudy sun perennials that want to flash every-thing they've got like cheap hookers. You have to look hard to find the pockets of beauty in my garden."

"Your garden?"

But Eudora was no longer listening. She strode ahead, slowing down when they entered an intimate fairy-tale forest. The path narrowed and switched to pale stone. Crazy paving, Tom would have called it—stone slabs haphazardly slotted together in a way that defied time, feet, and the extremes of weather. The formal, structured sweep of the Historic Gardens was replaced by a hint of controlled but wild beauty. Above the towering hemlocks, the clouds broke apart to reveal slashes of blue sky.

Eudora was right—so many pockets of beauty if you looked hard enough: trailing catkins and clusters of reddish pitcher plants that looked like rhubarb stalks with curling ends. (Such fascination he'd had for carnivorous plants after Tom had shown him a picture of a Venus flytrap in *Encyclopædia Britannica*.) A dead stick jutted up through the leaves; the sign next to it read "Northern Catalpa." He would research that on the Web when he got to the office. See if he could find a picture of it in full leaf.

"Here, smell this." Eudora had stopped by a small, unimpressive tree, but as Felix moved close, he spotted tiny pom-poms of reddish blooms. He had never seen anything quite so weird or wonderful. Ella should definitely plant one of those.

"Hmm."

"Witch hazel."

Birdsong surrounded them, and they ambled along a gravel path that meandered down a short flight of steps.

"This railing . . ." Felix reached for a red wooden handrail so shiny it glowed.

"Magnificent, isn't it? Believe it or not, I helped with the sanding. Heavens to Betsy, that was some job. Several weeks of eight-hour-a-day shifts."

Of course he believed it. Nothing about Eudora surprised him.

"Red cedar," Felix said. "Long lasting and slow to rot."

"And always the first tree to colonize when the land is no longer farmed. Very common in the North Carolina landscape."

"What's the finish?"

"Polyurethane. Come," Eudora said. "There are more rails up ahead."

The path snaked through the trees, and they followed in silence, passing through the endangered species garden and over a small bridge with more cedar railings. Such a simple, organic idea, yet so beautiful— not unlike the earrings Ella used to make. As he walked, his mind drafted design ideas for a new bridge to their house. He imagined the joy of working with his hands again. Of creating beauty.

The ground was hilly but the slopes gentle. Ahead, nestled in the leaves and sitting on the brow of a slope, there was a cedar shelter shaped like a giant bird feeder with benches. Presumably for bird watching. *How inventive.* More cedar rails led up toward it, the end post richer and darker than the others. Felix stepped forward. He couldn't help himself; he had to stroke the wood. For a moment, he thought of Harry. Always touching, unable to stop.

"This piece appears to have been burned at one time." It was as smooth as he'd imagined.

"Such stories in this one rail, and the flaws make it beautiful. All the timber came from Durham. From an old moonshine distillery, unless I'm mistaken." She touched his upper arm briefly. "Look," she whispered. "On the bird feeder."

"A woodpecker?" Felix said.

"A downy woodpecker. What a handsome fella."

They continued along the woodland path and down another flight of steps, and Felix paused to stare at a pavilion that overlooked a small pond. A flash of sunlight broke through the trees, turning the water luminous. To their left, a mossy nook closed around a circular stone dais with two wooden benches flanking a round stone table.

"A hobbit's grotto," Felix said.

"Isn't it just?" Eudora settled herself on one of the benches. Felix sat opposite.

"I think we've avoided the issue long enough," she said. "Tell me about Harry."

A squirrel shot through the leaves, and Felix raised his face to a flickering patch of sunlight. Harry was right; Felix always sat in the sun. And yet he'd talked Ella into a house that was tucked away in the shade. He lowered his head slowly and held Eudora's gaze.

"He left his laptop open with a message to his girlfriend on the screen. A message in which he called me a rather unpleasant name. I doubt he intended for me to find it. Harry is scattered but not malicious."

Eudora nodded. "I suspect his ADHD means he often leaves things undone."

"Did I tell you about that?" He frowned at her.

"No need."

"You don't miss much, do you?"

"At my age, I miss plenty."

Water babbled down a small waterfall sculpted from mossy boulders.

"We had a pair of red-shouldered hawks in the garden once," Eudora said. "Very protective of their nest, they were. One morning, we found them attacking a baby owl. Couldn't adapt, you see. Couldn't accept that little owl posed no threat, unlike his mama or his daddy." Eudora raised her eyebrows. Again, he was aware of hidden meaning in her words, a lesson he couldn't grasp.

Felix leaned forward and rested his elbows on his knees. "My son hates me."

"That's not true, hon."

"I haven't been much of a father to him."

"No." She patted her perfectly pinned hair bun, or french roll, or whatever an updo was called these days. "You haven't been."

"Thank you. I'm so glad we had this conversation."

"Mistakes are human. Learn from them, but leave regret where it belongs—in the past. It's the future we need to pay heed to."

Felix glanced at his signet ring with the Fitzwilliam family crest and motto. If only it were that easy—walking away from the past.

"When Dahlia died, I didn't think I could go on. Son, I was sure I couldn't. But then I thought about my remaining time on this precious earth. I haven't visited China yet, or New Zealand." Eudora paused. "I want my tombstone to read 'She Lived Out Loud.' You, hon, need to start living out loud."

"I'm not an out-loud person, Eudora."

"Golly bean, you do have some dusty ideas in that brain of yours." *Golly bean?*

"You can be whoever you want to be, Felix. No one is responsible for your happiness but you. What do you do for fun?"

Felix watched two small birds flit in and out of dead undergrowth on the forest floor. Would they be nesting soon, starting a bird family? "I don't have much free time. What I have is devoted to fixing up the house."

"Your house doesn't need fixing up. It's delightful. You've lived there for, what—sixteen, seventeen years? And all that time you've been modernizing it, decorating it, changing its very nature?"

Felix raked his fingers through his now permanently ungelled hair. "Trying to bring it up to standard."

"And will it ever be just the way you want it to be?"

In the forest behind them, the woodpecker hammered away. Rat-a-tat-tat; rat-a-tat-tat.

"No."

"Well, there you have it. Stop looking around corners, Felix Fitzwilliam. Enjoy the glorious now."

The sun disappeared behind a cloud; a sudden chill settled on his shoulders and slunk down toward his heart. "What if my wife is dying?"

"If that's the good Lord's intention, then even more so."

Felix stood. Why had he allowed that thought in his head? Why had he allowed it to come out of his mouth? Every day he spun in ever-decreasing circles, trying to eat his tail like the mythical dragon Ouroboros. How could he pick up his life and move on when this fear for Ella gnawed at him constantly? The forest slipped into full shade; the clouds had thickened and re-formed while they'd been talking. It would be dark early tonight.

"My last year with Dahlia was the happiest of my life because I allowed it to be. Did I have days when I wanted to scream and cry at the injustice of it all? I sure did, son. I'm no saint. But I didn't spend life waiting for death to show up on our doorstep. Her prognosis was very bad, but miracles happen. And those doctors? Heck, they don't know who's going to beat the odds and be in that slim percentage of survivors. If you're too busy worrying about what might be, you forget to enjoy what you have."

"I miss her—the real Ella. She shuffles around the hospital as if she's little more than a ghost."

"She's still Ella, hon, but she's been through a life-changing event. Well now, so have you and Harry. Y'all need time to heal. I can help out with Ella when she comes home, but it's you and Harry I worry about. You need to be looking after each other."

"And how do you propose I do that if he hates me?"

"Dang. For a smart guy, you don't listen as well as you should. Just because something's always been one way doesn't mean it has to stay that way. As I see it, some adapting needs to be going on, and I'm guessing that's not your thing. But life just handed you an opportunity. You've been given a second chance to be a daddy."

Felix stared at layers of decaying leaves piled on top of each other. Spring had become a distant fantasy. "Suppose I was never meant to be a father?"

"Bit late to decide that, don't you think?"

Felix smiled; he couldn't help it. "Is this your 'suck it up' speech?"

"Fatherhood doesn't come with an expiration date, and that delightful boy of yours will need his daddy until the day you die. This time next year, he'll be a young man thinking about graduating from high school. An exciting time, but terrifying, I'm sure, for such a homebody. And when he does finally fly the coop, he's got to know his daddy will have his back. Wherever life takes him."

"That's typically been his mother's role."

"No reason he can't turn to both of you. This isn't an either/or situation. And while I'm being so candid, you need to ease up on yourself. Life isn't perfect, and people sure as heck aren't. We're broken and messy and a hornet's nest of contradictions. And yes, that includes you, son. I think if your own daddy were alive, he'd congratulate you for being a true family man this last month."

"My father was a bastard," Felix said.

"But you, Felix, are not." Eudora gave him a withering stare. "You're a good man."

"I'd like to believe you, I really would."

"It's the gospel truth." Eudora stood slowly. "I don't lie."

They began walking again and emerged back on the sandy path that ran straight like a Roman road.

"Why are you helping us?" Felix said. "And please don't insult me with talk of southern hospitality."

"Does kindness need a reason?"

"In my world, yes."

Eudora raised an eyebrow, looking like an aged version of Samantha in *Bewitched*. (Tom had loved that show. One of the few American imports on the BBC in those days.) "Then we need to expand your world." She paused for a shallow sigh. "It was obvious to any person with half a brain that your family needed help and you were stubborn as a mule and bound to say no. Depositing myself in your garden to take care of things I was pretty sure didn't interest you seemed the best way to start. After that, it became apparent."

"What became apparent?"

"That you need more help than your wife and son."

Felix stood still as anger prickled through his muscles and up into his jaw. "Excuse me?"

"I don't know where your demons come from, hon, and it's none of my business. But I sure do wish you'd figure out how to enjoy that boy of yours. His heart, well, it's big enough to feed the world, the way I see it."

"My son is a disorganized mess."

"Powdered sugar on a doughnut. It's what's inside that counts. First time I met your son, I was carrying in groceries. He came rushing over to help." Eudora smiled the smile that took its time to unfold. "I'll never forget him leaping over my flower bed, arms outstretched, shouting, 'Wait! Let me!'"

"I hope he didn't crush any of the flowers on the way over."

"See. There's my point. That's why you need my help."

"What?" Good grief, his voice had become a parody of Mother's imperial tone.

"Seems to me you always have a mind to focus on finding fault, not celebration."

A young man in a bomber jacket trotted by and raised his chin in greeting. "Hey, Eudora."

"Hi, hon." She waited until he was out of earshot before continuing. "Now. What about taking a trip—just you and Harry? A weekend in Boone, maybe?"

"I don't have time for a jaunt to the mountains. But spring break is around the corner. I'm planning a college tour."

"With Harry's input, of course."

Felix tugged up the collar of his coat. Yes, there was definitely snow in those clouds. "Every time I raise the issue, he refuses to engage."

"I suspect he's scared."

A hawk cried and Felix tensed. "Of me?"

"Of his future. The threat of change can be a fearsome enemy. Would you like me to talk with him?"

"No, thank you. I'll give him one more chance, and then I'm moving ahead with my plans. Time is running out."

"Well, I'm sure you know best." Again with the smile. Underestimate it at your own cost.

I do; I'm the father here. And no offense, but you've never had children. The conversation had begun to annoy him, and he didn't want to appear rude.

"I should return to the office. Thank you for the"—he hesitated—"advice."

"My pleasure," she said, and walked back the way they'd come.

Felix marched in the opposite direction. He had wasted enough time. He needed to focus on Harry's future; more specifically, he needed to arrange a trip to Harvard. Harvard was the key to Harry's future, just as Oxford had been the key to his.

TWENTY-FOUR

Would Dad be up for a driving lesson this weekend, or was he still pissed? *Duh.* Turned with a knife in his hand and snarled no when Harry offered to help with dinner. 'Course, he shouldn't have suggested that it would be easier to chop the onion in the food processor. Dad 101: never make helpful suggestions.

As Max had said so eloquently at lunchtime, "You, my friend, are in some deep shit."

Dad hadn't spoken to him since last night. Questions about school, like "Do you have your lunch box?" didn't count. Did he now have the Dad Situation as well as the Mom Situation?

Going to Sammie's had probably been a mistake, but removing himself from the house had seemed the best plan. If he'd stayed, he might have thrown out something far worse than *Nazi neat freak*. Thing is, he wasn't angry anymore. Dumping on Dad had been surprisingly liberating. But worth it? Hell, no. The tension in the house was now heavier than southern humidity in August. With anyone else, he would have fallen on his sword. Apologized and been done. But this was Dad. The guy who'd taken to smashing heirloom glass. (Yeah, he'd uncovered the evidence in the garbage.)

Harry picked up a piece of graph paper from his desk, folded it into a paper plane, aimed it at the trash can. *Yes!*

If only he were outside shooting hoops, burning up megawatts of energy, but that meant walking through the dining room—the new Dad Work Zone. This Life Plan shit seemed to be a do-or-die deal, but weren't they all? And now that Dad's work had crept into the house, started taking over, everything felt prickly again. What had his psychologist said? "Behavioral contagion, Harry. Remember the mantra: this is not my stress."

Harry bounced up. Valentine's Day in two weeks, and he actually had someone to spend it with! If only he could get his license, he and Sammie could go on proper dates. He'd hated that her mom had to taxi them last night. Totally not fair on Mrs. Owen.

What could Eudora teach him to cook next? Mac and cheese, so he and Sammie could have a romantic dinner! For Mom's welcome-home dinner, he was going to make french toast. Mom's favorite! Their lives were so topsy-turvy—why not have breakfast for dinner? Dad had already given his approval—when he had actually been talking as opposed to grunting.

Harry grabbed his phone and texted Sammy: `whatcha doing`

`English essay.`

`i <3 you`

`Me too.`

`bored`

`Work.`

`can't`

```
Go bother your dad, not me. ☺
```

His stomach twisted. Was he bothering her? Did he text too much? Some of her replies were kinda short. But he did text her a lot. Like, all the time. Like, every few minutes when she didn't answer him. Like, nonstop. *Text less, Harry.* But his fingers started magically typing again.

```
haha right we're still only
exchanging guy grunts

Apologize.

him first

Aren't you always telling Max to
apologize and move on when he's
ranting about his mom?
```

Then she sent him a heart emoticon, and he sighed his biggest love sigh and everything from his toes up tingled. Also: instant hard-on.

How many hours till he could kiss Sammie? Harry counted. Too many. Ms. Lillian was on lunch duty tomorrow. She was cool, a great human being, but she had zero PDA tolerance. Would have to wait till pickup. Shit.

Harry fell facedown on his bed. That morning, Ms. Lillian had let him sleep on the couch in the staff room because Dad had done drop-off ridiculously early. Some important breakfast meeting with Robert. Before-school care was depressing. Not that Harry cared about being with little kids—so many degrees of adorableness—but it was a big, flashing statement about how much life had changed with the Mom Situation. He'd overheard Ms. Lillian arguing with the school director. They were trying to keep it down, but his hearing was freaky good. All his senses worked in overdrive. Never had figured out why. "Yes, I'm making an exception for this kid because his mother is critically ill," Ms. Lillian had said. The words *critically ill* rocketed back to hijack his brain waves.

Harry bounced back up. Bounced on the balls of his feet.

If only Sammie were here, snuggling and filling his world with supernova fireworks. Taking him outside the Mom Situation. For Sammie, he might have to start writing poetry. Love sonnets! When they were apart, it was like he was being stretched on a rack, bones snapping. Harry cracked his knuckles, tried not to imagine his fingers twisted through her hair, tried not to imagine inhaling Sammie. She smelled like summer.

```
off to apologize to dad but only for
you
```

He sent a row of heart emoticons—one, two, three, four, five, six! In assorted colors.

Harry pulled out a chair and flopped down at the dining room table. Messed with his hair, cleared his throat. The outside security light came on and flood-lit the patio. The deer must be out. If Mom were here, she'd be banging on the doors, yelling.

Dad looked up over his glasses, those blue eyes chilling. The Dad Vader death stare. Sammie was right. One of them needed to man up and apologize. Apparently, it was not going to be the parent. And people thought teenagers were immature.

"I'm sorry, Dad." Harry chewed the skin around his thumb. "I didn't mean all those things I said when we got back from the Nasher. I was just lashing out."

"My experience is that people normally speak the truth when they're angry."

Harry sighed. "Since things are heating up with this deal, how about we put off talking about the college shi—stuff until Mom's settled back home and your life's less manic? We could mark off a whole afternoon for a college summit." Okay, that was one huge olive branch. Even Dad had to accept it. And it would buy some time. When Mom came home, he would go to the source, consult the oracle on all things Dad. Mom would know how to fix this.

"Will you promise to give me your undivided attention?"

Harry raised his right hand. "My attention, my whole attention, and nothing but my attention."

"A week from Saturday."

"Done."

Dad pulled out his phone, typed in their date. "Noon."

Harry leaped up and pushed the chair back into place. *Look, Dad, I'm putting it in exactly the right spot. Happy?* "Are we good?"

"Yes, Harry." Now it was Dad's turn to sigh.

"Come on, Dad. Can't we just kiss and make up?"

Dad put both palms on the table. The tips of his fingers turned white, with half moons of jagged, angry red underneath. Which was ghoulishly freaky. Harry swallowed. Was Dad going to start smashing glass again?

"I gather you want to live with your girlfriend's family."

"What?" *What the fuck?*

"You left your laptop open after you ran off to Sammie's. I was attempting to shut it down when it sprang to life, and there on the screen was a message that declared your wish to go live with your girlfriend."

"You read my private messages?" His head snapped into that sideways tic again, the one that had started at the airport. Shooting pain filled his head, pain almost as hot as the anger boiling over in his brain.

"It wouldn't have been an issue if you'd turned your computer off. You need to learn to conserve energy."

"Conserve energy? Are you kidding me? Are you fucking kidding me? You invade my privacy, and you want to lecture me about the battery power of my laptop?" Right before she'd gone to Florida, Mom had joked, "When you go to college, you'll escape. I'll still have to deal with him." Why couldn't it be Dad in the hospital?

"So we're not *good*, then?"

"No. We're not," Harry said. "We're far from good. Intergalactic far. And I think it's your turn to apologize for once. I'm going outside to shoot hoops. And then I'm going to change all my passwords. Stay out of my room. In fact, just stay out of my life."

Dad muttered something, but at least two words were crystal clear: "With pleasure."

TWENTY-FIVE

Three hours of sleep did not make for a functional investment banker. Felix had achieved nothing in the last hour. Not so much as a doodle.

Yes, he was still miffed that he'd been cornered into an apology. It was hardly his fault that Harry had failed to shut down his ruddy computer, but as the parent, he had crossed a moral line, which was beyond reprehensible. Why had he not kept his mouth shut? Clearly, being a full-time father brought out the worst in him. Going for the jugular had been a deliberate move. Harry had accepted his apology, but their détente was, at best, shaky. From now on, however, he would imagine an electric fence around the nuclear wasteland that was Harry's room. Harry didn't want him inside? Fine.

Felix laced his fingers behind his neck. Damn, he was overdue for a haircut on top of everything else. He stared up at his office ceiling—the same pale gray as the walls, a shade lighter than the carpet, and two shades lighter than the desk. He was cornered in a monochromic world devoid of pictures, photographs, and cute desktop gadgets. He had chosen to not clutter his work space with the personal, and he'd never questioned his office décor until today.

Piles of paper lay everywhere—on the floor, on the table, on the desk—but the room was blank. How many hours had he spent alone in this space with the angular wall of glass that magnified the intensity of the afternoon sun?

The hands of the black-and-white clock on the wall opposite inched toward twelve thirty. Robert, as predictable in his adultery as he was in all areas of his life, would be out with the mistress until at least two. One partner should always remain in the office during market hours, but that theory was based on the assumption that the partner was present in mind as well as body. If a client called, Felix would be useless. He texted Katherine.

> Free for a quick coffee?

> Sure. I'm doing research at Duke
> today. Somewhere close?

How much research could a bodice ripper require?

> Scratch. The bakery on Orange
> Street. You know it?

> Be there in ten.

Felix buzzed the front office, and within seconds Nora Mae stuck her head round the door. Until Ella's heart attack, he'd found the office administrator's daily attempts at pleasantries to be an irritant, although listening to her ramble on had always given him a chance to contemplate the many cacti lined up on her desk. Their needles screamed *Don't touch*, but the bright desert blooms seemed to say, *Oh, give it a go.*

"I need to pop out for about forty-five minutes. Something related to Ella. Can you cover for me?"

"Sure thing. If Curt asks, I'll explain you had to go and see a client." She winked.

The strangest thing about crises—they revealed allies in unlikely places. The expressions Nora Mae, a widow and devoted grandmother, fired toward Robert's back whenever he left for a lunchtime special had long betrayed her opinion of extramarital activity. What Felix hadn't realized until the last few weeks was that Nora Mae also had no patience for phonies. This had proved useful, since whenever Curt was within spitting distance of Robert, he became more obsequious than Uriah Heep. Evidently, Curt had designs on a partnership. The one that belonged, at least for now, to Felix.

He had grown fond of Nora Mae. A gift might be appropriate. "I'm going to Scratch. Can I bring back a pie for card night? My treat." He would ask Liz, the young barista who always said, "The usual, Mr. Fitzwilliam?" for her recommendation, since he wasn't a pudding person.

"Oh, you're good," she said. "You remembered Friday is girls' card night."

"Indeed. I'll text you the specials."

"You're a gem. Thank you."

Head lowered against the cold and the murmur of incessant thoughts, Felix strode onto the brick-paved pedestrian street protected by arching, mature trees. He glanced sideways into the narrow alley that always reminded him of a medieval Italian street, possibly because of the huge terra-cotta pots. They were stuffed with what he could now identify as heucheras.

He looked right and there was Katherine, sitting at one of the metal tables outside Scratch, typing into her phone. She glanced up and smiled. The smile was the best thing that had happened to him all day, which was sad considering the she-devil's opinion of him. Antihero didn't sound like a desirable role, but he wasn't here to be liked or disliked. He was here for one reason: Katherine had earned his trust.

"I thought we'd be more private outside, but the temperature's dropping." She stood and pushed her funky green reading glasses onto her head. They mirrored the color of her eyes.

"Yes, it appears last weekend's spring weather was an aberration. It's definitely a little exposed out here." He craned toward the road at the end of the street, checking for Robert's silver BMW. Brilliant—he could add paranoid to sleep deprived.

Felix held open the glass door. A warm, spicy smell and the hubbub of chatter greeted them. "What can I get you?" Felix stared at the blue chalkboard wall. Lunch—real food—might be advisable, but he had no appetite these days.

Katherine marched up to the register, despite the spiky-heeled boots that seemed utterly impractical for walking, and smiled at Liz. "Cappuccino, please."

Decisiveness. A good quality. He was gradually coming to understand why Ella had chosen Katherine as a friend. She made things easy. There was no drama and no oversharing. She liked you; she didn't. She spoke her mind, and if you didn't agree, it was not her problem.

Felix ordered a cappuccino, too. Why not?

"Not going for the London Fog with Earl Grey?" Katherine nodded at the specials listed on the wall. "I thought you were a tea drinker?"

"That's my usual." Felix smiled at Liz. "But the parameters of my life appear to be shifting."

"Have you had lunch?"

He shook his head. Katherine turned back to the counter. "The snack plate with the assorted pickles, cheeses, and meats is locally sourced, I assume? Fantastic. We'll add one of those, please."

"I'm not hungry," Felix said. *Nor do I appreciate people choosing my food.*

"No offense, but you're looking a little malnourished."

His stomach replied with a loud growl, and Katherine raised her eyebrows. "I rest my case."

Felix paid, then hesitated by the glass display case, checking the pies before pulling out his mobile to text Nora Mae.

"Am I keeping you from something more important?" Katherine said.

"I promised to take the office administrator a pie for her Friday-night poker game. Liz?" Felix raised his head. "What do you recommend for a whole pie?"

"The chocolate chess. Always," Liz said. "Can I get you one?"

"I'll let you know before I leave."

Katherine hooked her hands into the back pockets of her jeans. "You're full of surprises, Felix Fitzwilliam."

"Meaning?"

"Still trying to figure that one out."

Meaning?

Katherine turned and led him to the table in the window, the table he would have chosen since the adjacent one was empty. She picked the seat with the view of the café. His view would be of Katherine and a brick wall, which seemed highly appropriate. He removed his coat; she unwound her scarf and unzipped her leather jacket. Felix resumed his texting.

"Which pie did she choose?" Katherine said, watching the counter. Was she willing Liz to hurry up so she could do this and escape?

Felix pocketed his phone. "The chocolate chess."

"Good choice. So tell me what's on your mind."

"I never thanked you properly for persuading Ella to see Harry. It made a huge difference to him."

"And to Ella."

He stared through the plate-glass window to the quiet street, to the empty concrete planters, to the cars jammed into the small parking lot beyond.

"I need to ask you a rather large favor." He was on a path of no return. Felix Fitzwilliam was going over the top, crawling out of his trench to be pinned down by gunfire in No Man's Land. He was issuing a formal invitation for help. Next he'd be opening his front door to salespeople. "I'm bringing Ella home tomorrow."

"I know this." Katherine leaned her elbows on the table, slotted her fingers together, and rested her chin on her hands. She wasn't going to make this easy, was she?

"I'm about to hit crunch time with this Life Plan deal. D-day is one week and counting, and I have no idea how much care Ella will need. I do know, however, that she's frightened of being alone. Eudora has offered to help out, and I was hoping you could fill in the gaps until the deal is done."

"Reverting to form, are we? Work comes before Ella?"

He crossed his legs and started swinging his right foot back and forth like a pendulum. Above Katherine, there was an alcove in the brick wall with a small window and a vase of colorless dried flowers. Dead flowers. "No. I'll take the night shift and continue to ferry Harry around."

Liz appeared with the snack plate. "Can I bring you some forks?" she said.

"Just one, thank you." Katherine smiled up at her.

Moments later, Liz returned with the cappuccinos, a fork, and napkins. Felix thanked her and then devoured the half biscuit smeared with pimento cheese.

"And what happens after this week?" Katherine dipped her finger into the cocoa swirl on top of her cappuccino and then sucked the foam off her finger.

"Once the Life Plan deal is done, I will be taking an off-ramp out of the partnership, which will allow me to stay with the firm, but in a less stressful role. After the transplant, I plan to set up on my own."

Katherine scooted forward to the edge of her chair. "Taking clients with you?"

"No. It doesn't work that way. I'll be taking nothing but what's left of my reputation." Felix wiped his mouth with a paper napkin. "And starting over as a corporate financial consultant."

"Is that what you really want?"

"Of course not. I love my job, but as Eudora has pointed out, it's time to adapt." Felix speared a pickle. Katherine was right; he was starving. He chewed slowly, savoring the vinegary taste, then swallowed. "I don't see an alternative, and this way I can be more in control of my working life. What I'm doing now, to get through this one deal? Cobbled together at best. And I have no idea what Ella's diagnosis will mean for the family long-term."

"What does Robert think?"

"He doesn't know. I haven't told anyone."

"Except for me."

"Except for you."

She tossed back her head, and her dangly earrings tinkled softly like tiny bells. How could she bear to wear such large earrings with all that hair? As if reading his mind, she combed her left hand through a few stray locks and smoothed them behind her ear. Katherine had fabulous hair, he'd give her that: layered, straight, and auburn, although the color was chemically enhanced.

"What's your take on Ella's progress?" she said.

"She seems more distracted than usual. And increasingly less able to do anything." Was he being disloyal?

"What does Dr. Beaubridge say?"

"That her lack of energy and mobility is normal for class three heart failure." Felix massaged his forehead, pinching the skin between his thumb and pinkie finger. Another headache was taking root. Most days, it was a toss-up between which bothered him more—his head or his stomach. "Everything is so fucking normal."

"I didn't think I'd ever hear you use the f-bomb."

"I didn't think I'd ever share my lunch with you." He pushed the plate toward her; she shook her head.

"Yes, Felix. I'll talk to Eudora and we'll figure out a schedule. And I'll help as much as you need after that. Caregivers burn out quickly, and I have no dependents, not even a goldfish. Use me as backup for whatever." Katherine raised her cup to her lips and then put it back down. "And the depression? What does Dr. Beaubridge say about that?"

"You've noticed it, too?" He helped himself to a forkful of something that looked like deviled ham.

"I'm familiar with the symptoms."

If they were friends, he would have asked for an explanation. Then again, if they were friends, she would have offered it unsolicited.

"She tells me everything is fine and she's anxious to get home." Felix glanced at the empty plate. How had he eaten everything so quickly? "Is that what she's telling you?"

"Yes, but she needs to talk to Dr. Beaubridge about an antidepressant."

"Katherine—" Felix tossed down his napkin. "She won't take any more drugs. Listen, I should head back to the office."

"Wait." Katherine reached for his arm. "If I order a piece of chocolate chess pie, would you share it with me?"

"I don't eat dessert, Katherine."

"Please? I need to talk to someone who might understand."

Felix nodded, and she left to order the pie.

She returned moments later with two forks and fresh napkins. Liz followed with a huge slice of dark chocolate pie. Katherine took the first bite.

"Oh God." She brushed a piecrust crumb from her bottom lip. "This is delicious."

Felix hesitated, then scooped up thick chocolate with the side of his fork and couldn't help but agree. It was heavy but light, sweet but slightly bitter. Katherine said nothing else, so he continued until he had eaten what he deemed to be his portion. He put down his fork with a satisfied groan. Her green eyes watched him.

"Did I miss something?" he said.

"I thought you didn't do dessert."

He shrugged and tried not to visualize Pater's bulge.

"I appreciate your not rushing me," she said.

"My new pastime is waiting for Harry to finish sentences."

Katherine smiled briefly. "My ex hated delayed confidences. He would have left the café by now. Mind you, marry an asshole and what do you expect?"

Felix wasn't sure how to respond, so he didn't.

"I wouldn't have survived my divorce without Ella," Katherine continued. "My husband fell in love with another woman and was gone. Fait accompli. Cataclysmic betrayal from a person who was meant to love me no matter what. I fell apart, couldn't figure out what was wrong with me." She stared down at the lacquered tabletop. "Part of me believed it was my fault, that I wasn't good enough."

"I understand better than you might think," he said.

She looked up and something fell into place between them. She was no longer the she-devil; maybe he was no longer the antihero.

"Sorry. I didn't mean to divulge . . ." She ruffled her hair. "What happened back then is irrelevant. The point is that Ella gave me the strength to pick up and go on. She turned me into a fighter. And now it's time to repay the debt and . . . I don't know what to do, how to be when I'm around her. I'm terrified that I can't make it better. I'm terrified that no one can. Most of all, I'm terrified she's giving up. And how can I be strong for Ella if I believe—"

"I know," Felix said. "Trust me, I know."

TWENTY-SIX

A bat swooped from the black line of ivy-wrapped tree trunks, and Ella shivered. Barely six o'clock, and the world was shrouded in night. The landscape lights, set on a timer, glowed like underwater orbs, but the house remained silent and dark. Had Harry not thought to welcome them home with lights?

Waiting with the passenger door open, Ella huddled in the jacket Felix had brought for the journey home. The jacket belonged to another life, her London life. For the last few years, it had been packed away in the back of the closet with cedar blocks to fend off moths. Felix must have dug through everything to find it—a romantic gesture only she would appreciate.

He crouched down and took her hands, rubbing them between his. "I'm sorry, I didn't think to bring gloves."

"It's fine. I'm just happy to be home." Anxiety crawled up her spine. Would it ever release her?

She wrapped her arms around Felix's neck and buried her face in his warmth. He lifted her as if she weighed nothing and carried her over the bridge. The wheelchair stayed in the car.

"You can put me down," she said when they reached the front door.

"And miss carrying you over the threshold, my bride?"

Such exhaustion.

An unexpected smell of cinnamon welcomed them inside. Felix eased the door shut with his foot and carried her to his orange Jetson chair.

"Wait here while I unload the car," he said. "Harry! We're home." Then he disappeared back into the night.

Whatever she had been expecting, it hadn't been this unlit echo of her former life. None of the lights were on except for the light under the range hood, which she never used. This house needed lights all the time, unless it was mid-morning with the sun filtering through the trees into their bedroom. Duke Forest kept the rooms cool and shady, kept corners dark. And Felix had chosen rich woodland paint colors for the walls—deep reds and Robin Hood greens. Ella had wanted white. She'd wanted skylights; she'd wanted huge, funky light fixtures that screamed for attention. She had wanted to open up the house; Felix had wanted to close it in and create his very own fortress.

Subtle changes—laundry piled on the sofa, papers and files spilled across the dining room table—had erased her presence. The dining room was now Felix's work space. It was one of his many contradictions: he demanded impossible levels of order in the hall, in the living room, in their bedroom, and yet his office looked like a set from a reality TV show on hoarding. Every scrap of paper had to be saved.

In the four weeks she'd been gone, the personality of the house had adapted to accommodate her absence. Everything was familiar; yet nothing was the same. The present and the past scrambled together, and suddenly she was the too-tall, uncoordinated girl praying not to be the last one chosen when teams were picked on the playground.

"Mooom!"

She wobbled up to a standing position as Harry threw himself into her arms with a gush of sound and energy.

"Sorry—I was on the phone with Sammie. You're home, Mom. You're home!" He gripped her so tightly that she could hardly breathe. But what did she care? She would never let go.

They clung to each other, and for the first time since he had been born, she had nothing to say to him. Then Harry began to jerk. Not a serious tic, but bad enough to break the hug. Ella pulled back, sniffed, and smiled. Harry sniffed too. He touched her right cheek softly, then her left. He was finding his balance.

"You look—" he said.

"Like three-month-old roadkill?"

"No! I was going to say a helluva lot better than when I saw you in the hospital."

The contrast between them must be horrific. Photos never captured Harry's beauty: those huge hazel eyes; those sculpted cheekbones; those full lips; those white teeth that had never needed braces; that thick mop of hair, naturally streaked, that was neither too curly nor too straight. Michelangelo could not have constructed a more perfect man-child. Genetics had been so kind—and so cruel.

Harry grimaced and blinked, grimaced and blinked. "I'm making dinner tonight. Dad said I could."

"Let me guess—french toast?"

"Mooom." Harry's shoulders slumped dramatically. "How did you know?"

"You've been practicing. I can smell it." She breathed through a wave of nausea.

"Yeah, I wanted to get it right, so I did a practice run. But I can do omelets if you'd like, with cheese and peppers and onions."

"I'm impressed." She wobbled again, and suddenly Felix was there, his arm around her waist.

"You've overdone it," he said, his voice weary. "Harry, let your mother lie down. Don't bombard her."

Harry's huge smile twitched from side to side.

"It's okay, sweetheart. I just don't have my energy back. Not yet, not—" She couldn't disguise the hitch in her voice.

"I'm sorry, Mom." Harry glanced to Felix and back again, and started cracking his knuckles. She'd forgotten how the sound grated. She tried not to flinch, but Harry never missed a trick.

"Sorry," he mumbled again.

Now it was her turn to touch his face, but she held it firmly with both hands, keeping her gaze level as he grimaced and blinked, grimaced and blinked. "French toast would be divine, my amazing son."

"I love you, Mom. I'm so glad you're home."

"Love you too." She wanted to say more, but words wouldn't form. Then she kissed his cheek, and with Felix guiding her, shuffled toward their bedroom.

She was asleep the moment she lay down.

Ella awoke sharply, heart pounding, chased by the edges of a dream she couldn't quite remember. Every waking moment, she was anxious; every sleeping moment, she was afraid. *Afraid to live, afraid to die.*

Where was she? In the hospital room? No, there was no artificial light glaring at her, and the cloud of pillows and bedding was too soft. She was home in her own bed. This—she tugged the duvet up to her chin—this she had missed.

Banging came from the kitchen, and light suddenly filtered under the door. Someone had turned on the hall lights. Harry started singing, his voice angelic enough to impress even Felix. Ella had no idea where this talent came from—certainly not from his unmusical father. Maybe it was divine compensation.

"Hey, Dad. Did you hear how long I held that note?"

"Indeed."

Ella screwed up her eyes. *Don't criticize, Felix. Don't criticize.*

"But let's keep it down so we don't disturb your mother."

"How long will she sleep?"

"I don't know."

"Can I go see if she's awake?"

No. Please don't. What was wrong with her? What *the hell* was wrong with her? How could she not want to see Harry? Her heart rate picked up. She lay still, on high alert. Had she overdone it? Should she call Felix? Did she need to go back to the hospital?

"No, Harry," Felix said. "Leave her be until supper is ready."

Gently, slowly, Ella spread her arms and waited for the panic to pass. Lying in semidarkness, she eavesdropped on her family. This was a new experience—being on the outside, no longer being the single parent with a high-maintenance child.

Every twist and turn of Harry's life had filtered through hers without a break and without a support system. Friends had been sympathetic, but none of them had really understood. How could they? If you didn't have a kid with a soup of issues, you had no point of reference. Another first-grade mother, who had two boringly docile kids, had once accused her of being a helicopter parent. But how could normal parenting apply to a child who kicked holes in walls during rage attacks and had tics as violent and dangerous as seizures? The tics had improved with puberty, but she had been forever locked into a cycle of concern for Harry's emotional and mental well-being. Since she'd been forced to step aside, to unplug from the minutiae of Harry's daily life, she'd had the opposite fear: Could she slot back into that world now that she'd become her own worst nightmare—a person lost in self-absorption?

Right after New Year's, when she had left to see her father, she'd been a healthy person in charge of her family. She had returned as someone else. What if she didn't belong here in this life anymore? What if she couldn't pick up where she left off? What if she were evaporating into the stranger in the mirror?

Everything was meant to be different when she got home. Coming home was meant to be the cure—instant and miraculous.

The quiet, contained knock on the door said Felix. It was not the musical rap-rap Harry would have been responsible for. She struggled to raise herself up out of the pillows, when all she wanted to do was sink back under the duvet and let it swallow her whole.

"Ella?" Felix opened the door, and the french toast smell wafted into the room. He put the light on, but it was dimmer than it should have been. He had reset the switch to the lowest setting. What else had he changed?

He frowned. "Ella Bella?"

"I'm fine, just woke up. Bit disoriented."

He moved inside and sat on the edge of the bed. "Do you feel up to eating in the kitchen?" He stroked back her hair. "Or should I bring you supper on a tray?"

"You're suggesting I eat maple syrup in our bed?" She put all her effort, as much effort as lifting a barbell, into a smile.

"I was suggesting you exert as little energy as possible. And eat over a tray carefully." He paused. "Maybe skip the maple syrup?"

"Felix," she whispered, "I'm not up for french toast."

"He's worked really hard," Felix whispered back.

"I know. But the thought of french toast . . ." The nausea never left. She had forced herself to eat in the hospital so they would let her come home, but nothing tasted right.

"Could you try?"

She nodded. "Could you sneak in a few crackers?"

Felix kissed her nose. "Our secret."

Our secret. Such rich, comforting words filled with promise. Felix slipping back into his original role as her guardian, her gatekeeper;

Felix saving her as he'd done when she had been drowning in grief, and he'd helped her find her way home.

TWENTY-SEVEN

Shift change! Katherine was giving Dad the Mom update in the kitchen, which meant Mom was actually alone. A rare event these days. Whenever Harry tried to talk with her, Dad always appeared and gave the you're-not-to-tire-Mom-out lecture. It was freaky—like Dad had developed ESP.

Harry ran down the hall and knocked on the bedroom door. Dad used to be the closed-door person in the house, but now everything was up for grabs. How weird was that—having to relearn his parents at seventeen?

"Mom!" he whispered through the door. "Mom!"

"Come in, sweetheart."

Mom was in the big chair, legs tucked up, with a book on her lap. But she hadn't been reading; she'd been staring off into the forest. *Never fake a faker.*

"How are you feeling, Mom?"

"Good."

Total lie. One look at her, and you'd think she was going through chemo. Everything about Mom had slowed to fragile, even her speech. She was in far worse shape than Sammie's dad. He was doing pretty well. Had even picked up some freelance work. Sammie wasn't sure how she felt about that—said it gave the family false hope.

"How was school today?"

"Usual. Tons of homework." Harry stopped mid–knuckle crack. Dad had been on his case about how annoying it was. Harry was trying to stop; honest, he was. It was just—well, half the time he didn't realize he was doing it.

Mom tried to pull herself up in the chair.

"Wait!" Harry grabbed a pillow, puffed it up, and stuffed it behind her back.

"Thank you, sweetheart. Something on your mind?"

"Can we talk?"

"I thought that's what we were doing." A flash of Mom humor. *Most excellent.* Unlike the Owen family, the Fitzwilliams had hope. Hope by the truckload!

Harry threw himself down on the bed. "Does Dad ever get mad at you?"

"Only when he thinks I'm wearing a path in the carpet from our bed to the bathroom door." She raised her eyebrows. "Why? Did you guys have a fight?"

"Nope." That sounded so lame, but he and Dad had agreed to keep everything stress-free for Mom. No way must she know about their bust-up. He and Dad were sort of okay, but it was hard to shake the specter of Dad hunched over his laptop reading Sammie's love notes.

Harry's elbow flapped. Lying to Mom was the worst. "We have a date to talk about college and, you know, I was hoping you could tell me what the magic is for dealing with Dad."

"Ah." She smiled, but it looked phony. "There is no magic, Harry."

"But there must be. You found it."

"I accept that Dad has certain ways of handling life. He's a deeply compassionate man who needs everything to be a certain way."

"Don't you think it's darker than that, Mom—like levels of craziness?" Harry started rubbing his palms back and forth along the duvet. Back and forth.

"Your father isn't crazy. He has control issues, but that's a small part of who he is. Look at the whole, Harry, otherwise you miss the good stuff."

Harry sprang up onto the balls of his feet. Either Mom had seen God in the ER or they were giving her too many pills. Where was the person who used to mutter about Dad being self-centered when he was a no-show for dinner because another deadline had preempted family time?

"Dad comes from a deeply dysfunctional family—you know this. What you don't know is that your grandfather was abusive. Even I'm not familiar with the details, but your father has scars. Physical as well as emotional."

"I know. I mean, I don't, not really, but I kinda guessed . . ."

Oh no, was she going to cry? He couldn't make her cry. Mom never cried. Except for that day he'd visited her in the hospital. And he'd been crying, so it had been monkey see, monkey do. Harry grabbed the tissue box off her nightstand, jumped up, and handed it to her. She waved it away.

"You don't expect people to judge you by your attention issues, Harry. You can't judge Dad by his control issues."

Harry turned one way, then the other. "Has he talked to you about the college tour?"

"College tour?" Mom frowned.

"Spring break college tour. He's planning the Northeast Ivy League blitz attack."

"He is?"

"He hasn't said anything to you about it? Nothing?" This was not good, very not good. If Mom didn't have his back with this shit, who was going to derail Dad from the Harvard plan?

"Not that I remember, but I have a hard time staying focused these days."

"I know, Mom. I get the whole focus issue better than most people."

"Sorry. Of course you do."

Harry almost said, *Who are you, and what have you done with my mom?*

Somewhere in the house, Katherine laughed.

"It's good that Katherine and Dad are becoming friends," Mom said. "Much easier for me."

"Will you talk to Dad about it?"

"About what, sweetheart?"

Harry cracked his knuckles, tried not to sound irritated. Irritated fell under the category of stressing out Mom. "The Northeast college tour."

"I thought you wanted to stay in state."

Harry paced the room. Would Dad accuse *him* of wearing out the carpet? "I don't know what I want, Mom, that's the whole point. But Dad won't give me space. It's like my future is something to check off his to-do list, like he has a gun to my temple and he's saying 'make a decision or we're playing Russian roulette.'" He should slow down, but he needed to talk. Needed to get this stuff out. His mouth and his brain were a pair of runaway trains racing over a cliff. "There's nothing for Dad but forward motion to Harvard, and that's the one place I know I don't want to go. Maybe you and I could do college visits in the summer when you're feeling stronger. But I can't do it now, not when I'm so worried about you. I'm scared enough about the future and leaving high school and Max and"—*and Sammie*—"and Dad's making it a gazillion times worse. Why can't he see that?"

"Wait a minute." Mom held up a hand. "Slow everything down and separate it out, Harry. No more worrying about me. Yes, I've had a bit of an upset, but—"

"A bit of an upset, really? You want me to believe this is a bit of an upset?"

"I'm making progress. It's just long, hard, and slow." Mom stared down at her hands. She'd knotted them into a tight ball and buried them deep in her lap. "And there's light ahead with the transplant."

He might have believed her if she'd made eye contact. But Mom had retreated into a timid shadow. She just wanted to sit in that chair and stare into the forest, and when she did leave this end of the house, which she hadn't done in five days, she panted like an old person hiking the Appalachian Trail.

"How can I not worry about you, Mom?"

"Have we switched roles?" Finally, she looked up. "Harry, sweetheart, I'm tough—you know that."

He used to know that. But now? Hell, all bets were off.

Mom stretched awkwardly, not with her usual grace. "And as for leaving home, everyone's terrified of going to college, but once you get there and find friends, it's the experience of a lifetime."

"Were you terrified?"

"Catatonic with fear. But that's how I met Anson, and if I hadn't met Anson, I wouldn't have moved to London, wouldn't have met your dad, and wouldn't have this wonderful son called Harry. Once you make friends, everything settles. And you make friends quickly, Harry. You'll be fine. But I don't think you should wait till the summer. I think you and Dad need to move forward with your plans for spring break."

But he and Dad didn't have plans. All that existed was Dad's college-tour manifesto.

"You need to see the campuses while schools are in session."

Harry frowned. "That's what Dad says."

Mom turned to stare through the sliding glass doors. A pair of psycho squirrels was playing tag on the concrete; in Duke Forest, a hawk screeched. Her attention, everything that had anchored her to the conversation, floated away like ectoplasm. He kept waiting for Mom to come back, the old Mom. She was everywhere but nowhere. A bodiless voice repeating public service announcements: "There's nothing to worry about. Regular programming will be resumed soon."

"Dad's under a lot of stress," she said.

"We all are, Mom."

She turned her head back toward him. "I know, baby. That's why I think it would be good for you and Dad to get away. Do something normal, like a college tour, that has nothing to do with me being an invalid."

"You're not an invalid!" He punched the air, willed her to do the same. *Glass half-full, Mom!*

"Harry. I've got a long way to go, and we can't all sit around waiting for the transplant. It's important to me that you and Dad take your lives off hold. College won't wait; your future won't wait. You need to do this."

Great, now neither of his parents listened.

"But I can't think it through because every time we talk about it, Dad makes me too stressed."

"Then just go on the tour to keep him happy, and use it to eliminate colleges you're not interested in."

"But that's a humongous waste of time and money and energy!"

"Not it if helps streamline your decision process."

"I don't even want to go to the Northeast, Mom. If I'm going anywhere cold, I want it to be in the Appalachians."

"See? You're already making decisions." Mom paused. "What if you did your own research on colleges in the Northeast and asked Dad to work them into the tour?"

"Please, Mom. I can't do this without you."

"You can, sweetheart. You'd be surprised what you can do without me." She heaved herself up to her feet. "You and Dad need to cut me out of the equation. Handle this yourselves."

"You mean in case something happens to you. Why do you have to talk like this? Why?" So much for not upsetting her. His leg jerked up and he touched his heel, a tic that had caused endless problems in kindergarten because of the teacher's ridiculous mission to create the perfect line of silent, nonmoving five-year-olds. Every freakin' morning.

"*Shhh*, baby. I seem to be handling this badly, but my thought process is less functional than a broken garbage disposal. What I'm trying to say is that my recovery is putting too much strain on the family. You and Dad must stop worrying about me and start moving forward with your lives. This is your junior year—the most important year of high school." She paused. "And you just released a tic we haven't seen since kindergarten."

He sniffed and wiped his nose with the back of his hand.

"Don't use your hand to—"

"I hate when you talk like you're giving up, Mom." Harry raised his voice. "Like you're stepping away from us." Mom had never let him give up—even when he'd been in a dark place with the rage attacks, even when he'd felt as if he were the worst person in the world, cursed by God. So why was she curling into a ball, waving a white flag, and staying there?

"Harry, sweetheart. I'm being a realist."

"You're not. You're giving up."

"I'm sorry you feel that way."

Someone knocked and the door opened immediately. Dad was right. There were way too many people in the house these days.

"Gracious, child," Eudora said. "What's all the hullabaloo?"

"Nothing that a trip to *Harvard* won't cure," Harry mumbled. "I have to go do my homework."

Mom shuffled toward him, but he couldn't hug her, didn't want to feel her bones. "You and Dad need to do this. You need to think about college visits, think about your future—"

"Why does everyone keep telling me what I need to be doing?" Harry sniffed again.

"I love you," Mom said, but already she was moving back to the chair, as if just looking at him was too much effort.

"I love you too."

With a glance at Eudora, he left. That was it. If Mom wasn't going to take on the college stuff, Harry was officially on his own with Dad. He ran into his room, tore through his bedding, found his phone. Sent Max a text.

    `code spongebob`

His phone rang immediately.

"What's wrong, dude?" Max said.

Harry heaved out a sigh. "You and I need a new plan for my life, 'cause this one sucks balls."

TWENTY-EIGHT

"I thought he reserved his door-slamming for me." Felix loosened his tie and pushed off from the kitchen island. "I should go and make sure he didn't upset his mother."

"Eudora's got it covered," Katherine said. "I'm sure she'll shout for reinforcements if she needs them, and I was hoping to say something to you before I left."

Felix dove into the fridge and pulled out a small bottle of Perrier for himself and a bottle of the ginger limeade that he'd started keeping in the house for Katherine.

"No, I'm good, thanks." She reached down for her bags.

He put the limeade back, twisted the cap off his bottle of carbonated water, and guzzled. No alcohol today, not when he was contemplating an all-nighter. Thank God he could still make sound decisions about alcohol. He'd never realized before how exhausting the role of caregiver could be. Having a caregiver buddy—or in his case, two—might be the reason he was still drinking for pleasure, not need.

Katherine wound her hair into a knot and then released it. "I spend a lot of time reading people," she said, "and apart from the husband fail, I thought I was a decent judge of character. But I have to admit I was wrong about you. I'd like to offer a carte blanche apology for every snide comment and evil glare. And I'd like to start over." She hoisted her bags up onto her shoulder. "Felix Fitzwilliam, it's a pleasure to finally meet you."

She held out her hand and he shook it. "Does this mean I'm no longer the antihero?"

"Well, let's not go that far." Her crooked smile was almost endearing. "How are things between you and Harry?"

He and Katherine updated each other daily on the basics of Ella's progress: she ate *X* today, her energy level was down, she slept for an hour this afternoon. The spikiness had disappeared from their conversations, but they didn't discuss anything personal. Katherine seemed ready to change that.

"Unlike you, Harry does not think he's misjudged me. I'm pretty sure he hates me."

"Aren't sons meant to hate their fathers and lust after their mothers? Oedipus and all that."

"Oedipus didn't hate his father. And he didn't know the identity of either of his biological parents when he married the queen."

"Right. Thanks for the potted history lesson." She smirked and he relaxed. Sarcasm from Katherine he could handle. "Look, Harry's a good kid; he'll be fine. He and Ella are just so close, and this has to be turning his world on its head."

"I don't know what he wants from me."

"Well, if my brothers' interactions with my dad were anything to go by, I'd say that's standard for a father-son relationship. My dad spent his life complaining that he didn't understand his sons."

"Your father's dead?"

"Both my parents are."

"I'm sorry."

She shrugged. "Ella's the only real family I have. Brothers are useless, you know."

He nearly contradicted her, but he wasn't ready to open up their relationship to include Tom. "How's the deadline coming?"

"Inspired by you, I asked for an extension."

"Did you get it?" Felix stretched out yet another crick in his neck. Working at the dining room table was killing his back, his neck, probably even his eyesight.

She nodded. "How's the deal?"

"D-day is looming. Which means enough pleasantries, woman." He smiled. "As we say in England, bugger off. I need to check on my wife and get back to the grind."

He started walking toward the bedroom, and then— pandemonium. Eudora screamed, Katherine dropped her bags—*Oh God, was that her computer smashing?*—Harry's door flew open, and Felix's gut said *Run.*

Ella and Eudora were huddled on the bedroom floor. Ashen, Ella clutched her chest. "Can't breathe . . ."

"Katherine, call 911," Felix shouted, tugging Ella into his arms.

Harry sank to his knees beside them. "Mom. I'm sorry! It's all my fault. It's all my fault!"

"No," Ella wheezed. "No . . ."

TWENTY-NINE

"Here, child." Eudora handed him one of Dad's fancy cut-glass tumblers. The reddish-brown liquid in the bottom stank of rubbing alcohol. "Moonshine from my medicine cabinet."

"As part of our intervention." Katherine smiled.

Harry's jaw popped and his head jerked sideways as if in some death spasm. Again and again. He looked at the rug in front of the black, empty fireplace. Everyone waited; no one spoke. They huddled around him like a blanket.

"I don't drink."

"I do," Max said. Max had arrived within minutes of the ambulance. Probably broke the sound barrier along the way.

"Best not say that out loud, child. The ding-a-ling in that yellow house across the way is a bit"—Eudora tapped her head—"cray-cray, bless her heart. She'd turn you in for underage drinking faster than I can reload Daddy's shotgun." Eudora nodded at Harry. "Sip it so you don't get tore up."

"Tore up?" Max laughed.

"Redneck for sozzled. My car mechanic's expression of the week."

"Man, that's disgusting!" Harry gagged.

"You'll develop a taste for it when you're older. I reckon this might ease those tics, though. That last one looked mighty painful."

"Yeah, okay." Harry held his nose and drank. Fire burned his throat, but he deserved it. And then warmth filled his insides, and his elbow stopped flapping.

"Good job. And one more," Eudora said.

He still felt like shit, but at least he felt loved. A loved piece of shit.

"When the ambulance turned up, I thought she was dying," Harry said. "I thought it was my fault."

Max draped his arm around Harry's shoulder. "So not true, dude." He took Harry's glass and had a gulp.

"Child, my mama used to have panic attacks all the time. Of course, they weren't called panic attacks in those days. I think they were called a case of female nerves. The medical profession has not been kind to women."

"Amen, sista." Katherine leaned forward and took the glass away from Max. "I've had them too, Harry. Given the stress everyone's been under, I'm surprised it didn't happen earlier. To any of us."

Dad appeared from the bedroom. He was still in his suit and carrying an overnight bag. He looked like an unloved piece of shit.

Harry jumped up, threw his arms around him. "Dad, I'm sorry. I'm sorry about everything. It's all my fault."

Dad stiffened, patted Harry's back, and then clutched at him like they were both drowning. "Hazza," he said quietly. "You did nothing wrong. Katherine and I both believed your mother needed help managing— managing . . ."

"Her emotional stress," Katherine said. "Harry, this is a good thing. They'll keep her for a few days' observation and probably send her home with an antidepressant. Felix, did you call Robert?"

Dad eased himself free of their hug. "I'm meeting him at the office in an hour—after I take this bag to the hospital." He grabbed the photo of toddler Harry sitting on his plastic dump truck and slid it into the bag's outside pocket.

"Dang. At this time of night?" Eudora said.

"Sadly, yes. Katherine, can I leave you in charge?"

Katherine nodded. "Stay in the office until you've met the deadline," she said. "I'll take over here."

Max raised his hand like an overeager preschooler. "I'll take Harry to school tomorrow. And drive him home."

"I'll make the best southern breakfast y'all have ever tasted," Eudora said.

"With biscuits and gravy?" Max said.

"And fried eggs, country ham, fried okra, and grits."

Max squealed.

"Now, you give me the number of that school, Felix, and I'll call first thing in the morning and tell the director that these two delightful young men will be in my charge until I'm done feeding them."

"I think I love you," Max said to Eudora.

"I'm mighty flattered, hon, but I'm a lesbian."

"Sick. Now I really love you."

Dad pulled out his phone, scrolled through his contacts, scribbled down the phone number for Eudora. "I have to go into work. Boys—Katherine is the parent in charge. Whatever she says goes. Katherine, you'll need to put clean sheets on the spare bed. I've been sleeping there so as to not disturb Ella."

Katherine gave Dad a long, hard stare. Mom hadn't shared news of the family sleeping arrangements? Funny, he'd always assumed Mom told Katherine everything, the way he'd always done with Max—until Sammie.

A yawn slipped out. Harry couldn't help it. The room seemed a little fuzzy, and suddenly all he wanted was sleep.

Dad squeezed his arm. "Go to bed, Harry. I'll see you tomorrow evening. No guilt, alright?"

"I'm on it, Mr. FW," Max said. "If he starts acting all melodramatic and contrite, I'll beat him over the head with his Darth Vader cushion."

Did Dad smile—at Max?

"Dad!"

Halfway to the front door, Dad swung around. "Yes?"

"Drive carefully. Be safe." Harry bit into his bottom lip.

"Always, Hazza."

"Heavens to Betsy," Eudora said, then swallowed the leftover moonshine in one gulp. "I'm such a *Star Wars* fan. If it weren't a school night, boys, I would suggest a movie marathon."

Max pointed at Eudora. "So much love for this woman."

THIRTY

Felix sat in a chair by the nurses' station to answer his phone. Why was Mother calling his mobile and costing both of them a fortune? She knew it was an emergencies-only number.

"Darling! How's my beloved grandson?"

Mother's one saving grace was her devotion to Harry. Although she blamed his energy levels and tics on lackadaisical parenting. As if she would know.

"He's fine."

"Terrible line. Are you in a wind tunnel?"

"I'm at the hospital. A minor setback with Ella. Nothing to worry about." His voice—flat, emotionless, disconnected—was not his own. "Shouldn't you be asleep, Mother?"

"After hours of tossing and turning I have simply abandoned all hope." She gave a labored sigh. "I decided I might as well start my day at three in the morning. Of course, my GP is responsible. That dreadful man is utterly determined to sabotage my sleep patterns and refuses to prescribe tablets. Personally, I think he's on the sauce."

"How about I send you some more melatonin tablets, Mother?"

"I suppose that would do. But the National Health Service is not what it was."

"Mother, you have private health insurance. If you don't like your doctor, find someone else."

"But the family has been with the practice for generations."

Felix tapped his palm. "I can't have this conversation right now. I'm in hospital with Ella."

"I thought Ella was back at home."

"She was. As I said, a minor setback. She's been readmitted for a few days."

"I suppose I could get on a plane if you need me to come and help out."

Help out. How would that work when Mother didn't cook, didn't clean, didn't parent, and hadn't driven since the eighties? She smoked, drank gin, and pottered in her garden shed. Tom dead at forty-one because his long-term partner had strayed once; Ella fighting for life at forty-seven because of faulty genetics; Mother in prime health at eighty-two despite her pack-a-day-plus-Hendrick's habit. Maybe all the cucumber slices soaked in gin kept her healthy.

"Felix, are you there?"

Felix balanced the phone between his shoulder and his neck, and put his thumb on his pulse. Yes, racing like the clappers.

"Felix!" she squawked.

"Yes, Mother?"

"If it's absolutely necessary, I can ask my travel agent to book a flight."

"Thank you, Mother, but it's not. Harry's in school most of the time and we're coping adequately, thanks to Ella's friend and one of our neighbors. Besides, I'm afraid there would be nowhere for you to sleep since I have decamped to the spare room."

"Did you say a *neighbor*?" His mother's tone was loaded with accusation.

"Eudora, yes. You'll approve—she's a retired horticulturalist. She also happens to be a gourmet cook." He emphasized the word *cook*. "We're eating extremely well."

"A neighbor is feeding you? Most unorthodox, indeed. I would like to point out that I am also retired. And I have the added benefit of nursing skills."

Retired from what? Mother had never worked—even inside the home. And volunteering in the cancer ward had hardly classified as nursing. One morning a week, she'd served tea and biscuits to family members and shuffled magazines around the waiting room.

"Mother, I appreciate your concern, but we're managing." *Somehow.*

"And just how poorly is Ella?"

"She's in heart failure and waiting for a transplant, which makes her pretty sick."

"Oh, dear me."

He had told his mother this several times. Maybe she'd been drunk. "Mother, I really have to go. I'll call you tomorrow when we can talk properly."

"Don't forget to post the melatonin. I need two bottles."

Felix said good night, hit "Call End," and sat. Just sat. He needed to get back in his car and drive to work—*the deal must go on*—but his legs no longer functioned. Maybe he could stay in a hospital corridor for the rest of his life. That would really push Robert over the edge.

"May I join you?"

Felix looked up and frowned at Dr. Beaubridge. "I had you pegged for a nine-to-five man."

"Hardly." Dr. Beaubridge sat next to him. His white coat made a rustling sound that took Felix back to Sunday matins at All Saints Church and the starched white surplices of the choirboys. The hell of sitting still, sandwiched between Pater and Mother; the pretense of being the family that deserved the front pew. "I'm glad you requested the ambulance bring her here."

"I'm sure our insurance will make us pay heavily for the privilege."

"It was a good decision," the cardiologist said. "How are you holding up?"

"I no longer know." Felix spread out his hands and looked at the hairs, the creases of skin, his wedding ring. "Stress can really do that to someone with a heart condition?"

"When your heart is weakened, anything can be the enemy: too much salt; an infection; emotional stress leading to a panic-attack type setting, as appears to have been the case with Ella . . ."

"Now what?"

"I know this is not the answer you want, but we continue to wait for a donor."

"But for how long?"

"I can't answer that. It could be months; it could be longer. In the meantime, I'd like to keep her in for a few days' observation, start her on an antidepressant, and then send her home again. Here." He handed Felix a card. "Waiting can be a difficult, frustrating time. There are support groups for families such as yours."

Felix wanted to rip the card into tiny pieces and scatter them like ashes. Support groups—the touchy-feely stuff of nightmares. Felix handed the card back. "We don't need outside help."

Dr. Beaubridge refused to take it. "You might change your mind."

"I'm not a fan of dissecting my feelings in front of strangers."

"I was that way." Dr. Beaubridge paused to greet a nurse. "Until my wife died."

A phone rang behind them at the nurses' station, and a patient's call alarm went off.

"How?" Felix said.

"Car wreck. Five years ago."

"Do you have children?"

"No." Dr. Beaubridge tried to smile. "My greatest regret."

Felix collapsed his arms onto his legs and hung his head. "How do you do this day in, day out?"

"I make sure I'm the best."

"Level with me. One husband to another." Felix rolled his head sideways and stared at Dr. Beaubridge. "How bad is this?"

"It's not a situation I would have hoped for, given how tenuous her heart failure is."

"Can you be more specific?"

"Given all that has happened in the past four weeks and today, Ella is now in the highest category of heart failure."

"Class four?"

Dr. Beaubridge nodded. "There's no way to predict whether she'll have another episode of heart failure or an irregular heart rhythm, either of which could prove fatal, or not. She doesn't meet standard indications for implantation of a device to predict irregular rhythms—an internal defibrillator—in part because she's not far enough out from her heart attack for us to know if the heart muscle will recover or not. And since she's stabilized, she doesn't yet meet indications for an LVAD, the implanted pump we talked about earlier. Bottom line? We're in limbo. And we could stay this way for months while we wait for a transplant. I'm sorry."

Felix put the card in his pocket and stood. "Thank you," he said, and walked away.

Finally, Dr. Beaubridge had been honest, and he had nothing worth saying.

THIRTY-ONE

Felix used to brag to Saint John that spring in North Carolina began on February 1. Not this year. February 8, and record lows had kept the furnace rattling all night. The weather was moving backward into the grip of full-blown winter. The house was definitely not constructed for such temperatures. Since the panic attack, Ella had complained endlessly of being cold, and Felix had bought several space heaters. The master bedroom was now stuffier than a National Health Service waiting room in a heat wave, and still, she couldn't get warm.

The humidifier made some strange gurgling noise and struggled to disperse moisture into the brittle atmosphere of the house. Felix snapped the new elastic band around his wrist and returned to his Dear Robert letter.

A week had passed since the Life Plan deal had gone through. It was time to step down from the partnership and offer to train Curt, and Felix wanted everything in writing. After ten years of partnership, he didn't trust his soon-to-be-ex partner. Nor did he trust Curt. Quitting in the summer was still plan A, part B, but that was a secret shared only with Katherine.

Ella coughed and appeared in the hall wearing her fuzzy gray slippers, yoga pants, and a ratty old cardigan he didn't recognize. She tucked the cardigan under one arm, then the other; it resembled a huge chest bandage.

"What are you doing out of bed?" Felix closed his laptop and jumped down from the kitchen stool. The wood floor was cold under his bare feet.

Ella smiled. Her face was gray; the roots of her hair were gray; she matched the gray Saturday morning sky beyond the sliding doors. "I thought I'd try moving around." She caught her breath. "Prove to Harry I'm not a sloth." She reached for the doorjamb.

"Ella, please, you're doing too much." Taking her elbow, he guided her back to bed. "Did you use the sleeping pill last night?"

"Yes, Papa Bear." She paused, her breathing still whistling as if she had asthma. "I am now the good patient who takes every pill known to womankind."

Felix was firmly of the belief that sleep deprivation had been a contributing factor in the panic attack. After she came home the first time, Ella had catnapped during the day and slept poorly at night. Dr. Beaubridge had prescribed sleeping pills, which she'd refused to take: "Because I wake up with my heart pounding, Felix. I wake up terrified and have to relive it all."

But sleep deprivation could be dealt with, could be fixed. Could be cured. This was a positive step involving forward motion. And now they were tackling the depression. It was early days for the antidepressant, and yet Ella seemed less adrift.

"Morning, Mom! Morning, Dad!" Harry skidded into their bedroom doorway. "Shall I make everyone french toast?"

"Lovely. Thank you." Ella's smile wavered.

"Dad?" Harry looked hopeful.

"Yes. Thank you."

Felix had eaten breakfast—brain food to help compose the letter—but Harry needed to feel useful. Felix had discovered this about his son. Besides, he could always skip lunch and squeeze in twenty minutes on the treadmill.

"I'll bring you a tray, Mom!"

"How about I do that, Harry?" Felix said as he watched Harry trip over nothing.

*

Two hours later, Felix was scrubbing the griddle that Harry had supposedly cleaned. Why, oh why, had he let Harry cook? Simple. Concern for his son's emotional well-being. He'd squeezed in an emergency appointment for Harry with the child psychologist after the panic attack, and everything had seemed fine. But you never knew. The young brain had a way of assuming guilt.

It was hard to say which came first—the doorbell or the sound of the front door opening. His house was no longer his castle.

"Yoo-hoo. Anybody home?" Eudora entered, followed by Katherine, who was carrying a huge Moses basket.

"Good morning, ladies." He wiped his forehead with his arm, brushing back his hair. Ella had told him she liked it longer, that it made him look younger, sexier. He wasn't convinced it was anything but untamed and irritating. "Did I miss something?"

"You and Harry are having the college talk today, right?" Katherine said.

His phone, buried in his jeans pocket, buzzed with a reminder.

"It appears so," Felix said. How had he forgotten?

"Well, hon, since Harry believes talking about college caused the panic attack, we thought we'd keep Ella occupied with a girls' day. English and southern style!"

Katherine dove into her huge wicker basket and held up two DVDs. "*Love Actually* and *Notting Hill*," she said.

Eudora rootled around in the basket, too. "Plus *Fried Green Tomatoes* and *Steel Magnolias*."

"Also, popcorn," Katherine said.

"Two bags, since I can't bear anyone picking at my popcorn. And this." Eudora pulled out a bottle of champagne.

"What's that for?" Felix said.

"The best reason of all, son. To celebrate life."

Harry came rushing in. "Hi, Katherine! Hi, Eudora! Dad, when we're finished with the college powwow, can Sammie come over?"

Felix glanced up at the ceiling. His quiet, secluded hiding place was suddenly bursting with women and busier than Clapham Junction.

"Why not?" he said, too exhausted for argument.

Harry rocketed off toward his bedroom, and after five minutes, rocketed back. They settled at the dining room table—Harry with a glass of milk and a six-pack of Krispy Kreme Original Glazed Doughnuts and Felix with a mug of black Earl Grey. Harry twitched through a concerto of tics, then devoured a doughnut. Felix lined up his legal pad and two pens—one black, one red.

"We'll start with a list of your top ten choices and go from there."

Harry turned beetroot.

"What?"

"I'd like to discuss an idea. I mean, a proposal. About college visits." Harry reached for another doughnut but pulled back.

Felix crossed his arms over his chest. "I'm all ears."

"Max and I have been doing some research," Harry said. "Brandeis—you know Brandeis, up near Boston?"

Felix nodded.

"Brandeis has an open house in two weeks, and we'd like to go. By ourselves."

Felix bolted upright into a coughing fit. "The two of you want to fly to Boston? A-*lone*?"

"Yup." Harry clicked his tongue against the roof of his mouth.

"You can't possibly expect me to agree."

"Why not?"

"A thousand answers, most of which hinge on two facts: you're phobic about flying, and you've never flown without your mother. What happens if you freak out and some airline employee assumes you're a terrorist?"

"Look at me, Dad." Harry's fingers strummed the air. "I'm a blond American teenager. No one could mistake me for a suicide bomber."

"Need I remind you about that appalling airline woman who wanted to call security because you were ticcing? What if something happens that's out of your control? Suppose the flight gets delayed or diverted?"

"Then I'd have to deal with it." Harry rocked back and forth in his chair. Felix put out a hand to stop him before he snapped the chair legs in half.

"You guys want me to be more independent, tackle my future, right? Then you have to give me the space to try." Harry fired a manic smile. "And let's face it, at some point I have to take my show on the road. If it makes you feel better, I'll type up little cards I can hand out to people on the plane that say, 'No, I'm not an escaped lunatic, I have Tourette syndrome.'"

"Let me get this right. You want to go on your first college visit alone. Even though you have no clue what to ask or what to look for?"

"How hard can it be, Dad? I listen, I ask questions. I like a place, I don't. After talking with Sammie, I've decided to investigate small liberal arts colleges. She's the one who suggested Brandeis."

"I will not fund any college decision based on where your girlfriend is going." Felix began tugging pills off his black cashmere sweater.

Harry clicked his tongue again. "I'm not asking you to. She wants to go to NC State, but she suggested I look at small liberal arts colleges. I think she's right."

Felix's lower leg swung back and forth, back and forth. He stopped when he accidentally kicked the table. "And what about Ivy Leagues?"

A part of him doubted he should even push for Ivy Leagues anymore. Could Harry cope with the pressure? Could Ella? But if you didn't aim for the top, didn't push yourself to be the best, what did you have except unfulfilled potential? And what kind of a father didn't want the best for his son?

"The way I see it"—Harry snarfed down another doughnut and continued to multitask through chewing and talking in a most unpleasant manner—"if I can't get on a plane without Mom, then considering *any* out-of-state college is pointless. And I'm not talking Russia. Boston's a plane ride away, and there are direct flights. I checked. And doesn't Mom's old roommate live in Boston? We could stay with her."

"I see you've done your research."

"If I can do this one college visit with Max, an easy trip with a direct flight, it could give me the confidence to think bigger." Harry's voice was high and slightly squeaky, a sign he was overstimulated. "Harvard bigger."

Felix paused before answering. "Do you honestly think you can do this, Harry?"

"Do *you* think I can do this?" Harry stared at Felix, his chest heaving and his eyelids blinking in rapid fire.

"Yes. I think you can. But here's the deal—if you take the trip with Max, you agree to a weeklong college tour with me over spring break. It's going to be in the Northeast, and it's going to include Harvard."

"Really?" Harry beamed as if he were standing on a winner's podium with a gold medal. "Rad! Thanks, Dad, thanks." Harry shot up and spun in different directions. "I've got to go call Max, I've got to—"

"Harry, please sit down so we can finish this conversation."

"Yeah, sorry, Dad. I'm just, you know." Harry grimaced and blinked, grimaced and blinked. "Excited."

Not a sentiment Felix shared. This was going to be expensive and probably a complete waste of time. On the other hand, Harry had used convincing logic. He did need to learn independence. Also, this would be a good test, a dry run before the real college tour over spring break. Although he had yet to raise the issue of a week's absence with Robert. Would it be easier or harder to negotiate vacation time as a worker bee, not a partner?

"Sit down and help me create a budget and a to-do list."

Harry squirmed and cracked his knuckles. Felix and Ella never discussed money in front of Harry, but he needed to man up and learn how to budget. The thought left Felix nauseated.

"Let's start with Max's home phone number so I can coordinate booking flights with his parents."

Harry gulped loudly. "Couldn't you just book the tickets and ask them to reimburse you?"

"No. I prefer to keep the finances separate."

Harry gnawed on his thumb.

"I promise to be on my best upper-class Brit behavior," Felix said. "How's that?"

"'Kay."

"Let's assume the two of you can stay with your mother's old room-mate. That will help keep the cost down."

Harry nodded.

"Do you know how to draw up a budget?"

Harry shook his head.

"It's a simple math problem that involves listing income and expenses, and then balancing the two. Since income is irrelevant here, we'll list your expenses, and it will be up to you to stay on target." Felix smoothed down the first page on his pad and wrote *Harry's trip*. "What's the date of the open house?"

"February twenty-seventh."

"I'll call the admissions office and sign both of you up for the tour."

"Great. That's great, Dad. Will you be okay—I mean, you and Mom, here by yourselves? If something should happen—"

"Nothing's going to happen."

The concern was surprising and sweet. But sweet could only carry you so far. Sweet also meant others could take advantage of you. Was sending Harry out into the world by sanctioning this trip a horrible mistake?

"Dad, there's a problem."

"Only one?"

"How are we going to tell Mom? I mean, I'm sort of terrified to tell her anything that isn't 'I'm fine, school is fine, Sammie's fine.' Will she freak out—about me going on a plane by myself, although I won't be by myself because I'll have Max and she knows I'm not nearly as anxious if Max is with me?"

"I have no idea, Harry. I'm making everything up as I go along."

"Does she know about you stepping down from the partnership?"

"No." Felix wasn't entirely sure why he'd told Harry about this when Ella was back in hospital, but after the panic attack he'd been more worried about Harry than Ella. Felix had wanted—needed—Harry to know that their lives would not spin out of control, that Felix wouldn't let things get worse.

Someone turned up the volume on the movie in the bedroom. Music played and Eudora giggled. Katherine joined in. Felix didn't hear Ella laugh.

"Why are we keeping stuff from her, Dad?"

Felix slumped back in his chair. "Because we're trying to protect her?"

"Like she always protected us," Harry said quietly.

Did he use the past tense intentionally? Felix fiddled with the family signet ring. "Do you want to sit in on a class if I can arrange it?"

"Yeah, thanks." Harry cleared his throat several times.

"A history class, I assume?"

"Nah."

"I thought you wanted to major in history?"

"Changed my mind. Psychology. I want to be a clinical psychologist."

"When did this happen?"

"I've been thinking about it for a while. History's kind of useless, you know."

"I read—majored in—history."

"I know, Dad. But there was a different world order when you were my age, a different world economy."

Harry had a point. Maybe his son actually did have a grand plan.

"Why psychology?"

"Why not!"

Felix sighed. So there was no grand plan.

"I think the world needs more psychologists," Harry continued. "Good ones. I mean, you never met my first psychologist, but she redefined useless. Also, I want to help people."

"An idealist, huh?"

"I guess I want to make a difference. Pay it forward. Tell messed-up people that life is peachy even if you're as weird as me." Harry stopped and scrunched his mouth into a thoughtful pout. "Dad, did you ever have a friend like Max?"

Sometimes the trajectory of Harry's thoughts was as mysterious as the unexplored depths of the ocean. "I didn't need one," Felix said. "I had a big brother."

"Most people wouldn't see that as a good thing." Harry grimaced and blinked, grimaced and blinked.

"I wouldn't have survived my childhood without your uncle."

"Want to talk about it?"

"The shrink is in?"

"I'm a good listener, Dad."

"But I'm not a good talker. I never talk about Tom."

"Yeah, but you've mentioned him loads since Mom had her, you know, thing." Harry's elbow flapped.

"Heart attack, Harry. She had a heart attack."

"I don't want to use those words."

"Weren't you the one who told me the things you're too frightened to face are the things that grow into monsters?"

"I guess."

Felix drew in a huge breath and closed his eyes. He exhaled slowly. To say the words, to shine a spotlight on his own weakness, his own failure, would change everything between them. He might just as well strip naked, show Harry his scars, and ask for pity. Felix opened his eyes. "Your grandfather whipped me. With a riding crop he kept in the bottom drawer of his desk."

Harry slammed his fists onto the table and Felix jumped. "The . . . the . . . bastard." Harry's head and upper torso convulsed. "The f-fucking bastard. I-I'm glad . . . I never . . . never met him."

"I'm glad you never met him, too, Hazza, because you're right. He was a bastard."

Out in the forest, a pair of hawks cried back and forth, their screeches bouncing off the trees like sonar. The tic passed, and Harry slumped back in his chair as if he were a punctured inflatable snowman, one of those horrendous holiday decorations that littered people's yards every year after Thanksgiving. Felix took off his glasses and rubbed his eyes.

"I hate him, Dad. I hate him for what he did to you."

Thank you. Felix slid his glasses back into place. "Now tell me what happened to your mother," he said softly.

"She . . . she had a heart attack."

"A big one. But she survived, and she's surviving every day." Felix sat up. "Just as I survived your grandfather's brutality."

Harry nodded.

"Your mother will move beyond this. And so will we, Harry."

A week ago, he and Katherine had made a pact: only positive thoughts ahead. And he was trying. God only knew how hard. But someone had blasted his life to smithereens with a cannon. What if the remaining pieces were too small and too fragile to glue back together?

THIRTY-TWO

Five days later, Felix stood in the hall holding up Katherine's sheepskin coat as she grappled to push her arms through the sleeves. She flicked her hair out of the collar and turned with a smile. "Right, I'm off to the store before panic shoppers clear the shelves. You'll remember to check the news for school closings when you get up, assuming we still have power?"

"The prospect of freezing rain doesn't bother me in the least." Felix walked into the kitchen and moved Katherine's wine glass to the sink. "Although I appreciate this means the entire Triangle will predictably shut down for days."

And necessitate cancellation of the school Valentine's Day dance. So much for the romantic dinner he'd planned for tomorrow night. The first time he and Ella would have celebrated February 14, and the weather gods were plotting against them. Well, his wife was bedridden and he could barely cook, so he used the verb *celebrate* with some irony.

"But you did go to the store and stock up?" Katherine said.

"I refuse to do so." Felix washed the glass, then put it upside down on the draining board. "Southern histrionics about the mere chance of winter precipitation are a turnoff for me."

The recessed lights in the kitchen ceiling flickered.

"They've upgraded to ice pellets." Katherine grabbed her bag from the floor and strapped it across her chest. If not for her designer coat— left over from her days as a fashion journalist for American *Vogue*, she'd told him earlier—she could have been mistaken for a grad student. "I don't remember ice pellets as a weather label before. Global warming's turning out to be one helluva bitch this winter."

"Global warming or climate change?"

"You say tomato, I say *tomah-to*."

Felix gave a breathy huh that was almost a laugh. "You're welcome to stay if you have concerns about the weather."

"Nah, I'm good. To be honest, I wouldn't mind being iced in for a few days. Provided we don't lose power. Think of all the writing I'll get done."

"I'm sorry."

"For what?"

"Adding to your strain. Messing with your deadline."

She held up her hand. "We've moved beyond this, Felix."

"If you change your mind, please come back. I've extended the same offer to Eudora."

"I'm assuming she also turned you down?"

"Indeed. I'm surrounded by stubborn women." Felix paused. "But if we do get inclement weather, you'll call and check in? Let me know you're alive?" He had meant to say *us*, not *me*.

She nodded. "Happy Valentine's Day. I hope Ella likes the ring."

"Thank you. And thank you for helping me choose it. Oh, wait." Felix dried his hands on the tea towel and retrieved a small gift bag from behind the bread bin. "I hate people opening presents in front of me and then gushing, so I'll say you're welcome, and please accept this as a mark of gratitude for all you've done for the Fitzwilliam family."

"Totally unnecessary." Her mock scowl disintegrated into a Cheshire cat grin when she peeked inside and saw the gift certificate for a massage. "But much appreciated. Thank you."

Clasping the gift bag to her chest, Katherine let herself out.

Felix sipped his single malt, then opened his laptop and clicked on the local weather website. The map for central North Carolina greeted him.

Oh shit.

Cracks and booms continued throughout the night, and they lost power around 2:00 a.m. A full-fledged ice storm, then. Ella and Harry slept through it all. Felix knew this because he checked on them numerous times. There would be no school today; there would be no work; there would be only the three of them trapped in a cold, dark house. What would this do to Ella's emotional stress level, something he now obsessed over as much as her ejection fraction?

Happy Valentine's Day, Fitzwilliam family.

Felix had never believed in fate, but the unpredicted severity of the storm did cause him to question whether there was some grand, insidious plan working to unravel his life thread by thread. Tonight was meant to be a rebirth, a renewal—a commitment to the decades that would follow. He'd bought shrimp and lobster tails and chocolate-covered strawberries. (Eudora had briefed him on how to grill the lobster and make the sauce for the shrimp.) And Katherine had helped him choose a simple garnet ring from Ella's favorite English jewelry designer. Garnet, the stone of love and devotion. The shipping had been astronomical.

At seven o'clock, daylight crept through the woods and across the patio. The natural world took shape, coated in a thick glaze of ice. The trees—white and feathery—were beautiful and dangerous. Most of the smaller pines were bent double; some would not survive. Felix counted three giant root balls in Duke Forest. Mature trees were down. Ella's camellias bowed toward the ground, dripping icicles; branches littered the patio as if tossed there by divine beings playing pickup sticks. Nothing moved or breathed except for the birds participating in a frenzy of activity on the feeders.

Felix reached for the phone to call Eudora. No service. It had been a mistake to let her leave last night. He would send Harry over to check on her later—provided he could be careful. Ice and Harry seemed a lethal combination.

Around eight, Harry shuffled into the living room, wrapped in his duvet. "Power still out? It's got to be, what, six hours at least?"

So Harry had known what was happening during the night but had chosen to deal with the situation alone. That was promising, showed backbone. The apocalyptic sounds of an ice storm could easily terrify.

"School's closed today. No surprise there. I took a few things out of the fridge last night and left them in a cooler for breakfast and lunch. Some ham, some cheese, some lettuce. The milk. Please don't open the fridge until the power's back on. And I defrosted a chocolate croissant for your breakfast. Obviously, it's not warmed."

"Thanks." Harry hurled himself onto the sofa. He grimaced and blinked, grimaced and blinked. "Do you think they'll cancel tonight's Valentine's Day party?"

Felix collapsed next to him. "I'm sure they have already." He glanced sideways at Harry. "Sorry."

"I've never had a date to take to a school dance before."

"Maybe you and your friends can persuade the school to reschedule?"

"I guess." Harry popped his jaw—open and closed, open and closed. "I was just, you know . . ."

Felix nodded.

"'Course, I can't dance, so maybe I've saved myself some major embarrassment." Harry held up his hands and jiggled his fingers like a gospel singer. "In the immortal words of some famous and rather wise dude, shit happens."

How could his moods be so mercurial? Had Felix been in Harry's position, he would have fallen into a bottomless funk.

There was a loud crack and a crash from the street, and Felix jumped. Please God, that was not a tree falling on one of the cars.

"I hope the cars are safe," Harry said.

Felix looked from the empty fireplace to the icy world outside the wall of glass. "We should have brought in firewood last night."

Harry shivered. "Temperature's plummeting."

"The house wasn't designed for brutal cold." All the glass didn't help.

Another crack that sounded horribly close to the bridge. If they lost the bridge, they would be trapped.

"Is Mom okay?"

"She's still asleep."

Harry blew into the air. "Look, I can see my breath."

Felix got up. "I'll see if I can start a fire."

"I'll help!"

"No. There could be live cables down, weakened branches, and—"

"I get easily distracted?"

"I don't want you to go outside until I've had a chance to reconnoiter."

Harry gathered his duvet around him. "I think I'll go back to bed. Stay warm." He shuffled off, clearing his throat.

Felix walked through the house to the side door, opened it, and then closed it quickly. A huge limb lay across the bridge, and the black walnut had split down the middle. Half of it was on top of the log pile. Terrific. He would have to hire someone to come out with a chainsaw.

"Harry!" he called as he retrieved his jacket and gloves and scarf from the hall. "I'm going to need your help after all."

Harry bobbed out of his room. "'Kay."

"But dress warmly and do exactly what I say out there."

"Gotcha. Should I go to Eudora's, see if she needs anything?" Harry grabbed his jacket.

"Let's do one thing at a time. We'll get a fire going, and then I'll go next door and see if I can bring her over here."

"Did you call Duke Energy? Report the outage?"

"Yes, Harry. That I did manage to do."

"What did they say?"

"They have no idea when the power will be back on." Why did that feel like a recurring theme in their lives?

The fire sizzled and popped as Ella leaned toward the faded board that was part of their fifty-year-old English Monopoly set. It had belonged to Tom. The guys had dragged the sofa over to the fireplace for her, and she was tucked up with more layers of bedding and blankets than a little old lady in a nursing home. Truthfully, she felt like a little old lady in a nursing home. Even the simple act of moving a game piece exhausted her.

Eudora, who had complained of not feeling well, had opted out and was asleep in the guest bedroom. Since she had seemed fine before dinner, this rapid-onset illness had to be a ploy to allow them a family evening. An extremely generous ploy, since their elderly friend had willingly forgone the warmth of the fire. Every other corner of the house crackled with cold.

Ella held the small metal top hat over the board. Felix had chosen the iron, Harry the old boot. If she landed on Mayfair, which Felix had covered with hotels, she would be sunk. She threw the dice and counted out spaces.

"No," she groaned, and landed on Mayfair.

"Just you and me, Dad," Harry said. "Prepare to lose!"

Her breath tightened. One of the candle flames guttered and went out.

"Mom? I think you need to lie back." Harry was at her elbow in a flash. "You've gone pale."

Felix squatted in front of her, hands on his knees, and those eyes locked on hers, those eyes that had always made her heart spin like a flamenco dancer. She tried to smile; he tried to smile. Harry tried to smile.

All God's creatures try to smile.

She was definitely losing it. Even armed with a daily antidepressant, she couldn't shake the sense of dread that followed her from room to room. A shadow of fear.

Ella watched the reflection of the fire in the stone of her beautiful new ring.

"Darling?" Felix said.

She practiced her deep, slow breathing the way the ER nurse had shown her after the panic attack. "Just a bit dizzy. This has been a wild and crazy night for me. More activity than I've had in weeks. And look. Still up at ten o'clock."

"Baby steps, Mom!"

"I know, but swallowing my own advice sucks. I'd much rather swallow more of that delicious lobster." She'd barely tasted the lobster—so much chewing involved—but she had forced herself to eat an amount deemed acceptable by Harry.

Felix gave her a sexy, intimate smile; Harry coughed loudly.

"Dinner was fabulous," she said. "Thank you."

After much discussion with Eudora, they had opened the fridge and packed the contents into coolers with Ziplocs of the one thing they had plenty of: ice. The coolers now sat on the patio, where the temperature rivaled that of a freezer. Felix had grilled on the barbecue; Harry had been the sous-chef.

"You sure you're okay, Mom?"

"I'm fine. You guys need to stop worrying about me every time I sneeze."

Harry cleared his throat multiple times. On school days, the house seemed to ring with his absence. She missed his tics, his noise, his energy . . . Felix retrieved her cashmere throw from the back of the sofa and draped it around her. He squeezed her shoulder, and she reached up to lay her hand over his.

"Do you need to go to bed?" Felix said.

"In a bit. I'm not ready for this evening to end. Not yet."

"Are you sure?" Felix said.

She nodded. "Cross my heart and hope to—omigod." The laugh rippled out. "Sorry. I'm so sorry, guys. That"—she laughed—"that was completely inappropriate."

Harry held it in for a moment, but then his giggle exploded. Harry's giggle had always been infectious. Even Felix joined in.

"Thank you," she said when she ran out of breath for more laughter. "Both of you. For this most perfect evening. I wish I could preserve it in a snow globe."

Harry sat down on the hearth and stared into the fire. Orange firelight illuminated one side of his face, as perfect as that of a Botticelli angel; the other side remained in shadows. Felix stopped laughing, and the atmosphere in the room shifted. The fire crackled, but the air became cold and heavy. Ella shivered. It was as if the house itself had stopped breathing. She glanced from Harry to Felix and back again.

"Dad and I had a really good chat about colleges the other day, didn't we, Dad?"

That had to be good, right? So why the dread clawing at the back of her neck?

"And we're going ahead with the spring tour. Want to tell her the rest, Dad?"

Yes, want to tell me the rest, Felix?

Felix moved in front of the fire and clasped his hands behind his back. "I've given my permission for Harry and Max to visit Brandeis University outside Boston. They will be attending an open house on February twenty-seventh."

"That's great." She pulled herself up on the mound of cushions and pillows. "I'm happy you're thinking about college. Are Max's parents driving you?"

"They'll be flying," Felix said. "Alone."

"Harry, sweetheart, you're phobic." Her heart began to thud. "You've never flown without me."

"I know, Mom, but my anxiety isn't as bad when Max is with me."

"And if something goes wrong?" She kept her voice level.

The log in the fire made a weird whistling noise, as if oxygen were trapped inside and could detonate at any second.

"Then I'll have to face my fear. Gotta live outside your comfort zone. That's where all the good stuff happens. Or so they say." Harry grimaced and blinked, and then gave a Harry shrug—quick and floppy. "And if I can do this, then I can consider applying to out-of-state colleges. Maybe even Harvard."

There it was, the elephant in the room. The one that had caused her to have a panic attack, that had brought back all those memories from the plane. She slowed down her breath, visualized the ocean— calm and flat.

"Dad thinks I can do it. And we were hoping we could stay with your old roommate in Boston. Dad doesn't want us in a dorm."

Ella's brain struggled to keep up even as her heart threatened to explode through her rib cage. Was this what happened when she made Felix the primary parent—he cut their son loose?

Felix moved back toward her and sat on the arm of the sofa. "We have to let him try this. We have to let him go. Isn't that what it means to be a good parent—to let go?"

No, she wanted to scream, *I've spent seventeen years holding on. I can't let go. I don't know how.*

"Maybe you guys should talk about this without me." Harry bounced up. "I'm going to call Sammie, see if they have power."

"No, you're not," Felix said. "We need to reserve our mobiles for emergencies. Besides, we haven't finished the family discussion. Ella, what are you thinking?"

What was she thinking? A mudslide of contradictions: she had to let go and she couldn't. She used to be the family anchor, but now she was the reason Harry couldn't use his cell phone. She was a potential family emergency twenty-four seven. Despite the sudden chill, she began to sweat. Thoughts of Harry on a plane, in crisis, needing her. Memories of being on the flight from Florida. The living room seemed to slant away from her.

She stared at Harry, her thoughts building like a migraine. She had once been the gravity of his universe, the focus of his unlimited adoration. Silently, she grieved for the little boy who had never been embarrassed by her, who had never ignored her when she'd volunteered at school functions, who had never dodged a kiss given at an inopportune moment. Who had never rolled his eyes and said, "*Mooommm. Really?*"

"I'm thinking how hard it is to let my baby go. I love you."

Harry grinned.

"What are we going to do when he leaves for real?" She looked up at Felix. *Make it better. Make it go away.*

Felix dipped toward her. "I think we'll figure it out, don't you?" His expression turned uncertain, boyish, like he was asking her on a date. And then, with a quirk of a smile, he leaned closer still and kissed her. A soft, gentle kiss that slowed her breath, her thoughts, and her heart.

She was okay; everything was okay. She was no longer the passenger in a driverless runaway car. Felix was in the driver's seat; he had been all along. Cupping his face, she rested her forehead against his.

"*Eeew*, guys. Get a room!"

"I'll leave the two of you to figure out the details." She pushed up and attempted to stand; Felix was by her side instantly. "But if you'll excuse me, I think I do need to go to bed after all."

THIRTY-THREE

Embers glowed on a pile of ash, but there would be no hope of sleep. Primeval instinct kept Felix alert. Left arm braced against the fireplace surround, he leaned in with the poker to kill what remained of the fire. He'd never been a pyromaniac; he'd never enjoyed igniting Guy Fawkes effigies on Bonfire Night. A fire was a poorly chained beast with the power to break free and roar out of control, and when you were teetering on the edge of hell, one spark could ignite and consume your world.

With Eudora in the spare room, he'd planned to sleep on the sofa, but the living room had become an icebox. He glanced toward the glacial nether region of the house where his warm wife was asleep in their warm bed under their warm duvet. His heart began to race; desire snaked through his body. He wanted his wife.

Disgusted, Felix jammed the poker into the ash and embers. He would stay out here and freeze. What kind of a lowlife thought about sex when his wife barely had the energy to drag her body to the loo?

Felix replaced the poker on the fire tools stand. The house echoed with sleep; dawn seemed an eternity away. He puffed up the two pillows he'd retrieved earlier from the hall closet and shook out the antique quilt that had been a wedding present from Ella's aunt. It smelled of the passage of time. Numb with exhaustion and cold, Felix settled down on the sofa and listened to his thoughts.

Would he ever make love to his wife again? Death had tried to claim Ella on that plane and had failed. But he needed to remind himself that death was irrelevant, because she had lived. And as Eudora kept reminding him, they needed to celebrate life.

He flipped onto his side, then gave up when his lower leg tingled. He turned onto his back.

Katherine had said, "We all struggle, but suffering is a choice. Your wife taught me that." He would choose to not suffer; he would choose to be positive and enjoy each day with his wife. Yes, they would make love again.

A cramp grabbed his calf muscle, and Felix launched himself off the sofa.

Don't scream, don't scream.

He wanted to scream.

Goddammit. He massaged the hard clump of muscle and gritted his teeth.

Forcing his weight onto his leg, he attempted to stand. As the contractions weakened, he grabbed the torch and began walking. Instinctively, he turned down the hall, flicking random light switches on and off, which was utterly pointless. If power were back, he would have heard the heat kick on.

Pointing the beam of the torch at the floor, Felix cracked open Harry's door. As his eyes adjusted to the gloom, Felix spotted a big mound of duvet and teenager. He eased the door shut and turned. His bedroom door was firmly closed. *His* bedroom.

Hand trembling, he reached for the knob. Was he about to do something incredibly stupid? If only his mind were as quiet as the rest of the world. Without the constant thrum of appliances, the house had become a sound vacuum. A silent, freezing tomb in which nothing moved but him.

He opened the door.

His wife was broken, and yet he had never loved her more than he did at that moment. She was nestled into the white pillows as if she had constructed an igloo around herself, but she had left one pillow on his side. Was it his Tempur-Pedic pillow? Had she left it there as a statement? He reached out to touch the cold, white linen pillowcase. Yes, it was his pillow. He knew the subtle—and not so subtle—ways Ella shut him out if she wanted to be left alone. This was a welcome card.

Felix tiptoed around the bed to the chair where he'd dumped his pajamas after changing the sheets for Eudora. Then he turned off the torch, so as not to wake Ella, and felt his way along the bedroom wall and into the bathroom. He brushed his teeth in polar water, and with a sharp intake of breath, lathered up soap and scrubbed his face. He stripped off his clothes, pulled on his pajama pants and T-shirt, and hurried back to the bedroom.

A movie played in his head of his first night with Ella, the taste of her, the smell of her, his hands shaking as he'd started to unbutton her black fitted shirt, which she'd left open to reveal a hint of lacy black bra. All evening at dinner, he had thought only of removing it. By the time they returned to the flat, Ella was drunk. Not fall-down drunk, but tipsy enough to raise the level of her giggle and cause her to sway against him as he fumbled to unlock the front door. Their first time was on the hall floor; the second time was on his flatmate's sofa. The third time, they made it to his bed, where they stayed all weekend. The toast crumbs had lingered longer.

He moved around the edge of the bed like a crab, hand over hand. The cotton sheet was as cold as steel, their Tempur-Pedic mattress as solid as concrete. Had it frozen? Slowly, he lay down and huddled under the duvet, his limbs desperately searching out pockets of warmth.

Once the blood started pumping freely to his fingers and toes, Felix eased himself up onto his elbow. Ella was curled on her side, facing away from him. He wanted to touch the back of her neck, to run his fingers through her hair, but he didn't.

On New Year's Day, he'd started a research file for their twentieth wedding anniversary—a trip of a lifetime that would take three years to plan. Tomorrow he would destroy the file. They would go nowhere. There was only one thing he wanted for his twentieth anniversary: for his wife to live. And to mark that, they didn't need to travel to the end of the world. All they needed was a weekend in bed that left behind a smattering of crumbs.

Felix pushed aside one of Ella's pillows and slid his arms around her waist. Gently, so as to not hurt or wake her, he eased her back against his thumping heart.

He curled his legs under hers, and his mind stilled.

The heating chugged through the overhead vent and the clock on the cable box flashed 6:00 a.m. Power was back, but Ella's side of the bed was empty and cold. Felix sat up and listened. She wasn't in the bathroom. Where was she?

He jumped out of bed and raced into the living room. She was sitting on the sofa, hands folded in her lap, staring at the dead fire. Her pose, that of a woman wearing stays, was oddly uncharacteristic. All those years spent hunched over pieces of jewelry had wrecked her posture. She never sat bolt upright; she rarely sat straight. She was a woman who tucked and folded herself into every chair.

"Ella, what on earth are you doing out here?" How did she get this far by herself?

"There are things I need to tell you," she said quietly. "Things I should have told you years ago. Things you have a right to know."

"And you want to tell me now?" Felix had never believed in spousal sharing. Marriage was more delicate than a hothouse flower. It should exist under a dome of glass, protected from the elements, not exposed to the storms of truth: *My father whipped me; I'm about to lose my job.*

Ella nodded but didn't turn. "The conversation last night, the realization that I can't hide from the future, that Harry will leave home and I won't be there to keep him safe. I'm not ready to let him go, Felix, to let the world dig its claws in. Adults get bullied, too, you know."

"Ella, keeping him close isn't the answer, either. It still singles him out as different. We have to let him do this."

"I know. He has to move forward and so do we—so do I." She paused. "I have to move through the rest of my life with no regrets."

"You have regrets?" He forced himself to swallow. She'd had an affair; she wanted to leave him; she didn't love him. Had she ever? He'd never deserved her, never.

"You've always had such faith in me, Felix. But it's a burden I can't carry anymore."

Felix leaned over the back of the sofa and dug his fingers into the padding. Whatever she confessed, he mustn't lose his temper; he must keep her calm. "Did—did you have an affair?"

"No, no! Goodness, no." She swung round and grabbed his arm. "But you think I'm such a good mother. And I'm not. I haven't been."

"Codswallop!"

"Please just listen." She guided him round the end of the sofa, but the moment he sat, she curled away from him, resting her head on the sofa arm.

"When Harry was little, I used to pray for him to sleep all the time, because the moment he woke up, I was in hell. He had no fear. He trusted everyone and he never stayed still. He was an uncoordinated dynamo—a wrecking ball. Other parents at birthday parties muttered about bad mothers unable to handle their kids. Strangers in supermarkets said the same thing. And during the rage attacks there were days"—she lowered her voice—"when I struggled to love him."

Felix kept still.

"I used to dream about having ten minutes to myself, ten minutes without being dragged into some crisis: 'Mrs. Fitzwilliam, your son kicked little Johnny.' And then we hit middle school, and I had a different set of worries. Would academic pressure trigger new tics? How would he cope with standardized tests? Could I get him extra time? Throughout school, I had to supervise, oversee, question. Did the school have enough backup meds; was the new teacher giving him the breaks he needed; was he getting enough sleep to manage his stress? Had someone made fun of his tics?"

Felix reached for her cold bare feet. He eased them onto his lap and started massaging warmth back into them.

"And thanks to you," he said, "our messy, unfocused son has a level of self-confidence I could never have imagined at his age. He's in love, he has devoted friends, and he's trying to take control of his future, all because you taught him to believe in himself. You laid the foundation for the young man who's developing before our eyes. He's going to be fine." *Provided he takes his afternoon Ritalin pills.* "You've given him the tools he needs to be Harry. Now you have to let him find his own way."

"There's more." Ella raised her head and glanced to the hallway, where a single night-light burned outside Harry's closed bedroom door. "During the rage attacks, I felt dead inside. I wasn't sure I could be his mother. I wasn't sure I could be anyone's mother." She lowered her voice. "I looked into a residential home."

"You"—*stay calm, Felix*—"considered sending our son away?"

Ella yanked her feet from his lap and sat up. "I have no excuse. Nothing I did worked, and I thought that maybe all those people who'd judged and criticized had been right—that I was the problem, that if he got away from me, he might have a chance. For so many years, I wanted to be a mom—and then I was filled with nothing but failure and doubt. What kind of a monster considers sending her child away?"

"Sometimes residential care is the answer. It's not a statement about parenting; it's a question of need. Imagine if we'd had other children to consider."

"I was grateful we didn't."

Felix threw himself back against the sofa. "You should have come to me—you should have told me what was going on. And I should have helped out more. I failed you and Harry in those years."

"No. You didn't. We made an agreement, remember? You did your job, I did mine."

And it was a bad agreement. He never should have accepted her terms. "Do you know when I fell in love with you—really fell in love?" He rolled his head toward her. "When I watched you become a mother. Nursing Harry, rocking him to sleep, singing to him. No one with my upbringing would ever want children, but you showed me something I'd never seen before—unconditional parental love." He reached for her hand and entwined their fingers together. "Ella, please never doubt what an incredible mother you are."

"There's more." Ella stared straight ahead. "I couldn't figure out how to tell you. And then I was scared you would overreact, and then I thought maybe it didn't matter, but it does. The heart attack has taught me that everything matters. And then Harry, talking about comfort zones. You need to know . . ."

"Know what, Ella?"

She drew in a deep breath and nodded at the painting above the fireplace, the vile picture of Ella distorted into *The Scream*. "That sums up how I felt after Mom died. And then I met you and the screaming stopped. When my thirtieth birthday came around, I knew what I wanted." Ella withdrew her hand and slowly turned toward him. "I wanted a child; I needed a father."

"Wait, wait." Felix shot up. "Are you telling me that the pregnancy wasn't an accident? You set me up?" To hell with staying calm.

"This is why I never told you. I wasn't trying to set you up. I was in love, I thought it was hopeless. You'd told me you never wanted a family, but I wanted a child desperately—and I was prepared to raise him alone. I never expected you to turn up in America with your grandmother's engagement ring. Once you were here, in the States, I couldn't risk losing you. After that, it all happened so fast—the wedding, Harry's birth, the craziness of life with a newborn. And then somehow it seemed irrelevant. We were a family. Did it matter how we became one?"

"But he's seventeen." Felix dragged his hands through his hair. "Why didn't you tell me after he turned five or twelve? We even talked about this while you were in hospital. I gave you the perfect lead-in." Yes, he was angry. He was flat-out furious. How could she have done this? He collapsed back on the sofa. "Good God, Ella, there must have been a thousand opportunities to tell me in seventeen years."

"But I chose you to be the father of my child," she said, and picked at her thumbnail. Even her beautifully shaped nails were split and broken these days. "Isn't that all that matters? I chose you, the person who caught me when I was falling. I chose you, Felix."

"You chose me," Felix repeated.

She chose me. All these years he'd been wrong! She hadn't married him because it was the best decision; she'd married him because she wanted him. *Him.* She had chosen *him.* He laughed and locked his arms around her like a safety harness.

"You're not mad?"

"Don't you see?" He was still laughing. "The pregnancy was the excuse I needed to get on a plane and follow you. I had no angst over my decision. I had nothing but relief, relief that we could be together, that I didn't have to wait for you to reject me. I chose you, too, Ella Bella. Don't you see? We chose each other."

"No, you did the honorable thing. You married me because you have an overinflated sense of right and wrong."

"I married you because I was passionate about you. Because you were the sexiest, most intriguing, most beautiful woman I had ever met, and for some unknown reason, you appeared to want to spend your life with me. I followed my heart, and I would do it again. Here, now, the morning after Valentine's Day, I choose you." He pulled her closer still. Breathing in lavender, he kissed her hair. "I choose you for the rest of my life."

She draped her arm over his thigh. "Even though I look like death on a stick."

"You're beautiful and sexy, and you always will be. You can't hide it, Ella. The only thing that prevents me from jumping your bones right now is the realization that sex would probably kill both of us." He stroked her cheek, smooth as porcelain, cold as marble. "On the other hand, what a way to go."

"Not for Harry. He'd find us."

"And need even more therapy. Ella, I'm sorry—for not being a better husband, a better father. For not being someone you could trust with the truth."

"Do you have any secrets to wipe clean?"

Felix eased himself out of her embrace, stood, and adjusted the thermostat on the wall. "Let's continue talking in bed while the house warms up." He held out his hand; Ella took it.

"It's been a while," she said, "since we just talked."

They stopped outside the spare room, and he put his ear to the door. "Snoring soundly," he said. This constant concern for others was a strange new feeling. He still couldn't decide whether to categorize it as good or bad. He made a move toward their bedroom, but Ella didn't budge.

"Forty-eight percent of women don't survive their first heart attack," she said. "Do you ever wonder why I survived, Felix—why I'm not in the forty-eight percent?"

"No. It's a statistic. Nothing more." He might have shared the truth once with Harry, but he would never say, *Ella, I'm terrified.* Fear had always been something he'd wrestled alone. Besides, from now on, he was choosing a different path, a different attitude.

"Tell me it's going to be okay," she said. "The future, I mean. Please."

"I can't." He kissed her—a kiss that wasn't a prelude to sex, to good-bye, or to hello. A kiss that screamed *mine*. From now on, he would kiss her every day—and take the time to do it right.

The house hummed back to life: the fridge gurgled, ice dropped from the ice maker, the hall floor creaked as if a ghost were walking toward them. The wind must have shifted. The flue was still open, and a sudden draft came from the fireplace, bringing a strong smell of wood smoke.

"Things might never be the same." Felix combed his fingers through her hair. "They might be a little harder, but you're still Ella Bella. And this—what we have here, right now—this is good."

"You've discovered mindfulness?"

"I've discovered the world according to Eudora."

Finally, Ella smiled. "Maybe she really is Mary Poppins."

They lay side by side, facing each other as the morning light filtered through the gauze blinds. Outside a solitary bird sang the dawn chorus.

"The wood thrush is awake," she said, turning away from him. "Do you remember why I agreed to buy this house?"

Was that a trick question? "Because the camellias were blooming?"

"That was part of it, yes." She turned back with a smile. "But it was also because of the light in this room. When the sun hits our bed around mid-morning, and Harry's in school and you're at work, it's my guilty pleasure to sneak in here and lie down for fifteen minutes."

"A power nap?"

"An excuse to shut out the world and just *be*." She exhaled—a long, slow release. "Felix. You've been amazing. Thank you."

"I have another Valentine's Day gift. More of an idea, really. I was thinking about turning the shed into a workshop for you."

"So I could make jewelry again?"

He nodded. "After the heart transplant, after you've healed. What do you think?"

Ella wiggled her lips from side to side the way she did when she was thinking. "I'd like that."

As the heat continued to vibrate through the ceiling vent, her fingers traced patterns on his chest. Felix closed his eyes.

"Take off your T-shirt," she said. "I want to touch skin."

"I don't think that's a good—"

Ella put a finger to his mouth. "*Shhh*. Take it off."

He did; and Ella burrowed into his naked chest. "Now it's your turn to open Pandora's box," she whispered between butterfly kisses. "Start by telling me why you disengaged from the family. It was long before Harry was diagnosed."

"It's hard to focus when you're . . ."

"Do you want me to stop?" Her voice sounded breathy.

"God, no," he groaned and, pulling Ella's face up to his, kissed her gently. Then he flattened his hand over her heart. "But your heart's running a marathon. We can't do this."

"I know."

She snuggled into him, and Felix started to talk. Words spilled out, about spanking Harry, about the fear that he could become his father. And then Ella asked, as he knew she would, about the scars, about whether Tom had them, too. And Felix told her everything. For Ella he relived the memories, even the one he'd never shared with Tom.

"Did your mother know?" she said.

"I have no idea. Marriages are full of secrets."

"Not ours. Not any longer."

He began to tap his palm, jabbing himself with his fingernails despite the pain. Ella reached for his hand and kissed the tips of his fingers one by one.

"What aren't you telling me?" she said.

"I stepped down from the partnership this week. After your transplant, I plan to leave and set up by myself."

"Felix, no. Your job means everything to you."

"You mean more. Things have changed, and I have to adapt. Something else I've learned from Eudora." Felix tweaked her nose. "What if we've been given a gift?"

"Are you serious? I have a near-death experience, and you become the family optimist?"

"Apparently so. Tom is turning in his grave."

Ella gave a wheezy laugh.

"What if this bizarre period in our lives is a second chance to help us find everything we've lost? Help me face my fear of being a father. Help you find your way back to that dream of a little jewelry shop."

She snuggled into his chest, and gradually her breathing fell into the gentle flow of untroubled sleep.

He'd had such hopes for Valentine's Day, and it had surpassed every one. Despite the circumstances that had brought them together as a couple, there had been nothing accidental about their marriage. She had chosen him, just as he had always chosen her. "I chose you, Felix."

Buzzed, Felix vowed to stay awake—the keeper of this most perfect moment.

THIRTY-FOUR

Harry jiggled from foot to foot outside the women's restroom. What was taking Sammie so long? The movie would be starting. Not that he really cared if they missed the beginning. Or the middle. Or the end. He was here only to sit in the dark and hold Sammie's hand. Maybe sneak in a kiss. For the first time since Mom's heart attack, life felt normal. He was on a date! Like every other hot-blooded American guy on a Saturday night. Except for Max, their designated chauffeur, who was wandering across the lobby shoveling fistfuls of popcorn into his mouth.

"Giving up my Saturday evening for true love," Max had said earlier. He'd also told Harry he and Sammie could sit in the back of the car and make out, but Harry had *some* pride. He let Sammie sit up front on the way there but leaned forward to hold her hand. Well, as far forward as the seat belt would allow. Touching Sammie meant anchoring himself in pure happiness. He wanted to be with her forever and ever and ever. Times infinity.

A cute emo chick by the concession counter eyed up Max. Harry tried to signal with his head.

"What?" Max said loudly, spitting out bits of popcorn. The emo chick made a face and disappeared into movie theater one.

"Cute girl was *sooo* eyeing you up, dude. Before you regurgitated half a ton of popcorn."

Max snorted. "We'll find plenty of hot babes in Boston. Still can't believe your parents said yes. This is going to be rad."

"I don't want a hot babe. I have Sammie. Besides, college girls aren't going to give you the once-over. We're high school juniors. The lowest of the low."

"I guess." Max slumped back against the wall with one foot propped up, looking every inch a rock star. Or maybe a beat poet. "You do realize if you go to college near Boston, you'll be freezing your balls off for six months of the year. And I won't visit to protect *mine*."

"You're such a southerner."

"Last time I checked, so were you." Max glanced at the women's restroom. "Ever wonder what takes them so long?"

"A more complicated process, I guess."

Max grunted yeah. "Hey, your dad's pretty chill these days. You never told me he was a Joy Division fan." Max slotted the popcorn bag under his arm and picked at his bright-blue nail polish.

"He is?"

"Yeah. Overheard me singing 'Love Will Tear Us Apart' and said it was one of the few songs he'd liked at our age. A man of most excellent musical taste."

"Dad's not really into music." Harry's phone blared with the clown horn that drove Dad nuts. Mom had started texting him again. Like, all the time.

When will you be home?

we just got here movie starts in five

```
Right. Sorry. Fell asleep. Dad had
to run into the office. Some crisis
with Curt. Eudora says hi. She wants
to know if you and Max will go and
see a sci-fi movie with her next
week.
```

Mom didn't really understand texting. Her messages were more like emails. Crazy long.

```
sure!!!
```

```
<3 Text me before you leave.
```

"Your mom again?" Max said.

"Yup." Harry put his phone on "Mute." "This trip is making her super nervous, and now I'm super nervous—and worrying about whether it's putting too much strain on her heart and if she's going to end up back in the hospital. Last night, she created all these scenarios of stuff that could go wrong and asked me how I would handle them."

"Yeah. You and me on a road trip. What's to worry about?" Max grinned. He hadn't inherited a single worry gene. "And your dad?"

"Seems pretty laid-back about the whole thing. Go figure."

"Did you tell either of them about the other part of your plan?"

"No way." Harry paused. "You didn't tell your parents, right?"

"Duh. I've been keeping your secrets since we were mere blobs in diapers, my friend. Mere blobs. Why change the habits of a lifetime?"

"We were out of diapers."

"Irrelevant." Max swept away the comment, apparently forgetting he was holding a large bag of popcorn. Kernels scattered over the carpet. "My life began the moment you shared your juice box with me on the jungle gym. Complete with a healthy serving of Fitzwilliam drool."

Harry gave him a high five, and then Sammie came out of the restroom and grabbed his hand and he nearly dissolved into a puddle of happiness. Life was looking pretty good about now. Even though he secretly agreed with Mom. A thousand things could go wrong with this trip, and underneath all those worst-case scenarios? He was scared to death.

THIRTY-FIVE

Wired—he was wired with heart-thumping, sweat-making, head-pounding nerves. Could a guy chew himself raw?

Harry threw his boxers into the bag and tried to pay attention to Mom, who was sitting wrapped up in the big chair. Supervising with a list. She used to give Dad a hard time about lists, but she was a list maker, too.

He chucked in the pair of backup shoes she'd insisted he take. He'd be gone three days. Why would he need a second pair of shoes? "In case anything happens to the first," Mom had said. Nope. Didn't get it. His elbow flapped; his tongue clicked against the roof of his mouth.

Mom sighed an overly dramatic sigh. "Shoes and heavy stuff should go on the bottom, sweetheart. Do you have your meds?"

"Meds! Right. Knew I forgot something."

Mom groaned.

Was Max here yet? Would Sammie miss him? How much would she miss him? Flash thought to the unopened box of condoms hidden in his bathroom.

"Nervous?" she said.

"A bit." He cleared his throat. Telling the absolute truth would make everything worse. Shitstorm worse. Panic-attack worse.

"If you get anxious at the gate, you'll text me, right?"

"Yup!" Lots of bravado crammed into that one word. Lots! "Ready for my swashbuckling adventure." *If I don't throw up my breakfast first.*

Mom twizzled her wedding band. "And if you get anxious on the runway, do the same. Even if they've told you to turn off your phone."

Another big, fake smile. "You told me this already, Mom."

"And don't forget to go to the bathroom before they start boarding."

Okay, enough. "Mom, I'm not a little kid anymore."

"Sorry, I'm turning into such a ninny."

"I can do this, Mom." Double thumbs-up.

"I know. You'll have a wonderful time, and Dad and I will be nervous wrecks."

Somehow he doubted that last part—about Dad. Although Max was right. Dad wasn't so bad these days. And it was a helluva lot easier dealing with him over the trip. Mom fussed about every little detail, made him twice as anxious.

Harry tossed in his black jeans. "I love you, Mom. And I'll be fine. Stuff never freaks me out when old Maxi's around."

Max never fussed. *Hallelujah!*

Mom's smile was as convincing as Dad acting out exuberance. "This is a huge step for you." She twisted her hands together. Around and around, like she was trying to create knots.

She doesn't think I can do it.

"I promise if anything goes wrong, even the slightest hiccup, I'll call home." Harry switched to his Darth Vader voice. "I'm off to fulfill my destiny." He paused. "But I'll worry about you the whole time." What if something happened to her while he was gone?

"I'll worry about you, too. That's what mothers do." Mom tugged her little-old-lady cardigan around her shoulders. "Time for a pact—neither of us will worry about the other one."

"Most excellent plan." Harry threw in his toothbrush.

"Uh, no." Mom sounded more Mom-ish than she had in weeks. "Put it in a Ziploc bag, Harry." She nodded at the pile of plastic bags Dad had left out.

Dad stuck his head around the door. "Can we speed it up? Max just arrived." He stared at the half-packed suitcase. "You do realize he's just going to dump it all in on the way home, Ella, which makes the packing lesson utterly pointless." He turned to Harry. "Money. Credit card. Phone charger. Do you have your photo ID?"

"Check, check, and check." Harry pulled out his new wallet and waved his learner's permit.

Dad scooped up the remaining clothes, put them in the bag, smoothed them out, zipped it up. "Let's go."

"Bye, Mom!" Harry darted at Mom and kissed her cheek quickly. Then he grabbed his travel backpack, the one he always took to England because it was superlight and squishable and could go under any airplane seat and still leave him tons of leg room, and ran after Dad.

"Wait, Dad!"

"What?" Dad turned with his Medusa stare.

"Do *you* think I can do this?"

"Pack a bag in a logical manner?"

"No. Get on a plane by myself and fly to Boston."

"You're not flying by yourself. You'll have Max."

"That's right, dude!" Max called out from the living room.

"But you think I can do this?"

"I hardly would have agreed to fund something I believed was destined to fail, would I? Yes. I believe you can do this. But whether you'll return with all your possessions remains to be seen. And please don't let some pickpocket steal your wallet."

Just once, wouldn't it be great if Dad gave a vote of confidence minus the critical add-on?

THIRTY-SIX

The plane rattled down the runway. Was it even airworthy? Would bits drop off? Harry imagined himself trapped inside some alien science experiment that shook humans around as if they were stones in a rock tumbler. Was he going to barf? Suppressing the urge to be a total wuss and grab Max's hand, Harry gripped the armrests. So many things could go wrong during takeoff. Even more on the final approach.

Sixteen percent of fatal crashes occur during takeoff and initial climb, twenty-nine during approach and landing.

What would happen to Dad if he *and* Mom died? Would Eudora look after him?

"Dude!" Max said. "Look at the view."

Harry shook his head. No, no, and no. That meant opening his eyes. Boarding hadn't been so bad 'cause Max had talked nonstop about how far he'd progressed in *Assassin's Creed IV*. But now they were in a metal tube in the air. About to fly too close to the sun and die.

"If humans were meant to fly, they'd have wings, right?" Like that had helped Icarus. Harry screwed his eyes shut even tighter.

Max leaned in close. "Your dad said I should remind you to take another Klonopin on the plane. You did, right?"

"Not working. Not yet."

"Pop another one."

"No, dude." Harry opened his eyes and stared at the headrest in front of him. He had a strange desire to kick the seat again and again, to see how many times he could kick it before the large businessman squashed into it noticed. "Took two already."

"Take a third."

"Can't. These are serious meds. Two is my max, Max." *Shit a brick.* He was going to die without holding Sammie's hand one last time, without smelling her hair, without tasting her breath.

"C'mon. What's there to get anxious about?" Max started humming Green Day.

Harry tapped his leg. Tap, tap; tap, tap.

"We're going to rock that campus. And hey—we're not in school! Love that a college visit is an excused absence." Max paused. "I need to get me a few more of these," he said in his best redneck accent. Max, with his finely tuned ear for any sound, had a whole repertoire of accents.

"When're you going to tell your parents the truth?" Harry said.

"About not going to college?"

"No, that you're pregnant. *Duh.* Of course college."

"Figured I'd wait until after spring break; otherwise, they'll stop me from touring with the band. Thankfully, they're not as anal about the college shit as your parents. Dad's too busy figuring out his soccer coaching schedule; Mom's too busy with some corporate takeover. When they're not doing either/or, they're pecking away at poor Dyly. He's much happier when he's alone with me. Our boy Dyly is pretty chill."

Maxi-Pad was a good big brother. The best. Dylan adored him. "The band really going to tour over spring break?"

"Yup. Well, Greensboro counts, right?"

"Sure does, dude." Harry never doubted that Max was going to be mega famous one day. "Why do parents have to make everything so hard?"

Max held up his fingers and curled them into animated bunny ears. "Parents know best."

"Your mom'll go apeshit when she figures out you're not on track to be the next Albert Einstein."

Max shrugged. He pulled out his iPod and scrolled through a play-list. "Math's great and all that, but who grows up and says they want to be a math teacher? Since I was five years old, I've been telling the parentals I want to be a rock star. It's hardly my problem they never listened." Max reached into his messenger bag and then scribbled in his lyrics notebook. "Idea for a song."

Knowing better than to interrupt pure genius, Harry started counting backward from one hundred in his head. He tried to focus on the soothing roundness of numbers and not the impulse to kick the seat in front of him.

"Here's the problem with the older generation, my friend." Max put his notebook away. "They don't understand passion. They just want to bring home the bacon. Yada, yada, yada. If I have the commitment to try for a career in music, and if I want to bust my ass trying, surely it's on my back if I fail. But I'm not—gonna fail." Max grinned. "Are you going to sing with us next Saturday?" He jabbed Harry with his elbow. "Sammie'll be impressed. C'mon, man, you have a great voice. Time to get you in the limelight."

"And what if I tic and send cymbals flying?"

"I'll walk you across the stage with my arms wrapped around you. People will assume we're gay. I'd be down with that."

The plane lurched and Harry hugged his stomach. "It's all irrelevant if we die in the air." Had Mom felt this way on the flight from Florida? Had her life flashed before her eyes? Had she thought of him and Dad before she'd passed out? Harry rubbed his eyes with the heel of his hand.

"Thinking about your mom?"

Harry nodded. "Can't stop, you know."

"She going to be okay?"

"I don't know, man. But I'm going to prove to her—and to Dad— that they can stop worrying about me. They make everything about me all the time. And I get it, I do. I know it's not easy being the parents of the kid who's different, but big newsflash: it isn't all about Harry."

"Amen, bro."

"And besides, I'm okay with this shit."

"I know you are, dude. I'm proud to have a best friend with seri-ously fucked-up brain wiring. Makes you fucking interesting. Now, some people think love of math and love of punk music both fall under the category of mental illness. Guess that makes me, you know, extra challenged. And the perfect person to share your Boston shenanigans." Max wiggled his head back and forth with his Frankenstein expression.

The second Klonopin kicked in, snipping the edge off all that worry. It was still there, but tucked away, like a chocolate bar you were saving to gobble after school. Yeah, they were going to have some she-nanigans. What could possibly go wrong?

THIRTY-SEVEN

Killer hike across campus to the freshman dorms. At least, it was when you believed you would never, ever be warm again. For the rest of your life. Harry looked up at the snowcapped, old-fashioned streetlamps and perfectly snow-laden trees. He and Max could have fallen through time into some made-for-TV Christmas movie. Although they stuck out like a pair of mutant misfits—the only people in the group of prospective students and parents not dressed in their Sunday best.

The tour guide led them through a decorative gateway that could have been the entrance to Saint John's crumbling historic mansion. Off to the left, the white spire of a chapel shone against the brilliant blue sky. Did everything here shine?

The campus was beautiful. Well, Harry knew that before he came; he'd done his research. Dad never expected him to have his shit together, but Harry was about to prove him wrong. *Very wrong.* He'd even taken the afternoon Ritalin pill so he could tone himself down a notch. Plus a Klonopin for the anxiety.

The thing about having anxiety issues was that you had to prepare, head things off at the pass. It was the opposite of the ADHD impulses, which made him super distracted. Sometimes he felt as if two warring ferrets were loose in his brain. Sometimes Tourette's was the easiest thing he had to deal with.

Harry shoved his hands into his jeans pockets. No way did he own clothes warm enough for this place. There was more snow on the ground than he'd ever seen in North Carolina. He had to swallow the urge to scream, "Look at the snow, y'all!"

Max had no interest in the campus, but he was still on the hunt for babes, which seemed utterly pointless since everyone was muffled in so many layers it was hard to tell who was male and who was female. Plus they had to be back in Boston at five o'clock. Mom's friends were taking them out for dinner.

Beautiful setting; didn't feel like him. Felt a bit daunting, if Harry was being truthful. Mom always talked about listening to her gut. He'd never really done that before—never really had to, since his life had been bound in Bubble Wrap. Yup, seventeen years of predictable, safe living, if you eliminated the rage attacks. No major decisions to make, ever. Now he had to find his own instincts.

What did he feel? Harry concentrated. *Freezing.* He imagined Dad's voice: "It's a bit nippy." Okay, different track. Could he see himself here?

No. He felt out of place. Maybe that was his answer; maybe that was his instinct.

The student leading the tour was pretty—not hot, not Sammie cute. A bit preppy. She stopped, and her eyes lingered on Max for a second too long. And just like that, Harry's decision was made. He was not interested in a place that could judge his best friend by the way he dressed. Yes, Max was a punk, but he was also a math genius. As smart as anyone on this campus.

The pretty girl swept her arm to the left and said something about the Science Center being shaped like an old Polaroid camera from the side. She caught Harry's eye, and he gave a restrained smile. He'd never cared what people thought of him—take me or leave me was *his* attitude—but pleases and thank-yous mattered. Both his parents had taught him that.

Maybe they should just break off from the tour, catch the shuttle back to Boston, feel their fingers and toes. Man, would he ever get warm again?

"She's hot," Max muttered.

Harry rolled his eyes. "She keeps looking at you as if you're a Martian."

"I know. How fucking cool is that?"

The boys giggled; the girl glared. Max yawned.

The girl started spouting facts and figures and dates. Then she said, "Let's walk."

"Yes, let's," Max replied loudly.

Harry giggled into his hand. Pretty girl was probably memorizing their faces, adding their names to some huge admissions blacklist. The admissions equivalent of Twitter jail?

"Dude," Harry whispered, "she's giving us the evil eye."

"You don't really want to come here, do you? Because I am not visiting if you apply and get in. Let's bag it." Max glanced toward one of the red-brick buildings, one of the freshman dorms. Music pulsed through an open window on the second floor. Two girls with long dark hair were leaning over the window ledge, laughing. People were moving in the room behind them. Quite a few people. Friday afternoon party?

A pudgy campus cop with gray, slicked-back hair leaned against a tree, eyes up, watching the same scene. Waiting for someone to screw up. Waiting to find fault, just as Dad always did.

"I can't, man," Harry said.

"I know. But you owe me big for this."

"If you want to go grab a soda, I'll text you when I'm done."

"No way, Jose. I'm going to stay and suffer, and then I'm going to make you feel so guilty that you'll have to perform with us on Saturday. You know, to thank me."

As they crossed the yard, the sounds of partying intensified. A group of students spilled out of the dorm onto the sidewalk. One of them clutched a red plastic cup. He glanced at the cop, dumped the contents on the ground, lobbed the empty cup into a trash can.

"Dude. Let's go party." Max pulled out his fake ID. "Maybe they're selling beer."

"Max," Harry whispered, "we can't head back into the city reeking of alcohol. Besides, I can't drink. I took another Klonopin this morning."

Max routinely chose to forget Harry didn't drink; everyone else assumed Harry drank because he hung out with Max. Amazing how people saw what they wanted to see without taking the time to look.

"Come on, dude. We're here to see student life in all its glory. I bet you'll learn more from talking to a bunch of students than we will from Miss Perfect Tour Guide. She's probably a senator's daughter."

"How do you know she's not a bus driver's daughter and just really, really smart? Like astrophysicist brilliant."

Max shook his head. "Wearing those huge glittery studs in her ears?"

"They could be fake."

"You're not turning into one of those nonjudgmental people, are you? Wait! I forgot. You already are one!" Max slapped his forehead. "Stop thinking nice thoughts. She smells of money." Max raised his hand. "Excuse me, miss."

The entire group stopped walking, and Harry hunkered down into his winter jacket.

"You look *sooo* familiar to me. Is your dad someone, like, mega famous?" Max never used the word *like* for the same reason he used perfect grammar in texts. He was role playing, acting the dumb punk.

"I prefer not to talk about it." Her tone was cautious.

"Let me guess. Senator—"

"Weinsteen. Yes."

Max gave Harry a look. "I rest my case. Go talk to the party animals, dude. I'll be back."

Harry rubbed his arms. He wasn't shy—he'd never been shy—but suddenly he felt awkward, and he just wanted to be home. With Sammie. And Mom and Dad. And Eudora. And Katherine. If someone played "Carolina in My Mind," he would cry.

"Max?" Harry turned around. "Max," he said in a stage whisper. Max had vanished.

"Is there a problem?" Senator Weinsteen's daughter said. All eyes focused on Harry, and he began to tic. Her smooth forehead wrinkled.

"I'm sorry. I have Tourette syndrome." Harry's fingers strummed the air. "And I don't want to disrupt the tour. I think it's best if I excuse myself."

She nodded, her face blank. Was she concerned or relieved? Or had she, like him, spent a lifetime masking facial expressions? Had to be tough being a politician's daughter. She probably had less control over her life than he had over his tics. And wasn't that the point, the whole reason that he and Max had taken this trip?

Yes, he was interested in small, liberal arts colleges, but not Brandeis. (Well, he might be after visiting yesterday.) Harry had come to Boston for one reason and one reason only: to visit Harvard and make a point to Dad. To prove that he was capable of being an adult—that he could listen to both sides, take his father's opinions seriously, but still forge ahead on a path of his choosing.

Yes, I will consider your feelings, but this is my future, and I will make the ultimate decision.

He had seen Harvard, and he didn't like it. This was not the school for him. All he had to do was grab Max—tear him away—and leave.

He couldn't see Max anywhere in the yard, but he didn't need to. Max would have followed the music.

Harry turned back across Harvard Yard and headed toward the freshman dorm that throbbed with life. The old campus cop was still there, acting the sentinel. But he pushed off the tree and watched Harry walk past. Something tightened in Harry's gut, told him it was time to leave. More instinct?

What was Sammie doing? Longing hit like a bullet through his heart. He wanted to be home so bad. Maybe they'd go out to Southpoint Mall again this weekend, hang out at Hot Topic, and catch another movie. Harry stopped, pulled out his phone, sent a text.

miss you

He added lots of smiley faces.

She couldn't text back, not in school, but she'd get the message on the way home. He wished he were in school, where everything was familiar and comforting.

Harry walked up to the main door of the dorm building, the cop's eyes still on him. He could feel them. Could the cop tell he didn't belong? Nothing about this place felt right. It was too big, too over-whelming. Twenty-one thousand students here according to the brochure. He would be lost among twenty-one thousand. Just another hyped-up, ticcing kid.

He stared at the keypad on the door. *Oh.*

"Hey," a girl with glasses said. She stopped and swiped her student ID, then pushed the door open. "Need help?"

"I'm supposed to be on a tour, but I lost my friend. I thought he might have followed the noise."

Something passed over her face. He must have started ticcing. At least she didn't ask what was wrong.

"I'm a high school student visiting from North"—throat clearing; yup, he was definitely ticcing—"Carolina. Sorry, I have Tourette syndrome."

She shrugged. "That's cool. What does your friend look like?"

"A punk. With dyed black hair and blue nail polish. Can't miss him."

"Come on, let's have a look."

He followed her up the stairs, and she chatted away. Was she flirting? He almost said, *I have a girlfriend.* Then realized that would sound stupid.

"What's going on in here?" Harry nodded at the packed dorm room.

"Pregame fever. I was supposed to meet someone." She gave a cursory glance around, as if she didn't much care whether she found the person or not. "Guess he's not here, either."

Harry wasn't sure what to say, so he shrugged.

She juggled the books she was carrying onto her hip. "I have half an hour till my next class. Want to go grab a coffee, and you can pepper me with questions about Harvard?" She gave a really big smile. A great smile. Not as great as Sammie's, though.

Why not? He'd come this far. Was he really prepared to walk away without even completing the tour? "I just have to t-"—Harry cleared his throat—"text my friend."

"It's got to be hard."

"What?" Harry typed fast: where r u

"Doing college visits with Tourette's. Trying to blend in and be anonymous when people stare."

"People have been staring at me since I was a toddler. Doesn't really bother me anymore. My mom taught me that the people who stare and make rude comments are the ones with issues. Not me."

"Good for your mom. I have a brother with cerebral palsy. People stare at him all the time. When I was younger, I hated being out in public with him."

"Maybe people were staring because you're beautiful."

Shit, why had he said that? This place—had to be this place making him all twitchy. "I didn't mean that in a creepy way. I have a girlfriend. But I don't always self-edit. It might be a Tourette's thing."

She held out her hand. "I'm Annie."

He took it. "Harry." Wow. College was going to be tough for him and Sammie. So many hot girls. And she would be surrounded by just as many hot guys at NC State. Where the hell was Max?

"Come on. Let's get out of here." Annie led the way back down the stairs; he followed. Like a lemming.

"Where're we going?" Harry said. "I need to tell my friend."

"What are you interested in for a major?"

"Psychology."

"We'll go to the café in the Science Center, then. The psychology building is straight down the road from there. I can show you."

"Cool. Thanks."

"No problem."

His phone made its clown noise.

Went for a piss, Max texted. Came back, and you'd gone.

meet me in the café in the science building

You ditched the tour? Max typed back.

yup

He nearly told Max about Annie, but suppose Sammie grabbed his phone, which she'd done before, and saw his texts. Would she classify having coffee with another girl as cheating? Had no desire to find out.

They walked down the stairs, chatting. That sense of responsibility Dad claimed he didn't have kicked in: *I'm here; I'm going to do this right.* He would do his research. Ask Annie lots of questions and write down her answers in the notebook Dad had suggested he bring for keeping track of his impressions. He wouldn't put it past Dad to double-check. Crap. He'd left the notebook in the bedroom where they were staying. Could visualize it on the nightstand. He'd have to make notes on a brochure.

They pushed through the door, back out into ice age cold. Harry tugged his jacket around his chest. The wind bit like a flesh-eating monster with sharp metal teeth. The campus cop was still there. The dude hadn't moved. He watched them, which was creepy as fuck. Talk about instincts . . . That didn't feel right. At all.

"Gorgeous day," Annie said.

For real?

"It's been such a terrible winter," she said. "That polar vortex was something."

"Yup. Our county got down to ten degrees one night."

"Ten degrees? That's all?" She laughed. They left the path and crunched through snow, which seemed like a really, really bad idea. She was wearing boots, but he wasn't. Would the snow come over the top of his Docs?

"Why do you want to come here?" Annie asked.

"I don't. But I have good SAT scores." *Actually, I have perfect scores.* "And a high GPA."

"Everyone here does." Annie smiled.

"My dad believes in striving for the best. He thinks anything less than perfect isn't—"

"Aha. Get it. You're here because your dad made you visit."

"Yes and no. He doesn't know I'm here."

"Intriguing."

"It's hard to explain. We have an odd relationship." Harry paused. "But it's getting better."

"Closer to your mom?"

"Yeah." Although maybe that wasn't quite true. Not anymore. He used to be closer to Mom. These days, he went straight to Dad for pretty much everything from pocket money to advice on Sammie.

They walked through another ornate wrought-iron gate. Lots of gates in this place. To keep people in or out? Two students on bikes pedaled by frantically, heads down. Harry looked up into the blue sky framed by leafless trees. No evergreens. If he were here, he'd miss the pines. The grand building off to their right was a doppelganger for the St. Pancras train station in London. *Freaky.*

"Since you bailed on your college tour, I'll tell you that we are now crossing the plaza, and I'm about to show you the best part of campus. Did you know Winnie-the-Pooh lives here?" She tucked her arm in his.

Harry wasn't sure how to react. Annie seemed nice enough. Open, his kind of person, but she was being a bit too friendly. Even by his standards. She stopped in front of a tree stump that had been turned into a little house. The wooden shingle roof was held in place with strips of tin, and a small hand-painted sign above the wooden door read "Pooh"—in red.

"It has its own caretaker, but the history of Pooh's Harvard home is shrouded in mystery. We thought we'd lost it when they cut down the tree in 2012, but it proved impossible to dispossess Pooh Bear. He just had to relocate for a while."

"Adorable." Harry flattened his hand across his chest. The cute factor alone was almost enough to make him change his mind about Harvard.

"I was a total Winnie-the-Pooh nut." Annie giggled.

"Me too," Harry said. A forgotten memory—reading *Winnie-the-Pooh*, but with Dad, not Mom. Dad reading to him at bedtime in Granny's house. From a battered old copy. "Tigger was my guy. Had even more energy than me." Dad had liked Eeyore.

"Definitely time for a hot drink." Annie shivered.

They entered the Science Center, and she paused to stomp snow off her boots. "Let me treat you. What'll you have? Coffee? Tea?"

Yuck. Harry shook his head. "Do they do hot chocolate?"

"I don't know, let's find out."

"Wow," Harry said when they walked into a towering atrium. Sunlight poured through the glass roof to create a play of light and shade on the brick floor. It reminded him of the Nasher Museum of Art, and Dad trying too hard and Harry not trying hard enough. When he got home, he would try hard enough.

"Imposing, isn't it?" Annie said.

Harry craned his neck to look up and around, and then down. "Love the red railings."

Annie smiled. "Come on."

Ten minutes later, they sat on stools at the counter inside the café, and Harry sent Max another text.

```
here but you're not

On my way, dude.
```

"What are you smiling at?" Annie asked.

"My friend uses perfect grammar in his texts. I don't."

"Life's too short?"

He couldn't help it; he thought of Mom. "Yeah, I guess. Thanks for the hot chocolate—and for taking the time to hang with me."

"My pleasure," she said. "I host visiting students all the time."

Harry ransacked his backpack to find something to write on. Pulled out all kinds of shit, including his math notebook. He ripped out a few pages from the middle. "Do you mind if I write things down? I get wild squirrelly and forget stuff." He started to doodle.

"Annie?" A voice came toward them, gaining momentum. Gaining force. "Annie! *Annie!*" The owner of the voice sounded pissed. "Why didn't you meet me in the room?"

A big guy with a military haircut and a seriously puffy jacket that made him look all torso and no legs bore down on them. He was carrying a Styrofoam cup. *How unenvironmentally friendly.*

"Hey." Annie smiled, but it wasn't a smile of happiness. Harry knew fear. He could read it, smell it, feel it, taste it from a mile off. Annie was scared of this guy. That wasn't okay.

The guy frowned.

"Harry, this is Steve." She said his name quietly, like it could sting.

"Her boyfriend," the guy said.

"Hi." Harry jumped up with his hand out, even though Steve seemed more of the hand-breaking than handshaking type. "I'm—" Without warning, his hand shot out in a tic, knocking Steve's Styrofoam cup into the puffy jacket.

"What the fuck!" Steve jumped back. Coffee dripped down his front. Annie went pale; the café went quiet; you could hear people listening.

Annie was on her feet, too, rushing at Steve with a ton of paper napkins. She looked terrified. A girl should never be frightened of her boyfriend. Harry stood up straight. If only Max were here. Max would know what to do; Max would defuse this.

"It was an accident," Annie said quickly. "Harry has—"

"Harry." Steve snarled his name and lowered his face inches from Harry's. Out of the corner of his eye, Harry saw the campus cop from the yard. Was it a coincidence, or was the guy stalking him? He really, really wished Max were here.

"What's your problem? You a spaz or something?"

A spaz? A spaz!

"No, you moron." It had been a long time since Harry had felt rage. Burning, I-will-kill-you rage. It came from nowhere. A sea of red; a wall of fire. "I am not a spaz. I have a neurological condition."

Steve sneered. He *sneered*.

Harry lunged at Steve; Annie screamed. A blurred movement, a smashing sound, a gasp, voices. Rough hands grabbed him, pinned his arms behind his back.

"Take your hands off me!" Harry yelled. "Get your hands off me!"

"Calm down, son," a deep voice said.

Harry's leg shot backward in some weird, contorted tic and made contact with bone. It was like someone pushed a remote control button and all he could do was flail. His limbs began swinging to their own rhythm.

He was on the floor. Facedown on a dirty floor. Someone heavy was on top of him. Harry couldn't stop ticcing. His shoulder was going to pop out of its socket.

"We have a kid out of control. Violent," a man said, and a reply crackled through a walkie-talkie. *The cop?* "Yeah. Kicked me. Call 911."

"No," Harry screamed as loud as he could.

"He's a fucking psycho," said Steve.

"He is not," Annie said. "He's a visiting high school student."

"He tried to kill me. He's crazy."

"He isn't, he didn't." Annie started to cry. He'd made a girl cry. And he couldn't stop ticcing. His head did the violent sideways tic and smashed against the floor.

"Calm down now, son. It's a serious offense to hit a cop. Show's over, everyone." The cop leaned into Harry's ear. "You're coming with me." His breath was rank with stale coffee; his body stank of sweat and cheap cologne. Harry nearly gagged.

Handcuffs clicked.

He was hauled to his feet. Everyone stared as if he were naked. He was used to people staring, but not like this, not like this. Voices blurred and the world turned slowly—images at the end of a kaleidoscope. He tried to open his mouth, tried to say, *I have Tourette syndrome.* Where were those cards he'd made up for the plane? His feet didn't want to move. His legs gave way.

Again he was hauled up. The cop's arm kept him upright. Without it, he would've fallen over. Tumbled to the floor like a piece of trash. Unwanted, thrown away. All he could think about was his bag. Dad had said not to leave things behind.

"My b-bag," he stuttered.

"You might want to be quiet now. Let's just get you out of here, and everyone can calm down."

Annie picked up his backpack.

"What's in the bag?" A second cop? Where did he come from?

Harry tried to speak, but it was too hard. *Woozy, so woozy . . .*

"I'm pressing charges," Steve called out.

"Steve, please let it go."

"Let me handle this, babe. He's a fucking psycho."

"No," Annie said. "I'm a witness. It was an accident."

"Why don't we take this somewhere quiet?" the cop said.

He was being hustled out. Max! Max was there in front of the Starbucks.

"What the fuck?" Max ran over. "What are you doing with my friend?"

"He assaulted a student and a cop."

"He has Tourette syndrome. He sometimes lashes out involuntarily."

"First time I've heard that one," the cop said.

Legs felt all wobbly. Turned back to Max. "Get Dad." The wall behind him was painted lime green. Bilious lime green . . .

"I feel—" Vomit spewed. Over the cop. Splat! Onto the brick floor. Splat! So much vomit. Like he was losing his insides.

"What the hell?" the cop said, jumping back.
And Harry went down.

THIRTY-EIGHT

Felix rifled through the mounds of papers on his desk, temper rising. Curt had been in here. The file he needed for his meeting with Robert was missing, and someone had rearranged his papers. This was not acceptable. No one touched his desk—including the complete wanker who was supposedly taking over his job. In the last week, he had discovered that Curt's ambition did not match his ability. He had no patience for the details of a deal; he was not partnership material. Staying with the company would mean fixing Curt's screwups seven days a week.

His mobile started ringing. Not a number he recognized.

"Felix Fitzwilliam," he snapped and, balancing the phone between his head and shoulder, sifted through another pile of papers.

"Mr. FW, it's me. Max. I got your number from Harry's cell phone."

"Max?" Felix stopped moving. "Is there a problem?"

"Harry's on his way to the hospital with a concussion."

"What!"

"Some fuckbag thought Harry's tic was a punch, and some rent-a-cop came on heavy and he bashed his head—Harry, I mean, Harry bashed his head, and—" Max gulped. "He was out cold, Mr. FW. He's in an ambulance and they won't let me ride with him, but the other campus cop, the nice one, said he'd drive me over and that Harry probably has a concussion and he'll be fine, but I don't know what to do. I don't know what to do, I—"

"Max. Take a deep breath. Is Harry conscious?"

"Yeah, yes!"

"Did he talk to you or anyone else after he came to?"

"I don't think so. He puked like a geyser, and then he collapsed. Wait! I saw him talking to a medic when they put the stretcher in the ambulance."

"Good, that's good. How long ago did this happen?"

Sirens wailed at the other end of the phone.

"Minutes, Mr. FW. Minutes."

"So he wasn't out for long?"

"I guess not. It felt like ages, though. I'm just waiting for the nice cop to come back and drive me over. Harry threw up *everywhere*. And the fucking fuckbag asshole is mouthing off about pressing charges, and there's this really cute girl involved, and they wouldn't listen to me about the Tourette's." Max yelled the last bit. "Ella, I mean Mrs. FW, always said that if—"

"I can't possibly get Ella on a plane, Max." Felix slumped into his office chair.

"No, no! You don't have to. Harry needs *you*, Mr. FW. That's why I'm calling. The only thing he said before blacking out was 'Get Dad.'"

Felix shot out of his chair and grabbed his car keys.

"When you know which hospital they're taking him to, text me."

Max sniffed.

"Can you do that, Max?" Felix slowed his voice down.

"Yeah." Max sounded like a little boy. "What are you going to do, Mr. FW?"

"I'll be on the first flight to Boston." He glanced up at his clock. "When I was making your reservations, I saw a JetBlue flight at six.

Assuming I can get a seat, I'll be on that one. I should land around eight."

Felix opened the office door and waved in Nora Mae. "I need you to be my eyes and ears until I can get there, Max. Can you do that?"

"Yeah, I think so."

"Good. Good lad. Now, when you get to the hospital and Harry is assigned a doctor, you're going to call me again—on this number—and let me talk to the doctor."

Nora Mae gave a small gasp.

"Okay," Max said.

"Harry's a minor. They need to talk with me about insurance, and I need to give them a list of his medications. I also need to tell them he has Tourette's. I don't want anyone thinking he's an epileptic or trying to give him drugs without my permission."

"Wait." Max's voice brightened. "I told the medic about the TS."

"Brilliant. You did brilliantly. Now all you have to do is sit with him until I get there. Tell the doctors you're his brother. I doubt they'll question it. But do not leave his side."

"Harry doesn't like hospitals."

"I know, but he has you. What is it he calls you? Max the Overlord? I officially dub you Max the Overlord, protector of Harry, until I can get there. You up for the challenge?"

"I'm on it, Mr. FW!"

"And Max?"

"Yo."

"Not a word about this to your parents. I don't want them to call the house and talk with Ella until I've figured everything out. Got it?"

"Got it."

The burning rage came from nowhere. A sea of red; a wall of fire. Felix stared out of his sloping glass window into the deserted downtown street below. He needed to chain the monster until he could get to Boston. Then he would kill the person or persons responsible. Beat them to death with his bare hands.

Nora Mae touched his shoulder. "Harry?"

"Has a concussion." Felix turned. "Book me on the next flight to Boston. Use the corporate credit card. If the only seat is in first class, book the ruddy thing. Check JetBlue first. I think there's a flight at six. Tell Robert—"

"Tell Robert what?" Robert appeared in the doorway. He was jacketless with pinstripe shirtsleeves rolled back tightly. Never a good sign.

"Harry's been in an accident." Felix tossed files into his leather briefcase and then slotted in his laptop. "I'm going to Boston to get him. We'll have to do this via conference call tonight."

"You cannot be serious. Curt is completely out of his depth on this deal. Someone else will have to go to Boston."

"And who do you suggest—my critically ill wife?"

At least Robert had the decency to blush.

Nora Mae scowled and said loudly, "I'll go book that flight."

"Thank you," Felix called after her, and tugged on his coat.

"Seventeen-year-old boys get into accidents all the time. I'm sure he's fine. You don't have to rush off like some superhero." Robert fiddled with his suspenders, and in that one second, Felix hated him in a way he had never hated anyone except Pater. Then Robert stood tall. "You can't leave. It's that simple."

"No, I'll tell you what's simple," Felix said with a calm he didn't know he possessed. "My son needs me, and you are in my way. That gives you two choices. Either you step aside, or I will break your jaw."

"But—but . . ." Robert flushed scarlet from the collar of his shirt up to his receding hairline.

"And now I'm going to ask you very politely to leave my office." Felix selected Katherine's number on his mobile. "While I make arrangements concerning my critically ill wife."

"You're going to reimburse me for that flight with interest," Robert said as he marched out.

"Fine," Felix said, and slammed the door.

Katherine answered on the first ring. "Hey."

"Are you sitting with Ella?"

"I certainly am," she said. "Do you want to speak to her?"

"No. Just listen and don't react. Harry's had an accident. He has a concussion, and I need to fly up to Boston."

"Uh-huh."

Good, Katherine understood.

"Tell Ella I have to pull an all-nighter at the office. She won't be suspicious."

"Uh-huh." Katherine varied the pitch of her voice slightly.

"When I know what's going on, I'll call you, and we can decide what to tell Ella."

"Excellent plan," Katherine said cheerfully.

"I'm sorry, I don't mean to put you in the middle again, but I don't how she's going to take this news, and there's no point upsetting her when I don't have the information."

"Oh, don't worry about us. We'll rack up your bill on pay-per-view. Don't work too hard."

And she hung up.

He typed a text.

```
Thank you.

Bring our boy home safe. Don't worry
about Ella. I've got it covered.
```

Felix opened his door. "Nora Mae?"

She was tapping away on her computer. "No seats on the JetBlue flight, but I'm working on something else. Go to the airport. I'll text you the flight details."

Then she shooed him away without raising her head from the screen.

As he ran to the car, he called Ella's friends in Boston and explained he would come by tomorrow to pick up the boys' belongings. Then he broke every speed limit between his office and the airport.

Felix paced the overlit, overheated terminal that was strangely devoid of people. Not a peep from Max since a two-word text with the hospital name: Mount Auburn. Felix had never heard of it.

A little boy with a metal airplane that was not even remotely age-appropriate toddled up to join him at the window, and Felix glanced around the gate. Was the child unaccompanied?

"Look, Mommy!" A pudgy finger pointed at a jet landing on a distant runway.

"I see," a young woman said, and resumed her phone conversation. How could she not be on high alert in a public place? How could she be so careless with her son's safety? Felix watched over the child until he returned to his mother's side, but even so, glanced back periodically to make sure he'd stayed put.

His mobile finally rang. "What have you got for me, Max?"

"Hang on, Dad," Max said with heavy emphasis on *Dad*.

There was some mumbling and scuffling.

"This is Dr. Ramirez. Your rather insistent son won't let me treat your other son until I've spoken with you."

"Felix Fitzwilliam, Harry's father. Harry is seventeen, has Tourette syndrome, ADHD, and anxiety that includes a phobia of hospitals and everything medical, which can lead to panic attacks. He takes Concerta and Ritalin for his ADHD and Klonopin as needed—up to two a day—for anxiety. How is he?"

"Other than a nasty bump to his head, I would say he's doing well."

"What's his prognosis?"

"We're assuming he has a concussion, but since he vomited and is having double vision, I would like to run a CT scan to make sure there's no bleeding around the brain."

"Is that possible?"

"Anything's possible with a concussion."

"I'm not sure how he'll handle a CT scan. He's claustrophobic. Can you delay it for three hours until I can get there?"

"No. That would not be wise."

The airline employee at the gate called first-class boarding. Felix dashed forward, waving his boarding pass. "Can Max, his—um—brother, go in with him? Talk him through?"

"Of course."

"Can I speak to Harry?" Felix said.

"Of course." The guy was all business.

Felix walked onto the jet bridge. It seemed to sway as the vibrations of his footsteps filled the narrow space.

"Dad?" Harry's voice sounded a long way off.

"Hey." Felix swallowed. "How are you feeling?"

"Killer headache."

"I'm boarding, so I'll have to turn off my phone for a few hours. I haven't figured out where the hospital is yet, but I should be there by nine. The doctor tells me you need a CT scan, but Max can go with you—do a song-and-dance routine to keep you amused."

"'Kay. I'm really sorry. Is Mom, you know . . . ?"

"She doesn't know, Harry. One thing at a time, okay?"

"'Kay."

"Hazza?"

"Yeah?"

"I love you."

"Love you too, Dad."

Felix hung up. He would not cry, not here in public with two flight attendants welcoming him onto the plane.

He began to cry.

THIRTY-NINE

Flying—definitely on a par with an unmedicated root canal. Silently, Felix cursed the Wright brothers and anyone else involved in the invention of flying. Man was not meant to leave the ground. And flying at night was the worst. Unless it was the overnight flight to England, and you could see dawn streaking out of the blackness, bringing the hope of morning. Felix glanced around the businesswoman in the window seat next to him. There was nothing but solid night outside the window. No city lights below, no lights from the plane. They were suspended in darkness.

He finished his whisky in one gulp, but even the warm buzz couldn't obliterate the image of an underpaid cop manhandling Harry. Felix sank back into his seat, heart pounding faster than Ella's defective one.

Could the plane not speed up?

He'd paid to use the Internet, not something he usually did, but he needed to stay connected. If nothing else, he could research the hospital, make sure the staff was competent. He scrolled through his email: one from Robert with no subject. Felix ignored it.

Could the plane not speed up?

What if Harry had brain damage? The British actress Natasha Richardson had barely bumped her head during a skiing lesson, had seemed fine, and then had died of an epidural hematoma. He logged onto the Web and started a Google search: *CT scan + brain.* Then he closed his laptop and flagged down the flight attendant for a second whisky. First class had its perks, provided you chose not to think about cost.

Felix raked his fingers through his hair, and his neighbor turned toward him. He closed his eyes on her. *Don't even think about asking what's wrong.*

Mount Auburn. He needed to figure out the location of the hospital. He sat up, flipped open his laptop, typed, and read.

"Mount Auburn Hospital is a vibrant regional teaching hospital closely affiliated with the Harvard Medical School." Harvard Medical School? He clicked on "About Us" for the address. Mount Auburn was in Cambridge? Why had Harry been sent to a hospital in Cambridge? Did he need special care? Or had the boys been in Cambridge when the incident occurred? Today was their down day, a day to sightsee around Boston. Clearly, they had decided to go into Cambridge. A flashback to Harry's apology for calling him a Nazi. Felix had said, "My experience is that people normally speak the truth when they're angry." Angry or upset.

What exactly had Max said earlier? Slowly, Felix replayed their conversation.

Max had mentioned a campus cop. Cambridge plus a campus cop added up to one thing—Harvard. The boys were at Harvard. Harry was on a college visit and he had included Harvard. But why? Why fight the idea every step of the way, and then go to Harvard in secret? Harry didn't have a devious bone in his body. What the hell was he up to?

The flight attendant came back with his drink, and Felix forgot to say thank you. He'd just lost the one good thing to come out of his childhood: perfect manners.

Harry's at Harvard; Harry's in trouble.

Everything that had happened between them since Ella's heart attack had boiled down to his own bullishness about Harvard. Why could he not get his mind off Harvard? Was it merely socioeconomic programming, the belief in the old school tie network and the do-what's-expected-of-you model that had been bashed into him during his formative years? Even now, was he still acting in ways that would have gained Pater's approval? Pater had sent him to hell, and still young Felix would have walked across broken glass barefoot if he'd thought it would have made the old man happy. All he'd ever wanted was to be the perfect son. Nothing he did was ever good enough for Pater; nothing Harry did was ever good enough for him.

Had Harry visited Harvard for the same reason Felix had gone to Oxford—to make his father happy? Felix thumped his head back into his headrest and stared at the airplane ceiling. Why could he not be proud of his son? A straight-A student who would likely graduate valedictorian. A straight-A student who was a good kid. A kid who just wanted to make his father proud. And where had it led him? To the ER.

Max's parents didn't care that Max looked like Marilyn Manson on a bad hair day. Why should he care that his son had Tourette syndrome and couldn't sit still through a movie? Why should he care that his son was messy and chaotic and an indiscriminate hugger? Why should he care that his son was not perfect?

Felix returned to his laptop, typed in *perfectionism*, and hit "Enter." He paused on the fourth listing: "Perfectionism—Personality Disorder."

Personality disorder? Like Pater? Tom had said once, "I don't know whether he's a psychopath, a sociopath, or he just has a personality disorder, but our father is not of sound mind."

Like father, like son?

Swirls danced across his laptop screen—a generic pattern he'd never customized.

His head spun; his heart spun; his stomach spun somewhere up near his throat. The ringing in his ears blocked out the sound of everything but his thoughts. Harry had accused him of being fucked up. What if his son had been right? What if he was stark raving mad? A genuine, certifiable lunatic?

No. Felix took a deep breath. He would be calm; he would be rational. He would be in control. He flexed his fingers and hit the "Return" key. The screen came back to life. He scrolled down. A book was listed: *Too Perfect: When Being in Control Gets Out of Control.*

He clicked on the reviews. One said, "Best book on OCPD out there."

What the hell was OCPD? A form of OCD? But shouldn't he know if he had obtrusive, unwanted thoughts? Wasn't that what defined OCD—you were a slave to thoughts you didn't want and couldn't control? He had no problem with order and control. It was everyone else who had the problem.

He read on: "OCPD is not OCD."

Oh.

Felix huddled forward and angled his laptop round so his neighbor couldn't see. He started a new search: *obsessive-compulsive personality disorder.* He swallowed hard. Personality disorder was the deepest, darkest level of insanity, a whole separate level from barmy, which was the polite British way of saying you belonged in a loony bin. Did he have a personality disorder? Did that make him a danger to society—someone who belonged in the Bates Motel?

Felix downed his drink.

"Can I get you anything else, sir?" The flight attendant took away his empty glass.

Alcohol—the coward's way out. Felix shook his head, shook off the fug of two whiskies. He wasn't a big drinker, didn't like to lose control. Control. His whole life, until Ella's heart attack, had been about maintaining control.

When being in control gets out of control.

He started to read online articles. Everything he could find. He read until the plane began its descent into Logan International Airport. And then he closed his eyes and tried to process the information.

OCPD was nothing he'd ever heard of and everything that was familiar. He had memorized the list of characteristics from the International OCD Foundation's website:

"Rigid adherence to rules and regulations." *Check.*

"An overwhelming need for order." *Check.*

"Unwillingness to yield or give responsibilities to others." *Check.*

"A sense of righteousness about the way things 'should be done.'" *Check.*

"Excessive devotion to work that impairs family activities." *Check.*

A long explanation followed about why OCPD wasn't obsessive-compulsive disorder. He imagined some exasperated person typing, *For the umpteenth time, no. OCPD is not OCD.* The bottom line appeared to be this: people with OCD knew they were crazy; people with OCPD didn't. People with OCD wanted to change; people with OCPD didn't.

He found information about hoarding and frugality, which he preferred to ignore, and a link to Tourette syndrome. All those years wasted looking for answers, for the root cause of Harry's tics, and everything led back to Felix, to the Fitzwilliam DNA.

His midair research had also revealed that most OCPD went untreated. Sufferers were too convinced of their own rightness to believe they needed help. Apparently those who did seek treatment did so only because desperate family members had issued ultimatums: get help or we walk.

Had he driven his family to desperation—caused his wife's heart to fail from the stress of living with him; pushed Harry into an action that had endangered his life? Was his desire for control *out of control?*

He was not losing his family; he was not losing Harry. Their relationship was just beginning—a new chapter, a new day in his life. He would not be Pater, who had died estranged from his sons. He would do whatever it took to be a good father—not a perfect father, but the best he could be. He would be there for his son today, tomorrow, and every day after that. And he'd read that psychotherapy held much promise for people motivated to change. Damn right, he was motivated to change. He was going to hire professional help—the best.

Felix barely noticed the landing, barely noticed the bracing roar of the airbrakes. His attention was fixed on the seat belt sign. The moment it dinged off, Felix was in the aisle with his laptop and his briefcase. He stood first in line to deplane and powered his phone back on. He was going to rescue his son, and nothing would stand in his way.

FORTY

To hell with squirrels in his linen closet—there was a troupe of them cartwheeling through his mind. Felix jostled around in the back of the town car. Anxiety, outrage, terror, shame—which was stronger? How could you mend a broken personality? Wasn't that the core of your being? Did it mean that inside he was defective and contaminated? Rotting away?

And there had been no update from Max about the CT scan. Felix needed those results. He needed to know Harry was okay.

The moment the taxi pulled up alongside the hospital, Felix had to stop himself from opening the door to vomit in the gutter. His hands shook as he paid the cabbie and texted Max.

I'm here.

Max responded with a smiley face that seemed slightly deranged.

Where are you? Felix typed.

Some room off the ER.

Not exactly helpful, but it told him enough. Felix catapulted into an emergency department for the third time in six weeks.

"My son, Harry Fitzwilliam—" He started talking before he reached the check-in desk. Or rather, yelling. He stopped in front of the counter and took a breath. "My son, Harry Fitzwilliam, was brought in five hours ago with a concussion, and I've just flown here from North Carolina." He paused to catch his breath; the bug-eyed receptionist smiled but did and said nothing. He flipped open his wallet, pulled out his driver's license, and pointed at his name. "I need to see Harry Fitzwilliam. Right now. He's a minor. You're treating a minor and I'm his father and I need to see him. Right now."

"Yes, sir." She consulted her clipboard. "Love the accent. Are you from Great Britain or Australia?"

"London. Where's my son?"

More consultation of the clipboard. "I'm saving up for a trip to England. I hear it's very expensive, and I want to see the whole country." She glanced up, her index finger marking a spot on her list. "I think five days should be long enough, don't you?"

Good God.

"Did my son come in with anyone?"

"Another kid. I believe he's still here."

"How about a campus cop?" Felix clenched his right fist. "And a female student?"

"Not that I'm aware of, sir. Do you have any recommendations for restaurants in London? Decent food, not too expensive."

"No. Is he through here?" Felix walked toward a door.

She leaned over her counter. "Hold on, there! I need to buzz you in first. Then turn right, and it's the third door on the left. How about hotel—"

Felix ran.

He opened the door without knocking. Max was sitting in a chair pulled up close to the bed, watching Harry sleep. A very pale Harry.

"Is he okay?" Felix whispered.

"Just dozed off, but I'm timing him. If he's not awake in"—Max glanced at his phone—"another ten minutes, I get to slap life back into him." Max grinned. Even when he smiled, Max was one ugly mongrel, and Harry was blessed, so blessed, to have him as a best friend.

Felix put his briefcase down quietly on the floor, yanked off his tie, and shoved it in his pocket. Then he tugged off his coat and dropped it onto the other chair. Since when had the lining been ripped? Ella had been pressuring him for years to donate the coat to Goodwill, to splurge and buy a new one, and he'd always argued it had years of wear left. Was this a marker of OCPD frugality? Would he suddenly question everything he did, search constantly for flaws in his behavior? *Not now, Felix. Shelve the thought.* He stretched out his neck.

"You've been brilliant, Max. Thank you."

"Here—" Max gestured to the chair. "You sit, Mr. FW."

Harry stirred.

"He's been drifting in and out. I'm not sure if it's the concussion or the shock."

"When did the doctor last visit?"

"A while ago."

"Have you eaten?"

Max shook his head.

"Are you hungry?"

"Famished." Max pursed his lips. "Also starving, ravenous, and anything in the thesaurus that means about to chew off one's fingers."

Felix pulled out a twenty-dollar bill. "Find a cafeteria and get something to eat."

"Thanks. Can I bring you anything, Mr. FW?"

Felix was about to answer no when his stomach growled. "A bottle of water. And, you know what? A bag of salt and vinegar chips if they have any." He handed over another five dollars.

"Salt and vinegar—my favorite," Max said.

"Mine too." *At least they used to be, until I developed absolute control over my eating habits.*

Max stopped in the doorway. "Don't forget to wake him in ten minutes; otherwise, Nurse Ratched will rip you limb from limb."

"Nurse Ratched reporting for duty." A slim brunette with multiple piercings entered the room.

Max turned back to Felix. "She's way tougher than she looks. A total ball breaker, *Dad*." Then he laughed and disappeared.

"You must be the boys' father. Max said we should expect you. I'm just going to take some vitals."

"How is he?" Felix asked.

"Fine, he's doing fine. We're just keeping him in for observation. I'll tell the doctor you're here, and he can go over the CT scan results with you."

"Please tell me—were they clear?"

She glanced toward the door and nodded; then put her finger to her lips and smiled. He could have kissed her. Felix stood up and moved out of her way.

"Harry, sweetheart," the nurse said. "I need you to wake up."

*

Harry woke with a sharp jolt. Shook his head hard. *Ow.* The nightmare still clung. Face shoved into a dirty floor; someone suffocating him. Stale sweat and coffee breath bearing down on him, crushing him. He gasped for air.

"It's okay, Hazza. You're safe." Dad's voice. Was Dad here?

The hospital. Not a nightmare after all. Worse than a nightmare because this was real.

Harry shielded his eyes.

"Are you still seeing double?" the nurse said.

"Yeah." His hand groped air. "Dad?"

351

"I'm here, Hazza. I'm here."

Never thought he'd be so happy to hear Dad's voice.

After the nurse left, closing the door quietly behind her, Dad scraped the chair around and straddled it. He leaned over the back and took Harry's hand. "How're you feeling?"

"Head hurts." Harry tried to pull himself up.

"Relax. We're not going anywhere until the doctor gives you the all clear."

Harry flopped back. "You came."

"You doubted me?"

No. "No. I'm just so happy to see you. When can I go home?" He wanted to be in his bed, under his duvet, away from this waking nightmare.

"Soon." Dad's hand was hot and sticky; he squeezed hard, then let go.

"Mom?"

"She thinks I'm staying at the office all night. Katherine's covering for us. We'll call home tomorrow, and you can tell Mom you're okay. She'll want to hear your voice."

"I can talk to her now."

"Let's wait until you're feeling stronger. Mom doesn't miss much where you're concerned. She'll hear hesitation and worry."

Harry tried to nod, but too much movement and his head might explode.

"Once they discharge you, we'll book into a hotel. You and Max can order room service and sleep in tomorrow. Then we'll pick up your suitcases and head to the airport."

"Are you going to sit up all night watching over me—to make sure I'm breathing?"

"That thought has crossed my mind. How's the head?"

"Sore. Can I get a Tylenol or something?"

"I'll ask the nurse." Dad frowned, then glanced at the call button. "Is the headache worse than before?"

"Holding steady," Harry said. "How much trouble am I in?"

"I'll take care of everything."

"No, I mean with you. Are you going to punish me?"

"Yes?" The nurse's voice crackled through a speaker on the side of the bed.

Dad slumped forward to reply. "Can my son get a Tylenol for his headache?"

"I'll be right in, sir."

"I'm sorry, Dad. I just wanted to impress you. I—" Harry closed his eyes, but opened them quickly. The pain was worse with his eyes closed. "I just wanted you to be proud of me. It was meant to be a surprise. I was going to come home and say, 'Look what I did, Dad.'"

"You did all this—the college trip, everything—to make me proud?"

Harry nodded.

"I am proud of you, Harry. So very proud."

"You are?" He was?

"What you did took real courage. You faced your fears, and you're an inspiration. On the plane, I was trying to figure out why I always want more from you. Why enough is never enough. Why I can't ever say well done. I think you're right, Harry. I think I have"—Dad stared down at the vinyl floor—"problems."

"All the best people do," Harry said. "Normal is vastly overrated."

"I'm going to find a therapist." Dad straightened up. "I want to fix this. I'll do whatever it takes."

"That's great, Dad. Really great." The pounding in his head intensified.

"I found this thing online called OCPD. I think that's what I have."

"Sounds like an STD," Harry said. "What does it mean?"

"I don't know, but I'm going to find out." Dad paused. "And I'm sorry, too. Sorry that you've had to wait seventeen years to hear that I'm proud of you. Sorry that I pushed so hard about Harvard. Sorry that I'm the world's most fucked-up father."

"Yeah, but you're my fucked-up father. The only one I've got. And I wouldn't trade you."

Dad smiled.

Harry rubbed his forehead and tried not to think about the pain bouncing through his brain like a beach ball with spikes. "Dad, can we take Harvard off my college list? I didn't like it even before I got hand-cuffed and knocked unconscious."

"Consider it gone," Dad said.

Talking—just talking—with Dad was good. The Tylenol had kicked in, and the doc was off working on the release papers. And Harry was never coming back to Boston. Not even if Max's band kicked off their first world tour in the city.

"You know the weird thing, Dad? I'm not that anxious about being in a hospital bed. I think I'm all anxiety'd out. Just incredibly relieved to be here and not in jail."

A muscle pulsed in Dad's neck. "Want to tell me what happened?"

Harry told him everything, twisting the edge of the hospital sheet tighter and tighter. "It was all a big misunderstanding, Dad. I didn't really hit a cop. I couldn't control the ticcing. I hit him because I was ticcing, and then I hit my head because I was ticcing."

"I'm going to sort this out, Harry. There will be no repercussions. I'll make sure of that."

"But what about Steve? The last thing I remember, he was mouthing off about pressing charges."

"I can assure you he won't be when I'm done with him." Dad's voice was cold.

Harry's elbow flapped. Maybe he should have downplayed Steve in the role of bastard asshole. After all, Steve wasn't the one who'd thrown the first punch. "Can we just pretend it never happened and hope it goes away?"

"No. You have a neurological condition, and this kid judged you. That is not okay. That will never be okay."

"I'm used to being judged, Dad. As long as no one's pressing charges, I don't care." Harry tried to smile. "How do we find out what's going on?"

Someone knocked on the door. A quiet little knock.

Dad turned. "Come."

"It's Annie," Harry whispered as the door opened.

Chewing her fingernails, she peered around Dad and then darted to the bed. Her eyes were puffy and red, and she hadn't buttoned her jacket right. He hadn't meant to cause her pain, hadn't meant for any of this to happen.

"Are you okay?" Harry said, and patted her hand.

She burst into tears. "You're asking me?"

Then it was hard to tell if she was crying or laughing, but Dad handed her a tissue, and she seemed to pull it together.

"Harry, I'm so sorry." She dabbed at her face with the tissue. "I told the campus cops everything—that it was an accident and Steve over-reacted. I don't think they're going to pursue it, but I made sure they have all my details if they need to contact me. Steve, he's . . . a thug. I've been trying to work up the courage to dump him for months. But what he did today—I'm just so sorry. And I had to check on you."

Oh dear, a fresh round of tears. Dad gave her the whole box of tissues this time. Then he looked at Harry as if to say, *No fucking clue, you?*

"And I tried to come in earlier," Annie continued through her sniffs. "But they wouldn't let me, and then I bumped into your friend Max in the cafeteria. He brought me back here. I'm so sorry, Harry."

Someone appeared in the doorway. Dad stood up; Harry gasped.

He might not be in uniform, but the old dude with really bad hair and a beer gut leaning in the doorway looked horribly familiar. "I was worried about you, kid. I wanted to see how you were faring." He puffed out his chest and spoke to Annie. "Thank you, miss, for setting the record straight. I've written up the incident as a jealous boyfriend overreacting. And apologies to you, son, for not believing your friend when he told us you had Tourette's. I can assure you I won't be making that mistake twice."

"Thank you," Harry said.

"And I brought someone with me." The cop reached back into the corridor. "Figured I'm not the only one who owes you an apology."

"Steve," Annie said, and held the tissue box to her chest like it was a bunch of garlic and her boyfriend was Dracula.

"What are you doing here?" Steve looked angry as fuck.

"So." Dad made a strange smacking noise with his lips. "You're Steve."

Steve didn't look so big and scary anymore. Definitely not Dracula. In fact, barely a cartoon bat from *Scooby-Doo*. He seemed to cower next to Dad, and almost lost his balance completely when Max pushed past him, saying, "Did I miss something?"

"Ah, welcome back." Dad's voice had lightened considerably. "No, you're just in time to hear this young man apologize to Harry. I believe he called him a rather insulting name."

Oh God.

"I'll wait outside," the cop said. "So I can take Steve back to campus when he's done."

"I don't think that's going to be necessary." Dad smiled. "I'm going to keep him for quite a while."

The cop shrugged and left.

"And you, young lady," Dad continued, "need a boyfriend who isn't a bully."

"I'm not—" Steve said.

Dad held up his hand. "I believe it's rude to interrupt, Steve, and I haven't finished. Oh no, I have a great deal more to say. You see, I have no tolerance for bullies. First off, let me tell you what's about to happen here. You are going to explain that you misread an innocent situation and, acting out of jealousy, made false accusations against Harry. Then you will apologize to him, and I will record the entire episode on my phone." Dad's grin was strangely malevolent. "This will be my proof of your wrongdoing. I'll keep it somewhere safe, and if Harry should hear one squeak out of you again, if you track him down on social media, if you make another ridiculous false claim against him, I will post this on YouTube, right before I create a hugely embarrassing scandal about how Harvard treats kids with Tourette's, with you at the center of my publicity campaign. Do we understand each other?"

"You tell him, Mr. FW." Max nodded in the background.

"And when you have finished your apology, you will sit outside in the corridor—with me—and read an online article of my choosing about Tourette's. Hopefully, this will penetrate your thick skull so that next time you encounter someone with Tourette syndrome, you can offer understanding, not dickish behavior."

Steve's face burned scarlet, but at least he had the sense to keep his mouth shut.

"Annie?"

"Yes." She turned big cow eyes on Dad.

Please be nice, Dad.

"Thank you for all you did to help my son."

She relaxed her shoulders. "You're welcome." Then she looked at Steve. "You know what? We're done."

"You're dumping me," Steve said, "because of a high school kid?"

Sirens wailed outside the window. More emergencies, and Harry longed for this one to just be over and done.

"I'm dumping you"—Annie looked at Dad—"because of your dickish behavior."

"Dude, this just gets better and better," Max said, rubbing his hands together.

"Annie, you can't—" Steve said.

"Yes, I can. I should have done it a long time ago." She kissed Harry's cheek. "Thank you for showing me that I deserve better."

Harry smiled and hoped he didn't blush too much. She really was hot. Not as hot as Sammie, mind. He had so much to tell Sammie, but probably not this bit. Or the part about upchucking all over the Harvard Science Center.

Annie left and Steve seemed to shrink into himself. Harry stared down at his hands while Steve squirmed through a brief apology that ended with a dismissive sniff. Even Harry felt sorry for him—until Steve glanced at him with pure hatred. Dad had read the situation well.

"Now—" Dad put a hand on Steve's shoulder and guided him to the door. "If you'll step outside with me, we can begin your enlightenment."

Max gave Dad a high five and then plopped down in the chair. As the door closed, he shoved his feet up on the bed. "That was a beautiful moment, man. And your dad? Fucking awesome."

"Yeah." Harry smiled. This time, his head didn't hurt when he nodded. "He was, wasn't he?"

FORTY-ONE

"Mom, I'm still fine." *Just like I was still fine when you called half an hour ago.* "Better than fine, really. Dad's been amazing. Yeah, I wish you could have seen him, too. Love you lots." Harry hung up and watched Max slouch off to the restroom.

Beyond the huge glass panes, snow had begun to fall sideways. Blowing horizontally at the airport windows, firing like a spray of bullets from a giant Gatling gun. Dad continued to pace, his expression set in a scowl.

Their flight had just been delayed by another half hour. And Dad had become distant, shut down. Impossible to reach. Anxious, if Harry had to guess.

Bored. Harry was bored. Which was fan-fucking-tastic. He'd never been bored at a departure gate before. Tense, frightened, ready to puke, yes. But bored? Was this a glimpse into the world of normal? Shudder at the thought!

Dad didn't look like he wanted conversation, but how Dad looked on the outside rarely reflected what was happening on the inside. One plus one didn't always equal two. Math was not the answer to the problems of the universe. Max would disagree, of course, but Harry had always found math too logical. Too cold; too right versus wrong.

He should say something. Say anything. Act like a Brit and discuss the weather. He tugged out one of his earbuds. "Weather's been total crap this year. Worst ever. I mean—a polar vortex? Isn't that something from a disaster movie? And a Valentine's Day ice storm?"

"I'm ready for spring. Snow in March?"

"Well, this is Boston, Dad."

Dad came over and plonked down in the seat next to him. "Maybe you should stick with a college down south. Better winters."

Harry smiled. That was a very Mom-ish comment. Totally un-Dad. Was Dad trying so hard to be like Mom that he had finally become her? Harry didn't know, didn't care. He liked this new Dad who could be scary as shit when he defended Harry's honor, but also vulnerable. Harry liked vulnerable. Vulnerable, he could do.

Dad crossed his legs, but one of them kept moving back and forth in a quick metronome beat.

Harry put his hand on Dad's leg. "You doing okay? You seem, you know, wound a bit tight."

Dad leaned in toward Harry. "I hate delays." He paused. "How are you doing?"

"I'm good."

Actually, he was good. And strangely calm. Just as well, since the ER doc had said no Klonopin. Or maybe he'd been through so much in the last few days that there was nothing left to worry about. He'd done a college trip without Mom or Dad. He'd been on a plane and he'd been admitted to the hospital—all without his parents. Okay, so the whole thing had been a disaster of near-biblical proportions and he'd almost gotten arrested for assault and battery, but he'd done all those things and survived. And now he was going home. He'd practically lived a whole decade in the last two days. Best of all—he was proud of himself. Maybe he really was ready for the scary stage of life labeled "College."

"I used to hate delays," Harry said.

"How did you cope?"

"Music." He pulled out his right earbud, put it in Dad's ear, hit "Play."

"'Waterfront' by Simple Minds." Dad cocked his head. "It came out the year your grandfather died. After the funeral, Uncle Tom and I took a road trip down to Brighton Beach. We listened to that song over and over on the drive. Tom loved it."

"I do too."

Dad sat back, crossed his feet at the ankles. A slow smile settled on his face. "Would you make me up a playlist when we get home? Joy Division, 'Love Will Tear Us Apart,' some old New Order, 'Waterfront.' That Coheed and Cambria song you're always playing."

"'The Afterman'?"

Dad nodded. "And anything else you think I might like."

Interesting turn of trust. Dad never let anyone choose anything for him. "How do you feel about U2? There's a song called 'Sometimes You Can't Make It on Your Own.' Bono wrote it about his dad. You do know who Bono is, right?"

"Really?" Dad raised his eyebrows, then glanced toward the departures board.

"The other trick—if you're getting super anxious—is to avoid checking the departures board. That gets you locked into the cycle of worry, so, you know, everything escalates."

"You're quite a professional at dealing with all this, aren't you?"

Harry watched his right leg kick to the side. He hadn't been aware he was ticcing. "I don't think about it, Dad. I mean, I've been doing this my whole life."

Dad looked at his hands. "Do people treat you differently when you have a label?"

"Depends. But some people are asshats no matter what."

"I'm not good at letting it all hang out. I can't see myself explaining to someone that I have . . . a handicap."

"Then don't."

"But you do."

"Dad, Tourette's isn't really something I can hide. Most people have me pegged as odd before I've opened my mouth. Tell people what you want them to know." Harry shrugged. "Or don't. It's totally up to you."

"How do you deal, though, when people judge you?"

It was as if the world had melted away to just them and the snowflakes dancing in the black void beyond the airport windows.

"I tell myself I'm not my diagnosis, that I don't really care what people think, just like I don't care that I have Tourette's. It's far more of an issue for you and Mom than it's ever been for me. There'll always be dicks like Steve in my life, but then I have friends like Max. Well, I don't have another friend like Max, but you know what I mean. I think if you do have this OCPD thing, it just makes us two messed-up guys against the world. I'm good with that. How about you?"

"Acceptance." Dad fiddled with his glasses. "That's an interesting concept."

Dad's phone pinged with a text. He shuffled around in his seat, pulled out the phone, slid it back into his jeans pocket.

"Everything okay?"

"Robert. No doubt he wants to talk about my job. As in, whether I still have one." Dad put his phone away.

"You're not going to answer him?"

"No. I'm having a conversation with my son about things that matter."

Harry rested his head on Dad's shoulder. He wouldn't embarrass him with a hug. Dad had his way of dealing with life; Harry had his. It didn't make one right or one wrong. It all boiled down to acceptance.

Dad rested his cheek on the crown of Harry's head.

Harry smiled. Best thing of all? Dad had finally stopped wearing aftershave.

FORTY-TWO

Felix turned off the engine, and Simple Minds stopped playing. What were the chances Harry and Tom would be drawn to the same song three decades apart? Was it merely a quirk of coincidence, or was it a present from the cosmos? Maybe the dead never really left; maybe everything circled round in a big blur, until endings became beginnings and the wheels of life started moving again. Or maybe he just needed sleep.

Extracting himself from Max's house had led to a new level of exhaustion. Max had insisted on a bear hug, and then Max's brother and the family dog had wanted in on the action. Apparently, Felix was now something of a star in Max's world. It was not an unpleasant experience, despite the hugs. Max's dad, Pete, had even suggested they grab a beer sometime. Felix had thanked him and accepted the invitation—even though he didn't drink beer, and Pete was definitely one of those backslapping types who favored sports bars.

Felix stared up through the windshield into the clear night. The stars glittered like polished gems; the moon was close to full, with a wisp of cloud streaked across it in the gentlest of paint strokes. Until he'd moved to North Carolina, Felix had never seen nights as bright and clear, nights that looked as if they belonged in a planetarium display. Beyond his sleeping son in the passenger seat and across the bridge, the warm lights of their house beckoned. Felix smiled. He had brought his son home. Nothing had ever felt quite this good.

Felix released his seat belt and leaned toward Harry. "Come on, Hazza. Let's go see Mom." Should he not have let Harry sleep in the car? Felix had run every worst-case scenario with the doctors before leaving Cambridge. How long, though, before he stopped obsessing over the chance of traumatic brain injury?

For once, Harry woke with a stretch and a yawn, not a jolt. "I'll get the bags."

"Be careful on the bridge," Felix said.

The tree limb that had fallen in the ice storm had taken out part of the railing. Next weekend he would start work on a new bridge using red cedar, and coat it in polyurethane like the rails in Duke Gardens to achieve that rich color. And he would encourage the ivy to wind up the bridge in the same way it wound round the tree trunks. To represent survival.

"Wow, Dad. What a night! Twinkle, twinkle, big galaxy. Or galaxies. Did you see that? Something orange streaked across the sky. What d'ya think? Meteorite or a comet?"

"Good question. Meteorite?"

"Yeah, that's what I think."

Harry gave him a knuckle touch, and they crossed the bridge as Ella's voice called them home. She was framed in the light of the open front door. Katherine was with her, but she withdrew as Harry rushed forward to hug his mother.

"Gently," Felix called out before he joined them and closed his arms around his family.

"I love you both so much," Ella said, and pulled back to ruffle Harry's hair. "There's someone inside desperate to see you."

"Sammie!" Harry squealed, and disappeared.

"Eudora's here too," Ella said. "Everyone's been so worried." Ella touched his face, her hand freezing. It was hard to tell in the moonlight, but she looked pale.

"You shouldn't be out of bed. Let's get you inside."

"I haven't had a breath of fresh air in days." Ella craned her neck to see the stars through the trees. "March first, and it feels as if spring is finally on its way. And the camellias are in bloom. Would you cut me a flower, and then I'll go back to bed? I promise. Katherine left the kitchen scissors by the door."

Felix grabbed the scissors and walked toward the biggest camellia, smothered in red blooms, its glossy dark-green leaves lit by the moon.

"That day on the Tube"—Ella's voice drifted through the night behind him—"I knew you'd be a good dad. And you are, my love. You're the best."

"Just one bloom?" He turned with a smile, but Ella's expression had changed. She looked bewildered. Confused.

"Felix . . . ?" she said, and crumpled.

This time, he couldn't catch her.

Ella was floating. Below her, Felix was standing over someone stretched out on their sofa. Katherine placed her hand on his shoulder. Harry flew into his father's arms.

A baby cried.

An organ played the wedding march.

A beautiful man with an English accent asked how he could help, and she thought, *Be mine.*

Her mother sang a lullaby.

Ahead, a column of white light emerged, as pure as the sunlight that broke through the trees and fell across her bed mid-morning.

A shadow stepped forward. *Are you ready?*

I'll never be ready, Mom.
The white light disappeared; the world went black.

FIVE YEARS LATER

Unseasonable May heat shimmered above the sidewalk and carried the scent of wild honeysuckle through the pines. Two cardinals whistled a duet; a mockingbird joined in. Ella watched, seeing but unseen: a whisper of light, a memory glimpsed from the corner of the eye.

It's almost time.

Gown flying behind him, Harry rushed from Kenan Stadium towing a petite blonde, a southern belle with a beautiful smile.

"Grad school, here I come!" he called to Max.

Harry stopped and rubbed his arm. He had sensed her echo as he had done many times in the last five years. Today was especially hard for him. Mother's Day always was.

Max understood. "Missing her, dude?"

"Yeah," Harry said. "But I'm good. Wow!" He looked up into the Carolina-blue sky. "A stunning day to start the rest of my life!"

It's almost time.

A girl tapped Max on the arm. "Can I get your autograph?" She giggled.

Even with the dark glasses, Max couldn't disguise his fame—the full sleeves of song lyric tattoos were such giveaways. The girl blushed and ran off, clutching a signed scrap of paper.

Sammie, Max's guest at the commencement ceremony, stepped forward to shake hands with Harry's girlfriend. Max watched, protective as ever.

Tell her, Max; tell Harry. Tell both of them how you've felt since the first day you saw Sammie Owen, the prettiest girl in tenth grade—moments after your best friend noticed her.

Max had given up so much for Harry, and no one knew.

Eudora appeared, wearing a huge hat covered in fake flowers. She pushed Ella's dad in a wheelchair. It hadn't been easy for him to make the journey from Florida, but he had been determined. Harry, a Morehead-Cain Scholar, had graduated from the University of North Carolina at Chapel Hill summa cum laude. Harry's granddad told anyone who would listen it was the happiest day of his life.

Finally, Felix and Katherine joined the group. They ambled, hands entwined, the Carolina sun sparkling off the new diamond on her fourth finger. Of all of them, Katherine's journey through grief had been the hardest. In the end, it had been Felix who'd kept her safe. Felix and his savior complex. There had been a small rift between them when Katherine started writing the memoir of her friendship with Ella, but after it catapulted to the bestseller lists, the celebration dinner had led to something else.

Everything was as it should be; a new story was about to begin.

Ella blew a breath of air at Harry's cheek; he reached up and touched his face. Smiled.

It's time.

The column of white light opened ahead.

I'm ready to let go.

Ella walked into her mother's embrace.

ACKNOWLEDGMENTS

Nothing about my third novel was easy, and without my agent, Nalini Akolekar, it might have become homeless. Nalini believed in me from day one, even though our first interaction came after I screwed up an email attachment. I will be forever grateful that she didn't say, "Take you on as a client? You can't even format a Word document." Four years later, she still has my techno-challenged back—and a knack for bringing calm to any situation with the potential to make my head do the *Exorcist* spin. Extended thanks to everyone at Spencerhill Associates.

Huge thanks to Jodi Warshaw and the team at Lake Union Publishing for welcoming the Fitzwilliams with open arms and being drawn to my "dark quirkiness." (I'm quite partial to it myself.) Extra-special thanks to Clete Barrett Smith, whose insightful edits gave me new love for *The Perfect Son*.

A shout-out to Emily Ohanjanians, who helped shape the first draft and was my editor for *The In-Between Hour*. I firmly believe Emily's brilliance is the reason my second novel was chosen by the Southern Independent Booksellers Alliance (SIBA) as a Winter 2014 Okra Pick. Endless gratitude to SIBA and to all the indie booksellers who were so supportive of *The In-Between Hour*, especially Jamie Fiocco at Flyleaf

Books and Sharon Wheeler at Purple Crow Books. My commitment to indie bookstores continues.

Group hug with my writing comrades at Book Pregnant/The Novel Factory, who cheer, cry, and vent with me every day. I'm raising my glass to the future bicoastal drunk fest.

Thank you to everyone who took the time to answer annoying research questions, and apologies for any facts I've garbled. Mega thanks to my medical consultant on call, Karen Perrizolo. For helping me understand issues of the heart—thank you to Dr. Andrew Greganti, Sherry Gorman, Becky Williams, and Dr. Marschall Runge, executive dean of the UNC School of Medicine at Chapel Hill. Dean Runge happily replied to more emails than anyone should ever have to answer. (You, sir, are a saint.) Special thanks to Stephanie Mahin at the UNC Medical Center news office for not giving up on my search for a cardiologist! Thank you to Daniel Kim and Kelly Hartog for offering fresh perspectives on OCPD—when I was beginning to fear there was nothing but gloom and doom. Thank you to Nancy Siebens and Densie Webb for the parents' point of view on Tourette syndrome. Air kisses to Julie Smith for sharing firsthand experience of concussions. And, as always, heartfelt appreciation for Dr. Pat Gammon, guru of all things anxiety related.

For attempting to explain the world of finance to a woman who can't balance her checkbook, thank you to Scott Cooper, Stephen Piercy, and Rob Rose. (Guys, I'm a lost cause. Sorry!)

Flight attendants—you rock. Thank you to Mike Wilson, Tricia Homan, Michael Tongko, and James Prentice. (Extra thanks to Buzzy Porter, Scott Wilbanks, Marci Nault, and Beth Lundberg for the intros—gotta love Facebook!)

Thank you to Annabel Garrett for the guided tour of Duke Gardens and for explaining the true wonders of the Blomquist Garden; thank you to Marcy Cohen for helping me research the Nasher Museum of Art scene and for riding shotgun on the great hunt for the Fitzwilliam house. Thank you, Josh Stallings and Diane Ritchie, for bringing the Harvard campus to life. Cheers to pals Lynn and John Pickles and Carolyn Wilson for answering pesky questions about all things British.

Phew. It really does take a village. Speaking of which . . . thanks to my entire transatlantic tribe: old and new buddies who answered random cries for help on Facebook; the Grossberg clan; the Rose family; Anne Claypole White; and—never forgotten—Reverend Douglas Eric Claypole White. Unending gratitude for Susan Rose, who caught my whopper of a mistake and saved the day. (And yes, her English bone china mugs full of history are fabulous.)

Much love to fellow writers Elizabeth Brown and Sheryl Cornett, who bravely waded through my second draft—on a tight turnaround—to provide ideas that shaped the story and my characters; and a wave to Laura Spinella for tackling my rubbish synopsis. To Barbara Davis, please move back south so we can continue our author support group of two.

A million thanks to my beta reader, Leslie Gildersleeve, who went above and beyond time and time again, and realized—before I did—that the manuscript needed a flashback scene with Felix and his father. You, my friend, are the best.

Mother-son hug for Oberlin sophomore Zachariah Claypole White: for answering every text that screamed "word choice emergency," for staying up half the night to read the third draft, and for providing a brilliant critique with a decorative note that read, "Never say this manuscript is crap again or I'll put a spider in your bed." (Nice try—you're more terrified of arachnids than I am.) And thank you to Zachariah and Danlee Gildersleeve, a.k.a. The Arcadian Project, for creating music that allows me to tune out the world and tune into my characters. Please remember your parents when you're rich and famous. (We expect the rock 'n' roll rest home.)

Biggest thank-you is reserved for my one and only—my emotional anchor, Lawrence Grossberg. Thank you for suffering through my craziness and for endless brainstorming that produced such genius comments as "What if Harry went to Harvard, Barbara?" Thank you for embracing domestic chaos and taking over huge chunks of our lives so that I could be a penniless dreamer. Most of all, thank you for believing that I could actually do this—again.

The following books were extremely helpful:

Too Perfect: When Being in Control Gets Out of Control, by Allan E. Mallinger, MD, and Jeanette Dewyze
Passing for Normal: A Memoir of Compulsion, by Amy S. Wilensky
Twitch and Shout: A Touretter's Tale, by Lowell Handler
A Family's Quest for Rhythm: Living with Tourette, ADD, OCD, and Challenging Behaviors, by Kathy Giordano and Matt Giordano

BOOK CLUB DISCUSSION QUESTIONS

1. No one in the novel is quite as he or she seems at first. Ella, for example, appears to be the perfect mother, but is filled with hidden doubts and insecurities; Felix appears to be a rigid control freak, and yet every decision he makes for the family pushes him beyond his comfort zone. As the story unfolds, did any of the other characters surprise you, and if so, in what ways? Do you agree that we are often too quick to pigeonhole a person based on one aspect of his or her personality?

2. Felix is a dark, unlikely hero. Even as Katherine warms to him, she calls him an antihero. How do you feel about Felix, and did those feelings change while you were reading the novel? Is Felix his own worst critic?

3. Were you shocked by Felix's flashback scene? Do you think we ever truly know what goes on in a family?

4. Harry does not have coprolalia—the involuntary and repetitive use of obscene language. Coprolalia is, however, the most common popular image of Tourette's, even though it affects only a small percentage of people with Tourette syndrome. Do you agree that fictional characters struggling with neurological or mental disorders are often depicted using stereotypes? Do any of your family members battle an invisible disability, and if so, what have you found to be the most challenging part of explaining quirky behavior to the outside world?

5. When parenting a high-maintenance child, do the lines blur between being a helicopter parent and being a child advocate? Does Ella's health crisis speed up the natural process of separation and boundary setting that she and Harry must experience?

6. How do Harry's relationships with both his parents change during the novel?

7. How did you react to Ella's attempts to distance herself from Harry while she was in the hospital? What would you have done in her situation?

8. Harry and Max have a unique bond. What did you like most about their relationship? Do you think they will be BFFs forever, despite taking such different life paths?

9. What do you think is the emotional core of Ella and Felix's marriage? Are they well matched or an unlikely couple? Do you agree with Felix that the two months following the heart attack are a gift—a second chance for them?

10. In chapter one, Ella refers to the stranger sitting next to her as the good father, and throughout the novel, both she and Felix question what it means to be a good parent. What do you think it means? Do you agree with them that the hardest lesson of parenthood is learning to let go?

11. Do you have a favorite secondary character? If so, who and why?

12. One of the novel's themes is that a person can find clarity and empathy in a moment of unbearable darkness. Does the Fitzwilliam family crisis bring out the best in all the characters, including the secondary ones?

13. Ella's journey is a solitary one, whereas Felix is drawn increasingly into a community of support, something he's never experienced before. What do you think about that?

14. Why doesn't Ella die on the plane? Do you think she ever believed she would get better?

15. We see various settings in historic Durham, North Carolina, from Felix's perspective. What did you learn about Felix through the different settings—especially the scenes at Duke Gardens and the Nasher Museum of Art? Why do you think Felix, a Londoner who loves the afternoon sun, was drawn to a house hidden in shade at the edge of Duke Forest? Do you think Felix will stay in the house?

16. How did you react to the ending?

A CONVERSATION
WITH THE AUTHOR

What was the inspiration for this book?

This story grew out of several unrelated moments in my life and, as with everything I write, comes back to my passion for poking holes in stereotypes of mental or neurological disabilities.

I've always wanted to create a character with Tourette syndrome, and I've long been fascinated by the 80 percent divorce rate among families raising special-needs kids. My son has battled obsessive-compulsive disorder for most of his life, and I'm active in a support group for parents of OCD kids. I've watched many marriages in that community crumble. After someone asked why my marriage had survived, I started researching a story about a broken marriage and a high-maintenance teen in crisis. Then three separate events occurred.

The first event was a routine medical procedure that went horribly wrong. I ended up in the ICU, and the strain on my guys, who are both empathetic, was unbearable. We got through that crisis, but a few months later, on a family trip to visit my mother in England,

I was struck down by a virus that manifested as asthma. I couldn't breathe, and the steroids I was prescribed made my heart race. Since I have genetic heart issues, it was hard not to freak out. One night, my husband sat up with me for hours, holding my hand while I chanted silently, "I am not sick, I am not sick, I am not sick." The next day, I wrote two pages of gibberish about a wife who has a heart attack. (I think that was therapy for dealing with my own fear.) The final incident happened on the flight home from a literary festival in Ireland when some poor guy collapsed three rows in front of me. (Yes, I was the bad person taking notes.)

I ditched the manuscript I was working on—which felt way too serious—and started fleshing out the Fitzwilliams. I'm drawn to dark humor, and the characters kept making me smile. Once I'd found Max, the punk / math genius who uses perfect grammar in his texts, there was no going back. From that moment on, my life was all about Harry. (That was my working title, *It's All about Harry*. But of course it isn't really . . .)

Your characters have severe medical, neurological, and mental problems to overcome. How did you research this novel?

I'm a research-heavy novelist who conducts many one-on-one interviews. I also read memoirs, do Internet research, lurk in online groups, and watch endless YouTube videos (okay, so some of the music videos might be distractions . . .). With this novel, however, I found my research difficult and overwhelming. Ella's medical journey provided the framework for the story, but it took seven months to track down a cardiologist willing to talk with me. Until that point, I was constantly second-guessing her storyline.

The research into the neurological and mental disorders came with its own challenges, since many of the firsthand sources focused on more extreme cases. I nearly abandoned OCPD because most of the accounts came from disillusioned ex-spouses who said, "If you're married to anyone with obsessive-compulsive personality disorder, run." I reminded myself that my characters are not their disorders, and that we all have individual brain chemistry and unique life experiences that mold us into a mess of complexities and contradictions. As one mother told me, if you lined up a hundred kids with Tourette syndrome, the Tourette's would manifest differently in every child.

I'm not trying to create cardboard cutouts that say, "I am OCPD" or "I am Tourette's." The fun part for me is always thinking outside the box of clinical definitions to find the person behind the label. Hey, people with messed-up brain chemistry and wiring still need backstories and well-rounded personalities!

During the writing of this novel, did anything surprise you?

Everything surprised me. Even though I forced myself to create a detailed outline, nothing went as planned. I started a story set in Chapel Hill, but it skipped over to Durham; I thought I was writing about a marriage in crisis, then it became a father-son story . . . and finally, I realized it was about a family finding acceptance. Harry decided to fall in love, Max announced he didn't want to go to college, Katherine became a good guy, and the ending reversed in the second draft.

The characters' emotional arcs surprised the heck out of me. I loved that Harry, who had never learned to establish boundaries with his mother, took charge of his life by learning to confront his father. And Ella evolved in ways that I hadn't anticipated. Her revelations about the pregnancy and her doubts about being a mother? I never saw those coming.

I'm not sure that discovering the real Felix was a surprise, but it was the most rewarding part of writing this novel. I heard Felix's voice from the beginning, but he presented huge problems. He's not an obvious hero, and until you understand his layers, he presents as a judgmental control freak. When an early reader said, "I didn't want to like Felix, but I did," I finally began to believe readers would stick with him.

Tell us about the setting. Your first two novels have lush rural settings, but this time you switched to the city of Durham, North Carolina. Why?

Once again, I wanted to set the story in rural Orange County, but Felix isn't a country person. So I moved the setting to an established Chapel Hill neighborhood. That didn't work, either. (Felix is quite picky!) And then I was driving around the older, tree-lined streets of Durham by Duke Gardens, and I had a lightbulb moment: I had found Felix's home. While parts of Duke speak to Felix of his time at Oxford, he's also drawn to the sense of rejuvenation at the heart of historic Durham. There's a creative, cosmopolitan, slightly funky energy to the downtown that reminds me a little of London, and Felix is a Londoner. By putting the house at the edge of Duke Forest, I could also sneak in references to light through the trees, which is my favorite writing image.

Felix is your darkest hero yet. What drew you to his character?

James Nealy, my beloved OCD hero in *The Unfinished Garden*, came from my darkest fear as a mother: What if, when my young son grew up, no one could see beyond his quirky behavior to love him for the amazing person he is? Since James, I've wanted to go deeper and darker, and that desire led to Felix. Felix is ruled by a rigid personality that makes him hard to like sometimes, but Eudora's right—he's a good man. I love that contradiction.

Tell us about Harry and Max's relationship, which seems unusual for two teenage boys.

My son and his BFF—"Thing One and Thing Two"—have been best buddies since they were toddlers. Nothing and no one comes between them, and I've always been extremely grateful for their bond. All is well in my world when those two are together, and man, are they a creative force! They used to build huge worlds out of Legos, make movies, and go on epic adventures in the forest. Now they write and perform music that inspires me. I firmly believe they will change the world. (I think Max and Harry will, too—Max through his music, Harry as a psychologist.)

Where did Eudora come from?

She popped up in my head one day, wearing that hat from the final scene. I put her aside for a future novel, but when I was spewing out my stream-of-consciousness first draft, she appeared in Ella's garden with a pair of pruning shears. Given my love of gardening and eccentric characters, I knew she had to stay.

Do you have a favorite scene?

Not really, but I'm quite fond of the moonshine scene, which came out fully formed. As a reader, I love secondary characters who steal the show, and that scene belongs to Eudora and Max.

Why do you include a listening guide with your novels?

I started writing seriously as a mother on the go, which meant I had to learn how to tune out the world instantly. Music allows me to do that, but only if the song speaks to me of my point-of-view character's emotional state. With my iPod and earbuds, I can write anywhere. Huge chunks of *The In-Between Hour*, for example, were written in the child psychologist's waiting room and in a parking lot during my son's Tuesday night guitar lessons. Because of that training, I managed to write a very difficult chapter of *The Perfect Son* on a transatlantic flight. (The wine may have helped.)

If I had to pick one song to listen to over and over while reading this novel, it would be "The Kids from Yesterday" by My Chemical Romance. The reference to lights makes me think of Ella, and the line about how your heart has to break before you can hear the music always says Felix to me. The hardest part of writing this novel was figuring out Felix's relationship to music. I knew he would ask Harry for a playlist, but it took a while to figure out when and how. That's the best part of writing—finding the pieces and watching them fit together.

LISTENING GUIDE

My Chemical Romance, "I Don't Love You"
New Order, "Bizarre Love Triangle"
Coheed and Cambria, "The Afterman"
U2, "Ordinary Love"
Coheed and Cambria, "Pearl of the Stars"
Tears for Fears, "Woman in Chains" (with Oleta Adams)
U2, "Every Breaking Wave"
The Arcadian Project, "Hey There, Pretty Girl"
Joy Division, "Love Will Tear Us Apart"
Everything But The Girl, "I Don't Understand Anything"
The Airborne Toxic Event, "The Fifth Day"
Gnarls Barkley, "Smiley Faces"
The Airborne Toxic Event, "This Is London"
My Chemical Romance, "Planetary (GO!)"
U2, "Sometimes You Can't Make It on Your Own"
The Airborne Toxic Event, "The Way Home"
Coldplay, "Fix You"
The Strokes, "Reptilia"
Simple Minds, "When Two Worlds Collide"
The Smashing Pumpkins, "1979"

The Arcadian Project, "The Windmill"
Leonard Cohen, "Anthem"
My Chemical Romance, "The Only Hope for Me Is You"
Heaven 17, "Let Me Go" (extended version)
Our Last Night, "Skyfall"
My Chemical Romance, "The Kids from Yesterday"
The Airborne Toxic Event, "The Graveyard near the House"
Green Day, "Troublemaker"
James Taylor, "Carolina in My Mind"
Simple Minds, "Waterfront"
Muse, "Exogenesis: Symphony Part 3 (Redemption)"
U2, "Kite"
The Arcadian Project, "The Disappearance Symphony: One Last Question"

ABOUT THE AUTHOR

English born and educated, Barbara Claypole White lives in the North Carolina forest with her family. Inspired by her poet/musician son's courageous battles against obsessive-compulsive disorder, Barbara writes hopeful family drama with a healthy dose of mental illness. Her debut novel, *The Unfinished Garden*, won the 2013 Golden Quill Contest for Best First Book, and *The In-Between Hour* was chosen by SIBA (the Southern Independent Booksellers) as a Winter 2014 Okra Pick.

For more information, or to connect with Barbara, please visit barbaraclaypolewhite.com.